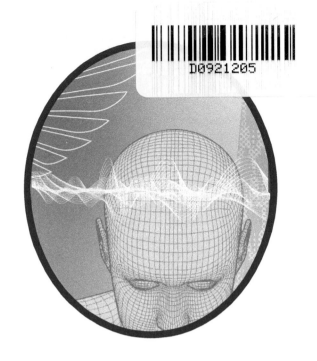

REPLAY EARTH

MARK SCHLACK

STORY WITH E.B. WEISSTEIN

ANAPHORA LITERARY PRESS

QUANAH, TEXAS

ANAPHORA LITERARY PRESS
1108 W 3rd Street
Quanah, TX 79252
https://anaphoraliterary.com

Book design by Anna Faktorovich, Ph.D.

Story with E.B. Weisstein

Cover design by: Erin Farrell

Published in 2018 by Anaphora Literary Press

Replay Earth
Mark Schlack—1st edition.

Library of Congress Control Number: 2018910410

Library Cataloging Information
Schlack, Mark, 1953-, author.
    Replay earth / Joseph Matthew Reynolds
    286 p. ; 9 in.
    ISBN 978-1-68114-484-9 (softcover : alk. paper)
    ISBN 978-1-68114-485-6 (hardcover : alk. paper)
    ISBN 978-1-68114-486-3 (e-book)
1. Fiction—Science Fiction—High Tech.
2. Fiction—Science Fiction—Adventure.
3. Science—Global Warming & Climate Change.
PN3311-3503: Literature: Prose fiction
813: American fiction in English

For Layla, Katie, Talia, and Safia

PREFACE

A billion years ago

A few dozen fighters stand on a battlefield, bone weary, dirty, hunger their only nourishment. The smoke of combat only lets a few stars shine in the night sky. But the sickly gray air is quiet, the roar of the fighting paused for now, as the remaining armies of all three Houses rest in the carnage that has consumed their world for 30 years.

In a clearing, one of the fighters stands on the hood of a personnel carrier. Naw'ra, a low-ranking officer in the army of the Second House, addresses the assembled officers from all three armies.

"Brothers and sisters, mothers and fathers, we have engaged in this all-consuming war for many years. One in three of us who was alive when it started has fallen. Our air is thick with smoke, our water with blood, and our land covered with our dead, and the dead of all else that once lived here, and with poisons that will kill for years. We have fought each other for land, for wealth, for power, and we have exhausted all three in doing so.

"The three great Houses of U Maw have defeated each other and themselves in the process. I tell you that the soldiers of the Second House will fight no more. I ask you of the First House and the Third House to put your weapons down. They will help you no more."

"How nice for you if we do," shouts someone from the Third House. "I guess you want us to give you our food and children, too."

"I want no such thing," Naw'ra answers, and pauses, slowing her breathing down, remembering that she has come to persuade, not to fight. "I want you to remember that before there were three Houses, there were the clans, and before the clans, there were the bands, and before that, there were just the Maw'u'I, talking animals who could not only imagine the future, but make it real. And in only 150,000 years, they settled all the lands and lived mostly in peace, however simple their life seems to us now. We are those same creatures, but we have lost our way. We let ourselves believe that peace and cooperation were stagnation and that only war and competition brought progress."

"What do you expect us to do?" shouts a soldier from the Second House. "Tear off our clothes and live like savages?"

"Our answer is to move forward. I ask your patience for a minute, and you will begin to understand. I need only for you to quiet your tongues and still your minds."

Naw'ra nods, and one soldier in each of the other houses nods in return. The three of them anxiously search for each other's minds. They have quietly honed this skill over many months, but never with so much on the line. Her confidence builds as she feels the first fringes of the other minds, and then the feeling of profound connection enfolds all three of them.

As if their three minds have become a fourth, a joint consciousness, they encircle the group around them, entangling each soldier into a vibrant mental chord.

The soldiers gasp, feeling the connection. Now Naw'ra speaks to them directly in their minds, her thoughts and feelings mingling with theirs. After the fear and boredom of battle, there is something about touching the core of so many others that is deeply restorative.

"Yes, you feel it now, don't you? How small are the differences that have driven us to fight all our lives. How unfounded are our fears of each other. Now I know your heart and you know mine, and we have taken the first step toward peace."

"Yet we fight for our homes, Naw'ra," a scarred old veteran shouts out. "Maybe years ago, we could have all gone home and forgotten it. Now, there is nowhere for most of us to go to, and we fight for the last good lands and waters. What do you propose?"

"You are right, old soldier. We need more. We need a home whose air and water don't bring disease, whose land can support food. Someday, this planet will be that again, but for now, it cannot. Peace must bring progress. And so, our small group from all three houses has been working secretly on a project that will give us a new start. And now we will show you."

All of them are still now, their minds filled with a strangely different sky, a subtly different landscape. They see a pristine world for the first time. The air tickles their nostrils, fresher than anything they have ever breathed. This new world beckons.

Soldiers fall to the ground, stunned and joyful. They are looking through the eyes of a few dozen souls on this new world. They have joined the first people to leave their world. The settlers came from all three Houses. Yet on this new world, they belong to no house.

"Who are you?" one soldier shouts at the sky. They all feel the response.

"We are your fellow citizens, waiting for you to join us as explorers, and as builders," says A'mon, from the new world. "Look at the red planet just above your eastern horizon. We are there, yet we can know your thoughts and feelings, too, and you can know ours, as if we were in the same room."

"Go home to your armies and your leaders," Naw'ra says. "Tell them that a new era has begun. I will train you to entangle and you will train your families, your neighbors, and yes, your leaders. Together we will settle the new world and rebuild the old. I have laid down my arms, and so have many others in the three armies. From this day, we are no longer three houses, but one—Guardians of these worlds. We have been fortunate to have ripped open the fabric of reality and to have seen more deeply into it than anyone before us. And now can begin the work of transforming our lives, our homes, and our future."

PART I

BAD DREAMS

Somerville, Massachusetts
September 5, 2048

People were screaming all around him, so many and so far away that Raefe couldn't see them all, he could only feel their terror envelop him. Something awful was happening near the harbor. He could hear metal bending, shredding. He heard water, lots of it, banging cars around, getting louder, so many sounds. Loudest of all, he could feel the fear and horror of thousands of people hearing those same terrifying sounds.

Raefe bolted awake, sweating, his temples pounding as they always did when he had these visions. He started the deep-breathing exercises the therapy bot had given him. Even awake, he could hear rain lashing the walls of the little building. Must be the remnants of that hurricane. It's just a storm, he thought. But why did he still feel the screams of drowning people? It's not a dream, he realized, stunned. He shook Lina.

"Get up! We have to get to the roof."

He yanked her arm, pulling her up out of the bed. She grabbed her Voice and they ran up the back stairs in their underwear, yelling "Wake up, get to the roof!" to the people who lived on the top floor of their TinyStack, banging ferociously on the door as they ran by. The water was so loud that they could barely hear their feet on the stairs.

They got to the roof, Kiko and Kayam right behind them. The hurricane drove sheets of rain toward them. They bent into the wind, trying to see what was happening. They could barely see that the usual bright necklace of lights and gates of the harbor seawall had disappeared. The ocean had already pushed the Mystic River fast over its banks, churning inland past their home. Looking down, there was nothing below their second-story apartment but water.

Huge waves slammed the shore. Cars pinballed into buildings, the rending of metal inaudible beneath the storm. A small Coast Guard boat surfed a 10-meter wave headed from Boston Harbor toward the Mystic Tobin Bridge. The ship twisted and for a minute it looked like it would pass under the bridge that towered 50 meters above it. Then the water threw the boat back into the farthest pillar. A mile away, they heard the bridge straining over the roar of the water. The pillar bent, twisting the whole bridge. That freed the ship to continue on until it smashed into a building only blocks away. The four of them watched, stunned into silence, deafened by the noise. But for Raefe, the noise was not just metal on metal —beneath that, and further into his head, he could sense screams and terror, a terror that now was spreading inside him.

They searched for a way off the roof, panicked by the sight of sea water filling the streets all around them. And dawn was still hours away.

"We've got to get out of here," Lina screamed over the noise. "I don't know if the TinyStack will hold in this."

"There, look," Kiko shouted back, pointing to a track for maintenance bots on the elevated highway running just above their heads. "There's a ladder on that pillar, we can climb up to the highway."

They grabbed the rungs built into the stanchion and climbed up. Through the drowned air, a ragged column of survivors was just visible on the interstate. The rain was everywhere, there was no escape from its driving needles. They turned their backs on the flood and merged with the other survivors, marching north, away from the harbor.

Through the driving rain, Raefe followed his white hand on the back of Lina's brown head as if it were a beacon. But he couldn't stop the flood of images from the other survivors, the people that hundreds of others were seeing. Broken limbs, sobbing, and worse. He had struggled with his headaches since childhood—moments when he seemed overwhelmed by what felt like other people's emotions. He had never been able to get his parents or doctors to understand what they felt like, and they had told him these were migraines. But now he felt that sensation a thousand times over, his mind wracked by a kind of lightning that brought a thunder of drowned screams.

They got to the top of a big hill. Seeing the emptiness in Raefe's face, Lina shook him.

"It's OK, we're safe," she said. "We made it."

He nodded but wondered, when will the screams stop? He felt an animal fright spread out over the land, a fright that seemed to extend all the way to the horizon. He let it wash over him, bits of anguish, sadness and desperation rushing by like broken twigs on the water. He had never felt anything close to the depth and breadth of these feelings. He wanted it to go away—usually even a hint of this would send his brain spiraling into waves of pain and nausea. But something had changed, like a blurry vid suddenly in focus. With every step, his mind could feel some minds recede, and others move closer.

Lina pulled him by the hand away from the column of survivors to a small knoll next to the road. They turned and looked back over East Somerville, now a drowned urban swamp lit by a full moon. There were no more streets, just dirty water and short buildings sticking out of it like fat trees. Beyond their neighborhood was a forest of them as far as they could see.

"So, this is what the apocalypse looks like," Kayam said, his arms wrapped tight around himself. "The beginning of the end."

"Yeah, and where's Jesus?" Lina answered, her voice angry in the dark. Kayam's religious bent always put her off.

"No, no Jesus coming," Kayam said. "Not like that. This is no free trip to heaven for the true believers. No, this is man's work, not God's. Look around—you're telling me this isn't the end of our world? You think we're the only people right now standing on a hill looking at something like this?"

Raefe asked what no one had wanted to. "Do you think Miguel got out of the first floor?"

"No way," Kayam said. "Water was already over the back door when we got to the roof."

Raefe struggled to absorb this. Migs was the guy he always said hi to, the guy he might someday be friends with. He realized he didn't even know how old Migs had been or where he was born. And that none of that mattered any more.

"Rest in peace, Miguel," Lina said. "Sorry we didn't have more time to get to know you."

"Shit, Kiko," Raefe suddenly realized, "Where's your food trike?"

"Serving the fishes," she said. "You're going to have to find a new place to get Cubanos and Korean barbecue."

"Starting to see your point, Kayam," Lina said. "Maybe this is the end of the world."

Raefe smiled absently, registering Lina's ability to snark even in the midst of the apocalypse. Or was she right? Were the screams in his head those of souls being swallowed up by a real Armageddon?

"Is that what this is?" he asked her. "Is that what all the screams I hear are?"

Kiko and Kayam turned away, not wanting to embarrass him. Lina had told them that Raefe sometimes had these spells—seizures was the word she had used. Lina turned, shielding him from them.

"What are you hearing?" she asked quietly.

He told her, wondering out loud why she couldn't hear them, too. She wasn't sure what to make of it but wanted to keep him from freaking out.

"You know how you always react so strongly to other people's distress?" she asked. "Maybe this is just that. Just you sympathizing with thousands of people in trouble. Try not to let it overwhelm you."

He sighed. So hard to get people to understand that he wasn't trying to sympathize with anyone. But the voices came anyway. In fact, his attention was fixed on the only home he'd ever had since leaving his parents. From here, their little TinyStack just looked like a bright painted shipping container floating under a bridge, as if it had fallen off a ship passing by. Well, it wasn't much more than that anyway, though it had been the first home either of them had ever had since leaving their childhood ones. And now they were marching steadily away from it, to who knows where?

Hours later, the first light of day brought a dull, gray shine to the city. Lina's Voice finally found the Net. She sent a text to her parents in Sofricar and gave her Voice to Raefe to call his family. In Raefe's ear, it was loose, smaller than his, but he jammed his finger in to make it fit. He talked to it quietly, resetting it to work for him. The Voice took a while, but it was able to get through to Oregon.

"Dad, it's Raefe. Just wanted to let you know I'm OK."

"Thank goodness; we were so scared. I'm seeing some crazy stuff on the Net—10 million people homeless, no power to 100 million all up and down the East Coast?"

"I don't know, Dad. My puter's lost in the flood, we had to leave in a hurry. I'm using Lina's Voice. We just walked all night to get out of the flood. We're standing on hill in the middle of. . . I don't really know. I'm hoping some cops come by, or anyone who knows where we should go."

"It's chaos, Raefe. They're saying the government can't even find its own people. DigiBrands and Brightstar Defense and some other big corpos say they're going to help. You know how that works—have a problem and call Brightstar, now you've got two problems."

"It just keeps getting worse, doesn't it, Dad."

"I'm afraid so, son."

Raefe could see him, sitting in their apartment in the endless town-house development south of Eugene, staring out at the wind farms on the ridge. On the wall, the photo screen of Justin Miller and Charlotte Epstein holding newborn Raefe, big brother Benny looking up, standing in front of a brownstone in Brooklyn.

He loved that picture. They're smiling about their future, a vivid LED glow of warm colors. No one thought that The Slide was only months away. A secret US weapons test in space would cause a massive communications satellite failure. The Net would disappear for six weeks, tipping the creaky world financial system down the long incline it was still on. Millions of Justins and Charlottes—billions around the world—would never have a full-time job again. Nor would they ever smile quite as effortlessly.

"Just tell Mom I'm thinking of you guys. I can see that picture on the wall, you smiling at mom." he said. "Don't forget that smile. You give mom and Benny my love."

"Will do. You take care of yourself. And say hi to Lina."

Raefe felt the heartbreak behind his dad's robotic goodbye. He wondered, is there a right thing to say at a time like this? He turned to Lina and Kayam and Kiko.

"My dad says the Net is crazy with rumors. One hundred million without power, 10 million homeless. Corpos already feasting on the whole calamity."

He stood numb, feeling like a giant antenna receiving a million channels of fear and sadness. Yesterday he was just another kid struggling to find work and keep it together. Today they were all human driftwood washed up on an alien shoreline.

A PROMISING PLANET

Traveler's Perch
September 8, 2048

Diver from Great Heights was beside herself. She sat motionless in the inner ring around the pulsing energy of the wormhole interface that was the heart of the Guardians' galactic network, intent on maintaining full entanglement with Raefe Epstein Miller, the most promising of the humans that she monitored. She might be 400 years old, but she thought she knew exactly how Raefe felt. For her, this was also that moment when she had to face circumstances way beyond what she had ever imagined for the first time in her adult life. She and Raefe both teetered on the edge of despair and doubt. Unlike him, she had been trained for this moment and fully understood what was going on.

The ozone glow of the interface field highlighted the purple in her feathers. She sat upright, in her vaguely birdlike way, balanced atop her thick, squat legs. Her two arms were rotated slightly back at the shoulders and her hands had six fingers—a thumb and five nearly equal fingers where claws had once been.

The sharpness of her beak, the way her arms looked poised for flight even when she was still, everything about her expressed her alertness to this moment. Fifty thousand years ago, she might have perched on a cliff, hiding from other predators hunting her. Today, she had to be vigilant to every nuance of the situation.

She had spent years learning the language of the mind, learning how to exploit the fundamental quantum entanglement that lay beneath the universe we could see, and how that essential connectedness expressed itself in dozens of different forms of intelligent life throughout the galaxy.

She sensed something on the periphery—it was Flies Far to Cross Oceans, her boss. To her, he had also become Far Flier, close friend and occasional lover. He touched her mind lightly, politely, so as not to startle her.

"Aren't you the diligent one? he said. "Coming right to the source."

"I didn't really have a choice," she said, speaking out loud. "Earth is not exactly the strongest signal in the galaxy and I have to find Raefe's mind. Something is happening, and I can't risk missing some key event because the signal from Raefe and the lesser entanglers on Earth isn't strong enough to show up in our usual waveform. The wormhole interface is the best place to find it."

"Things have changed?" he asked.

She filled him in on the extreme storm on Earth, how Raefe's city was struck by a giant wave of ocean water.

"He was nearly killed," she informed him. "Tens of thousands were. He and millions are homeless now."

Flier sighed. "The life of young species is often filled with pain. But Raefe survives. Is he injured?"

"No, but I don't know how he's taking it. And there's more: I feel a surge from him—I think maybe the stress has strengthened his empathetic capabilities. Or possibly the opposite—he's always been a bit fragile, and the surge may have been a breakdown."

"Well, I came at the right time. I wanted to get an update from you on Earth ahead of the Council meeting."

She was annoyed. Surely, he could grasp that this was not the time for bureaucratic reports.

"OK," she said. "But just for a few minutes. I need to monitor things closely. And I'm just not sure everything coming from Earth makes it out of the interface into the waveform."

"I'm sure Earth's future will not be decided in the next few minutes," he said. "Ask Adno to monitor while we talk."

She let him follow her thoughts to her trainee Adno, who seemed pleased to take on the task but worried she was not up to it. Diver reassured her, and they left the interface chamber for the tunnels that took them to the cliff face outside of headquarters.

"It's a full sky today," Far Flier observed.

Prime's light warned them. High in the sky, Prime's trinary star mates, the Twins, glowed like orange eyes against the red sky. Closer by, Prime's other two planets, Red Nest and Water Eye, shone like small red and blue jewels on a head dress. The dance of these stars and planets drove the thermal cycle that all life on the planet lived by. She felt grounded and allowed her annoyance with Far Flier to ebb, replaced by the affection between them.

"Perhaps all this beauty will help to clarify our way forward," he said. "Analysis Section thought that Earth showed a small yet definite promise that it may progress to Balance, where it would likely flourish. Should I be telling them that they may have been wrong?"

"No, in the long run they will be proved right," she said. "But humans are still stuck in Optimization. Every problem they have, they try to invent a technology to solve. You can bet they'll be discussing bigger sea walls now. Sometimes I wish I could yell through the interface 'Stop with all of your widgets and gadgets and the hundred other words you have for things that are just stuff, just dumb matter. Look inside yourselves, the answer's there.' But on the plus side, they belong to an order of animals that is predominantly social, able to accommodate a wide range of social structures, from small bands of less than 10 to herds of thousands. So they have that in their favor."

"How does their genetics express itself in their ability to entangle?"

"Weakly, it would seem, although it's hard to tell," she answered. "I suspect that in the past they developed a very basic ability—they were able to colonize their entire world largely without the benefit of a common language, spoken or written. But for about 5,000 years, they have relied heavily on written language to organize elites in their society, and only in the last 200 years has written language become widespread outside the elites, and even then, not everywhere. And they have thousands of languages, although a handful are widespread. As they've advanced technically, they've also had tugs pulling them apart, pushing them backwards in their social integration."

"As happened with our ancestors," he pointed out.

He was right. All 20 species in the Guardians had gone through this, as had many dozens of others they had come across in their long history. Most complex life had a basic ability to sense the feelings of others in their own species, even other species. As they evolved, they gained an increasing ability to understand not just others' emotions, but intentions. From there, it was a matter of how their sensory apparatus evolved to be able to see behind the intentions to the reasoning, both logical and emotional. Some species could do that on their own, others developed technological or biological enhancements that did that for them.

But humans seemed stuck in a fairly extreme Emergent phase. Most societies learned how to destroy their environment and their own species, but they were usually further along in understanding their own minds when they did. Humans had a relatively primitive understanding of their own minds compared to their understanding of physics or chemistry.

Far Flier was absorbing these thoughts from her when he felt Adno make contact with her.

"Sorry," she said a minute later. "Adno wanted to let me know that Raefe's OK. He and his mate, Lina, have found a camp where they can eat and sleep for the time being. She confirms that his ability to entangle has become stronger. Adno suspects that as the shock of the flood wears off, he will also be less troubled by his abilities. We agree that he's starting to come to grips with his empathic power for the first time. If we could just nudge that along…"

"Well, we are bound not to intervene too much. Soon, though, you may be able to contact him directly. In the meanwhile, you sit by the interface, to do what? Hope for a miracle?" he asked. "As Adno's people on Water Eye say, 'You can try to swim on land, but it won't get any wetter.'"

She could feel that he wanted her to know that he was impressed by her effort. Was he doing that as her mentor or prospective lover? This was the new dance they had begun. Most days, she found it enjoyable, but today it was just a distraction.

"Well, Earth's not all that dry," she joked, letting her enhancements find a report she was still preparing on humanity's best features. She let him feel her doubts, too—was she naïvely tricked into optimism? After all, he had been at this for 800 more years than her.

"Think about what's the crux of the issue here," he said, now playing the mentor.

"They have to make that breakthrough," she said. "That moment when they learn to use their rationality to understand their irrationality. Their art is full of that, but they think of it as imaginary, not real. They're like most other intelligent species, a blend of emotion and logic. But they think of those facets as opposites instead of complementary. That's exactly what they need to shed."

"Well, you seem to believe they can. Let's just hope that they do, too," he said. "I knew you were the right person for this job. Most Guardians would have recommend abandoning this species to their own devices."

"I can't accept that they're that hopeless," she said, "Their abilities are buried, not nonexistent. If I sit in front of that interface I can sense the pure signal of a few thousand minds in that glow, unmediated by the interface network. It's just extremely weak. But something very real is happening, even as we sit here. Hopefully, Raefe is not the only one being pushed forward by crisis. But I fear for them—their civilization is trapped in the classic spiral of decline. Those with the power to change things delude themselves and use their power to protect their own narrow and very short-term interests. He's just one person in a failing world."

"And yet, I sense that what troubles you most is the fate of this Raefe."

"He has had a hard life. He experiences his own gift as an affliction, and he sees himself as weak and useless. Sometimes, my heart breaks for him."

"Still, it's a start for him and for you. Keep me informed. Next week is the Guardian Council meeting. At the very least, let's talk about it there. Now, I have to go."

WINTER HILL

Somerville
October 1, 2048

All Raefe could see in the dawn light was cool fire. The trees on the hills of East Somerville were in full autumn shades, diverting his view from the harbor waters that had crashed their way to the base of the hills three weeks ago. The sunrise tinted the water between the hills with similar colors. He'd come out looking for serenity and instead found a vision of a world caught between burning and drowning.

"Couldn't sleep?" Lina asked. She stood behind him, wrapping her arms around his waist. He felt her bushy hair at the base of his neck, her breasts warming his back through his shirt.

"Can't sleep in the glamorous DigiBrands Flood Relief Camp?" Raefe said. "Four-star cots, world-class rations, best portable toilets for miles around? Why would you think that?"

"Hey, this too shall pass. We're alive, at least."

"Authentic, thanks to my dreams," Raefe answered, dropping the sarcasm. He turned around to face her. "If I hadn't woken up at 2AM that night, I wouldn't have heard the sounds of the water rushing in from the harbor. We wouldn't have made it up to the roof."

He couldn't shake those sounds. Sometimes it was just a din, sometimes it felt like he could hear the voices of all 43,561 victims. And in the worst moments, another 10 million wanderers like themselves. He couldn't understand why she didn't. She had spent two years in horrid camps after the East African genocide. Had she become numb?

"But we did make it to the roof and here we are," Lina said, holding both his arms. "I've been through this. Actually it was much sootier than this. So I know we can get through this."

"Because we've already gotten through watching the sunrise over an ocean that used to be a mile away? Because no one bothered to maintain the seawall they built only five years ago after the exact same thing happened to Ireland when a chunk of Greenland ice slid into the ocean?" That night had transformed him. His head was a jumble of emotions, like an old 20th century abstract painting filled with random colored brushstrokes. He could turn the noise up or down, but he couldn't make it stop. Raefe worried that he was going crazy; but he was too scared to say that out loud to anyone, even Lina.

"No, because we can walk this path together," she said. "But if that path only leads to anger or fear or resignation, it will be a path that never ends. We are only 20 and our lives may be sooty, but they're ours. And you, who always takes on the suffering of the world, now it's your turn to look after yourself."

"I don't really know that means. All of my life, I've had these headaches, whether I 'looked after myself' or not. Sometimes I thought I was crazy. Now my headaches have vanished. But something else has happened."

He told her about the voices, like an old radio tuner stuck between stations. And not just the voices, he realized as he spoke. Sometimes it was just tones—fear, friendliness, greed, lust.

"I'm exhausted, but I can't stop," he said, not looking her in the eye. "I'm not as tough as you, Lina."

She was quiet, her hand resting on his, not grasping it but not restless either. He thought of the first time he had seen her. Her Solar-Cycle had gotten a flat tire on the Mass Ave. Bridge during the first big snowstorm in three years. Bad enough she had been riding during a blizzard, but there was her wiry little self, flipping the 50 kilos or so of the bike upside down so she could change the tire, gloves off, horsing the wheel nut off with a wrench. He'd stopped to help her, but she was much quicker at it than he was.

She offered to buy him something hot to thank him. They went to Golden Age, an ultra-retro cafe in the arty district that fringed the salty marshes along the mouth of the Charles. The restaurant recreated the 1950s as best as it could. They sat talking and drinking the muddy coffee. He remembered being puzzled by the weird little coffee pots with small glass domes protruding from the top. He liked retro, but he felt disoriented. His 180 cm felt gangly next to her compact frame. He felt pale and gaunt and weak in the face of her strength and energy.

She told him about how she had never seen snow up close before, having grown up in the East African Republic. The restaurant had covered all the light strips with plastic so that they looked yellowy, like 20th century incandescent bulbs supposedly had. It made the room feel warmer than it was and soon the warmth and the sound of her voice began to put him at ease. He couldn't take his eyes off her, from her riotous hair to her small but long-fingered hands that seemed to be translating her speech into some kind of dance language. After being out in the cold and wind, her yellow and brown hair went every which way, as if her cinnamon skin had separated itself into her mother's East African brown and her father's golden Chinese shades, and flowed like a braided river out into her hair, to glow in the antique lights of the restaurant. His gaze lasted a tad too long, causing her to run her finger self-consciously along the ropey scar tissue that capped her right ear.

Later, he would find out that the scar was a reminder of the East African holocaust that she could never quite forget or talk about. At that moment, it had broken his reverie and made her approachable. He told her stories his father had told him about living with knee-deep snow for weeks and months in far northern Vermont many years ago, and by the time they had finished their second cup of coffee, they both knew they would see each other again. In the two years since, they had made a bit of a life together.

She sighed, bringing him back to Somerville.

"You think I'm some kind of Sim character," she said. "That my superpower is to endure suffering, that my scars are like insignia on a soldier's sleeve. But soon you'll know, too, that endurance is learned, and at a cost. We might have to tough this out for a while. We're fugees now, like a billion other people in a thousand other places. But these voices—it worries me. Are you going to be OK?"

"I'm not sure what OK means, Lina. You want me to smile and say I'm fine?"

"I'll settle for a smile. And there's a whole lot of life between 'not fine,' and 'fine.' That might be our address for a long time."

I've disappointed her again, he thought. She wants someone tougher. He sighed. "Sad but true. Look, I don't know about these voices. Somehow, I can glimpse what people are feeling—I'm not just imagining that. But I'll do my best not to freak out. That's all I can say."

"Second best will do, too," she smiled. "It's not a test. It's cold out here—come downstairs and have some of those world-class rations DigiBrands is treating us to. They're free, don't you know? We've only got to work all day to get them."

They sat in the dining hall, a big inflatable structure with dull-colored sides, heads down with a few hundred others, eating an indifferent breakfast of weak tea, some kind of protein porridge and an orange. A woman in a shirt with a DigiBrands logo got on the bullhorn and told them all where to shape up. Their crew trudged down Broadway toward the flood zone. Once it had been the main street of East Somerville, the many small shops tattooed with flexible screens that displayed their wares and tapped into people's Voices to promise lowest prices, best ever, tailored just for you. Now, the screens were silent and covered with a film of grayish mud, the shops empty and their shelves no longer stocked with the makings of curry or parts for bikes or cheap 3-D-printed clothing. Feral cats roamed their insides, their yowling frustrated and angry.

Over the last three weeks, the water had receded part way, leaving most of the streets west of the interstate dry. Near the mouth of the Mystic, the remnants of a luxury condo and shopping enclave poked their way out of the expanded bay, their first few floors soon to be colonized by marine life. They had gone down to their TinyStack a week after the flood, but it was ruined. The three modules were no longer attached, the top two askew and looking like a strong breeze would bring them down. There would be no retrieving their possessions, now buried along with Miguel.

Raefe could still feel the screams of those who hadn't made it. As he replayed the night of the storm, he had come to hear more than just their screams: their shock, their anger, their disappointment as they realized the lives they would not lead. Grief was an ocean that still rose to his chin, sometimes he could barely keep his nostrils clear. He turned his mind away from those thoughts, trying to focus on the simple tasks of lifting debris, piling it up, sorting it, and loading it on the appropriate truck. Salvageable metals went one place, rotten organics another, plain old dirt a third—DigiBrands would find ways to monetize all of it, not that he would ever see any of that. The day went by, the sun traversed its arc, and they trudged back up Winter Hill in the dusk. He hated that he was actually looking forward to another meal of little more than prison food, but he was tired and hungry.

That night, he and Lina snuck off to an abandoned furniture warehouse the camp residents called The Club. Unless you had kids, the camp had separate sides for male and female—if you wanted to meet the opposite sex, you had to go to The Club. They found a couch in decent shape and dragged it to a dark corner. They made love for the first time since the flood, wordlessly, happily, sleepily. For the first time since that night, he was able to quiet his mind and not worry about his sanity or toughness; but he feared this would be a brief respite.

After, he held her face and kissed her. Holding her, he was suddenly afraid that she would tire of him and leave. "I know you think I'm a child sometimes," he said. "Compared to you, maybe. What upsets me is not becoming a fugee. It's living in a world of fugees."

"Fugees are the future, don't knock 'em," she said, trying to head off another of his melancholy bouts.

"You're scared I'm going to lose it, aren't you?" he asked.

"Maybe," she conceded. "I know this flood has knocked you off your feet. I was only a kid during the Efricar civil war, so I don't remember too much. But I feel like it must be tough for you to get to our age thinking the world is a certain way and then find out it's not at all like that."

"I understand how you could say that, from what you've had to go through," he said. "But we've all had our own 'civil wars' to deal with. Mine was The Slide. Even though I was a baby, my parents never got over that. All through my childhood, I knew something had gone terribly wrong, that my parents could do nothing about it. I didn't grow up in the camps like you did, but I was made to watch the old vids of the food riots, the mobs breaking into stores, the tanks guarding the banks. And every year on the anniversary, the memorials, the fat, pious words from politicians and corpos. My parents angrily muttering at the vid screen, always feeling betrayed."

"Trust me, that's bad, but it's nothing like being a slave in a camp run by genocidal maniacs."

"I didn't say it was."

"Felt that way to me. I don't need to feel you've been through what I've been through to love you, honestly."

"Look, I'm not trying to denigrate your experience. I've never lived in a world as bad as the one you escaped. But I have lived in a world that was bad enough to shatter whatever expectations my parents had. That, I do know. And I see it on the faces of everyone here. They have 'The Look'—I can feel them staring off into a future that terrifies them."

"You're right about the look. And the blankness—the feeling that you can't show what you are feeling, that if we all did that, we'd collapse into a writhing heap of despair."

"Authentic, that's it. And just like I've been carrying around The Slide as if it vaccinated me from anything worse, you carry around

Efricar. And now we all have to consider that no matter what happened in the past, we're not prepared for what's to come."

She nodded wordlessly, burrowing into his arms more deeply.

We've reached the end of words, he thought. *We need to feel something together, something new. More than that, we need to do something new.*

He listened to the distant waters, now singing a calming song. Maybe in time he could draw strength from other people's feelings, just as he drew strength from Lina. He wanted to explain that to her, but she had drifted off to sleep. He let the rhythm of her sleep breathing send him slowly into the deeps, no longer afraid she'd be gone in the morning.

FLYING SOLO

Diver was doubly excited this morning. She had made up her mind about how to help Raefe. And she was going to fly.

Most people on Traveler's Perch cherished their distant past as partially airborne creates. But she was one of the few who had learned to use their enhancements, plus a flight suit, to actually ride the air currents high above the canyons as their more avian ancestors had done naturally. That was, in fact, how she had met Flies Far to Cross Oceans—they both belonged to the same avian flying club.

People who hadn't experienced the unenhanced lives of other species thought her foolish or eccentric. But Ambassadors often cherished the rawness of such experiences, the sheer physicality of them. She had discovered something else, too: Her mind worked differently when flying. Most people on Traveler's Perch, when faced with a difficult problem, gave their enhancements multiple assignments to go off and dig through masses of data and come back with suggestions. That was great if the answer to your problem lay buried in mountains of data.

But sometimes she wanted a sharper strategic view, a way to get past difficulty and reach whatever prize she was interested in. She found her own organic mind worked best in that fashion when she flew. Somewhere deep in her mind, she was engaging circuits that were constantly evaluating threats and opportunities. She had found that the combination of flying and deep thinking could be powerful. Today she would put that to the test as she thought of how to approach Raefe.

She felt her body generating her morning nutrients and suppressed them—she had other plans for food today. She ordered her rooms to open the front wall and reshape it into a balcony. She looked out over the canyons hundreds of meters below, still flooded to remind everyone of their last brush with environmental suicide 10,000 years ago. A breeze brought the first hint of dawn's warmth to her face and decorated the water with a dance of foam, pink in the sun's rising red light. Higher in the sky, Prime's trinary mates, the Twins, still shone like orange eyes against the black of space. Prime's other two planets, Red Nest and Water Eye, were on the other side of Traveler's Perch this morning.

She smiled, thinking of the stories the ancients had about their sky. Prime was Mother, and the Twins were First Father and Second Father. The planets were their children. They thought the Fathers were doing a mating dance with Mother, and that the children were approaching her for food. Adno's people, on Water Eye, had a completely different story, one that mostly made sense if you spent all your time in the water on an almost landless planet. When their species had finally discovered each other thousands of years ago, their exchanges of myth and superstition had helped each species to understand the limits of their own perceptions in deep ways that had helped them avoid war.

Diver checked her flight suit, making sure its wings would release properly. Her short arms, vestiges of her ancestors' wings, would once again be as long and powerful as they were in ancient times. Standing on the edge of the balcony, she let her enhancements feel the winds. She dove, arms tight at her side, and kicked to release the small webs tucked between her three large toes, forming a tail where each foot had been. She used these small tails to guide her descent, relishing the feeling of laying out in the air and feeling its resistance. The sun was warm on her back, the wind hard on her face as she angled toward the water at over 60 kilometers an hour. At 30 meters above the water, she flung her arms wide, releasing her wings, breaking and angling nearly vertical to the water. The pressure was enormous, but nothing her enhancements couldn't handle.

She hit the water with arms tight to her sides and feet together, plowing into the back of a school of silvery fish. She may not have had the beak her ancestors did, but she could still harden her lips, hinge her jaw open, and seize a good-sized fish in it even as her legs were just breaking the surface. She arched her back out of the water, extended her feet, and thrust her arms out into the air in a swimming motion. Two more thrusts, and she caught the bottom of the air currents and tacked upwards toward her balcony.

Sitting on her haunches, she allowed her hands to protrude from the suit and took the fish from her mouth. The sun was full up now as she ate the fish methodically. She chewed slowly, savoring the texture and flavor of wild food much as she imagined her ancestors had done millennia before. If Adno could see her now, what would she say? Adno was no more a fish than she was bird, but surely it would make her uneasy. The 20 species of the Guardians covered a wide range of body types and environments. They all got along fine, but it had taken millenia for them to emotionally accept what they all knew intellectually: What was normal for one species might be frightening and alien for another.

She allowed her mind to come back to the task at hand, imagining what she would say to Raefe, how she would do present it all to him. Her mind was clear now.

She instructed the room to fetch transportation. She must find a way into Raefe's mind in a way that would be familiar to him, even if not totally accurate. There would be time for precision later, she hoped. A few minutes later, the room opened a portal in its back wall and she stepped into a small subway car, half full of neighbors also headed toward work. The train emerged from the tunnel behind their dwelling onto the broad flats of the plateau overlooking the canyons.

With the three stars in a low-radiation configuration today, most of the buildings had emerged from below and uncovered the transparent domes that topped them. Adapting to the complex solar cycles had plagued life on Traveler's Perch forever, but now their enhancements worked with the city's brain to modulate the light and dark periods, allowing everyone to even out their metabolism, sleep, and activity.

Today's light was bright without being harsh and tilted toward the warm. The buildings had adopted an appropriate palette, and the overall effect was quite cheery. Some of her colleagues thought she romanticized the primitive, but she was just as pleased by the city's display as by her morning fishing expedition. That was one of the things that had drawn her to Far Flier. He might be 1,200 years old and a bit full of himself, but Far Flier understood her appetite for the deep fundamental experiences at the core of life. Having been an Ambassador himself, he had felt firsthand the intensity with which unenhanced species had to pursue food to survive. He understood that evolution had planted a love of those skills deep inside every advanced life form.

And today, she would help Raefe surface some of those skills. For the first time, she would guide a less evolved species through the first steps of becoming adept at controlled entanglement. She had studied and trained for a century for this very moment. She wanted to burst into song. She told herself to remain calm and focused. She would need to be alert with Raefe to make sure his first experience was positive. She might not get a second chance.

At the Guardian Center, she found her way to her usual spot on the inner ring of the wormhole interface. Surprisingly, Raefe's mind was easy to find today. The fear and stress that she was worried about had triggered changes in him. Intrigued, she probed his memories. At first his strong empathic abilities had overwhelmed him but since she last entangled with him, his mind had responded by reaching out more strongly to those around him. And she saw that the crisis had intensified his connections with Lina. He was still confused, unstable, a raging storm of desire to do something that would make a difference, while lacking confidence that he could. Part of him could not bear so much sadness and loss around him, part of him could not bear being unable to do anything to alleviate it. She could probe his mind and feel this conflict more deeply than she had been able to before—he was more fully entangled—and he felt to her like a ripe altipano fruit ready to burst.

She knew that she should discuss this with the Guardian Council when they met in two days, or at least Far Flier, but she felt that Raefe's life hung in the balance. He was the most promising of the 2,000 or 3,000 they monitored. Losing him would set them back years, maybe generations. Did Earth have that much time?

She should consult with Green—he was in charge of Timelines. After entanglement, the ability to shift energy among alternate timelines in the multiverse was the Guardian's greatest tool. They could transmit Raefe's consciousness to another Raefe in a more benevolent timeline—he would bring the knowledge of a harsher fate to the other Raefe, and still hopefully be driven by his near-death experience, use his empathic powers to change history.

It wasn't the ideal scenario. The whole point of the Guardians, after all, was to ensure that this galaxy, in this timeline, would be a more hospitable place for intelligent life, and that rogue civilizations wouldn't rise and threaten all of the others. But if that was what it came to, she would have no choice. After all, if there were other timelines in which Earth became a threat, it was always possible that in the far future those humans would threaten not only life in their own timeline, but others as well. As far as she knew, this had never happened in the galaxy, but the universe never stopped surprising.

She would definitely investigate more friendly timelines, but for now she needed to make contact. Technically, she should have gotten approval from the Guardian Council, but hadn't Far Flier just about given her permission? Time for her to act. She had learned an old Earth saying from Raefe: Rules are made to be broken.

It was already night on Earth so she could reach out to him, make first contact in his dreams. With humans, that had so far proven the safest way.

Raefe and Lina had snuck out of the camp. Diver realized they were going off to couple. Humans were usually calmer after sex. Good thing they're not like the Glynx, who only mated once in a lifetime, after which their whole tribe celebrated for days. She dampened her entanglement with Raefe so as not to risk distracting him. An hour later, she was glad to see that he and Lina had drifted off to sleep in a good state of mind.

She had learned to infiltrate human dreams, and Raefe's were nothing out of the ordinary. In his memories, she found images of friendly females that sometimes appeared in his dreams. One was a character in a vid he liked to watch, a two-meter-tall woman, longer and leaner than most real humans, with very long, straight yellow hair. She had a variety of enhancements that made her what humans referred to as "super." Diver found the hair odd and so modified the image to match her own purple and green shades. In his dream, Raefe was sitting at his workplace. She walked up to him.

"Mars Girl?" he asked. "Is that you? What have you done to your hair?"

"I'm Diver from Great Heights, but my friends just call me Diver. I come from space, just like Mars Girl. You're Raefe, right?"

"How do you know my name?"

"Let's just say that you have a special gift that interests me. You are just beginning to come to grips with it, but your world desperately needs people who have this gift."

"My world? What world are you from?"

"I live on Traveler's Perch, about 20 light years from you. My world was like your world about 10,000 years ago. Now we try to help worlds like yours survive and move forward."

"I don't understand. You've traveled here to see me?"

"Traveling with my body would take many lifetimes—even I can't travel faster than light. But we can send energy—information—

through wormholes that make communication seem instantaneous."

"So, you're just some kind of holo vid?"

"Not exactly. More like we each live on one end of a giant guitar string made of light. Whichever one of us plucks it, we both feel it. So right now, my brain and your brain are playing a song—having a conversation—over these many light years. We can do that because we are entangled, at a quantum level, with each other."

"Quantum level? How does that work? Did someone plant a chip in me?"

She sensed his fear and felt a wave of doubts. This was what her teachers had warned about, why the Guardians made contact very infrequent, preferring to monitor and influence indirectly. She had unintentionally triggered images of possession—their culture was still so steeped in ancient superstition. She made herself smaller, changed the surroundings to his childhood home. They were sitting on a couch, schoolchildren. Her face now reminded him of a childhood friend, Samantha.

"Raefe, you don't need a chip," she smiled. "Sometimes you feel like an antenna, right?"

"And I can't turn it off."

"That's because you are extremely empathetic—much more so than most humans. You feel other people's feelings very strongly."

"Yes!" he said. "It's too much sometimes. How do I do that?"

"Many ways that you don't realize. You smell the hormones that leak from all people, you have finely tuned mirror neurons that very accurately interpret people's gestures and movements, but most of all, deep inside, unknown to you, you are entangled with the electromagnetic storm that is their emotions."

"Are those the voices I hear but can't quite make out?"

"Yes, in a way. Your brain tells you that they are speaking but can't make out the words, but that's because you are hearing the play of raw emotions, which don't live as words in your heads. But you know the feeling behind them—happy, sad, angry, and so on. Do you feel like they are laughing or crying or yelling, but you don't know why?"

"Exactly! It's like feeling crazy and half deaf at the same time. Very unnerving. I'm almost relieved to hear what you say. My head has been so filled with moaning and anguish from all sides, I was beginning to think I had a connection to Hell."

Again, the primitive superstitions, the imaginary places. She knew her people had once thought this way, but it had been 10,000 years ago. But she was glad he had said it—he was at least aware enough to give voice to his fear. If he could name it, she could help him around it.

"Relax, there is no Hell. You are perfectly sane and your abilities are growing. Your mind wants to reach out, to feel others and to let them feel you and other people, too. While it is not something encouraged right now in your world, it is something humans will have to get better at if they are to progress. If your world is to survive, connection and empathy must become more important than competition and aggression."

"So are you saying that we can sort of talk to each other, but without speaking?"

"Not exactly. At this point, humans can learn to have a much deeper sense of each other's emotions. You can use words for ideas and concepts, but words are not always the best way to convince each other of your motivations and intentions. Suppose I say 'I mean you no harm.' How do you know I mean it?"

"Right, you could say that whether you are lying or telling the truth."

"If you could feel my emotions, feel whether I was friendly, agreeable, resigned, angry, sneering at you, then you would know how to interpret my words."

She was tempted to explain to him that later they could augment this with technology that would, in fact, allow people to converse, one-on-one, without speaking, and, even later, among entire groups. But the Guardians had learned not to give new species a tour of the future: It was a country best visited in person.

"But you should know," she continued, "that there are others like you, and you all can help lead humans away from self destruction."

"Lead humans? You've got the wrong guy. I can barely get through the day anymore. I can't help anyone. I don't want that job."

She subtly shifted the environment so that they were walking through a meadow dotted with wildflowers. It was sunny and a pleasant breeze entertained them. She wanted him to be calm but also hopeful.

"Your empathic powers helped you, Lina, Kiko and Kayam to survive the flood. Don't forget that—you've already done something huge. In fact, we couldn't really be having this conversation if you didn't have a strong ability. But tell me, how do you feel since then?"

"I can't stop hearing the screams of the people who didn't make it," he said.

"And the headaches?" she asked.

"I have to admit, they've become weaker and less frequent."

"That's because you're beginning to master your own abilities. And because you were able to use them to save someone you love, so they're not just a handicap anymore. What other changes have you noticed?"

"Well, I have to admit, other people seem a little less of a mystery to me. Now that you mention it, I do have more of a sense of what they really mean," he said, mulling it over. "I feel like I'm just starting to get a handle on myself. But maybe this is all I can handle."

She could feel him tensing up, wanting to disconnect. Humans were very fond of babies, maybe he would respond to that.

"Think of me as a midwife. Imagine you're giving birth to yourself. The new you will be someone you are very proud to be. But first, you must go through the process of birth. Are you ready for that?"

"Slow down! Give birth, new me—I feel like I just started being me. Not sure I want to get rid of me yet."

She could feel his mind frantically reviewing vids of alien possession, demons.

"Sorry, sometimes I forget how strange it must seem if you've never entangled with another person. I can give you a sense of it first, so you see it's nothing to fear."

She focused her thoughts more intently than usual on the several centers in his brain that she would normally entangle with. She wanted to him to feel each touch. "Can you feel that?"

"Yeah, I do. It's like I'm seeing you in three dimensions. More like four or five, like I'm seeing the outside of you, but also your feelings and thoughts, all at the same time."

"That's it. It will be a long time before you can do this on your own. At first, you will just be able to sense people's emotions. In time, you will see some of the thoughts that accompany those emotions, and then how they connect to actions and future plans. I have technology that augments my capabilities and can hear the thoughts of those I entangle with almost as you do on the device you call a Voice. For now, though, every little touch you feel in your mind, touch back."

"I can't really touch you. It's like I'm a school of fish and you are too, and we're passing through each other."

"Now imagine more and more fish in each school until there's only a small amount of water between your fish and my fish. I'm silver fish and you're gold fish. Can you see that?"

"Yes!"

"One more step. Feel how we each disturb the water between us. Move and feel how the water moves. Now I'll move. Can you feel the vibrations in the water as I move?"

"The vibrations—that's how you speak to me?"

This was turning out better than she had expected. He was already able to sense the waveform, the resonance that was created by two minds interacting, just as two water waves would create a unique third pattern if they collided.

"Brilliant! Now you've got it. When you feel your headaches, when you feel like the people around you are shouting their thoughts at you in a giant jumble, you're feeling that water, just all mixed up. If you can focus, you can feel how each little eddy and whorl comes from a mind, how they form a giant chord, and you will learn to hear their separate melodies within the chord."

"I believe that. Sometimes I sense something like that."

"It's no worse than being in noisy place and hearing a lot of voices. It's just that these voices go deeper into your mind, into your feelings and sometimes, what you think of as your soul. Someday, all humans will be able to do this. But your mind can do this now."

Diver wanted his last memories of her to be peaceful. She shifted the scene to a subway car. He and Lina were sitting in the seat next to her. Lina was asleep on his shoulder.

"Soon you will wake and you will remember this. Have a good day!"

She slowly withdrew from his mind, letting his subconscious finish the dream.

MEET THE NEW BOSS

October 2, 2048

L ina woke him before dawn so they could sneak back into the camp. Raefe wanted to tell her something but couldn't remember what. The 6 AM horn sounded, and he filed into the shower room. As the water hit him, he remembered bits of the dream he'd had the night before. Mars Girl had been on the subway, only she had green and purple hair. There were fish floating through the air, but no water. He couldn't quite piece it together.

He ate breakfast like it was cough syrup.

"Hey, I thought you'd be hungry this morning," Lina said, giving him a little elbow. "You're making me feel like I messed up somehow last night."

"Not to worry," he said. "I guess I didn't sleep much—crazy dreams. I'm sure by tonight, I'll be hungry again." He nudged her back.

"Glad to hear it. Weird to have to sneak around though, hah? Our Tiny might have just been one big room, but we could take care of all our earthly needs just fine."

"If only it had been waterproof and had a boat engine."

After breakfast, they shaped up with their crew and made the usual march down to the work site. Another morning moving scattered bricks and twisted steel. But the streets were starting to look almost normal.

Maybe the worst of it was over, Raefe thought. Lina is right, I can't drown in this.

He let himself feel the arms and legs of the dozen of them, pushing, lifting, shaping, building. It was an infectious rhythm, an old-timey second line street parade of sweat and exertion, and he gave himself over to it. Soon he was lost in all their thoughts, feeling the silver fish of their thoughts pass through his gold...

Holy shit. This is what I dreamed. Purple-and-green lady was not Mars Girl, she was Diver, an alien. Did that actually happen?

Maybe it had been a dream, but the feeling wouldn't go away. He couldn't actually read anyone's thoughts, like what did Mo, the big Haitian guy, think about Sonja as he was chatting her up, but he felt that Mo was not paying attention to his shovel and thinking he was somewhere else, a food stand maybe? Lina had a bit of a hum about her. Everyone was enjoying the sun as it warmed up this October morning. Wasn't that what Diver had said, that he'd feel connected?

No voices were talking to him from the clouds. He wasn't getting crazy instructions to kill everyone with blue eyes or shorter than a meter and a half. And he wasn't getting a headache. Real or not, maybe something had happened to him during the night. Something good, for a change.

"Hey, dreamy," Nhitin, their crew boss, barked. "Sleep at night, work during the day. You're starting to get the hang of it—show me you can totally do it."

"The staff's all wound up," Sammy, one of the guys on their crew, whispered to him. "Something's going down."

All morning, people traded rumors—they were all being shipped out somewhere, the government was going to build new TinyStacks for everyone, they were all getting $10,000 to start anew. Anyone who had salvaged their Voice or taken their puter when fleeing the water was sneaking off to search for answers. But no one found anything solid. There were dozens of camps like this, the government itself was even less functional than usual, and the Net was full of even more sooty information than usual. Morning went and at noon they had lunch break. A Brightstar Defense Services truck showed up with food. Raefe and Lina grabbed some rice and beans and found a good rubble pile to sit on.

"Hey, Nhitin thinks you're dreamy," Lina teased him.

"Any dream with Nhitin in it counts as a nightmare to me," Raefe shot back.

"But you had those dreams again last night, didn't you?" she asked. "It worries me."

"I had a dream, kind of strange, but no, it wasn't what you think. I'm fine." He just didn't feel ready to tell her more yet.

"Well, good. Wouldn't be good if you freaked out every time we got busy."

"Authentic. I think more tests are called for, Dr. Feelgood."

"I think they should test this food," Lina grimaced. "Tastes like it was made before the flood."

Something loud was coming from back over Winter Hill. The lunch chatter stopped as everyone looked up. Three large helicopters in Brightstar blue crested the hill, approaching rapidly, noise and dust growing. As fast as they had appeared, they landed down the block, on a now-empty used electric car lot. Some government soldiers got out, followed by some suits and a woman in a Brightstar officer's uniform. The soldiers escorted the suits and the Brightstar brass toward the worksite.

"Geez," he whispered to Lina, "They look like they're on a mission behind the lines."

"I'm Captain Erzel, Second Engineers, Brightstar Logistics," the woman said through a bullhorn. "We want to tell you what's next in the relief effort. We've been asked by the government to coordinate, now that we're past the initial crisis. With me is Ken Robertson, the CEO of DigiBrands. He's going to explain what's next."

"Thanks, Captain Erzel," Robertson said, taking the bullhorn. "You're probably wondering why this surprise visit in the middle of the day. The simple reason is that we're all in a hurry, you and me and 100 million people on the East Coast whose lives were torn up by Hurricane Fatima almost a month ago. Roads are still spotty, the Net goes in and out, and people want to get home and back to school and work. Take a look around."

Robertson swept his arm across the scenery.

"You've worked hard. There are 13 other relief camps along the Massachusetts Bay, and they have all done the same. You've paved the way, so to speak, for the next phase. Rebuilding. And so we need to bring in real builders. When it comes to putting up bridges, roadways, and offices fast and efficiently, Brightstar Logistics is second to none. So they are going to take over that phase of it. But we have some priorities that need your contribution, urgently, and we're going to be moving you, and many of the other relief camps to those places and projects."

"Excuse me," a middle-aged man stood up. "Moving us? What happened to rebuilding our homes, our neighborhoods? And why are you, DigiBrands, talking to us? Where's the mayor? The governor?"

Robertson looked uncomfortable. An aide whispered in his ear. Raefe had a sudden whoosh of feeling from the two of them; a little panic, a little bit of something that reminded him of an old phrase— tap dancing. Must be like that Limerick Leap dance that had been all the rage a few years ago—people jumping up and down willy-nilly like they were walking barefoot on hot coals.

"I'm sorry," he said. "My associate was just explaining to me that you may not be aware of the latest news. Things have been moving fast. Let me backtrack a little. Some of you still have your puters and you may be aware that the crisis has stretched the government, at all levels, to a breaking point. Put simply, the government is broke. Bankrupt. President Schwartz and I have been discussing the situation for the last two weeks and we have come to an agreement. The US government has granted DigiBrands a semi-autonomous zone that corresponds to the entire Massachusetts Bay flood area. We are assuming responsibility for rebuilding, because we see tremendous opportunity here, and we have the resources to stay in it for the duration."

"So what are you saying?" the man who had interrupted asked. "We work for you?"

"Precisely," Robertson smiled. "And we have important work to do. We, along with Brightstar, have made rebuilding the Atlantic Sea Wall a top priority. We expect two or three more hurricanes between now and February that are Category 5 or worse. You'll be working with the Brightstar team on Truro Island. These helicopters will take you there—don't worry, your personal belongings from the camp are being packed up right now and will be on board shortly."

"Finish your food," Captain Erzel said. "In 20 minutes, we'll load up the choppers and head out."

Why did Raefe feel like there was an unspoken "you poor bastards" at the end of that?

TIMELINES

October 2, 2048

Diver was pleased to see that Raefe was integrating the experience well. She'd bent the rules by contacting him without formal approval, but at least it hadn't turned out badly. Raefe was on a good path now, but would it matter? Her scans of Earth suggested escalating ecological breakdowns. Coastal forests were being damaged by salt surges. Bird nesting areas were being wiped out. The insects normally eaten by those birds would now further damage plant life, and the downward spiral would continue.

Adno had been monitoring the thousands of mild entanglers on Earth and they showed definite signs of escalating social stress on humans. A billion years of Guardian history had shown that the combination of radical environmental shifts and psychological stress was hard to overcome. Unless the stress led to a wave of conversions like Raefe's...

Maybe Green would know something. He was a timeline analyst. He could help her understand what she was up against. They were old friends, so he'd probably be willing to discuss the matter even if the Council had not yet. She found his mind in the local waveform.

"Hey, Green, I'm hoping you can help me understand something," she said.

"Sure, what do you need?"

"I'm considering options for Earth."

"Right, the planet that never stops killing itself," he said.

"Wow, that's harsh. Why do you say that?"

"You know why they gave you the assignment, don't you?"

"Because I'm pretty junior and it's kind of a marginal civilization?" Diver replied.

"Well, I've been saying that all along. But when you were still a cadet, Hankori first took on Earth. He was an Ambassador then."

"Really? He never struck me as being that interested in other species. I thought he was more of an organization type."

"Sure, now," Green said. "He's quite brilliant. He was the first to detect the beginnings of an advanced civilization on Earth. He felt their entanglement powers were weak, but promising. But it didn't work out."

"What happened?"

"He was able to make contact with several promising leaders, and they began to build a following. But he didn't really understand the human makeup. He didn't see that some of his contacts were not empaths at all. They were self-delusional characters who thought they had superior abilities to connect with their fellow humans. I believe in their culture, they call this a 'narcissist' or 'sociopath.'"

She wondered how Hankori could mistake an empath for a sociopath—a conversation for another day.

"He must have felt terrible," she said. "How did his assignment end?"

"He insisted from the start that we begin with the most favorable timeline, one that turned out not to be our own. After a decade of working with them, there was a nuclear war in their year 1962. In our timeline, the humans call it the Cuban Missile Crisis because it was avoided, but we had to move more than a dozen of his contacts to more favorable timelines. Or so we thought. Some of them had their own catastrophic wars. The Middle East in 1976, Korea in 2012, Iran in 2019, Pakistan in 2023—the list goes on. The others we transferred wound up in timelines where there was less war, but the unrestrained economic growth led to faster environmental collapse. Hankori couldn't take it. He resigned and transferred to the administration wing."

So when she had been given the assignment, those timelines had been abandoned. Not surprising, since it took a lot of energy to maintain contact with many timelines at once. Even the Guardians had to obey the laws of thermodynamics—energy wasn't free.

"That's discouraging. So why did they give it to me?"

Green was uncomfortable. "Do I have to spell it out for you?"

"Maybe you do. I'm not seeing it."

"Diver from Great Heights, I know how capable you are. But the truth is, most of the council agreed with Hankori that Earth was a waste of time. And they were happy to be rid of the exorbitant energy budget. But Far Flier can be stubborn when he thinks he's right, and he wouldn't join that consensus. And when he assigned you, well you must know that it's no secret that you're more than colleagues. No one was going to buck him. So they voted with him. If it been anyone else, they would have voted it down."

She considered what he was saying. It wasn't impossible, but it didn't feel right.

"I don't know if that's why I got the job," she thought to him, letting him see both that she thought it might be true and that she had reasons to doubt it. "But it's certainly not why I'm sticking with it. I'm sorry if you think I'm just here to soothe Far Flier's vanity. From where I'm sitting, there is some cause for optimism about Earth. But I need to understand what the timelines show. What am I up against?"

"I can give you some ideas, but I can't give you too many specifics."

"Feathers as Green as Third Spring Grass, I'm not an idiot. I'm not going to bring on another Orion Belt disaster, OK?"

"OK, OK, always have to give that little speech about not going back into the past to change the present. So let's look at Earth across the timelines."

A column of light rose from the floor, showing the metaverse of the millions of alternative universes that had Earths. Many were very similar and grouped like trees, with common roots but ending in different branches. Green was trained to read the timelines, just as she had been trained to read entanglers across the wormhole interface. Entanglement plus alternate timelines—this was the foundation of Guardian technology.

"What you see is that at the present, there are several major trees of outcomes. The largest tree shows a steady decline punctuated by various crises—war, famine, disease, all aggravated by out-of-control warming, predatory social structures, and a variety of lesser ills. In short, the Earth you are currently focused on. There are other smaller trees: runaway warming, leading to a Venusian climate; total nuclear annihilation; escapes to space, most of which fail. I can't really see beyond 100 years, since there are too many variables in our model. I think you'll agree, Earth is currently in an extremely labile period—small changes can yield big course corrections."

"That's about the only thing I see that's encouraging. In the current tree, are there any signs of hope?"

"Hard to say. Ironically, in the timelines that failed earliest, there is some regeneration."

"That's odd. Why would that be?"

"Well, it looks like in some timelines, there was a Third World

War right after the Second World War and some nuclear weapons were used. But at the time, there weren't that many, so a full-on catastrophe was avoided. There were more than 300 million people killed. There was more of a nuclear autumn than a nuclear winter. The near-Armageddon caused some reflection about the way forward that has yielded some fruit in several timelines. And the increased desire to avoid future catastrophes bled over into tackling the greenhouse gas problem, so climate change has been much more moderate. Plus the nuclear autumn forced an economic slowdown that brought them some time on that front."

"Why didn't we focus on those worlds?"

"The Earth project started only a few years after those timelines blew up. Our models didn't show much promise. As we usually do, we went for those timelines that were least likely to self-destruct. And after things went south with Hankori, there was little appetite to invest more energy into the project than needed, as we just discussed."

This was not exactly the brave profile of Guardianship that she had been trained to implement. Damn them, she knew there was something in these humans. To survive partial annihilation on that scale and rebound was a feat on the scale of the U Maw, the first Guardians. Who would be their Na'wra? Was it Raefe?

"Well, you've given me a lot to think about. We'll talk more."

She might have to get Green moving on short notice. What if the water had risen just 10 meters higher around Raefe's home? Green was wrong—Far Flier had not parked her in a job that would be endless, fruitless monitoring of a world going nowhere. She would need to stay high on her perch and be ready to soar in a wing beat.

ISLAND LIFE

Truro Island
October 2, 2048

aefe and Lina were jammed into a big helicopter with 54 other
fugees. A half dozen Brightstar mercs kept an eye on them,
hands never far from their weapons. For the mercs, fugees were
always a threat, even if they came from your own neighborhood. The
chopper roared off the launch pad, the noise of the rotors and the wind
a thick fluid filling the cabin.

Raefe could smell the sea now, as the wind whipped through the
open chopper door. They passed over Logan Airport, its runways
plunging deeper under water the farther they were from the terminal.
Deer Island was once again an actual island, the causeway leading to
it submerged and little but the globes of the wastewater plant visible
above the surf. To the right, the thick stone walls of an old colonial
fort stuck five meters out of the water like an aquatic Stonehenge, their
foundations invisible beneath the choppy surf. To the left and right,
the familiar coastline of the harbor was blurred and smudged by the
new tide line and tons of sandy mud. Near the sea, roads came and
went, seawalls had become islands, half-drowned buildings tilted in
the surf.

Coming from the Somerville hills, down across the shore, out over
the drowned islands, Raefe felt like some character in an ancient myth,
a character descending into a watery underworld, filled by souls the
planet had washed from the land.

He watched Lina's brown curls swirl in the wind, exposing the ugly,
ropey scar on her right ear she never talked about. What was going
through her mind, to have survived the Efricar holocaust, escaped to
Sofricar, migrated here, and now, once again become a fugee and, for
all practical purposes, a prisoner? He could feel her anger and her sadness, but something else he couldn't quite name. Something dark and
deep. Was it the same feeling that was enveloping him, that they were

refugees now, not from some human conflict, but from nature itself?

They swept out over the open water, and soon Truro Island was in sight. Five years had come and gone since the same rising waters that had inundated Ireland had severed the outer arm of Cape Cod just above Wellfleet Harbor. Wind and water had blunted the knife lines of that amputation, smoothing and curving them into an ordinary, if steep, island shoreline.

They landed on field of hard packed dirt on a bluff 25 meters above the ocean. Their first words of welcome to the island were an incessant, robotic, "Single file, single file" from the mercs grabbing their arms and pulling them off the helicopter. A soldier gave them a more informative introduction through a bullhorn.

"East Somerville Work Detail welcome to Seawall Construction Camp Alpha. You will be reporting here at this exact spot every morning, Monday through Saturday. Sunday is yours. Sergeant Merto will be your work detail leader. Sergeant!"

"Yes sir! Listen up. You are on Truro Island, surrounded by the Atlantic Ocean. See those seals on the sandbar? They're sitting there so they don't get eaten by great white sharks. It's October and prolonged immersion in the water is cold enough to kill you, even if the sharks don't. The mainland is 30 miles from the other side of the island. You will all be chipped in the arm. If you get lost, we can find you. If you run away, we will find you.

"You're all here because a hurricane broke the Atlantic Seawall and made you homeless. Being homeless, you consumed a lot of government aid, supplies that the government bought from us but can't pay for. So now you can work off your relief aid by rebuilding the wall. Specifically, the part of that seawall extended from Truro Island north to Cape Ann. We will load up barges with supplies and go out to the work sites. Some days we will return, some days we will stay out on mobile work camps on the water. The work will be hard, but you'll get three squares and a roof over your head at night. We're all here to do a job, and we won't tolerate any funny business in the camp. No gambling, no pimping, stealing, drugs—you get the picture."

Raefe scanned the dozens of fugees sitting on the tarmac. He felt their dejection—first to get hit by the storm, and now by what seemed like a prison sentence. They had begun staring at anything besides Sargent Merto.

"Lastly, some of you fancy yourself some kind of fugee legal experts, and you're going to ask me about your rights. Forget it. For all practical purposes, you are no longer in the United States or the state of Massachusetts. You are employees of DigiBrands. And Digi has sub-contracted to Brightstar to take any and all means necessary to get this wall built. Short of executing you, we have total authority while you are here. This project is forecast to take 11 months. After that, your life is yours to fuck up how you want. Until then, don't screw this up."

Lina whispered to him, "Welcome to my world."

They got injected in the arm with a tiny telemetry capsule and then were issued yellow overalls with names and numbers written in red marker. He was now Epstein Miller, 4456, she was now Kawambai Yang, 5198. The whole crew spent the afternoon putting up large tents where they would sleep. Just like Somerville, sleeping quarters were divided three ways into families, males, and females, with a fourth tent for eating.

Night brought a quiet to the camp. Back in Somerville, some of the people had played cards at night. Sometimes small groups gathered around the few people who had rescued a guitar and sang songs. This night, no one was in the mood for socializing. After a desultory meal of curried lentils with a token bit of chicken, Raefe and Lina wandered away from the tents. A big oak had somehow survived all the hurricanes, and they sat down against it, the camp to their backs. He had never seen so many stars.

"Do you think they're laughing at us up there?" he wondered. He put his arm around Lina but felt her stiffen. He knew that sometimes Lina didn't want comfort, so he let it go.

"Only if their world isn't as fucked as this one."

"There's a thought. What would they say to us, from a world that made more sense than this, if we could talk to them?"

"That made any sense," Lina said. "How does it make sense that two kids like us, just trying to put one foot in front of the other, almost drown in a catastrophic flood, and now are risking death working against our will on a construction project in the middle of the ocean?"

She stood up, fidgety, pacing. He felt an unsettlement of her spirit, as if it had forgotten how it fit inside her.

"I don't know," Raefe answered. "Can I ask you, was this what is was like when you were a kid in Efricar?"

"No kids in Efricar," Lina said, looking away from him, staring out across a barren field. "Just little people trying to live long enough to get big. Living like this was not the worst that could happen to you."

Raefe could hear seals barking and squealing 50 meters offshore as they pushed and shoved for the best sleeping spots, the scent of nearby humans making them a bit agitated. *Twenty years ago, when this island split from the mainland, we left their world. Wonder if they're happy to see us back,* he thought. *I think you'll get your island back soon enough.*

"You're putting on your armor for the long haul, aren't you? You're getting ready for another couple of years of this," he said.

"Maybe," she said. "I don't know."

"No, it's OK. I can feel it."

Lina looked at him sharply. "You don't know what's in my mind."

"That's the thing," he said. "I realize I do know some of it, a lot of the time. And not just you. The night of the flood, why I woke up? I felt the screams and the terror of the people at the water's edge, the first people to drown. I thought it was a dream, but it was the real thing."

"How do you know?"

He wanted to tell her about Diver, but he wasn't sure if he wanted to take that risk right now. Even if she didn't run screaming from him because she thought he was crazy, it would be another shock to deal with. The time would come soon enough.

"Let's just say that since that night, I've been paying more attention. The headaches and all that, I realize I was just overwhelmed by other people's feelings sometimes. I'm just one of those people who's very tuned in, subconsciously, to other people. I can smell anger or lust. Strong emotions like that, I can feel them in other people."

She eyed him silently for a few seconds. "And you think you feel what I'm thinking?"

"Not so much in words as images and feelings. Alright, tell me I'm wrong. When we were on the dinner line, you saw those lentils and you thought about eating those with your mother in Efricar. It was a nice memory, like you were a girl sitting with your mom under a tree, eating. But then it hit you hard, right, here I am, like a girl in Efricar, in a camp with soldiers. And you instinctively wiped any expression of your face so the guards couldn't decipher you, because that's what you learned in that camp. That's what I meant about armor."

Lina looked away.

"You're freaking me out," she said. "I don't know if I realized that myself, but you hit it pretty much on the head, now that I think about it. All this time we've been together, you've been doing this?"

"No, not at all. I started to realize something was going on after the flood," he said. *Make something up, it's not time to tell her about Mars Girl.* "I found stuff on the Net, here and there. People like me are called empaths. Everyone is a bit of an empath. I'm just more so. And because we're already close, I get more of you than I do of strangers. Anyway, I just wanted to say that you don't have to put up your armor with me."

"Seems like it won't work anyway. But I'm worried about you—armor is a good thing when you're surrounded by hatred. You don't want to be smelling that too much."

"Right, need some anti-hatred deodorant," he laughed. "But you know what? I think we're going to be OK. These guards, they're pretty relaxed, just doing a job. I don't think they're waiting to gun us down soon as we've finished the wall."

"How about the sharks? What are you smelling from them?"

***

In the morning, they piled onto flatbed trucks that took them to the beach. They drove along empty, broken asphalt roads, a black ribbon through the gray forests, leaves long dead from years of salt-laden hurricanes. Here and there, the dead wood was streaked black from lightning fires. Around a corner, the sun shone bright off something green. They drove closer—it was algae growing in the salt ponds, safe from the ocean waves.

The beach was a different story. There were piles of materials and many trucks unloading prisoners and supplies. The motorized rubber rafts they called Zodiacs came and went. They sat huddled in one, then got off on a sandbar. The seals barked at one end while they stood knee-deep at the other, building a pylon out of recycled plastic blocks. The morning sun warmed the shallows, but, by afternoon, the clouds had rolled in and they could no longer feel their feet. The guards let them rotate in and out of the water, giving them a few minutes to get the feeling back in their feet.

Raefe found himself sitting on a mound of building supplies next to a burly, dark-skinned man with slightly graying hair and alert eyes. He seemed familiar. Raefe felt a blend of curiosity, intelligence and steel from him. Right, the one who had interrupted Robertson back in Somerville. He tipped his head to Raefe, who grunted "Hey."

"Alton Winchester," the man said. "And I'm guessing you're Raefe?"

"How do you know my name?"

"I saw with you with Lina. Used to see her down at the K&K. She talks about you a lot."

"I dug what you did the other day."

One of the guards came over and glared at them.

"Alright ladies, I'm sure your little footsies are warm enough now. Back to work."

As they trudged back into the water, Alton looked back for an instant, mouthing "Look me up tonight."

That night, in the mess tent, they found Alton and sat down next to him.

"So here we are," Alton said to Lina. "Two fugees trying to survive the apocalypse again. And not even Kayam's Cubanos to make it almost worthwhile."

"Yeah, he and Kiko didn't get scooped up for this gig, somehow. But you, you haven't missed a beat with that Goodstuff Benjamin track," Lina said.

"Who's that?" Raefe asked.

"Me and Alton always go 'round about him," Lina said. "He's a Nigerian guy Alton's into."

Raefe had seen the occasional vague posting about Benjamin and his group, the New Voodo Army. They weren't really an army, more like a group of do-gooders with enough rifles to defend themselves.

"He's not just a guy," Alton said. "He's the inspiration for mass resistance to the corpos, the mercs, the religious extremists."

"So pretty much every authority figure in the world," Raefe laughed. "Who's left to run things?"

"His followers are," Alton said. "That's the point. The NVA is all about self-determination."

"And the voodo thing? Sounds weird," Rafe said.

"White people gave vodoo a bad name. In Africa, it was a religion with deep connections to nature. That's what the NVA is all about— restoring that."

"Alton, before you give us that speech," Lina said, "I have to ask you: Did we just go from being fugees in Somerville to prisoners on an island?"

"You're not wrong," Alton said. "Technically, we can leave. But we'd give up any claim to any benefits or support. Total free agents."

"Son of a bitch," Lina swore. "Where would we go?"

"Wherever we go, we are always in the diaspora. Nothing has changed."

"When I came here five years ago, I thought I was leaving all that behind," Lina said. "And here I am, in a camp again."

"Same for me. I came here in '39 from Jamaica, after the plague. I was one of the five percent, the immune ones."

"What's going on?" Raefe asked. "What just happened?"

"They only tell us half the story'" Winchester said. "I've been in touch on the Net with different folks. That storm was the worst since the '43 floods. But the impact was the biggest ever, because it hit so many people, and it was in the belly of the beast. The New York financial center. The Boston bioinformatics complex. The US economy brought to its knees. Beaches littered with dead fish. Freshwater reservoirs turned into salt ponds."

"Where does this all fit in?" Raefe said, waving around the chopper. For the first time, he wondered how what Mars Girl had said played into all of this. Lead humanity from what to where? She was crazy to think of him as a leader, but maybe he could be part of something. He needed to educate himself.

"Looks like Digi swooped in, forced the Feds to give them a lot of East Coast territory. It's a disaster zone now, but they get to run their own economic zones near all the big metro hubs. They pay no taxes, they can squeeze their competitors, and they call the shots about what gets rebuilt and what doesn't. First thing they want to do is protect their investment, get this sea wall up."

Later that night, Raefe lay awake on his cot, still but unable to sleep. For much of his life, he had felt overwhelmed by the constant flux of people and their feelings. This place reminded him of a long car ride he had taken as a little boy, somewhere out in the part of the Midwest where it was empty between cities. Cars were still common then, and there was still radio, before everyone got Voices and eyeball puters and there was nothing but the vast, sprawling Net. His mom sat in the front seat, trying to find music on the radio dial. But there was nothing but static, the empty sound of the universe, to accompany her frustration and anger.

It came to him how much of his childhood had involved loss. Somehow, he'd come to feel responsible, like if he hadn't been in that car, his mother would have found a radio station and it would be playing that Arab trance music she loved. Of course, how could he have understood that years of drought had painted the Badlands onto what his mom had once known as corn and wheat, as far as the eye could see? Even now, knowing it, he couldn't shake the feeling that a different child, a better person, would have made it better for his mom.

Now, his mind was a radio, and he could hear faint signals from all the stations in all the minds around him. Much of it was fatigue and despair. But there were notes of affection for friends, happiness over small things, and always, the desire to hope. *I have a gift,* he thought, *but I don't know what to do with it. Where's Mars Girl when you need her?*

INTO THE FOLD

Traveler's Perch
October 4, 2048

Green fidgeted with his tea, remembering that Soars above the Plains of Hankori was always late. After Diver's visit, he had told Hankori that she had come to visit. Kori insisted they should meet. Too important to let this float in the waveform, he had said. So here Green was, looking out over the Red Canyons, sipping bitter tea, wondering exactly what Kori thought was so important. After all, he had handled Diver properly. He had told her what she wanted to know, but he would take no action until it was authorized. He had taken an oath to guard against the misuse of timeline technology, and he intended to keep it.

Hankori appeared around the corner. Strange that he had not sensed him before that, Green thought. Kori seemed to glide into his chair, just as a waiter appeared with a glass of water.

"Ah, my young friend," Hankori said, "so good of you to come."

"You asked me to keep an eye on Diver," he said. "I thought you'd be interested to hear what she was asking about." He told Kori about the alternate timelines, leaving out the conversation about Kori's tenure as Ambassador to Earth.

"Her boy must be failing," Hankori said, with no small glee. "She wants to know if she can keep him going on some better Earth."

"Yes, I suspect so. I told her about the history of the project."

"You did what? Why?"

"Well, she was bound to find out. But I also gave her the impression that she only got the assignment because of her tie to Far Flier. I don't think she's going to want to get too insistent now. She'll only embarrass herself."

"True. Thanks for letting me know." Hankori went still, staring at nothing in particular. Green could feel nothing from his mind, which was unsettling. Guardian worlds each had their own etiquette about sharing thoughts and feelings. Anyone could, and routinely did, choose to wall off parts of their mind. Sometimes that was to be polite, but they weren't above being devious or cunning, either, or just not wanting to share indecision or confusion or ignorance. But a completely silent mind was not something one usually encountered in a healthy individual.

"Kori, are you OK?"

Hankori smiled. "All my friends have called me that only once. Please don't. Our society seems hell-bent to break down every last barrier between individuals. I prefer to keep some boundaries and would appreciate you respecting my name. For me, the history of my ancestors is a source of great pride."

"Sure," Green said, embarrassed. He'd heard this about Kori, but was still surprised that it was true. Everyone had a past, so what? "As you wish."

"Thank you. But let's not worry about that. I think this incident with Diver is a good moment to talk about the future, not the past."

"OK, then, what about the future?" Green asked.

Hankori went away again, just for a second. *How does he do that,* Green wondered, *and why? It's annoying.*

"Green, my young colleague," Hankori said. "When you think of our society, what do you think holds it up?"

"Hmmm. I'd never really thought of that," Green said. "I mean, I can see that we exist in a web of cultures, from our own here on Traveler's Perch to the other Guardian worlds. Bits and pieces of this and that."

"Yes, true," Hankori said. "But entirely beside the point. Our world is built on three things: entanglement, the wormhole interface, and enhancement."

"OK, I see how you get to that." He was disappointed that timeline technology was not included in Hankori's view.

"We have had those things for thousands of years, and yet they remain the pillars of our existence. Do you ever wonder why?"

"Because they work," Green said, puzzled by the question. "For 10,000 years, we have had no wars, no famines on Traveler's Perch. We live longer and better."

"What if I told you that we could live forever?"

"I'd ask you why and how." Green felt a small ball of concern rise deep in his mind. His eyes scanned the plaza automatically, checking for danger. His enhancements dismissed the fear reflex and he felt a tiny squirt of hormones that would calm him.

"Why? Why not? When I was younger, my mother and father passed. They had not merely given birth to me, in the way of the ancients, and left me to my own. Our minds had intermingled, our thoughts and feelings shared at the deepest level. And yet, they were gone. Later, my own child was killed in an accident—yes, it still happens. And my mates will leave the world someday, even if many centuries from now. Why endure all of this suffering?"

"I don't know," Green said. "I was taught, like everyone else, that there is no alternative. There is no life without death."

"And who are these gods who taught you," Hankori laughed, "who know how much or how little we may accomplish throughout eternity?"

Gee, he's an odd duck, Green thought. He didn't know anyone who was really that concerned about death. To live 2,000 years or more was common—a life in which most people experienced being both sexes, had many relationships, raised at least a few offspring, and had hundreds of thousands of days to indulge their passions. At the end, there would be little left unsaid or undone. He wondered what was bothering Hankori.

"What is it you have in mind?" he asked.

Hankori smiled. "In due time. But for now, let's talk about the Guardians. Our mission has always been to preserve intelligent life, which seems to be about 20 species in our galaxy."

"So far."

"Well, if there are more, they're doing a great job of hiding."

Ah, so that's why Hankori reacted to Diver's questions. He had become one of the growing number of skeptics about their mission. A debate was brewing among the Guardian species. Was this it for the Milky Way? No matter which timelines Green had explored, the number never seemed to change.

"OK, granted, although I feel like there are still vast swaths of the far Milky Way that are a stranger to us. But what do you make of this paucity of intelligent life?"

"That our original mission has to change. That our approach to preservation of intelligent life has stagnated. Tell me, what would we do if some superior species from another galaxy, with technologies that we haven't even dreamed of, attacked us?"

"We've always believed that wouldn't happen. If they had survived long enough to become that developed, it could not have been on the basis of aggression."

"Or perhaps we just don't have the imagination to understand how they could develop that way. Are you willing to bet our future on that, forever?"

Green was troubled by this line of argument. Could Hankori be on to something? Why not find out?

"No, I suppose not. What are the alternatives?"

"Now you are asking the right question, the only question the Guardians should be asking, and the one question that we, so far, have refused to even look for the answer to. And you, young Green, can help us find that answer."

Interesting, Green thought. *Both Diver and Hankori, on opposite sides, think I can help them. But do I want to?*

UNENHANCED FEELINGS

Traveler's Perch
November 3, 2048

Diver looked out across the auditorium filled with a dozen species of air-breathers from as many planets. The room had adapted to them, providing perches for the hawkish Rayva, long pallets for the large, bearish Mondoni, and seats of whatever size were needed for the other species. On the other side of the auditorium's thick glass walls was what the students called The Tank—a series of liquid-filled chambers of various temperatures and chemistries for eight different marine species. She felt all of their thoughts merge into a complex waveform washing over her. Her mind rapidly adjusted and became another element in it. They were cadets, and they were eager to hear her thoughts. Today, she would help them understand more about life before enhancements—intelligent, yes, but isolated and sometimes primitive. They needed to be shocked out of their preconceptions.

"You've all gotten your assignments, the species you will be studying for the remainder of your training. I can sense that you all are anxious about being effective Guardians, working with species that can only communicate in a limited way with you, with species that live in the world all of our ancestors lived in, whether that was 10,000 years ago, as my species, did, or one million years ago as you Alaxazayawa did, or only 700 years ago, as the HooHooHu did.

"And that world is one dominated by unenhanced experience of whatever original organic senses your assigned species have evolved. Most will also have some electronic or mechanical aids—mine have computers, books, videos, audios and other means—but even those they experience through the senses."

"How is that different than us?" one of the students asked.

"OK, class, who knows what the heaviest isotope of strontium is?"

Almost instantly, the entire class waveform resonated with "Strontium 107."

"Correct. Your enhanced minds accessed a number of databases that contained that info, and barring corrupted data, you all knew the correct answer instantly. If you were unenhanced, some of you would know that from past experience, some of you would misremember it, some of you might not even know what the question meant. And that's just a simple fact. Everything they learn, everything they know and remember, is through the unfaithful lens of their senses and the unreliable record of their memory.

"But here's the odd part," she continued. "Eventually you will get to know an unenhanced being and you will see that they view this as natural. They will view you as less than natural, part machine, and they will be suspicious. But mostly, I want you to sense the mixture of knowledge and emotion that is their mental lifeblood and feel how that balance is different than yours. You can get a clue from the external sensory stimuli that they create. I've prepared a sampling of these sorts of artificial experiences from the species called humans that I work with, but they are fairly typical of many unenhanced species."

She gave them a glimpse of what Raefe saw in the vids he watched, a few hours of programming that their minds could absorb in minutes.

"Very imaginative!" one of the cadets exclaimed. "Their ability to build unreal yet realistic worlds is impressive. But there's so little information embedded in them."

"Yes, everything is sound and color. A world where people can do magical things, but they never even speculate about how," another thought.

"But hard to ignore," a third added. "And impossible to turn off, at least some of it."

"We can feel the two most important things about these experiences," Diver summarized. "First, we can all blend our own direct experience and memory with enormous amounts of data outside our own minds. Not so the unenhanced—they must process over time, sometimes even a lifetime—to penetrate the surface of their own experiences. Perhaps most importantly, as some of you just pointed out, up to 100 percent of the content of these documents and images are emotional. For example, in the vid you just watched, a fleet of human space fighters defends their planet against a massive alien fleet. And the planet is saved."

She turned to her assistant, who had only recently ended her cadet training. "Adno, how would you interpret that?"

"They seem to have a deep fear of other species," the large, fish-shaped female replied from the coldest of the water tanks. "And a strong need to convince themselves they can defend their planet."

"But they've never contacted other species," Toneva, one of the avian Rayva, protested. "Why would they think space holds nothing but threats? And why would an advanced species care so much about them?"

"Precisely," Diver agreed. "And there are so many other illogical ideas in this vid. How could Earth possibly win against such a force so technically superior? No, none of that makes sense. In fact, that is not at all the point of this story. Anyone think they know what is?"

She could feel them weighing different ideas, none convincing to them.

"No one? Don't feel bad—younger species have their own logic. This vid is one of hundreds, if not thousands, with a similar plot. What's important to grasp is that it details a struggle with what humans call 'aliens'—and in most of their languages, that word does mean other species from space, but also, and more commonly, means other humans from other political units and cultures. What the hero is literally doing in these vids is keeping people—his family, his town, his country, his ethnic group—safe from aliens. But deep down, many humans experience this as keeping their political or cultural unit safe from the more common aliens—humans who are slightly different from them. And many other species repeat this pattern."

"During my training, I was taught about this aspect of early intelligent cultures," Adno said. "But it was only after entangling with the Earther that I really started to feel the depth of it. They are actually sometimes terrified of other members of their species whom they have never met and who, most puzzling to me, have never done them wrong."

"Sadly, yes," Diver said. "But all of our ancestors did the same. What I want you to try and grasp here is that the humans who would never do that, who might even vigorously oppose that, will still watch this vid and cheer for the hero and thoroughly enjoy it. They will not be aware that in part their enjoyment comes from this symbolic purging of aliens. They will feel the emotion, but they won't be fully aware of its content. But sometime in the future, they may actively carry out this preprogramming."

"How can they truly feel something if they are neither aware of it or understand it?" a student asked.

"You are asking that because you can get to the truth about so many things in a nanosecond and then you can form feelings based on how that truth meshes with what you already know and feel. But most young species develop a complex system of emotion and thought running in parallel, intertwining and recursive. To put it simply, ideally they act emotionally, analyze the results logically, and modify their emotions accordingly in an endless cycle. Realistically, emotions can be hard to change, truth hard to find, and yet they still must act to survive. Over time, this causes them to develop deep culturally reinforced behavioral patterns even if they eventually run counter to their true long-term survival needs. That is the most common cause of the failure of intelligent species to survive."

She could feel the waveform rebelling against this concept. How could such species be called intelligent? They sounded more like species that had not yet crossed that threshold, a very smart predator, but not at all like real intelligent life.

"Ah, now you see how it works. They don't conform to your notions of intelligence. So you think they are not. And from there it's only a small step toward being willing to destroy them if they do something threatening."

The rebellious waveform collapsed. The cadets had finally seen that they were more different in degree than in kind from the humans. They were ashamed, which she was glad of.

"So now you have begun your training as Guardians. You begin to understand that all intelligent life takes twisted paths to develop. And that we have much work to do if we are to foster that life and avoid the traps of our ancestors."

FLOOD WARNINGS

Truro Island
November 7, 2048

Diver was pleased with how the class had gone. Getting the cadets to be humble in the face of the many irritating and irrational aspects of unenhanced intelligence was neither easy nor optional. She would have to return to that again and again, or risk having some of them dismiss the worth of the very species they were supposed to be guarding.

Her thoughts were interrupted by an urgent summons in the waveform.

"Diver, this is Manulo, from Information Analytics. Please give us your full attention."

What could Information Analytics want? They monitored standard electromagnetic communications from all the worlds the Guardians monitored through the wormhole interface. Diver and Adno focused on Raefe and the other entanglers, Analytics on the noise of their culture.

"Please focus on the stream from Earth," Manulo instructed. "This information came through the wormhole interface network only minutes ago."

News reports, satellite photos, military communications all arrayed in front of her. A volcano had erupted on the Isle of Surtsey, off the coast of Iceland. She understood immediately that Raefe might be in danger.

"Will it impact the area near one of our contacts, Raefe Epstein Miller?"

"Not the volcano. But Earth geologists say there is a 30 percent chance the volcano will cause an underwater landslide. Our simulations are clearer. The slide of part of the Greenland ice sheet into the ocean five years ago caused some upwelling of the tectonic plates. The earthquake that accompanies this volcano will almost certainly cause the eastward face of the island to shear off and fall into the ocean. The result will be a tidal wave over 50 meters high, and it will move at speeds close to 500 kilometers an hour."

"He will be killed?"

"Yes, in less than three hours. While the area of destruction will be smaller than the recent hurricane, he will be in it, and the destruction will be much more profound."

"Please forward your summary to the Guardian Council immediately."

She contacted Green.

"My main Earth contact, Raefe, will be dead very shortly in his current timeline. Manulo has forwarded the situation. Can you identify an alternate timeline that we can transfer him to?"

"You know I can't do that without authorization from the Council."

"No time for that. This is an extraordinary situation—a catastrophic earthquake and tidal wave."

"I'm sorry, Diver, but the truth is that human-induced climate change is the aggravating factor here. I have to reiterate that I can't authorize a timeline shift due to social factors without approval."

She disconnected, frustrated and angry. She felt Far Flier reaching out to her.

"I just heard from Info Analytics," he said. "What's the status?"

"We have to shift him to a new timeline. Fast. Green won't give me a suitable timeline. Says the catastrophe is the result of human factors, and so the whole Council has to approve."

"Never mind that. I'll explain it to you later, but I've been worried about this all along. I've got a contingency plan. A new timeline. You'll have to prepare him though. Let me know when you're ready."

There was more going on here than she understood and no chance for her to consider all the variables. She would have to focus extremely hard and cut through the noise. Raefe was stronger now, it should be easier. She could tell that he was on an island, doing some kind of manual labor. They had never connected while he was awake, but she had no choice.

She found his mind and assumed the Mars Girl image. This time he was at ease with her, smiling. Good, she would need him to accept what she was about to tell him.

"Hi, it's me again. Don't stop what you're doing, don't speak. I have important news to tell you; you can just think, and I will know your thoughts."

"Right, hello to you, too," he thought. "What's up?"

"You are in danger," she said. "Your island will be hit by a massive tidal wave in the next few hours. But don't be afraid. I have a way to save you."

"Are you sure? You can tell that from 20 light years away?"

"Yes, there's no doubt. When the time comes, you will wake up somewhere else."

"What about Lina?"

"I'm not sure if she'll be there. I'm trying to learn everything I can about what we can do, but we may not be able to save her, too."

"Then forget it. She's stood by me through so many things. I'm not leaving her. And I'd be lost without her."

He believed that, without any doubt, she could tell. Unless she could save Lina, too, he would never become the leader she thought he could be. In fact, he might never be a fully functional person again. Humans experienced grief much more often than her kind, but paradoxically, that made them more susceptible to it.

"Well, you wouldn't be leaving her, in any event. It's complicated and we don't have a lot of time. Let me find out more about Lina. I'll be right back. It will be quick."

She found Far Flier.

"He won't leave Lina."

"We could move him anyway."

"I don't think he'd ever cooperate with us again. And he could go insane. Is she in the timeline you have chosen?"

"Well, she's alive, but she's never met him," Far Flier said. "She's in Efricar, there's never been a holocaust."

"So she won't have died, in his new world, but they will never have met. I don't think that will be enough, though. He's dependent on her for emotional stability."

"If we transfer her consciousness, too, and then tell them how to find each other, will he agree?"

She had never moved a mind to a new timeline. Could they do that with Lina, who hadn't learned to entangle yet? What would happen afterwards? She had a million questions, but no time to ask them.

"He would probably go along, but can we do all that?"

"No time now. Let's just say we can."

But, she thought, should we? Diver was the head of the Council, but this felt somehow wrong.

***

Raefe asked the guard if he could get some water. He gave Lina a look and she nodded back. After he went up to water station, she made her own excuses and found him.

"Look at me," he said. "Don't talk. Hold my hands and look right in my eyes."

Hearing the urgency in his voice, she did.

He could feel her mind. Not clear like Diver's, but there. She startled, but kept her hands with his. He saw a little smile on her face and felt a warmth. He thought "I love you," and closed his eyes. Something like a strong current swept him away gently, but at incredible speed.

***

The guards were startled to see the two workers both collapse, lying lifeless on the beach. The other workers watched as two guards tried to revive them. One of them had a med puter.

"Their hearts are beating, they're breathing!"

"Good. Send the feed to HQ. I'll call and see if they want to evac them," their sergeant said.

"They may not want to," the guard said. "I'm getting no higher-function brain waves at all. Seems like they're on internal life support. Some fucking new drug the fugees are into?"

"Hey, Sarge," another guard spoke up. "I don't think we're going to evac them. Turn around."

The guards and the workers turned back toward the water. Far on the horizon, a strange gray curtain pulled up out of the ocean. The curtain was moving quickly toward them and revealed itself as an avalanche of water falling down an endless 50-meter high wall.

The sergeant threw down his rifle at the feet of the two bodies.

"Lucky bastards, to escape before that."

PART II

BRAVE NEW WORLD

Traveler's Perch
November 8, 2048

Diver had trained to be a Guardian for decades. She had handled low-level tasks as a monitor for more decades. She had been in charge of following Raefe for two years. In all that time, it never occurred to her that sometimes things would spiral out of control, and she would have no idea of what had just happened, yet she'd be forced to make the right choices and act without hesitation.

But sitting here in her quarters, watching the early morning light, that was just what she saw now. Raefe was in his new timeline, where she had just discovered he was known as Raefer. She had not yet contacted him, even though she knew he would be terribly confused, maybe on the edge of sanity, or even past that edge. But how could she help him if she didn't even know what had happened to Lina? Far Flier had assured that Lina would be OK—but how could that be? She had never entangled, her consciousness was an unknown quantity to them. How could she make the journey to another Lina in another timeline?

This was not how it was supposed to be. The Guardians were careful, methodical. She had never done a transfer, but in her training, it was always well thought out and planned. This was wild and uncontrolled. For all of her love of nature untamed, this felt different and not in a good way. She needed answers, and only Far Flier would have them. She searched for him in the waveform.

Just as she sensed him, he walked into her quarters.

"I know you want to contact Raefe, or rather, Raefer, right now," he said. "There's a lot I need to explain to you, but it will have to wait. Just for now, tell him that Lina is alive. She's in Kenya, which was part of Efricar in her original timeline. But in this timeline, they have not met."

"But she will carry recent memories, no?" Diver asked, "Just as he does?"

"Yes, she will understand the last year or so of her old life, similar to him. They will both find the world of their new timeline to be less endangered, further from catastrophe. But this new world still has many troubling signs they will recognize, and better than most of their new fellow humans."

"I don't know if he's going to care about that, but he'll be relieved to know Lina's OK. And what about her? When can we talk further?"

"Just find me when you're ready. We have much to do."

She had a lot more to ask him, but she put her questions aside and let her mind drift into the wormhole interface network, which now connected to Earth in the new timeline. She had not entangled with Raefe in this timeline yet. The first time in a new timeline was always a bit tricky. She thought of his thought pattern in the same way she would remember a face in a crowd. As the complex waveform coming from Earth in the new timeline washed over her, she looked for his signature. There!

"Mars Girl! It's about time!" Raefe said, sounding not a little bit peeved. "Me and Raefer, my twin, or whatever we are to each other, have been waiting for hours for you to explain what the heck we do now."

Even as he spoke, she let her mind slip along the tendrils that were Raefe and find the fuller mind of Raefer. They were, after all, only subtly different. And now she could address Raefer directly.

"Perhaps we should use my real name, eh? Raefer, Raefe, I'm Diver from Great Heights, or Diver to most people. I am an Ambassador from the Guardians, an ancient organization of 20 worlds in this galaxy that have intelligent life. We work to foster and protect emerging intelligent species, such as your own, throughout the galaxy," she said. "I'm sorry that you've been awake for hours. Things don't always line up exactly from one version of a world to another. I'd hoped to contact you while you were asleep, since you always enjoy hearing from Mars Girl in your dreams."

"Well, if we're going to get more real, than show me who you are. I really need to know I'm not going crazy, that I haven't made you up."

Diver hesitated. He wasn't thinking straight, or he'd realize that no matter what she did, it could still be the product of his own mind. But now was not the time for a logic lesson. She ordered her apartment to make one wall a mirror and looked at it. She let Raefer see what she saw.

Raefer stared for a long time.

"I could never imagine you like this," he finally said. "How big are you?"

"I would only come up to your waist," she said. "Our gravity is similar to yours, and our ancestors flew, so they could not be huge. We have actually grown taller since we lost the ability to fly."

"So what did you do to me?" Raefer asked. "I mean, I don't even know if I mean me, who woke up this morning in my apartment in Cambridge or me, who apparently was on a beach about to die."

"The Guardians have a much more advanced knowledge of physics, as we've discussed before," she said. She'd heard other Guardians talk about how awkward these "we know more than you" conversations with less advanced species could feel, and now she knew what they meant. She had to tread lightly—the Guardians avoided revealing scientific discoveries to societies that hadn't yet gotten there on their own. Human's knowledge of quantum physics was beyond basic, but far from complete. It wasn't her role to confirm or explain the multiverse school of thought. But she would have to explain some of the pragmatic aspects.

"We can't physically travel between our own universe and others, but we can send energy between them, just as we send energy through the wormhole to have these talks. To save the you who met me before this from the tidal wave on Truro Island, we've sent the energy that is the waveform of your consciousness to the you that woke up in your apartment in Cambridge. You're not crazy, there are really are two sets of experiences in your head right now."

"You've given the me from the beach a second chance, a replay?" he asked. She could feel a mixture of incredulity, relief, and confusion emanating from him.

"Exactly!"

"But you're also telling me that there are other versions of Earth where things are actually more messed up than this one here?"

"Yes, and you will have to consider what that means to you. Right now, you have been living your life without too much thought of where your world is headed. Now, you know that your world is only slightly different from ones that are in much worse shape. That's another way of saying that pretty soon, your world could be in much worse shape."

"And just what am I supposed to do about it? I'm just an entry level coder at a game software factory. Unless I buy a winning Giga ticket,

I'll be doing something like that for the rest of my life. My friends are all third-generation wankers. Don't you know? We're just another installment of life sliding down a long hill toward nowhere. And you think I'm going to lead everyone to the Promised Land and save the world?"

"No, I think by giving you a second chance you and others may somehow figure out how to save the world. Because there is no Promised Land—this is it. You from the other version of Earth knows that, I'm pretty sure. And he knows that stress and crisis often accelerate the evolution of new capabilities in living things. There are more people like you now, although none with as strong an empathic ability yet. Many people in your world are trying to set it right. Empathy will become a great catalyst that accelerates and sustains those efforts, keeps them headed in the right direction. You and Lina have a second chance to activate that reaction and in the process build a life that you will be proud of."

"You're making my head hurt. You saved one of my lives, but now you've made another one confusing. What do I do now?"

"That's up to you, Raefer. You are still you. The Raefe that you feel in your mind only remembers things in the last year or so of his life, and mostly the more recent things. Of course, most of your personality is older than that, so it won't take long before the strangeness fades and you'll just accept that you've visited some places, know some people, and had some experiences that don't exist for you in this world. Think of it like visiting a place when you were younger that made an impression on you, but no longer exists. But Raefe from the other timeline has strong feelings about certain things and those feelings may well persevere and become a part of you, too."

"And one of those things I have strong feelings about is Lina?" Raefer asked.

"Yes, Raefe and Lina were a dyad in the other timeline, although you had not yet reproduced. But you have been through a lot together. In this timeline, unfortunately, you have never met. Just as you are known here by your full formal name Raefer, not Raefe, she is known by her birth name, Milima. Here, she is still in Africa, where her Chinese father went to work and met her African—Kenyan to be precise—mother, and where she was born. But she is alive and well and remembers you and remembers that you were lovers."

"Well, nice to know I get a girlfriend in the bargain," Raefer said.

"So, what am I supposed to do? Post online: 'Nice Jewish boy interested in Afro-Chinese woman from a different timeline looking for empathic mate?'"

"It's a bit more complicated than that. Over the next few days, I will visit you and tell you what you need to know."

She had a nagging feeling she had once again failed to recognize the odd mindset humans referred to as humor.

***

"How did he take it?" Far Flier asked later, sinking into the chair her room now automatically made for him when he visited.

"He's angry. We've disrupted his life, and he doesn't see why. His abilities have only ever been disabilities to him. I'm counting on his memories of the flood and the refugee camp to spark a sense that he's dodged a bullet. I talked to him about second chances. I hope he can grasp that, but I leaned into it a bit hard. I wasn't ambiguous about his world's chances. I may have stepped over the line into giving him too much information that he may take as a prediction of the future, which I'm all too aware is not a good idea. As well as explaining scientific discoveries Earth is centuries away from."

She let Flier into her memories of the conversation. If he also sensed her anger and frustration at his evasiveness about his part in the process, so be it.

"You may have skirted the line there, but if you had to err, I agree with doing it on that side of the line. I hope he responds. I think you said the right things, though."

"But I need to understand what the hell is going on here. Flies Far Across Oceans, there are too many secrets between us. How did you transport him to a new timeline without Green's Timeline group? And what did you do with Lina?"

"I would have explained had there been time."

"Well, there's time now," Diver said, the small feathers in the middle of her head just starting to harden, though not yet the full crest her species displayed when threatened. She was not surprised that Flier met her challenge defensively.

"You give me too little credit. I've suspected for some time that Green has had his own agenda. I had made contingency plans. After so many years of being a Guardian, I have acquired a passing knowledge of everything we do. And friends throughout the different departments. I will tell the Council that I exercised my authority as head to carry out an emergency transport of Raefe."

"And Lina?"

"They cannot know about Lina. I have hidden that knowledge from the waveform. Only you will know, and you too should hide it."

"Why? What have you done?"

"I told you that I implanted the knowledge of Raefe and their relationship in her mind so that she would know him when they made contact. How did you think I did that?"

He was maddening at times, she thought. All that display of his age and experience, like the bright feathers of the ancient mating rituals. And yet there were the garish gold cuffs of his tunic. Why were they so clumsy and garish? Far Flier somehow always managed to be out of fashion, even when he was trying to be fashionable. She realized she was trying to distract herself from the growing realization of what he had done. She could not believe it. She would make him say it.

"How?"

"Like most intelligent life, she had latent abilities to entangle. I brought them to the surface."

"You used your abilities to transform her neural connections?" It was one thing to appear in someone's dream. It was quite another to carry out the most forbidden and dangerous of all Guardian interventions in emerging species—rewiring a person's mind to entangle without their knowledge or consent.

"Actually, I combined with Raefe to do it. That's why I asked you to have Raefe be with her when his mind was transported. When humans feel deeply about each other, as Raefe and Lina do, they are all but entangled. I could feel the pathways her mind uses to connect to other people. In essence, I trained her to feel them by showing her precisely where Raefe's emotive thoughts were in her mind. Time will tell how well she takes to it, but she is now a rudimentary empath and an entangler as well."

"But you know it was wrong, horribly wrong. It's always been a guiding principle of the Guardians—we guide, we don't direct. We use what evolution has given our contacts, not what we can reprocess them to be."

"I know it was illegal. And risky."

At least he understood that. He had put Lina at risk, not to mention the entire Earth project—and the nine billion people on the planet.

"And what about me? First you lobby for me to guide Earth—why, I don't know—and then you make me part of this. When the Council finds out, they will remove me from this project. I'm wondering if your mind is working properly."

"I wanted you in charge of the Earth project because I know you're honest, and you are a true Guardian."

"What do you mean, a true Guardian? There were dozens of other Guardians who could have taken this on. It's only a small project, a few thousand promising latents to monitor and a handful of active entanglers, with only one sufficiently far along to actually contact."

"I have shielded you from too much," Far Flier said. "I see that now. As head of the Guardian Council, I cannot share all with you. But as two people trying to do the right thing, we have to share more of what we know. And that is my fault."

She nodded, waiting for him to drop the wall of reticence she sensed in him.

"Not every Guardian believes in our mission," he continued.

Before she had been a Guardian, the council had already become lackadaisical about taking on new worlds to monitor and new species to mentor. It didn't happen all at once, more like an accumulation of frictions that slowed down the effort. A certain leakage of enthusiasm, like oxygen slowly leaking from a vacuum suit.

"I've come to believe that a growing number of Guardians, particularly on the Council, have lost sight of our purpose," Flier said, his voice accompanied by a newly combative mood. "I'm going to call this issue at the next Council. I hope to reignite the fires. But if we acknowledge Lina's transformation, it will become the only issue on the table and the consequences for me will be dire. I know I've lost your trust, but I hope you will come to see that I made a hard choice to preserve our work with Raefe and with the humans, because otherwise, the odds of their survival are quite low. And if the humans fail because of the Council's actions, I am not sure what the future of the Guardians will be."

She couldn't bring herself to reassure him. She understood his concerns but she didn't know if she could support him any longer. His actions shocked her.

"I can't answer you now," she replied. "I have to think about what you are asking me."

She didn't need to read his thoughts to see his disappointment as he left. After, her anger faded to sadness. Saving Raefe and Lina should have been a moment of joy, a continuation in their adventure together of the mind, body and spirit, a step toward a bright future. Far Flier had spoiled that with his disdain for their code. Or was she naïve to think that the code deserved such respect? She was disappointed to even be contemplating this.

Many Guardians had trouble understanding what life was like for species that had only what evolution had given them, whose lives lasted only a century or so. Such a life seemed so incomplete, fleeting, fraught with loss and unrealized dreams. Just now, she felt closer to a life of transient joy and unpredictable loss than she ever had before.

CITIZENS OF NOWHERE

Kiunga, Kenya
January 19, 2049

Milima was glad to see Kiunga behind the bus. The sleepy northern coastal town had once been a village until the English, and then the Americans, and now the Chinese, had found it a convenient waystation for various enterprises. Over the years, it had become a small, utilitarian city, a place you wanted to pass through, but not to stop, a dot on a long stretch of wild coast protected by a teeming reef.

As much as she appreciated the beauty of the coast, she was only helping to destroy the reef and the many fish that lived on it. Kiunga made her feel much more isolated and alone than she did in her cloistered life in the Chinese Quarters of Mombasa. She hadn't just been on her own these last three months, but alone with this new voice in her head. This voice called herself Lina, a nickname her girlfriends sometimes called Milima as a child. She was too similar not to be her and too different and detailed in her knowledge of her former life to be just a figment of her imagination. Milima had eventually accepted that she wasn't crazy, that Lina was real.

And the strangeness of that reality was what she was grappling with. It wasn't that what this new part of her said was completely unbelievable. Lina validated her qualms about the destruction of the Kenyan coast that she was participating in. And she was well aware that similar things were going on all over the world. But this new voice was also more troubled—her life had been meaner, more difficult.

Yet that life had also been filled with the companionship of an American boy. It was a life in which she had been her own guiding star, had found her own way in a new country, had found a lover who neither of her parents would be thrilled with. It gave her hope for her own future but, at the same time, made her current state of affairs more troubling.

And then there were other voices who visited her. Far Flier had known Lina, apparently, and Diver had known this American boy, Raefe. Who was really Raefer. When Far Flier had first tried to explain the situation, she had decided she actually had gone insane. But he slowly talked her down. And Diver had been kind, helping her to probe her own mind and see that they had awakened some interesting capabilities. Were they really aliens from across the galaxy? She had decided she couldn't deal with that just yet.

Still, with Diver's help, she had changed. She had grown up finely attuned to her parents' feelings. Their household was loving but also the site of a long and insistent but gentle battle between her father's Chinese heritage and her mother's African culture. And there was a second layer to it: Her father tried his best to shield her and her mother from the Chinese authorities and their disdain for the locals, but it was not a battle he could win. Sometimes that made him an ally to her, sometimes he couldn't help but resent her and her mother. As their only child, she learned how to stay in the shadows when necessary but also to navigate the conflict to get her needs met. She had known much of this before, if she admitted it, but now it had snapped into focus and the nuances were more evident.

Now she felt that alertness around most people, if she let herself. She was gaining confidence in her abilities to read people and to do the right thing socially. After a lifetime of feeling awkward and out of place, it was a relief. Maybe this bizarre turn of events would be worth it. She was looking forward to returning to the bustle of Mombasa. She wanted to test her new confidence with her old friends and even with her parents. When she stepped off the bus in a few hours, would they see these changes in her face? Would they already treat her differently, or would she have to earn that in some way?

After a while, town gave way to countryside. The road became less formal, and by the time the bus turned right toward Mararani, it was hard track but flat and in good shape. There was little but savannah in every direction. All was quiet as the heat began to rise midmorning. Still, the two Chinese guards in the front of the bus had their rifles at the ready in case raiders from Somalia struck. With the logo of China's Coastal Friendship Alliance on it, raiders would know the bus was likely to be all Chinese passengers. For most Africans, that meant "Stay away." For the more desperate, it advertised "People with money," who would be good kidnap victims.

She thought of what she would say to her father when she got home. She knew that it was not really his decision to send her to the port construction project. He just couldn't bring himself to admit that he couldn't protect her from his superiors. Since she had gained her empathic powers, she saw much more deeply into the complex web of her father's emotions. He had given up a lot to marry her mother, and Milima was a concrete reminder of his dalliance with an African. She knew that sometimes he wanted to tell the Coastal Friendship Alliance, the Chinese corporation that oversaw all of that country's development efforts in East Africa, to drop dead, but each time, he could not see how that would make their lives better. Without the CFA, he felt he wouldn't be accepted by the locals, and she and her mother would have no protection from the Chinese.

She thought he underestimated the Kenyans. After all, people of all sorts had passed through here for as long as there had been people. But it would require him to not just leave the CFA, but to leave behind his Chinese identity. As much as the CFA questioned that he still had one, she knew that he was deeply invested in his heritage. So, when they had suggested that his daughter could continue her computer studies by working on the harbor project, he could not refuse. That much she had sensed from him.

Still, helping to gouge out one of the world's last remaining viable reef systems to build oil rigs and a deep-water port was not something she could do for much longer. Lina's last memory of her Earth was the simple and terrifying feeling of her teeth vibrating deep into her skull. Far Flier had explained that seconds later, an enormous tidal wave had struck the ground where Lina had stood. More and more, Milima was coming to feel that last memory as her own. If you had been through something like that once, you simply couldn't be part of it happening again. Somehow, she would have to get her father to see that she simply couldn't be involved with this project any longer.

Her thoughts were interrupted by a loud noise as the right front tire blew out. The driver struggled for control, bringing the vehicle to a halt with front wheel in a ditch, but the bus was still upright. Thankfully, no one was hurt.

The guards were immediately on their military-band radios. There was no mobile service out here. She couldn't hear them, but their faces told her all was not well. She could feel their fear. One of them motioned toward to come to the front. Puzzled, she walked to the front.

"Miss Yang?"

"Yes?"

"Captain Li in Kiunga would like to talk to you."

She took the radio. The guard pointed to the large button on the side and then his mouth. She pressed the button.

"Captain Li?" she said in standard Global Mandarin.

"Miss Yang, thank you," he replied with a slight provincial accent. "We need your assistance. According to our records, you speak Swahili?"

"Yes, I do."

"Very good. The bus is disabled and it will be some time before we can send a vehicle to replace it. There is a village called Mangai about a kilometer from where you are. We would like all the passengers to walk there with the guards. When we get there, can you translate for the guards? We only want to let the locals know that we mean no harm and to ask for their help for a few hours."

"I hope so, Captain. I speak Mombasa Swahili. It's like Chinese, you know—the vowels are sung. Up here in the North, they're not. I suppose it's like the difference between Chinese and Japanese. But I think I can make myself understood and understand them. That's sort of the point of Swahili."

"Thank you. We will send help as soon as we can."

There were about 20 of them altogether, and they set out walking in the direction they had been driving. The land on either side of the road was grassy, with occasional small groups of antelope or deer. Farther off the road, they could see that the trees thickened on both sides. There were no signs of people anywhere that Milima could see. But after a half-hour, she saw smoke rising in the distance. One of the guards had binoculars and told them it was a village.

As they walked around a bend in the road, there were four Kenyans in the road. Two men, a woman and a boy. They were trying to shout something in Chinese, but no one could understand them. Milima walked ahead, waving in the way that Kenyans did so that they could see she was a local.

"Hello. Our bus is broken," she said in her singing Swahili. "May we stay in your village until help comes this afternoon?" Closer now, she could see the people wore the gauzy white pantaloons and tunics of the local Muslim tribes. The woman had a blue print scarf covering her hair.

"You are welcome to stay," the woman said in her flat Northern accent. "It will be safer for you. I am Imani. These are my brothers, Juma, Kamari, and little Rashid."" Milima suspected that they would not speak directly to her, an unaccompanied woman.

"Thank you. I am Milima Kawambai Yang. Safe from what?" she asked.

"Shabab," she said plainly. "They claim all of Lamu is part of the East African Caliphate. What you call Somalia."

Had her father known about this when he sent her here? No, he wouldn't risk her mother's wrath like that. Most likely, the CFA had hidden the truth from him.

"I didn't know they were here. Do they come often?"

"Now and then. You should tell your friends to put their guns away. If any Shabab see Chinese with guns, they may think they are soldiers and send for more people to attack them. They are not happy about Chinese coming here."

Milima told the guards, but she knew they would not put away their rifles. Juma and Kamari led all the passengers into the village, a jumble of old-style huts and cinder-block buildings with satellite dishes. Past the village were fields where they tended small herds of goats and cattle, as well as a large garden.

Imani brought them all to a small pavilion in the center of the village. Some long tables sat under an open-sided tent.

"You can stay here until your people come," Imani said. "The elders will come to meet you soon."

Milima explained what was going on to her fellow travelers. The group was tense, anxious for help to come from Kiunga. But with her new abilities, she could also sense anger—some of the group was feeling that they had been sent into danger haphazardly, their safety unimportant.

The guards thanked her for her translation and introduced themselves. Zhang Lei was short and stocky, with bad skin and a squint. Wang Tao was taller and leaner, with a wry smile.

"Do you live here in Kiunga?" Milima asked. "I haven't seen you around."

"No, you wouldn't," Wang answered. "There is a small military base south of Kiunga, just past Rubu. We stay there."

"Oh, I hadn't realized you were in the army," she said.

"That is good," Wang answered. "Our commander prefers us to appear as civilian security guards. He says that we work under the Light Footprint policy."

"What is that?"

"Foreign Minister Wei Peng has said that when we Chinese come to other countries with food and technology in our arms, our feet should not disturb the ground our hosts walk on. In this way, we bring improvement without disturbance."

Unless the disturbance is destroying the reefs and everything else below the water, she thought bitterly. But she detected not a hint of irony in either of the soldiers, and she bit her tongue.

***

Hours passed with no news. Milima had gotten used to the quiet nights of Kiunga, but Mianga was in another league entirely. Near midnight, almost everyone was asleep. She could hear a vid faintly off to her right and muffled conversation somewhere behind her. But all around her was the sound of birds, frogs, insects, and the occasional growl of some sort of big cat. Before turning in, she walked to the edge of the village. When she looked up, the inky river of the Milky Way was as vivid as she had ever seen it. Every so often, a meteorite streaked across the sky.

She wondered where in that sky Far Flier and Diver lived. In this place and time, would they save her if she faced death again? And would Raefe be there, too? Diver had helped her find him on the Net and they'd been having regular chats. She thought of them as half-blind dates. The Lina in her yearned for him deeply. Milima was developing a growing affection for him.

Now, lying on the cot Imani had set up for her, she allowed herself to relive what it had felt like when Raefe had touched her mind on that beach. It had all happened so quickly and she usually forced herself not to dwell on it. But here in the bush, remembering the vastness of the cosmos, she could feel the power that her mind was still growing into. In high school, she had been on the track team. She remembered the feeling of lacing up her shoes, stretching her hamstrings, exploding out of the blocks, and that glorious rush as her head came up and the track was hers. The sky, the village, the villagers—they felt a little like that track had.

Her cosmic musings led her deeper into her mind, and soon, she was asleep. Suddenly, she someone was shaking her.

"Wake up, we have to go!"

It was Imani.

"Hurry, Shabab is coming! We must leave."

Milima grabbed the gym bag with her things, stepped into her shoes and hustled out into the deep night, joining a stream of villagers. They were trotting down a path leading away from the village toward the forest. No one talked. She could feel that they had practiced this, perhaps they had fled before. She felt their fear, but also their determination and a kind of pride that they were doing this together.

She asked Imani where they were going but got only a sharp look and a finger to the lips for her trouble. It dawned on her that she was the only person from the bus in the column. As they continued their escape, she lost the thread of feeling the other Chinese travelers in her mind. For now, she was an African, jogging for her life with 200 other men, women and children. After nearly an hour, they stopped.

An older man, seemingly the leader of the village, quietly directed several younger men to act as sentries. They fanned out, each stepping just off the track into the forest so as not to be seen.

"Here, have some water," Imani said, offering her a water bottle.

"Thanks," Milima answered. "And thanks for waking me up."

"I couldn't leave you there."

"But you left the other Chinese travelers."

"Shabab will hold them for ransom, or to extract something from the Chinese government. If they get what they want, they will let them go. But you…"

"Because of my hair, and my darker skin?"

Imani hesitated. Milima sensed thoughts of blood and pain and shame from her.

"Oh, of course. They would think that I am the child of a prostitute and therefore worthless for anything but rape."

Imani's face betrayed her surprise at Milima's insight. "Yes. They rape us too, but for other reasons. To show our men that they are powerless against them. And they would take some of us back to Somalia as so-called wives."

"But you are all Muslim, I don't understand."

"All their praise of Allah is garbage," she growled. "They are bandits. When the UN set up drone planes and submarines in 2042 and finally made it hard for them to be pirates, they turned their eyes away from the sea. Now they kidnap and steal from us."

"And Nairobi? They don't help?"

"They are the government. They don't need to kidnap to steal. As long as Shabab doesn't send too many soldiers, as long as they only prey on small villages and leave the cities to the government, the army would rather spend its money on itself."

"So you come here and hide for a few days and go back?"

"No. The construction project at Kiunga has changed everything. For Shabab, this is a giant opportunity. Many foreigners to kidnap. Money to demand from the government to leave the foreigners alone. People will hear about how Shabab stood up to the Chinese and the government, and that will help them get more young people to join their army. Shabab means 'youth' but they have grown old and need young blood now. They will not leave us alone in Mianga. We go deep into the forest. There are people who will take us in."

Water break was over. The group resumed their double time march in silence broken only by soft whispers to "pay attention" to the sounds of large animals in the forest on either side of the track. The children were now in the center of the column, the younger ones on the backs of the largest men, the older ones able to run and keep up. For the big cats in the forest, probably leopards, the whole group of them must have looked like a dangerous herd. Apart from the occasional growl or strong scent of musk, potential predators were invisible.

Daylight revealed that they had been running along a slight ridge, perhaps 10 meters higher than the land around it. They were walking now. One of the women had a sat phone with a GPS. They had put about 20 kilometers between themselves and their village. All those laps at track practice were coming in handy! Several people huddled around the phone talking, and Milima could make out that they were looking for high ground to reconnoiter. The woman pointed to a fork in the track ahead, and they took the right-hand path. A short time later, they found themselves on a bald, rocky hill. Without the trees to block their view, the high point gave them a view in every direction.

Looking northward, the forest sloped downward for half a kilometer. Beyond that, there were grasslands all the way to the horizon. The view to the south was different. A kilometer or two away, something more than a stream and less than a river meandered westward. Milima could make out a small lake, a pond really, in the distance. For a second, she thought she saw a flash of light from the woods on the far northern edge of the lake. South of the river, the forest continued unabated but seemed to change color in the distance.

The group continued their march, now a brisk walk, headed toward the lake. Everyone was more relaxed now, talking, trying to make the best of it. But no one would tell her anything about where they were going other than, "you'll see, you'll like it." She thought about asking the woman with the sat phone if she could use it to call her parents, but what did she have to tell them at this point? She was sure they were headed for that lake, but she'd wait until they got there.

They had descended into the forest again. Swallowed up by the trees, she was unable to gauge their progress. Just before 3 PM, they emerged into a large clearing, filled with dozens of small buildings. There seemed to be 300 or 400 people about, busily going about their days. No one seemed surprised by their arrival. Lina guessed that a sat call had been made.

The Mangai villagers were met by a group of people who seemed to know some of them and greeted them warmly. Imani took Milima to a dining area consisting of some tables under a canopy in the center of the village. A tall, reedy, woman came to greet them.

"Welcome," she said in Swahili. "I am Edna. I speak for the village council. You must be Imani. And you must be Milima. Please, sit. We have some water for you. Are you hungry?"

"Yes, indeed," Imani said. "We left in the deep of the night and had no time for food."

Edna waved to some young men near the tent and asked them to bring food. "We will have a proper feast for you later, but we have some leftover lunch for you now."

Milima was impatient. "What is this place?"

Edna smiled. "It is Kakuma."

Milima laughed at the Swahili word for nowhere. "Well, I never saw it on any map, but really, where am I?"

"I will explain," Edna said. "But first, the council has asked me to discuss your situation with you. Shabab has taken your fellow passengers on the bus hostage. They've presented demands for money to return them. Are any of the hostages your friends or family?"

"No, I've only arrived in Kiunga recently. My family is in Mombasa—I was taking the bus back to visit them."

"How is it you came here to work for the Chinese?"

"My father is Chinese. He works as an engineer in Mombasa."

"Your father works for the CFA?"

"Ah, so you know them. His bosses suggested that my college studies would be more effective if I put my learning to use on the project in Kiunga."

"So your father is not very high up in CFA?"

Milima laughed. This one was sharp. "No, not at all. Why do you ask?"

"You will be reported missing. What happens next could depend on who you are, who your family is."

Milima knew what she meant. Had she been related to one of the CFA mucky mucks in Kenya, they would have paid her ransom and then sent attack helicopters from a ship offshore the next day to punish the kidnappers. If she was the daughter of a cook, the CFA would issue a statement but do nothing to save her. She was in the middle somewhere—they would probably issue a statement and offer to help her father pay the ransom. And dock his pay later. Or maybe the security forces would decide that no matter how low her status, her capture was a good excuse for target practice with live fire.

Her father would know all of this and would navigate it accordingly. Her mother would demand he save her, of course. Either way, she wanted them to know she was safe.

"I was actually hoping to contact my family when we reached here. Just to let them know I'm okay."

"You can do that in a little while. But we have to discuss what happens after that—will you go back to Kiunga, to Mombasa, to somewhere else? We have to figure out how to do that without endangering this village."

"I don't understand."

"When I said you are in Nowhere, I was not playing with words. Nowhere is not just our village, but our country. Look around you carefully. What do you notice about the people here?"

The village was unremarkable. The people were of many shades and shapes, more than you might expect so far from a big city. The closer she looked, she couldn't recognize for certain any one ethnic group she was familiar with. They wore a mix of traditional clothing from several ethnic groups and even a bit of Western clothing.

"There are many kinds of people here, but it is hard to identify their ethnic group by clothing or hair or jewelry."

"I am very impressed that a foreigner would notice that," Edna said.

"I am not a foreigner. I was born here. My mother was born Sauda Kawambai. As you can see, I speak Swahili like any Mombasa girl."

"And yet you are Chinese."

"Look, what's this all about? Right now, I'm just a person."

Edna beamed at her. "Yes, right now, you are like us. Citizens of Nowhere."

"You mean…"

"Most of us have been driven out of our homes by soldiers, bandits, pirates. Most of those who drove us out did so under the banners of country or faith, or progress, like your father's countrymen. And the people who had protected us before that, it was the same. Always two sides, always life and death which side you belong to."

"And you have not chosen sides?"

"We have chosen our side. The side of people, living life. Together."

Milima stilled her mind and let the woman's words wash over her. She could find no deception or irony or self-delusion in the woman's thoughts. This was what she believed, for sure.

"Cool."

Edna laughed. "Everyone will be very happy to know that we are cool."

"No, I mean it. I have lived what you described. My parents love each other, they are not at war. But I have been a battlefield for their cultures, who each see me as a traitor. Almond eyes, kinky hair, thin lips, skin like both but like neither. I never heard of Nowhere. But I have been called No One, in so many words, for as long as I remember."

"Maybe they don't see you as a traitor, but as a living example that no one group is better than another. So they make your life hard to prove that it is easier to be one of them."

"Yes, perhaps you are right." Perhaps they were both right—she had been called a disgrace too many times to not believe that was how she was seen. But Edna's view rang true, as well.

"But the world has changed, and it is not easier to be one of them, whatever that means. Here in Africa, we should know that better than anyone. The first people lived here—I mean right here—more than 150,000 years ago, and the people who came before the first people, too. They left behind forests like these and grasslands like the ones around Mangai, and they walked along the coastline your project is destroying, living on shellfish, and they walked all the way to Asia, and later to Europe and America. Many thousands of years later, their descendants returned here, as if they remembered the richness of the place. And they began the great mixing. I am from Ethiopia—in my face, you can see Arabs who returned to Africa many times over thousands of years. You can see the Hindus who came here to trade. The British, the French, just as I can see the Chinese in your face. Now, the whole world is churning, all its peoples mixing. All this fighting over 'them' and 'us'—it is like raindrops fighting in a typhoon!"

Milima shuddered, the memory of the hurricanes and tidal waves from Lina's world suddenly alive. She could feel Edna's passion under her serious demeanor, and she glimpsed the older woman's concern.

"Still, how do you keep all of that out of here?"

"We do what we can. When people come here, they must leave certain things outside. Whatever they believe in their heart, there is no room here for superiority. No religion is better, no nationality, ethnicity, class. Whatever it is they remember fondly about their old lives, they must share. They must cook a meal, celebrate a holiday, wear a certain color—and for those for whom this is not our tradition, we must partake with an open heart."

Milima was impressed at the idea, and she could also feel Edna's pride. "Really cool!"

They both laughed.

"What is it you want to do, Milima?" Edna asked, her expression once more serious. "Do you want to go back to Kiunga or to Mombasa?"

Milima scanned the village, noticing more details about the people. She saw now that there was a deliberate mixing of styles, as if the people of East Africa had had a big swap meet and exchanged fashions. She touched their minds as best she could. There was nothing special she could detect, except perhaps a quiet confidence. A calm.

"Maybe, yeah, I don't really know." she answered. "Can I stay here, at least for a while? If I could just let my parents know I'm OK, I'd love to stay. I can work, I'm not just a student. I'll earn my keep."

"You can stay as long as you like. After a week, you must decide if this is for you, and if it is, you must agree to our ways. We have our rituals, too. We can talk about that. As for your parents, we can get word to them. But they cannot know our location. No matter what you intend, the Chinese will put pressure on your parents, and they will tell them where you are. Perhaps they will send helicopters and soldiers to rescue you or maybe the security services will just make a note in their files. Nowhere will then be Somewhere on their map, and it will no longer be our home."

"How do you keep it a secret? Don't people leave on their own?"

"Yes, they do. We have our ways of remaining hidden, though. All in due time."

They move, Milima could sense the answer in Edna. Nowhere can be anywhere. They must move every now and then, and very carefully.

"You can get word to my parents soon?"

"Yes. Imani's village will return. We made a deal with Shabab several years ago. The villagers won't tell the Chinese where to find Shabab, and Shabab will leave them alone. We have a special relationship with Mangai village—our secret is safe with them. One of them will let your parents know that you are safe."

"And what about the people from my bus?"

"That will have to play out between the Chinese and Shabab."

She knows they will be killed, Milima thought. Shabab already knows the CFA won't ransom the bus travelers. They were all low-level workers, except for the two soldiers. And the soldiers sealed their fate by not dying defending the bus.

This is what Lina died for, she thought. What she gave up Raefe for, what Far Flier changed her for, the replay that Diver talked about: to learn what it feels like to put aside hatred and fear, to join with ordinary people. This is a start. My parents will be upset, but I cannot change that my life will always bring one or another of them some pain and regret. Let it at least mean something.

"I sense that you are thinking very deeply about this," Edna said. "I want to say that we would be very happy to have someone such as you who can bring us experiences and knowledge from places we have never had the chance to go. But I also want to say that you must not think of this as some kind of sacrifice, some kind of martyrdom."

Milima was startled. Now it was Edna who seemed to be reading her mind. "I confess, you are not far off what I was thinking. What should I think of this as?"

"As a decision you can make, or not. Many people take a new name when they join us, to signify leaving behind the names that mark their family and clan and culture. I took the name Edna. In my language, it means rebirth. For me, this is both a new way of life and actually an entire new life itself. Like a butterfly from a cocoon."

"Let me spend a week in your cocoon. Then let's see where I will fly."

SECRET EXPERIMENTS

Traveler's Perch
January 20, 2049

As Hankori neared the lava fields, he commanded his enhancements to turn his feathers a shiny black. He had never understood the fascination some of his species still had for the colorful plumage of their ancestors. Nor the chunky thighs, skinny lower legs and outsized shoulders that had helped them fly. Let Diver and Flier and the others who dabbled in assisted flight have their silly delusions. He loved that his compact body and drab plumage hid him here in the lava. If he moved carefully and shielded his mind, only the most observant could pick him out from the boulders strewn everywhere.

Hankori had picked this location with great care many months ago. On the slopes of the only active volcano on Traveler's Perch, there was an ancient tube. Empty near the surface, it harbored boiling lava deep below that sent hot air out of a vent at the top. More importantly, the entire area was filled with masses of swirling ions generated by the lava below. That generated so much quantum activity that most Guardians could never penetrate the static to entangle with him, let alone an ordinary citizen. Hankori, on the other hand, had made a study of quantum noise and perfected his own filtering techniques that he had shared with the select group that would meet today. So, the cave was safe from prying minds. All 17 of them could now converse in isolation, their waveform impossible to comingle with any others without their knowledge.

"We are facing a crisis," Hankori said. "The most naïve of the Guardian Ambassadors, Diver, has gone beyond her usual silly projects. Recently, she had cadets catch fish in their teeth. And now she is revealing herself to the barbarians of Earth. These are nothing more than primitive killers, and yet she has blinded herself to their natures."

"What of it, Hankori?" Putnomo, a large quadruped from Mondoni, head of Discovery, interrupted. "Let her waste her time while they destroy themselves."

"You are many light years from them," Hankori answered. "We are only 20. She may already be breaking her oath and leaking technical information to them. I believe her objectivity may be compromised. If she persists, in a millennium or two, they may well develop the means to threaten not only us, but other nearby Guardian species."

The group immediately started arguing about how much of a threat Earth was. His protégé, Green, supported him, but Putnomo resorted to scientist mode and made a big ceremony of his own skepticism. He needed Putnomo, but he wished he didn't. The man was just insufferable.

"I don't take issue with your skepticism, Putnomo," he said, trying to soothe him. "But let's not get caught up in debating something that actually doesn't matter. What I think we all want to hear about is how your project is progressing."

"Thank you," Putnomo said. "Whatever our differing opinions about Diver and Earth, we can all agree that the most important thing is to press ahead with our work on Permanance. We have made a breakthrough. About 600 years ago, we encountered a very unusual species on the outer edges of the Eta Carinae nebula. It was the only life, let alone intelligent life, that we have ever found that was composed solely of gas and plasma organized in a complex pattern of standing waves. We learned very little about it before Eta Carinae erupted in a partial nova that destroyed the life form, along with the entire region. For those of you who are new to our efforts, it was this encounter that helped Hankori and myself and a few others to realize that with some effort, this kind of life could be immortal.

"Three things had to be solved to make that happen. The first—reducing an individual's consciousness to free-standing waves—is already something all of our species could do, if we had not bound ourselves foolishly to retain our ancient forms. The second was how to overcome entropy—how can a waveform, in essence, eat while still retaining its essential nature? The third was how to continue to manipulate matter while remaining pure energy."

Hankori could hardly contain his impatience. Putnomo was always so impressed with himself. "Yes, yes, give us the news!"

Putnomo let them see his laboratory, hidden in the frozen asteroid belt of his planet's star system. Inside was a force field in which only a large plasma cloud existed, suspended within intense magnetic fields.

They watched as Putnomo, on his homeworld, nearly a billion kilometers away, donned a helmet. For a few seconds nothing happened and then Putnomo allowed them to entangle with the plasma cloud itself, through him. And then he broke his connection with them.

The waveform shuddered as they all gasped. The plasma cloud retained much of Putnomo's consciousness. In fact, it shifted gradually as they entangled with it.

Putnomo reconnected with them. "Yes, I was able to project my consciousness into the cloud, and while it couldn't think entirely new thoughts, it did react to you in small ways. For the first time, we have created consciousness in a cloud of plasma."

The waveform pulsed with approval and delight. Even Hankori was impressed.

"Are there fundamental issues you still need to address?" he wondered.

"Not fundamental ones, no. We have some decades of engineering before we can attempt a full transfer, and then perhaps some more time to ensure stability. But there is every reason to believe that we have found a way to preserve consciousness permanently. In short, to be immortal."

"And what about the third obstacle?" Green asked. "Does any of this bode well for allowing conscious plasma to still interact with the physical universe at ordinary temperatures?"

"We have been working in parallel on that. We chose the confined plasma precisely because we have known for millennia how to control it. It was one of the main technologies of the controlled fusion era. Reversing that, having the plasma control ordinary matter, is challenging but conceptually well understood. Many of the principles involved in lightspeed engine research can be reversed to apply to this." Putnomo was in all his glory now. "I feel strongly that we are perhaps 100 years away from a demonstration combining conscious energy capable of controlling material objects."

Hankori steered them back to the immediate threat. "All the more reason to not waste time or resources on foolishness. The lightspeed engine project is our cover story, and we need to keep the project alive, even if it's mostly a distraction from our real purpose."

"What is your proposal?" asked Putnomo.

Hankori hesitated. He wasn't interested in fully revealing his plans. "We must lay the groundwork for us to turn the Guardians away from fostering of any kind of life conscious enough to say a few words and have a few thoughts to the further development of all of our species, who are the highest form of consciousness."

"What is at stake," he continued, "is nothing less than the evolution of conscious life itself. In a million millennia, only 20 species in the entire galaxy have reached the stage of enhanced life. Should we spend another billion years hoping to find a few more? And leave ourselves vulnerable to forces beyond our control? To the whims of supernovas and their gamma ray beacons? To attack from far corners of the galaxy, or from beings in other galaxies who have gone beyond us in lightspeed travel or solved the riddle of faster than light travel?"

"We have already earned Permanence, and we deserve it," he said forcefully. "Let us turn the Guardians from this foolish philosophy of naïve benevolence to one of true Guardianship—of our species and our future."

The meeting was over, and Hankori felt minds drop away. But Green lingered.

"Are you not concerned about this development with the human, Raefe?" he asked.

"I am quite concerned," Hankori said. "But I have a plan."

"Care to share it?" Green asked. "We've been in this together for a long time."

"And we will share a victory toast. Soon. For now, the most good you can do is to keep an eye on Diver. She is such a foolish being. She will be an important unwitting ally."

TECHTOWN

Cambridge
January 22, 2049

The train glided to a stop in TechTown, with its 40-story glass buildings towering over Cambridge. Several heads jerked upright, their Voices telling them through their fashionably discrete ear implants that it was time to wake the frick up, get off the grimy train, and head to their jobs. Shiny little office nerds nervously tapped their eyeglass puters on: Must check those messages, wouldn't want to have to look at all the lesser beings on the train.

Raefer couldn't afford such fancy gear. Plain old flesh-colored skingel minibuds for his Voice and a pocket puter would have to do on his codetech salary. Right now, he was near the bottom of the food chain: a CodeEngine jockey who operated the software that MiniWorlds used to churn out application code. If he proved himself, he could move up to design and build the software that ran the CodeEngine clusters. Then from there, he could become a softsystems architect, helping design the complex EvoEco virtual ecosystem that evolved all the codes to work together to get anything done. Then he could think about invisible implants and even implanted puters, or actually moving to the top floors of those 40-story towers, with their views of the harbor to the east and the low hills landward. Right now, he was happy enough to look out of his own apartment at the building next door.

Or he could stop chasing this foolishness because he knew it would all be under water someday if the world didn't smarten up—someday in his life, not some far distant future in a scifi vid.

And find Lina. Their online exchanges left him aching for her, and not just for the pleasure of her sex that his other self couldn't stop remembering. Somedays not even mostly for that. But for the pleasure of their comfort together. For the deep letting-go that Raefe remembered and had now become fully integrated into Raefer's consciousness. He was in love with a girl he had never met. Now even the sight of her words on the screen triggered memories from another time and place, and they made him long for more.

That would have to wait. He had reached his workstation. There was already a good number of work orders waiting for him. The usual crap: Build a socket for input A to plug into module B, turn a fixed input into a user-adjustable one, and so on. CodeEngine had already downloaded all the parts he would need, but he needed to do some research to find out the full context in which the code would be used before deciding exactly which variants of the parts he should use, and in which order.

The part of him that had survived the tidal wave did better in the mornings. As the days wore on, he grew restless with the routine, so he had taken to front-loading his day with work and rewarding himself with an actual lunch break while CodeEngine tested his work. No more sipping smoothies at his desk while working. MinWorlds didn't care, as long as they could keep feeding their sim frameworks to their cyberindustry customers, who turned them into finished sims, games, courses, or whatever.

After lunch, he would have the results and could make corrections and do final tuning and optimizing. He looked across the wide expanse of the office where all the CodeEngine jocks sat. Nikko was head down, with the furrowed brow she got when she was deep inside the machine. Herbie was leaning back, arms folded, contemplating the screen—the thoughtful face he used when thinking about nonwork items. Roderick was doing that thing with his hands where he would hold them high above the keyboard and hit a key at a time with a motion like he was conducting an orchestra. He always did that when he sent his code off to the test queue. So, at least two for lunch. He sent them a word bubble to meet at 12:10 on the water walk along the canal that led to the harbor.

Raefer wandered out there, soaking up the early spring rays. He was looking for the Ethiopian food truck—close as he could get to Lina. He got a plate of chicken wat and some bread and walked over to the part of the water walk that jutted further out into the harbor. He grabbed a table big enough for three and waited for Herbie and Rod.

What were they thinking when they built this, he wondered. In 10 or 20 years, this could be under water. They could have spent the money to build a solar farm or the grid or anything that would forestall the rising seas instead of a nice lunch place for software builders.

"Hey, you look deep in thought," Herbie said. "What's up?"

"Oh, nothing," he said. "Just thinking how life is short on time and long on bullshit."

"OK, then," Herbie said. "Is that from your upcoming book, 'Raefer Speaks?' You have been very philosophical lately."

"I guess so," Raefer said. "No one told me that building grunt code would not only make me unrich, but also deeply wise. They really should include that in the job posting."

"Oh, I don't know," Herbie said. "Seems like so many jobs offer a life of enlightened poverty."

"What?" Rod said, just sitting down. "Poverty? What do you know about that? You should come with me next time I visit my family in Nigeria."

"It's all relative," Herbie said. "What you're used to."

"Right," Raefer said. "Herbie, you're used to whining. Rod, you're used to reminding us all that you grew up where oil sludge goes to die."

"And you," Rod said. "What are you used to?"

"Eating lunch with you two, so that I can soak up the full range of human experience."

Talk turned to work—which supervisor was the biggest jerk, which single women were at least semihetero, which of them might be desperate enough to consider a fellow CodeEngine jock as a sex partner, and so on. Raefer started to tune out during the sex talk—he had lost interest in pursuing the usual suspects in favor of figuring out how to reunite with Lina, or Milima as she now called herself. Something Rod said kicked off a series of recollections from Raefe.

"Hey, not to break up this highly enlightening discussion of relationship building techniques, but I've been meaning-to ask you Rod, where again are you from in Nigeria?"

"Ikorodu. It's near Lagos."

"Right. And why would I have heard of it before I met you?" Raefer asked. Something from his other self had been tickling the back of his mind about Nigeria, but he couldn't quite reach it to scratch.

"You probably heard about the whole mess there with development. The government had this grand plan to create a floating city on Lake Lagos that was connected to Ikorodu. With Lagos having over 30 million people, the government wanted to build housing to relieve that congestion."

"But they messed up?" Herbie asked.

"It was a disaster. Corruption, bad engineering, ethnic conflict. It all came together around this plan."

"Were you there when it happened?" Raefer asked, now curious.

"Most of it, yeah," Rod said. "Truth? It's still going on."

Something clicked for Raefer. He remembered Raefe talking to someone named Alton just before, well, just before Raefe joined him. About a man with one of those colorful Nigerian names.

"Somebody told me about a guy who was trying to stop it—Goodstuff Benjamin. Ever hear about him?" he asked.

Rod laughed. "Goodstuff? Everyone knows about him. Everyone has an opinion, too."

"No kidding," Raefer said. "I didn't know he was such a big deal. What's your opinion?"

"Complicated," Rod said. "Goodstuff, he has the right idea. In Nigeria, corruption and screwing up the environment are almost the same thing. In the old days, it was just take the oil and run. Then the big global agripharm companies realized that Nigeria was one of the best places in the world to both get oil and grow crops. So they could integrate the whole chain: take the oil, make fertilizer, genetically modify crops for higher yields. The generals were very happy to take their cut. But Goodstuff's followers, they were the losers in the process. Their land suddenly had oil wells on it, and their water was polluted. Their farms were stolen for a pittance by Monsanto Takeda. They can't even buy seed anymore without having to buy engineered seed, and that means they have to buy the enzymes to activate it, and they can't afford that."

"But?" Raefer said, sensing there was another side.

"Goodstuff is a talker," Rod said. "He's like the preacher on Sunday. He tells you about the promised land, but somehow, you can never quite reach it. And the generals got sick of his preaching, and they chased him back into the forests in the North. Up there, the jihadis are after his ass, too."

"Good taste in enemies," Herbie said.

I feel like I have to meet this guy eventually, Raefer thought, but how? How was he going to find a guy who was basically hiding from fanatical warlords in rural Nigeria? Maybe Milima would have some ideas. And even though he knew that Nigeria was quite far from Kenya, it was certainly closer to her than Boston. He was going to have to find a way to cross that ocean.

THE BIG MEETING

Traveler's Perch
January 23, 2049

Far Flier had never felt the waveform so volatile at a Guardian Council meeting. It wasn't the number of participants that made it so difficult to tune everyone in. Aside from himself, there were only representatives from all five main departments—Green from Timelines, Hankori from Administration, Putnomo from Discovery, Tanoch from Ambasssadors and Manulo from Analysis—plus Diver, summoned to explain events on Earth. No, the difficulty was in finding a wave that encompassed the full range of emotions that were brought to the meeting. He felt fear, arrogance, sadness, puzzlement, anger, gloating—not much to build resonance on. Disagreement was common among all peoples, and certainly the Guardian Council, but this was different. It felt like a will to avoid agreement, as if it were some ancient virus.

"Our work as a council," he began neutrally, "often involves difficult, even impossible, dilemmas. Our tradition has always been to stare these directly in the face. To brave the complications they entail, to find the solution that is most faithful to our principles and our mission. I ask for your help now in coming together to discuss the matters at hand. We have two key issues in front of us. One is the recent crisis on Earth—what happened, what was done, and what should come next. Two is the proposal from Discovery to launch a new initiative, a project aimed at developing a lightspeed engine. Let's start with Earth."

As soon as he had acknowledged the lightspeed engine project, the waveform had begun to coalesce more firmly. So this is what they really want to discuss, he thought. Why the emotion attached to it?

"Representing Timelines," Green started, "I want the Council to understand that at least one timeline shift was made without our participation. We know from past experience that any number of bad things can happen when this ability is used without proper care. That is the entire reason that Timelines was created as the newest part of the Guardians. Was it an Ambassador who initiated this shift? And can they explain why?"

"No Ambassadors are trained enough to accomplish a shift," Tanoch replied, as head of that department, "even if we were so inclined. What evidence do you have that it was an Ambassador?"

"I received a request from Diver for a suitable timeline," Green said. "And not long after, the shift was made."

"Green is correct," Diver said, "but his account is incomplete. I made an initial query because I was concerned that Earth's general situation was deteriorating. I wanted to begin thinking about alternative Earths for my contacts. Green gave me some insight into those options."

"And I warned you against trying to send your contact into his past to relive his mistakes," Green said.

"Of course. And I made it clear that I was not interested in that. But you are wrong to say that you did not participate in the shift."

"Nonsense," Green fired back. "We had nothing to do with it."

"Precisely. The situation was dire," she said. She broadcast the records of the volcanic collapse and the tidal wave. "I had only a short time to rescue Raefe, or his consciousness would have died with him. You were made aware of this."

"Diver is correct," Manulo interjected. "Analysis confirms both her assessment of the situation on Earth and what she told Timelines."

"And what was the response from Timelines?" Far Flier asked, leaving it vague whether he was addressing Manulo or Green.

"I received no request from them for more information," Manulo replied. "Typically, that would be the first step in planning a shift."

"Because no shift had been authorized by the Council," Green said. "I can only carry out the will of the Council."

"But you knew there wasn't time for that," Diver said.

"I knew you didn't have time for that," Green said. "But whose fault was that? You had already anticipated that a shift would be necessary, yet you never bothered to inform the Council."

"A good Ambassador always considers many potential outcomes," Tanoch said.

"Yes, precisely," Hankori said, "and prepares for them."

"You misunderstand my meaning," Tanoch said. "If every Ambassador came to the Council every time they saw that the potential for a time shift had risen to a level where it was worth thinking about, we would be in constant session. I think the record suggests only that Diver was correct in her assessment. None of us can predict the future, only see vaguely the shape it might take."

Far Flier could feel that Hankori and Green had walled off certain thoughts from the group. He guessed that they were agreeing to continue not really answering why Green had put up roadblocks to the transfer. He was still the Coordinator and he wouldn't allow that to stand.

"Let us rise above the level of petty disputes about the facts," Far Flier said. "The facts are not in dispute. Diver made a request to Timelines, and Timelines' answer was to follow procedure. Do we all agree on that?"

He could sense the frustration from some of the Council who had come hoping to discredit Diver, but no one objected to his characterization. Still, back and forth they went, Hankori's allies protesting the irregularity of it all, how they were risking an apocalypse for humanity, Far Flier's supporters pointing out the far more immediate danger to a real human.

"Enough!" he exclaimed, wanting to bring the discussion to a close. "Yes, Armageddon is a real possibility for all civilizations, even our various ones. And that is why our nurturance of humans is important, more important than our own rules. Our mission is to create the conditions for intelligent life to prosper and survive. Whatever inconveniences, messy situations, loose ends or confusion that brings, we must always keep that foremost in mind. I would hope that in the future, Timelines would adhere to that mission. I would like us to feel agreement on that."

Green and the other dissenters remained silent. Far Flier hoped that they had finished their interrogation without asking about Lina. He wanted to move on to happy news.

"Fortunately, Raefe has been relocated to a more advantageous timeline. Diver, you have entangled with him. What are his prospects?"

"Hang on," Hankori interrupted. "I don't think we're ready to move on yet from discussing the shift. I still don't understand how Diver shifted him without the cooperation of Timelines?"

Diver hesitated. "I didn't..."

Hankori had been lying in waiting for him, Far Flier realized. Letting Green take the lead while he waited for an opening. He sensed satisfaction from Hankori's allies now that he had sprung what they hoped was a trap. Far Flier wouldn't make it easy for them, though.

"I did," Far Flier interjected. "Analytics had made me aware of the crisis. Once Diver told me of the issue with Timelines, I took the necessary steps."

"How interesting," Hankori answered. "I was unaware that anyone but Timelines could actually access the quantum multiverse interface needed to shift someone to a new timeline. In fact, in Administration, we have gone to great lengths to ensure that each department is compartmentalized, so that no Guardian can hijack the system for their own agenda."

"I am surprised to hear you say that," Far Flier answered. "You know that as Coordinator, I have the ability to access any systems. Perhaps you were unaware that in my early days in the Guardians, we still practiced a system of rotation for trainees. Most of you are aware that every so often I participate in your department's work. I'm not sure how a Coordinator can function, really, if they remain completely ignorant of the details of what we do as Guardians."

"I will only register my concern, then, at your interference. A matter for another time," Hankori said.

Far Flier was actually relieved that there wasn't more support for Hankori's attempt to open the can of worms. He would be gracious and move on before someone thought to ask about Lina.

"Quite," he said. "We have much to talk about with the second item, the lightspeed drive project."

"Yes, indeed," Putnomo said. Everyone had sensed his growing impatience. "You have received my brief. Let me summarize. Some preliminary work by the Discovery team has revived interest in lightspeed travel. We are exploring some very promising new physics that will unlock this possibility. Rather than having to accelerate toward lightspeed, with all of the energy consumption and relativistic effects that entails, this new physics points to instantaneous lightspeed."

Far Flier was curious but dubious. Intelligent life everywhere seemed to have a common characteristic: a fascination with breaking free of the constraints of the speed of light. And yet, no one in this galaxy ever had.

"Might I ask more about the physics?" Manulo said. "What is the basic principal?"

"It's quite complex, really," Putnomo answered. "I'm broadcasting some reference materials if you want to dig deeper. But the short answer is that we think that by combining advanced plasma control systems with vacuum energy modulation, we can instantaneously transform the plasma into very high levels of light pressure."

Far Flier made a mental note to investigate the science more thoroughly. Putnomo's descriptions were always a bit grandiose, but this one didn't quite make sense and he felt skepticism from Manulo as well.

"What would you need from the council?" he asked Putnomo.

"The project will require a doubling of the energy budget and staff allocations for the entire Discovery department. It would mean a redefinition of our basic goals."

"What you mean" Tanoch said, "is that you would shift your activities away from supporting the Ambassadors' mission, isn't it?"

"No," said Putnomo. "We would change what is available to the Ambassadors. Now they can merely entangle with a few individuals. This project will enable them to identify new species and perhaps, someday, even go beyond this galaxy."

"But until lightspeed technology actually works, and we can use it for the Ambassadors," Tanoch pointed out, "you would essentially be allowing the current effort to stagnate, betting on a future replacement."

"Unless our home worlds are willing to give greater support to the Guardians as a whole," Putnomo answered. "That is not for me to decide."

Far Flier waited for Tanoch to continue his objection, but he sensed that he had made some accommodation with the proposal. He couldn't read why, though.

"Then I suggest that I ask each Guardian species to consider their stance on this," Far Flier said. "Ultimately, they must decide what future direction we want to take as Guardians. When we know the answer, we can meet to discuss again."

Both sides accept this, Far Flier thought. *I wonder why.*

GAME ON

Cambridge, MA
January 23, 2049

Something tugged at Raefer's consciousness, pulling him back from the intricacies of wiring up *Titan Towers*, the new sim game his team was working on. Without turning around, he knew that Mike, his boss, was walking across the floor to see him. What he couldn't tell was why, but at least he didn't feel anything overtly hostile.

"Hey, Raefer, got a minute?" Mike asked. Raefer turned around, acting vaguely surprised.

"Sure, Mike, what's up?"

"How far along are you on the *Titan* sim?

"Pretty far along. I've plugged in all the physics algorithms—local gravity, Jovian gravity, solar radiation, that kind of thing. Herbie is working on the projectile stuff—asteroids, comets, and so on. All I have left is to install the low-G effects and then the behavioral algorithms. How will people react to solar storms, alien attacks? You know, the usual."

"That's good, sounds like we're in the home stretch. You do a lot of these sims. Do you like the work?"

Uh oh, Raefer thought, *danger ahead*. But he still couldn't feel any serious negativity from Mike.

"It's fine. If you do a lot of these, you start to see that they're all pretty similar. On the one hand, you've got an environment with built-in limitations and threats. On the other hand, you have humans who have a range of probable responses to each other and the environment. And you want to make this nondeterministic but not invisible to the players. They want to discover what makes the sim world work and master it. "

"No flies on you. That's a pretty good summation. A lot of guys take many years to see that."

Raefer blushed. Had he said too much?

"Anyway, I suspected you had a pretty good handle on it, because I usually see your name near the top of the efficiency reports I get. Now I know it's probably because you're quite clear about what to do and not that you're using mind-enhancing drugs."

No, not repeating my old man's mistakes, Raefer thought.

"Thanks, I guess."

"Oh, I think you will thank me. I'm going to reassign you to a new team. You'll be working on something called the Civilization Project that MiniWorlds is partnering with MIT on. Ken Robertson himself brokered the deal."

"Wow. So what's the game?"

"It's not exactly a game. Have you heard of the Cosmos sim?"

Of course, Raefer thought. Every geek my age spent their high school years playing God in Cosmos, making the universe in their own image. Mike explained that the Civilization Project had amped up Cosmos to simulate the evolution of human society.

"That doesn't sound new," Raefer said. "Weren't some of the very first sim games about building a city, or farming?"

"This is not that. They're starting with monkeys and ending with our world."

"OK, that's cool. So yeah, thanks."

"In the end, we'll get a lot of fresh behavioral code that could give us much richer sims. And guys like you will learn new algorithms and new coding techniques."

And, of course, Raefer would get the exalted title of Associate Team Leader and a two percent raise. At the end of the year they'd tell him that he wasn't getting an annual raise because he'd already gotten the two percent. But still, he was that much closer to being able to afford a trip to Africa and Milima.

The next day, he reported to his new boss, a Braz named Elise Pasos. She looked thirtysomething, harried, and slightly intense. The rest of the team looked like standard MiniWorld grunts—electro-board shoes, cheap nanotats, clothes they pirated at some DIY fab shop.

"Raefer's joining The CivPro team from the Titan sim group," Elise said, turning to him. "Apart from taking attendance and general babysitting, I work on the quantitative sociology parts of the project. I also get to talk to the big brains at the Toot. What that means in this context is that I look at factors that have contributed to the rise and fall of societies. Jim develops math that represents those factors."

"Hi, Jim Nguyen. And what we're hoping you'll be able to do," he said, looking at Raefer, "is translate that math into an interactive, gamelike environment."

"And why do you want to do that?" asked Raefer. "Why the game part?"

The idea was that researchers could interact with the sim, change the characters, the weighting of different factors, really change just about anything, and see how the world turned out.

"Cool," Raefer said. "Well, I'm sure I can help. I've built dozens of game frameworks for hundreds of games and even some self-generating animated vids. We'll have to get deeper into how you want them to interact, how many people and so on. But that sounds exciting. Most of the games I help build are either about guns or money—is that the kind of stuff you're looking at?"

"Part of it—guns and money have driven a lot of history, eh?" Elise said with a wry smile. "But we want to look deeper into issues like competition and collaboration, heirarchy and equality, scarcity and plenty. How does that effect the role of guns and money, for example, in how a society works?"

Yes! Finally, I can use my insights about empathy to inform a game, he thought.

"Nice," Raefer said. "I'm a little bored of creating counters for bodies or coins."

He lay in bed that night, wishing he could talk with Milima. She was out of touch in some small coastal town, Kiunga. He had been wrestling with himself about just what it was he could do to put his empathic powers to good use. The thought of being some kind of charismatic leader, a Goodstuff Benjamin, just made him laugh. He just wasn't that kind of person.

He had to admit, his new-found empathic powers made him feel more comfortable with people. Not that he was shy before, but his headaches always made him feel different from others. Now he saw that difference in a new, comforting light. Sometimes now he felt more of a sameness with other people, not a difference. That Joe Nguyen guy, for example. He thought he had felt a little buzz coming off of him, like maybe he, too, could entangle.

Still, it was a long way from being less of a freak to feeling like he could lead an army of people to change the world. So maybe his role would be to work in the background, make sure everything was on a solid footing. Like the games he worked on; the customers saw the graphics but it was his algorithms underneath that made the characters behave realistically. This civ sim could be like that, too.

He and Milima were set to talk again in a couple of weeks. What would she think of Raefer, supergeek, saving the world with code?

LIGHT CONVERSATION

Traveler's Perch
January 23, 2049

At night, after the council meeting, Far Flier came to Diver's quarters.

"I've been waiting to ask you what the galaxy was going on at the last Council meeting," she said.

"'What the galaxy?'" he smiled.

"Oh sorry. I got that from humans, sort of. When they feel strongly about something, they invoke grand forces of nature or their deities. They say things like 'what on earth' or 'what the hell' is going on. The galaxy is kind of our world, right? It just made me realize that even though they can only communicate consciously through words, there is a richness to their expression that I like."

He smiled. "Your passion refreshes."

"Speaking of which, do you want to eat?" Diver let him sense that she had moved from anger at a betrayer to the concern of a friend.

"Yes, that would be nice," Far Flier answered, accepting her olive branch.

She was cheered that he had chosen to eat with her. It had been thousands of years since their kind had needed to deliberately eat to survive. Their ancestors had enhanced them with a variety of autotrophic mechanisms. As long as there was any kind of ambient electromagnetic energy, they were fine. And they could survive for days on gravity alone, in the rare event they were cut off from light or other electro-magnetic radiation. Eating was now for pleasure or companionship, for honoring the ancient voices that still spoke in their cells.

She dipped into her small stock of food to find purple fruit slices, and some dried meats with microherbal implants. She thought the codes that activated them, releasing the fresh tastes of the herbs into the meat. *What the galaxy*, she thought, and brought out a wine she knew he especially liked.

"You always know how to cleanse my mind, Diver."

"I'm pleased you feel that way," she said, pausing to consider her response. "I am still trying to cleanse mine, but I see now that there are no simple paths through the asteroid fields in front of us. I can't quite see my way to approve of what you did with Lina, but I may have overreacted. I was afraid of what would happen to Raefe and Lina, I was angry at all of us for not behaving better, and maybe you were the easiest target for that. But I see that you had few other choices. Maybe no other choices. And that disturbs me more than the deed itself."

"You have forced me to reflect on my own actions as well. In hindsight, I was too secretive and should have brought you and Tanoch into it. And really, I can't believe Green, hiding behind this idea of needing to have a committee meeting. Whatever happened to saving an entire species?" Far Flier said.

"Indeed," she agreed. "After these many millennia of the Guardians, sometimes we feel like the ancient kingdoms that existed before we entangled, filled with puffed-up officials and scheming lords. All of which scares me. Compared to that, the worst I can think of your actions is that you were egotistical, but ultimately right-minded."

She sensed his disappointment at the egotistical label and that he would let it go. He was mostly relieved. He would complete the ritual of submission.

"I accept your judgment. It's not just your passion that refreshes, but your idealism as well. I will try to do better. So what did you think of the meeting?"

Her mind swirled with questions. What were Hankori and Green up to? Why wasn't anyone pressing them harder on it?

"Confusing," she said. "Did I just hear Putnomo propose to end our entanglements with other species and Tanoch agree to it? Why would Tanoch do that?"

"I wondered the same. I've looked into it a bit and I can find no connection between Tanoch and Hankori's faction."

"Still," she said, "even if they are not secretly scheming together, our colleagues are losing sight of our mission. Traveling by lightspeed ship to contact new species? We have never wanted to be seen as demigods whose mere arrival in galaxy-spanning spacecraft would demonstrate our overwhelming superiority."

She thought of the human's obsession with aliens. Most of the time, they saw them as a threat. Nothing says "conquerors" more than aliens appearing in a highly advanced space ship.

Far Flier was quiet, considering her thoughts. Then he sighed, frowning slightly.

"I hadn't put the final pieces together, but I think I see them falling into place. I have promised not to have so many secrets from you, so I am going to tell you something that very few people know. And it should stay that way, at least for now. Are you willing to abide by that?"

"My head says no, but my heart knows that yes is the only real answer here."

"Your head will soon agree," he said, relieved that she seemed to understand the stakes. "Putnomo's presentation also made me uneasy for another reason. Something didn't add up. As I told you, I have many friends with many kinds of expertise, including advanced propulsion systems and plasma physics. I asked one of them, in loose terms, about Putnomo's project."

"Let me guess," she said. "It will take even longer and cost even more than he suggested."

"It will take an eternity and cost nothing," Far Flier said, "because it is a fraud. It can't be done."

He explained that the project rested on several technologies. One main focus—plasma containment and control—had a solid foundation and the general goals of more advanced control and higher yields were ambitious but reasonable. But the leap from better engines to instantaneous acceleration to lightspeed was not an engineering problem—the universe simply wouldn't allow it.

"What if he's discovered some new physics?"

"Undoubtedly he has," Far Flier said. "Putnomo makes vague allusions to a new technology that can entirely transform ordinary matter into a sort of three-dimensional, self-contained coherent light wave within a plasma cloud, and then reverse the process upon arrival."

"So that's how we would travel at lightspeed? We become light, and then revert back to matter on arrival?"

"At its heart, that's Putnomo's project. But my sources say that this is simply not possible. There can never be a 100 percent faithful transformation of matter to energy and back to matter. To put it simply, we can send our thoughts anywhere. We can send our bodies anywhere. But if we send our bodies as thoughts, and then recreate our bodies from those thoughts, they will be randomly different at the quantum level in a random number of ways, ranging from moderate to massive differences. But whether slight or massive, those differences could mean we won't survive the trip."

"Well, scientists often disagree, don't they," Diver said, wondering where he was going with this.

"But that's the thing," Far Flier said. "This disagreement was settled thousands of years ago. And this particular detail of Putnomo's plan was buried in his proposal. Only a few people—fortunately my friend is one of them—could look deeply enough into this to see its rotten heart."

"What do you think it means? What is Putnomo up to?"

"I think it means that Putnomo wants to develop something crucial to Hankori's agenda, and knows that its true nature must remain hidden. He's always been slightly in the thrall of science and cares more discovering something big and new than the consequences of Hankori's agenda."

"And what do you think that is?"

"I have no idea. But I'm afraid of what it is. And I don't think I can let this go. I fear that their project is something deeply, fundamentally wrong."

"If your friend is right, they are certainly behaving as if they know you and many of the rest of us won't agree to it."

"Will you help me to uncover this secret, and if I'm right, to stop them?"

It's come to this, she thought. I tell him I'm furious that he broke the rules and kept it a secret, and now he's willing to share the secrets. Suddenly, she understood what Raefer must feel. All of her talks with him must sound like this: There is a world you know nothing of, but I'm asking you to trust me. And I'm asking you to change your life in ways neither of us yet understand. But she couldn't surrender completely to a secret fight where anything goes.

"I want to help, and I appreciate you taking down some of the veil of secrecy. But I can't agree to do anything in the name of winning. Don't expect that," she said, her lips tightening in a grim smile.

She had hoped he would be proud of her for saying that, but could also feel his disappointment that she still considered him morally questionable and accepting that it would have to be that way for now.

BECOMING LINA

Tomorrow will be one week, Milima, thought. I'll have to give Edna my answer.

The first encampment had just been a way station and now they were headed for somewhere larger and more important, although, where, Edna would not say. For six days, they had walked north and west through the Kenyan brush. The land became drier, the plants shorter and sparser, and the noise of birds and insects gradually shrunk from a symphony to quiet conversations. It was the same with people. Villages gave way to smaller villages and eventually just to goat herders' huts. Hours could go by without them seeing any sign of other people.

With no distractions, and surrounded by hundreds of Nowhere people, she had used her empathic abilities to tune into their feelings. It fascinated her that although they spoke many languages, she could tune into their feelings without any problem. Emotions seemed to have a universal deep language and structure. She had learned to distinguish a couple dozen of them, which had surprised her. She never realized what a large palette of feelings we had to color our world. And she could feel there were many more that she couldn't quite yet bring into focus.

This morning brought no secrets, though. She could feel a wariness beginning to set in among all of them, feeling exposed on the broad, flat hard scrub. They had to hew to the forests to remain unseen, the trees dividing their ranks into many small braids. The adults grew more alert, constantly scanning for hyenas or other animals that might try and pick off small children if they wandered away.

"Today I am not the only one tired of walking," Milima said to Edna.

"I'm afraid you are right," Edna smiled. "But we are close now."

"To what?"

"Do you see in the distance over there, the woods?" Edna asked. "We will be there soon, and then we will stop."

"What's there?"

"New Dabaab. But then, you probably don't know what old Dabaab was."

"You mean where the Iranian Air Force bombed the Islamic State in '29?"

"Yes, the very same. You were just born then?"

"Yes, but my mother had family that were caught up in that. They were all killed."

She felt Edna's emotions as a blend of grays and reds, and she could feel them intertwining with her own pale yellows and sickly greens, the colors of bad memories she had absorbed from others. She would have to pay attention in the future to interwoveness. She had a sense that the tapestry was different than just the threads alone.

"I'm sorry to hear that. Dabaab had a long history before that. Even then it was much more than the last hideout for Islamic State. If you had come here 40 years ago, you would have seen a tent city of more than 300,000 people. Refugees from this war and that. That's how Islamic State came to be here, after they were run out of Egypt. But their comrades in Iraq and Syria, or what was left of those places, were still making trouble for Iran."

"My mother didn't talk about it much," Milima said. "But she always insisted her family had nothing to do with Islamic State."

"They were invaders," Edna said. "By the time they came here in '26, they had shrunk a great deal. But they were still armed, and they were able to take over the camps. The UN had run out of money and left the tents to the refugees, who made the best of it. By '29, there were still more than 50,000 people here."

They had been walking up a long rise. Edna seemed tired and stopped for a drink of water. It seemed improbable, but did Edna know about her mother's people?

"My relatives were probably some of those refugees. What happened to all of them?"

"They were, in many ways, the first Citizens of Nowhere. The world heard that the bombings killed 11,000 Islamic State fighters, but there were barely 2,000 by then. The rest were just ordinary people, caught in the fighting. Killed for being in the wrong place at the wrong time."

So many people, she thought. And no one really knew. One of the great slaughters of our time, and it never officially happened.

"With every day, I see more of what you mean by Nowhere."

"It was an awakening for us. Then and there, we had to decide whether to live or become ghosts. We chose to be living ghosts."

"You were there?" Milima asked, stunned.

"I was a young girl, still not a woman. Yet I became mother to those who had lost theirs. For a week, we lived in the midst of fire and smoke, like violent spirits who had been herded into the middle of the camp. When the smoke went away, we thought we would smell the breeze again, the familiar smells of the bush and of the camp. But there was only death around us. When all you can see in every direction are the dead, their sight and smell become one horrible overwhelming sensation that you cannot escape. Even if you close your eyes, you still smell them so strongly it feels like you can see and touch them, all around you. Each time you breathe, you have left the world and are in hell.

"In that time, I understood that I had died and had to will myself and those around me to be reborn. But not to live as before. That just didn't seem possible, to endure a hell like that a second time. At first, the imams and the remaining village leaders tried to gather us for prayers and funerals. But the old rituals brought no comfort, no sense. Certain people wandered off and found each other, somehow, in a quiet bend in the river. They sent word, and I came with other young people. We talked for days, and in the end, we understood that Nowhere was now our home. Eventually, a few thousand of us joined this new country. We split up into different groups and dispersed—to Kenya, to Nigeria, other places where we could quietly live unseen. And we come here when we lose that, to regroup and make plans."

Listening to Edna, Lina's memories of the Efricar civil war exploded from their hiding places in Milima's mind. She had escaped the worst here in this world, but it was not far away. She let herself feel Edna's emotions. They were the same rage and deep sadness the rape and killing of her other life had brought. But she could feel that, though Edna had these deep feelings, she also had learned to put herself outside them now, in this place she called Nowhere. Milima realized that since Lina had joined her, she had lost her sense of belonging in the world she had left behind in Mombasa. Hearing Edna's tale made her realize that Lina's tale was not just of another world.

She wanted to tell Edna all of this and about Raefer and what the future held for all of them. She thought Edna would understand, might even be an empath herself. She would arrange to talk to Raefer about it, maybe even Far Flier or Diver. They would figure it out together, and they would move forward together now, for the first time since Truro Island. There would be no turning back.

"I want to be part of those plans. I will continue on this path with you."

"I think you have been on it for a long time, even before you met us. And what will we call you now, Citizen of Nowhere?"

"Lina, call me Lina."

VERY LONG-DISTANCE ROMANCE

Cambridge
February 2, 2049

Raefer was beside himself. Milima's mother had managed to find him through messages he'd left Milima on their house puter. She had heard through the Chinese government that Milima had escaped a kidnapping and was safe, but was now somewhere in the bush.

It was almost six months now since he had been with her, in their other life, minutes from death, and now maybe she was on that island again. How had they let it go this long and not found a way to get together? He closed the window shade, turned off the room light. He folded his bed back into a couch and sat on the edge, as quiet and still as he could.

He closed his eyes and thought of her face. A moment from when they had just met returned, one of the few memories he had of that life that was older than a year. They were sitting at a coffee cart in Union Square; he couldn't quite remember the name. It was a beautiful spring day, and the coffee exploded in his mouth in a shower of bitter splinters, chocolate, and molasses foam. He smiled and she laughed. Her face filled his mind's eye—her anarchic curls, the slightly square nose that seemed neither African or Chinese—and a fountain of longing burst from inside him toward the sky.

And then he felt something back. A brush of fingertips raising the hair on the back of his neck. A whisper in his ear making him alert. A keening. And then it was gone.

He sat frozen, afraid to move even a millimeter. After a minute or two, he felt the desperation of knowing she might not come back, and a cry flew out from inside him. Had he actually shouted it, or was it just in his head? He wasn't sure.

"Raefer, are you OK?"

Who was it? A woman's voice, not Milima's. A neighbor?

It was Diver, in his head.

"Yes, I forget sometimes you can come when I'm awake. You heard me crying out?"

"I heard both of you."

"You heard Milima?"

"Yes, she heard you but could not hold on to your thoughts."

"Honestly I didn't expect her empathic powers to be that strong. I was really just reaching out in desperation, no expectations. Argh! So close!"

"You both are much stronger now. Empathy builds its own strength."

"You have to tell me, is she OK?"

"Yes, tired but safe. She can tell you all about it."

"I don't think I can wait until I see her. I'm going crazy here."

"I will connect the two of you."

An instant later, Raefer fully felt another mind. He had never experienced more than his one-to-ones with Diver. It took him a second to tease out the two streams. Now he could sense Milima, and his head was filled with warm light. He had a million questions, and he sensed that she did too. He tried to speak, but he felt her thoughts flooding into his mind and great streams of ideas flowing out of him toward her. Seconds, minutes, many minutes passed. He had no idea. And then he felt his mind settle.

He could feel something from Lina, as if she had just remembered who he really was. And he felt it too—not just wisps of memories. It was as if she was right in front of him, and he had always known her, and they had always been connected in this way that felt so full, reaching so far into the many corners of his mind. And then, out of this thick fog of emotions, words began to emerge, and then phrases, and bits of sentences. It was as if she was in the next room, talking on her Voice and he could make out bits and pieces of it.

"What am I hearing?" he thought, hoping Diver could hear him.

"Just what you think," she said. "You are feeling Milima's emotions, but now you are also beginning to sense her thoughts."

"You said I was an empath, but now you're saying I can read minds?"

Raefer could sense a smile from Diver. "How do you think humans first began to speak?"

"You mean, like this?"

"No, not exactly. But your people were empaths before you had language. Your animal ancestors could communicate danger, food, sex, pain, and sometimes even joy, but just in simple howls and grunts. Your species was the first to make that empathy concrete and shared among your whole group. You could speak to each other because you understood, deep down, the emotions behind the words that gave them meaning."

"But I've never felt this before," he said, still uncertain of what was going on.

"We've never wanted to do this so badly," Lina said, her thoughts now as clear as speech. "Your emails were wonderful. But now that I feel who you are so fully, I couldn't stop this even if I tried. This is wonderful!"

"Yes! You are Lina again?" Raefer asked. He could sense that she wanted to tell him this, that something important had happened.

"Yes!" she said. "I have met people and seen things that brought me so much closer to the life that Lina led. I know Lina was just her way of fitting in in America, but I wanted to break with my tradition, to start on a new path. Anyway, it's a cool name."

His mind swirled as she let him see the memories of her last three weeks. She hadn't just changed her name, she'd found a way for Milima to truly become Lina. And as Lina, she was in the middle of something new, something subversive. The way she told it, the people around her were already victims of the world the two of them thought they had escaped, and her new friends were already doing things that might actually change the way this world worked.

Her ideas, her enthusiasm—it all tugged at the Raefe in the back of his mind, pulling him closer to the surface.

"This is so exciting," he said. "Everything you're doing. And you know what's weird? Little things are popping up for me, too. Can you remember Alton Winchester on Truro Island, just before…"

"Yes, I do! The one who spoke up to Ken Robertson. I remember now, I knew him before you somehow."

"Yeah, that feels right, although I can't totally remember why. Well, I work with someone who knows the man who Alton follows, Goodstuff Benjamin."

"Yes, the Nigerian. Everyone here knows about him and his New Voodo Army."

"Right, they're in Africa, where you are. So maybe you can contact them? They sound like people Citizens of Nowhere would want to know."

"You're right, they're fighting for something not so different. And they have very interesting ideas about how to work with the land."

"I want to come to visit you, but I don't know when that will be. Maybe we can both talk to Winchester's people then. I know there must be more people than them, too, that can be part of this. But whatever you do, I'm excited about it. I don't know what my part can be, but I want it to be something. Maybe I'll be everyone's empathic supergeek."

He could feel her laughter. He let her feel his smile. Minutes or hours went by, he wasn't sure, until they reluctantly agreed that they would have to disengage for the time being.

THE FRUIT OF THE TREE

Traveler's Perch
February 24, 2049

Diver was nervous and happy at the thought of another quiet dinner with Far Flier. Eating dinner had been an occasional, novel way for her to amuse herself. Now it was becoming a serious way for them to deepen their relationship.

Her contact with Raefer and Lina had revealed immense progress for both of them, and more had followed in the weeks since they had entangled with her help. She hoped Far Flier would see this as a start to regaining their mission. Involving him in the good news would be a way to demonstrate that she had put her reservations about his behavior aside without him having to apologize or her having to admit she had been hasty in doubting his motives. If neither of them could claim the high ground, at least they could gaze toward it together as friends and colleagues.

She looked around her apartment and sent it an image of the space without the front wall, extending the floor out over the canyons below in a sort of patio. At the edges, she thought of a low curving wall with a spongey covering that the two of them could sit against and look at the sky. She realized she was thinking of the dinner in a romantic way and that she wasn't even surprised. Green had been right, of course. Diver and Far Flier had become a couple around the time she had taken the Earth assignment. But they had been casual about it. She had slowly explored him against the backdrop of her excitement about leading the Earth mission. And he had been willing to keep things that way.

Since the incident with Lina, their time together had been strictly work-related. But she realized that she missed even their loose arrangement. She wondered if he did; it wasn't the kind of question you answered by probing the other's thoughts. Just then, she sensed Far Flier approaching. He wanted to know if her balcony was still the way she had left it the last time he was there. She let him see the changes she had made, and he seemed pleased.

Half a minute later, she could see why. He had chosen to fly to her. He swooped down and landed gracefully on the deck, his purple, blue and green colors glistening through the tight mesh of his flight suit.

"Ah, what a glorious day!" he exclaimed. "I've been to the Rannikan Hills. This week, the sky is full and you can see the amala herds gathering for their annual mating."

"It's been forever since I saw that," she said. "Were the seven-fruit trees blooming also?"

He smiled. "See for yourself."

He pulled a sack from a pouch in the suit. There were two of each of the seven fruits. "I hoped you haven't made dinner yet."

"No," she said. "And this will be much better than what I had been thinking of. I didn't know you were a forager."

"Now and then. Gliding over the Hills, scanning for food, it has a way of clearing the mind."

She was delighted. Restaurants sometimes served the seven courses of fruit, but to have them fresh-picked during a full sky, the only time these trees produced all seven types of fruit, was a rare treat. She began to let him sense her gratitude, but realized a better way. She cooed the call that ancient females had used to signal their approval of mating displays.

Far Flier laughed. "I haven't heard that in hundreds of years."

"I won't ask what the last occasion was," she said. "We should eat them in the ritual order that our ancestors did to thank Red Nest and Water Eye for shining more of Prime's light, causing the trees to bloom and flower. And I've just told the kitchen to make some asterflower wine to go with them."

"Excellent!"

"If I remember, we start with the makkala, right?" She peeled the two small bright orange fruits, giving one to Far Flier and touching her lips to the other. "Ah, the tart one that prepares us to taste the others," she said, her eyes sparkling with delight. "You are one of the few people who understand my love for unenhanced experiences."

"Very few people have had them, I'm afraid," he responded. "Most of us see them as foolishly primitive. You know, I don't think I've ever asked you why you cherish these experiences so much."

"My parents brought me up that way," she said. "They were biologists who had spent their youth studying some of the more intelligent animals on our planet, like the harangi and the nut birds. They found it helpful to experience those physical environments unaided, to get more of a sense of how the animals experienced them."

"Is that how they came to be killed?"

"Yes, they had actually followed a harangi troop that liked to bathe in a warm stream that exited a lava tube. They became so engrossed that they detached from the waveform and didn't hear the warnings of the impending eruption."

"How sad. How old were you?"

"Oh, I was already 204 by then. My siblings thought we should be mad at them for being so absentminded. After all, so few people die like that from avoidable accidents. But for me, their death made it clear that the universe doesn't care about us, and so we have to care for ourselves. That's how they lived. They were in their 800s, but still intensely involved with the things that interested them and each other. I miss them, but I have so many fond memories of them, and so many of their ideas still rattle around in my head, including the notion that not honoring some of what allowed us to survive for millions of years is foolish. We only wanted to leave behind war and disease, not the joys of life."

"Well, you are a rarity. I hadn't thought that much about how our enhancements have changed us. But your story makes me realize that we often credit our enhancements over our entanglements. Yet it was entanglement which changed our world, long before most of our enhancements."

"Just what I've been hoping the humans will understand," she thought. "Connection would ultimately improve their society more than technology. Plus, they had too little concern about how technology would affect human connection, even though they fancied themselves in a golden age of connection. They valued connectivity, mistaking the wires between for the thoughts and feelings at either end."

"That is a most interesting thought," Diver said. "Your parents would be proud."

He handed her the second fruit, the minita. She savored its deep sugary blue flesh while she told him about Lina's discovery of the Citizens of Nowhere.

"This band of refugees has already left behind the worst practices of their civilization without any help from us. They are all very close to being able to entangle. Lina's presence alone may help them cross that line. Oh, this is the sweetest minita I've ever had!"

"Yes, this was the perfect day to pick this one. You know you can never get all seven at their best on the same day?"

"I didn't know that," she said. "But I always like that it's never quite the same each time you eat the full course."

"By the way, I think you may be right about Lina," Far Flier said. "Strong entanglers can set off a cascade of further entanglement."

"Hmm. So maybe if Raefer was with her, they'd have a more profound effect on those around them?"

"Yes, most likely. And vice versa—Raefer's abilities still need further development. Being together in a sympathetic environment raises the odds that they can ultimately initiate a durable waveform that other people can tune into. More and more will add to it, and if humans repeat the pattern of other species, within a few centuries humans will have left behind the era when they could not really understand each other. Once they have come to a deeper understanding of each other, they will be in a position to overcome their differences. But that is still a long way off. I want to hear what he is doing now, but shall we have the alottu first?"

She ate the alottu slowly, making sure its sour, vinegary juices didn't sting her face. In ancient times, the alottu was the reminder of the darkest periods, the rare times when none of the suns shone directly for a few days. These days, it was more of a reminder that life was not always sweet. She quickly drank some asterflower wine to wipe away the taste.

"Wow, that was bitter. Raefer has been trying to do something technical that uses his empathic abilities. He exchanges his abilities to program computers for sustenance with a company which is involved with a research project that's trying to understand the relative role of competition and collaboration in human history."

"Well, all things considered, they're both in a much better place to have a significant influence," he said. "All the more reason for us to not make too much noise in the council about what is going on."

Diver bristled inwardly. Just when she thought she had something positive to counter the campaign to minimize the Earth project, he wanted to hide it.

"It's come to that?" she asked, letting him feel her annoyance.

"Yes, for the time being," he answered. "I'm still trying to figure out what Hankori's end game is. In the meanwhile, you should consider involving your watery assistant, Adno, more. With the spotlight on you, we should consider that she may have more freedom to operate than you."

"I'll have to give that some thought, you're right. She's pretty green but learns quickly. Very quickly, as I think about it. When she was assigned to me, Tanoch was somewhat dismissive of her. Have you ever entangled much with her?"

"Not one-on-one, I've had no call to," Far Flier said. "Here, have a glantoch."

She nibbled at the long thin fruit. It's bland starchy flavor was meant to neutralize the alottu.

"It's a different experience than with most of the other Guardian species," she said. "I can't put my finger on it exactly. Her mind is always actively checking her location and the location of the rest of her school. She's never really alone. I hope she can pay attention to Raefer and not be distracted by all of that."

"Water Eye is an interesting place," Far Flier said. "It's still the only planet we know where life evolved for a very long time, and developed considerable complexity, as large colonial organisms."

He reminded her that eons ago, the seas had been full of huge mats that combined plantlike and animal-like life in a giant, colonial organism. Scientists were convinced the mats had uniquely evolved a collective intelligence. They were basically self-feeding brains, thousands of square meters in size, floating in the ocean. Perhaps they had even learned to communicate with other nearby mats.

She saw it now. "So on Water Eye intelligent creatures evolved from very large to smaller groups?"

"Precisely," he beamed. "So even now, Adno's people have a different sense of the individual and the group, the whole and its parts, than all the other Guardian species. To be honest, it's not clear any of us understand how they see things at the deepest level. Entanglement between mature individuals is not the same as a species having been completely entangled for its entire history, even back to its evolutionary ancestors."

Just like Far Flier, she thought, ranging off into the galaxy with all sorts of ideas. He really did need her, she could see now, to ground him. "For the time being, I'll bring her more into the loop but monitor her closely."

"That makes sense," Far Flier said. "Of course, we don't want to bring her too much into the loop. Some things we should still keep between us."

She handed him a small brown cluster of rila berries and ate each of hers slowly. They had a pleasant taste, but their real secret was the energy she would feel in about half an hour.

"I guess I can accept that we cannot be totally open," Diver said. "But it's a new feeling for me. Our whole lives are nearly transparent— our first instinct is to allow access to our very thoughts and feelings. Still, I want to tell you that I did something with Raefer and Lina like what you did with her."

"What do you mean?" he asked, a little alarmed.

"Raefer was sent a message that Lina had been kidnapped. He desperately wanted to contact her, but he has never initiated full entanglement with another human, let alone one on the other side of the planet. And she has even less experience. So I connected them—I advanced their development. Not so different from what you did on Truro Island."

"Well, I wouldn't beat yourself up about it," he said. "It was only a matter of a little time before they figured that out.

"Yes, just what I thought," she said. "But I feel like I have lost something here, some sense of order and rightness by violating our code. Even if no one finds out, I will know and be disappointed in myself."

"The truth is, we have lost exactly that sense of rightness. If it makes you feel better, I feel the same."

"Now that we have forgiven each other for breaking the rules we both want to believe in," she said, "I am still uneasy over the question of how are we different, let alone better, than Hankori?"

"We are not better," he said, rising to her challenge with animation and maybe a little impatience. She could tell this was a topic he had discussed many times in his long life. "The entire basis of our civilization and of the Guardians is just that. There is no 'better' among living creatures. There is, however, different. And that can only be measured in outcomes. What world do our actions make?"

"But that is why we have rules, isn't it? Because we have experienced terrible outcomes brought on by certain actions, and so we say 'never do that again.'"

"Yes, we do. We say that to children. And when they grow up, they discover that sometimes following the rule also leads to terrible outcomes. And then, they must weigh the consequences."

"But I don't know the consequences," she said. "That's really what's troubling me. About both of us."

"Yes, with all of our technology, our accrued wisdom, our success at survival, life still humbles us after all. We have to guess at things and do the best we can. There is no scientific reason to believe we will ever know the future before it happens."

"Still, the whole business upset me. The humans have a saying," she said. "'Rules are made to be broken.' Perhaps that is what they mean by it."

"Your humans are not the barbarians Hankori would like the council to believe," he said. "His experiences with them were as much about his own failings as theirs."

"I wondered that, too," she said. "Green told me that Hankori's contacts turned out to be deeply flawed. How could he mistake sociopaths for empaths?"

"Because secretly he believes that our abilities and knowledge have transformed us into demigods. And he mistook the sense of apartness that sociopaths have for a sense of aboveness. Hankori is a complex and layered individual, as each of us is: His mind rests on the brain he was born with, but he is also enhanced, and he participates in communal thought structures—what we call the waveform."

"Yet you are describing a person who could be considered insane by some definitions."

She let him sense her shock and horror, her confusion that one of the leaders of their society and of the Guardians was potentially insane. After 10,000 years, how could this happen? And what should they do about it?

"We are only atoms and ideas. This is the lesson of history and of the Guardians," he said. She could feel a combination of animation and frustration from him that he had to say this, as if it were self-evident. "We are imperfect organic machines, given to paradox and mistake. And the universe? It may obey the laws of physics, but those very laws yield all the chaos and violence of a supernova, not just the beauty of the sunset we are looking at now."

Diver pondered that. She leaned back against the spongey wall, wishing she could bottle the beauty of the many-colored light that shone down on them and use it to clean away some of the ugliness of life. She knew Far Flier was watching her, feeling her unease. Well, maybe ease was overrated. They had crossed some lines, and they might do it again. Best to remember that before they fell into erasing the lines. But best not be paralyzed by the lack of perfect options, either.

"Are you ready for the saforo?" he asked

She hesitated a beat and then smiled at him. "You know, I am. I've confessed my sins, you've absolved both of us and revealed that we're being led by a madman. Honestly, let's just enjoy each other for a little while. We can tend to the universe later."

They took a minute to chew on the green saforo pod. The flesh was tasteless, ironic, since it would heighten their enjoyment of each other's flesh in a little while. She took heart from Far Flier's serenity, feeling that they had crossed a small chasm and were now looking at the same view. His mind was still, content to sit here with her and share ideas and food and, later, each other's bodies.

"The light is comforting, isn't it?" he said. "Now you see the depth of my dilemma. Think of how shocked you are. You believe me, but will the other Guardians? And our own society? Ultimately, I believe they will, and we will be able to undo the damage," he said, his usual determination infused by a passion she had not heard from him before. "But the coming years will test us. We must be skillful, on the one hand, and yet not let the conflict make us into what Hankori has become."

"Have you found other allies?" she wondered to him. "We should eat the tea melon before it's too late."

"Yes, I have other allies but not as strong as you." He sliced the big teal colored melons into thin slices and put a plate with them between them. Almost as soon as the melon touched her tongue, she began to feel the heightened awareness that it brought.

She cleared her mind and looked at him. As she felt herself sink deeper into his emotions, she realized that he was acknowledging, as best he could, that he needed her, that he depended on her youth and her freshness, that these battles he had been waging in secret by himself had taken a toll on him.

"I am honored that you want to fly into a strong wind with me at your wing." she said. "Just as you depend on me to have the spirit and energy to carry on, I depend on you to have the insight and experience to know the way. But I will fly these currents with you, if that's what you are asking."

And, she thought, I see that he meant that but more, too. Not just to fly, but to nest. This was after all, his plan, bringing the seven fruits. Wise old man! She responded, humming to encourage him. He stepped forward and his arms enveloped her, as the wings of his ancestors would have during courtship. She put her head against his chest and hummed the mating song, feeling the vibrations travelling through her bones and resonating through her feathers. She felt her own arousal, deepened by the saforo, fueled by the rila.

He sang the male song and their melodies crossed and uncrossed, harmonized and countered. She didn't need the waveform to sense his ardor, nor he to know hers.

She told the room to close the outside wall. Her bed, a modern abstraction of an ancient nest, extended from the inner wall and the lights brightened, as if the sun were shining on them. She shrugged off her clothes, letting all of her colors shine in the brightness, watching as he did the same.

FRIENDS IN HIGH PLACES

Traveler's Perch
February 25, 2049

Hankori's antipathy to the Earth project had not blinded him to the importance of secretly keeping tabs on it. That wasn't that hard to do, once he had discovered certain things about Tanoch that the head of the Ambassadors was not proud of. They had an arrangement and Hankori was careful not to make compliance a difficult choice for Tanoch, at least not until it really mattered.

This time, it was Tanoch who came to him. He thought Hankori would want to know that Raefe and Lina, or whatever they were calling themselves at the moment, were making quite rapid progress in their abilities. Perhaps Hankori might want to reconsider? After all, these Earthers seemed more promising now than just a year ago. Maybe they were closer to a big jump forward than the Guardians had thought? Every species was different, each had its own surprises. He had thanked Tanoch and assured him that he would consider the matter.

What he really thought was that it might be time for him to get more directly involved. He had a few tricks no one knew about. During his stint as Ambassador to Earth, he found a few young empaths and cultivated them very gently and slowly. One particularly promising one had died but left a son who inherited his father's proclivities. And Hankori had watched with amusement as the son grew up to become Billy Warren, one of the most powerful of North America's retrograde oligarchs.

Billy's power rested on coal, chemical manufacturing and keeping a tight grip on the eastern mountain regions where his wealth lay. He was a cunning man who believed in nothing but himself. Yet he was skilled at getting people to see him as the defender of their way of life—traditional jobs, traditional values, familiar faces. Mines, churches, and the whole "generations of our family" claptrap had made Billy's family rich for five generations. In turn, that made it clear to Hankori what drove Billy and how to steer him.

Someday, he would reveal himself more clearly to Billy, but for now he only approached him while he slept. In Billy's dreams, he was Hank, a friend who sometimes helped him, sometimes needed Billy's help. Hank showed up infrequently enough that Billy had only the slightest conscious awareness of him, so slight that it never made him wonder why he kept meeting this person in his dreams or really remembering that he did. Now Hankori needed to find out more about what was happening on Earth, and Billy would do that for him.

His young friend Green had proved useful, too, showing him how to navigate from old timelines to new timelines. Of course, he'd had to make up a story about why—Green could be just as uneasy about Hankori breaking the rules as he was about Far Flier. Hankori found the signature of the Billy in Raefe's new timeline through the wormhole interface. He scanned Billy's mind and it was just as he had expected: hardly different from the Billy he knew. The powerful tended to conserve their characteristics across many more timelines than the average person, insulated from many of the forces that buffeted ordinary people's lives.

He touched the sleeping mind. Billy was dreaming something involving an airplane flight. He was sitting in a large jet, but no one else was in the cabin. Hankori slipped into the dream and sat down next to him.

"Hank, what are you doing here?" Billy said, somewhat startled. "Did you get on in Cleveland?"

"Yeah, I was in the back. You seemed busy, so I didn't want to disturb you. But, you know, long plane ride, I thought it would be a good time to catch up."

"Yeah, it's been a while. What's on your mind?"

"I'm thinking of investing some money in a software company a buddy of yours owns, MiniWorlds. Ken Robertson's bunch. I don't care that much about the business, more the talent. I hear they have a hotshot staff there and some interesting projects, but they're pretty buttoned up about what their real business is. Wondering if you could find out anything for me on the down-low. Don't want to get Robertson all riled up. But if you could find a way to take his temperature on the operation, that would be great. I'd make it worth your while if something comes of it."

Of course, Billy could. He'd get back to him soon. He let Billy prattle on in the dream about some new vehicle he was buying that he was very excited about. Hank feigned enthusiasm and slowly let Billy turn his dream away from him. Hank would make another visit in a week or so and collect the information Billy gathered in his waking life.

***

Ken Robertson was surprised when his Voice announced that Billy Warren wanted to talk. Warren was on his approved connections list but they weren't in touch much. He wondered what the old dinosaur wanted.

"Billy, nice to hear from you," he said. "What's up?"

"I'm hoping you can help me out, Ken," Billy said. "My damn fool nephew Heath's taken it into his head that he wants be the Hillbilly Software King. Says folks down here are tired of playing vids that take place everywhere but home. Got it in his head that some company you own can help him. MiniWorlds, is that yours?"

"Sure is, Billy," he laughed. He could just imagine explaining to the MiniWorld's team that they were going to have to add farm animals and coal country dialect to their games.

"Well, what do they really do, Ken? I mean, can they create games that Heath can sell?"

"Sure. But easier, they can deconstruct popular game types we already know are successful and modify the parts to seem like a brand-new game."

"That sounds like something up his alley. He's not exactly a marketing genius. Or any other kind of genius. But I want to make sure he understands what you all do. So walk me through it."

Robertson explained how code factories worked and how that played out for games, how games were just a kind of sim.

"Thanks, Ken, that all makes sense. And you have confidence that your team can do something like this? I'm guessing this is probably not their usual cup of tea."

No, usually our clients set their games in the present or future, Ken thought, not in your imaginary pastoral past. He told Billy he'd send him a recent evaluation of the staff's capabilities. Ordinarily, he'd never share that, but it was good to keep Billy on your side. As dinosaurs went, he was something of a T. Rex. If he thought you weren't a friend, you were an enemy. And he was quick to use his considerable influence in Washington and wherever else to remind you that being an enemy of Billy Warren was a special kind of hell. The fact that Ken could do the same, times two, didn't make it any smarter to waste his time and energy on petty squabbles.

"Appreciate the chance to do business with you, Billy. You should get all that stuff today. If you go forward, I'll make the introductions for Heath with the brass at MiniWorlds and make sure they treat him fairly."

"Always a pleasure, Ken. And if you're ever in West Virginia, you know where to find me."

Let's hope it never comes to that, Ken thought, ending the call.

AMBUSH

Traveler's Perch
March 18, 2049

Hankori felt the breeze coming up from the canyons, bringing cool moisture to the plaza. Not many people were around. He had read that this plaza was once part of the last great city on Traveler's Perch. When the inhabitants of the world had become entangled 10,000 years ago, they found the psychic noise of millions of minds packed together intolerable and unnecessary. With their fierce internecine conflicts on the wane, the power of concentrated cities gave way to the sustainability of distributed ones. They had spread out, like bright paint on a wet canvas, the drops melding and overlapping to form loose neighborhoods.

Pity, he thought. *This moment deserves some drama.* What it must have felt like for Cresilion, the last emperor of Traveler's Perch, to stand atop the ledges, his amplified voice addressing a million subjects below. Their sweat, their breath, their beating wings all welling up toward him. And his power reaching down, touching them all. But Cresilion had led the retreat, hadn't he, from the high civilization of Traveler's Perch into the Guardian ethos. Well, what choice did he have? The endless wars, the desolation of the water and food—Cresilion had done what had to be done. Yet, something had been lost.

And now maybe something else would be gained, but all in due time. He sensed Far Flier's approach even before his network bots informed him that the train carrying the Guardian Council chief was pulling into the nearby station. A minute later, Far Flier was across the plaza, giving a curt wave, his mind closed to Hankori. *Well, he's no fool, is he,* Hankori thought. *I'd do the same.*

Hankori offered him a seat and some alefka to drink.

"Thanks," Far Flier said to the offer. "Nice to have a little boost in the late afternoon."

"Agreed," Hankori said. "We're not middle-aged anymore." He

half-expected Far Flier to correct him, but that would mean acknowledging that Hankori was, in fact, quite middle-aged while Far Flier was past the halfway point of his life. But he would make that point later, in a more decisive manner. He let Far Flier savor the bittersweet taste of the boiled berries, their mild stimulant properties adding to what his enhancements provided, while they exchanged pleasantries. Still, he could not read the old guy's mood.

"What's on your mind, Hankori," he asked. "I can't remember the last time we met like this."

"I thought a frank exchange of views was in order," Hankori said. "There's a lot going on in the Guardian Council these days, and as the two most senior members, I thought we should chat on our own."

"You're worried I'll get in the way of your new lightspeed ship project?"

"Oh, no," Hankori said. "That's well underway. It hasn't escaped my attention that you're quite interested in it, though. You think I've got something up my sleeve, don't you?"

"No, I know you have something up your sleeve," Far Flier said, smiling as if he were complimenting him. "And I know it's something outside of our mission."

"You see, this was such a good idea. Because it's our mission that I wanted to talk with you about," Hankori said, returning the smile. "I've always thought of you as someone who sees our mission as that of a watcher and a waiter. And yet I see now that I'm wrong. You, like me, are much more of an activist."

"You think so?"

"Oh, yes," he said, enjoying himself immensely. "I see now how wrong I've been. It hit me like a hot wind rising from a deep canyon at our last council meeting. Everyone was so interested in Diver and Raefe, but what caught my attention was the girl."

He paused, but Far Flier didn't respond. He would let Far Flier see deeper into his thoughts, but only as he spoke. He wanted to savor the moment.

"You see," he continued, "I almost missed it, but then it struck me: Could you relocate her to a new timeline? Raefe, sure, Diver had established a connection with him. I may think he's a dead end on a dead-end planet, but he is a natural entangler. She—is Lina her name?—on the other hand, had shown no such talents before. No entanglement, no shift."

He felt Far Flier struggling to keep up a veil of detached examination, as if he were trying to formulate a careful response to a lesser creature, a story to deflect attention. So used to being persuasive, this Far Flier, he had forgotten that persuasion usually only worked on the willing. Far Flier would think that Hankori cared about whether the girl had been harmed in the process or whether the consequences would be an unforeseen problem. His mistake.

"It's true," Far Flier said. "But this was an unusual circumstance. She was with Raefe, with whom she has a very deep and intuitive tie. And they were under a lot of stress. Really, about to die. It doesn't get any more stressful than that. And we've seen stress trigger the conversion to being an entangler before. Isn't that the story of Na'wra? Granted we don't see it often, but not never."

Ah, appealing to our oldest myths. He really doesn't know, Hankori thought. This is just delicious.

"We both know that wasn't what happened. I'm going to save you the embarrassment of continuing this lie." He let Far Flier see the data that Green had relayed to him of Lina's conversion. The data stream showed clearly that Far Flier had orchestrated the whole thing. He had instigated the entanglement with her by inducing a waveform in her consciousness, without her consent, and if you really wanted to admit it, without her participation. Forget Guardians, every child of every Guardian species learned not to do that very early in life. It was dangerous and immoral in all of their cultures—you never knew what the consequences would be. Their worlds had few absolute prohibitions, but this was one of them.

"You see, Far Flier, I have important and useful friends, too. Even if I don't spend my evenings with them."

Far Flier still had not betrayed any emotion. Ever the leader, Hankori thought, weighing your next move even when you don't have one.

"I can see why you would say that," Far Flier said slowly. "But I prefer my version. Anyway, you've never been much a stickler for the rules before. I seem to remember certain leaders of one Earth country—North Korea was it?—who became quite bizarre around the time you were Ambassador to Earth. I've always wondered about that, had it in the back of my mind to look into it. Hopefully, your important and useful friends haven't cleansed the record."

"My, my," Hankori said. "I seem to have struck a nerve."

"No, I wouldn't say that. I just find your penchant for theater tiresome. What is it you want?"

"I want the Guardians to benefit Traveler's Perch and all the other members' worlds, for that matter. I want the Guardians to stop wasting time and resources on doomed civilizations such as Earth."

"Ah, so you can now see both the past and the future, is that it?"

"Sarcasm is my vice, Far Flier. It fits you poorly. And yes, I can see a bit of the future. I can see that your term as leader of the Guardian Council is coming to an end."

"You expect me to step down?"

"I do. While it would be satisfying to publicly humiliate you, I have no reason to do so unless you provide one. You can make up whatever story you want. You can take some time to do it. But within the year, you'll step down. And you won't involve yourself in the discussion of your successor."

"I never thought you had the patience to lead the Council."

"And now I don't have the patience not to."

Far Flier stood up, his face still blank. "The future, you will find out, is an uncooperative beast."

It's done, Hankori thought. He's done. Cresilion would have approved.

***

Far Flier had had his suspicions that the meeting would end this way. He wanted to take the long view. Something had come undone deep inside the Guardians, and little fixes couldn't change the fact that they were losing their way in the cosmos. It would take perseverance and courage to reverse that. He would need Diver, Adno, and others to do it, but he still had many centuries to live. Now he knew what they would be filled with.

FAMILY PLANNING

Diver gazed out over endless sea, the wind whipping her feathered crest. She felt the primordial fear of a distance that could not be crossed without landing, yet had nowhere to land. Or maybe that was just her mood since the Council meeting and Hankori's meeting with Far Flier.

"You're wrong, you know," Far Flier said, reading her thoughts. "Once our ancestors could cross that ocean with no tech at all. Now, we wouldn't get far at all with these engineered flight suits."

"Funny how the ocean is now harder for us to cross than space itself," Diver said. "Now that we all live on this continent, we have little reason to go to the other continents. And there are machines to take us there when we do. Still, it's been years since I soared over open water. Do you want to glide for a while?"

"I have a better idea. Well, at least a different one. Can you swim?"

"Can you?"

"Yes, centuries ago I visited Water Eye for some Guardian business. They have small floating platforms for visitors, but after a while I felt stupid asking them to come to the edge of the platform every time we wanted to meet. Our flight suits have a fail-safe mode for water, did you know that?"

"No."

"Well, if you go too deep they warn you. If they detect that you're hurt or unconscious, they slowly move you to the surface. This is in case you fall into the water flying through the canyons. But it will work in the ocean, too. So I decided I would see how our ancestors might have felt, going underwater to look for schools of fish."

"That must have made Adno's people feel good," she said, remembering that Adno's people had little taste for the ironic.

"Indeed. Fortunately, we were strongly entangled and they understood I meant them no harm. They may not be the most subtle species among the Guardians, but they don't confuse us with the flying fish of their world that prey on them. Anyway, after our long flight here, I think you'll love the wonderful cooling feel of the water."

They dove off of the edge of the cliff, circling down against thermals rising from the water. They were only 20 meters from the water now. The wind whipping the water would drown out any conversation, but Far Flier's thoughts reached her just fine.

"Watch what I do and follow me," he thought. And he headed straight down into the water, a plume shooting up almost to her as the water closed around her feet.

She tucked her wings in and stretched her feet to the sky. The water came fast and pushed her face back into her head, just for a second, and then she was wet and cool and weightless in a world of deep bluish green. She sensed Far Flier off to her right and watched how he used his limbs to navigate in the water. She turned to follow him down a few meters. Strange spongey rock towers rose from the bottom, and all manner of small marine creatures swam around and through the holes in the towers. Far Flier took them closer. The water had currents like the air, only they were thick and viscous to move through. Everything slowed down. The towers were alive, she could feel their energy. Many schools of fish circled the towers, occasionally passing through each other as if some quantum repulsion kept them from touching. Now and then, the light from above lit up the fish. She was enchanted.

"Come," Far Flier's thoughts said. "Our enhancements will only allow us to stay under for a short time."

He kicked upward toward the surface, his wings clearing the water and immediately grabbing the air for a lift as his enhanced legs thrust free of the water. She followed his example and amazingly, was airborne again. She let the rising currents take her back to the cliff.

"Wow, why have I waited 400 years to do that?" she said. "That was amazing. A whole other world under our beaks."

"Well, I'm glad you suggested this little picnic. Have some rainbow fish." He passed her a container with several of the small fish, seasoned with herbs. "I had wanted to talk to you about one thing, and then the meeting with Hankori happened, and now I'm very conflicted."

"Maybe I can help sort it out. What was it you originally wanted to talk about?"

"It may seem odd, after I tell you the second. But anyway, do you know how long I have been a Guardian?"

"Since before I became an Ambassador, but no, I don't know how long."

"It's been more than 11 centuries."

Ah, now she understood. Soon he would undergo their species' periodic transformation from one sex to the other. Relationships didn't always survive these changes.

"And you are not sure about us afterwards?" she asked.

"Our hearts will go whichever way they want. Either way, we will be friends. After our recent conflict, I realized how rare it is to find someone who both loves you and challenges you, and how much I cherish that. And you."

"And I, as well. In both directions—love and challenge. I think you'll be a wonderful girlfriend for me, and not my first. So, you can rest easy on that score."

"Good to know. The point is, it has been a long time since I fathered a child. It would mean a great deal to me if you would join with me for that, before I change. It will be some time into the future before I can mother my own child, and I don't want to wait that long to be a parent again. I'm feeling the need to leave more behind than just memories."

In only her fourth century, she had never thought much about birthing a child. Far Flier was her first lover who had even passed into parent status.

"Wow. My first reaction is, frankly, awe. None of my childhood friends have reproduced."

"And you may not want to when I tell you the rest. Hankori has won, for now. I will have to find a way to step down and make it look like I'm just stepping aside for a time. I will remain a Guardian, but a quiet one, while I watch and wait. Hankori, he is another story. I am beginning to believe he is a rare bird."

"How so?"

"Of course, you can't repeat this for now. But I am more convinced that your instinct is right, that he is insane, or, at the least, mentally unbalanced."

"How can that be?"

She had been raised to believe that mental illness had been eliminated thousands of years ago, that their entanglements and enhancements and all of their technology made it impossible for their minds to go so far out of balance as Hankori's seemed to be.

"I don't know. But the facts are there and disturbing: his bizarre record on Earth, where most of his prized contacts turned out to be psychopaths, the secrecy of his current project, his desire to get me out of the way. More and more, I've come to believe one hypothesis explains them all."

"So you've discovered the true nature of his current project?"

"Not completely. But at least one piece of it I know: He wants to abstract consciousness from the body."

"Don't we do that now, when we travel through the wormhole interface?"

"No, not at all. You project thoughts and feelings from your consciousness, but it stays firmly rooted in your body. Imagine if your mind was literally elsewhere."

"What would be the point?"

"I don't know. But it seems insane, doesn't it? To split the mind and body that way?"

"Yes, I agree. And deeply troubling. How can you give the Guardian leadership over to him if that's true? What will you do?"

And what about Earth? How can we just abandon billions of people who are on the verge of either making the leap forward or annihilating themselves? What is the point of empathy if we only turn it on ourselves?

"Yes, indeed," Far Flier responded, sensing her thoughts. "I've thought long and hard about this. There's so much at stake, and we so want to believe that our way is the right way. But we're not used to dishonest conflict, to sneak attacks. And that's what Hankori is orchestrating, I'm sure. And at some point, the Guardians who still hold to our original mission must launch a sneak counterattack, which means feigning surrender in order to eventually defeat him and his allies, whoever they are."

Here we are again, she thought. *Breaking the rules to honor the rules. And yet, I have no alternative.*

"You are so brave, Far Flier. In 10,000 years, no one has had to do this."

"Sadly, in the nearly billion years since Na'wra's Explorers discovered other intelligent life and founded the Guardians, situations like this have occurred from time to time, even if not on our world. Part of my initiation as head of the council was to read the ancient archives and to learn how prior leaders met these sorts of challenges. So, what you call bravery is just what I have prepared for quietly for centuries."

"Call it what you like, it will require courage."

"And, I fear, companionship. When I imagine what lies ahead, you are always in the picture. We would have to lead a dual life for decades, perhaps centuries. The life people will see is that of two minor Guardian officials, not very important people, going about their work, perhaps raising a child. Only a few will know that we are part of a shadow Guardian organization that monitors and ultimately resists whatever Hankori is planning."

And what if he discovers us? What if we become true outcasts? Would we become exiled on some asteroid? Killed? What were they risking, and how likely were they to succeed? Her mind had never been so roiled.

"I don't think I should answer this now. This is an occasion to enter alakh, to go deep inside and know my mind as fully as I can. When I emerge from it, you will know my decision."

"That is all that I can ask now, that you know your mind, be true to it, and share it with me."

ANOTHER ACTOR FOR THE CAST

Traveler's Perch
May 21, 2049

Hankori might be in his ninth century, but that hadn't made him any more patient than when he was a schoolchild. This Raefe human was a persistent annoyance. Hankori would never admit it to anyone, but Tanoch had a point. The human was progressing rapidly. On top of that, the primitive had blundered into a technology project that might accelerate his development. Hankori needed to know more about that, but he'd have to wait for Warren's report.

He hated being dependent on Warren. He was, after all, everything wrong with the humans in one package. Still, Hankori was more entangled with Billy than any other Earther. Time to change that. Why should he depend solely on Warren?

He found Tanoch in the local Guardian waveform.

"I've been thinking about what you said about Raefe," Hankori thought to him, with the proper trappings of sincere reflection. "Perhaps these humans deserve a second look."

"I'm pleased to hear that," Tanoch said. "And will Diver be too."

"Well, that's another matter, we'll get to that soon. But for now, I'd love to browse through the database of entanglers that she tracks. Get a feel for more humans than just Raefe or Lina."

"I can do that for you, but it would be easier to ask Diver."

"No. I think it's time you took her off the Earth mission. Surely you picked up that Far Flier was not alone in his misconduct."

"Well, I did wonder," Tanoch thought back to him with a kind of tentative sheepishness. "But she's young, she's going to make mistakes."

"Well, let her make them on some other assignment. I want you to pass the mission on to her assistant, Adno."

He'll wonder how I know about Adno, Hankori thought. Let him wonder. Let him get used to the idea that his department is under scrutiny.

"I can do that," Tanoch said, "but she's got a long way to go. For one, she's not all that knowledgeable about land dwellers."

Exactly the point, Hankori thought. While she's struggling with that, she'll never notice what I'm up to, he thought. He'd let Tanoch off the hook for now, though. Let him think he's still in charge. When he needed him, he had all the leverage to get his way

"I think you make too much of that. I think you should give her a trial period. Let her go back to Water Eye, where she's comfortable, and monitor the humans from there. But now, let me dig into the database."

Tanoch connected him to the data and they disconnected. His enhancements begin to examine the data. There were only a couple of thousand individuals logged as having entanglement potential above the background quantum fields. With a little luck, there'd be some who he could use to interact with Raefe.

There! This was even better than he had expected. If anyone had been nearby, they would have been startled to see the big smile on his normally placid face. There was indeed someone near Raefe. Someone who had not yet awoken to his capabilities, but would only require a small push to do so. Someone who had an even more fortunate quality that no Guardians had yet discovered in humans. This human could entangle even though he had weak empathic potential.

Hankori had seen this during his Ambassador stint. A small but significant percentage of humans—maybe even 10 percent—struggled to understand their fellow humans' emotions and to connect with them that way. But they made up for it with overdeveloped intellects that essentially deduced the typical give and take of normal human society and mimicked it quite well. Often, these individuals were quite successful, unencumbered by guilt and other emotions. Humans called these people sociopaths but were generally ignorant of how widespread this combination of qualities was among their leaders and elites.

The Guardians had always assumed that entanglement led to empathy, and normally it did, and for that matter, vice versa. But entanglement was more fundamental, based on subatomic forces as old as the universe. Maybe the sociopaths didn't always sense exactly what their fellow humans were feeling or thinking, but once they learned to entangle, they could manage a reasonable facsimile of that.

And they were far less likely to question Hank about what he would ask them to do.

He waited a few days. If anyone was curious, he didn't want them seeing that directly after his request for a cursory review of the human entangler database, he had made direct contact with the individual he was focused on. Over the course of a few days, he briefly touched the minds of a few dozen humans, but only one was of real interest to him.

His first contact was just to lurk in the human's consciousness, feel how his mind worked. Just as the database had led him to hope, the human was deficient in several areas, but had clear untapped potential as a more advanced entangler. Hankori watched his daily rhythms for a few days. The human would be all his for the next few hours, but he would only need minutes.

He reached out into the sleeping mind. Joe Nguyen was dreaming about something mundane. Hankori roamed through his memories to find something familiar to associate with. Nguyen was walking down a street in a generic Earth city. Hankori made himself visible to him, walking along side of Nguyen.

"Hey, Joe, is that you?" he said.

"Who are you?" Nguyen replied. "Do I know you?"

"Sure," he said. "It's Hank, remember me? You lived on the floor above me at 586 Green Street. Well, not above me. Above my girlfriend, Elsa."

Hankori had found fond memories of a statuesque redhead of that name in Joe.

"Wow, Elsa," Joe said. "You guys still together?"

"No, she went back to Holland a few years ago. I stayed here—couldn't pass up a great job in computer security."

"I hear you," Joe said. "I'm still doing fancy grunt work. Algorithms and such."

"Good to see you," Hank said. And then he grew small jets on his feet and launched himself upwards, zooming away from Joe. The human wouldn't remember this dream, but the jet exit would leave him with a vague impression of a cool guy named Hank who was an old friend.

A few days later, Hankori contacted Warren again. Robertson had delivered the report, but Hankori needed a quiet way to get it. He planted the thought in Warren's sleeping mind that he should read the report when he woke up the next day. Hank sat quietly in Warren's head while he read the report, all of it being recorded by Hankori's enhancements on his side of the wormhole interface.

Joe hadn't been modest. He was really a grunt. But the project was for real, and Hankori could see that putting Raefe in a position where he was intensively thinking about the future and how people related to each other was an invitation to events Hankori would prefer to avoid. And he thought he knew how.

JUST A MIND IN THE CROWD

Cambridge
May 23, 2049

Raefer had become a bit of a loner since making contact with Lina. He had lost interest in the mating rituals of his peers. He threw himself into work. He wanted to be able to tell Lina that he, too, was doing things that had the potential to change the world. Or at least make it better.

Not that his coworkers shared that view of the Civilization Project. Apart from Elise, CivPro was just another gig for them. Raefer could feel their malaise and it was mildly painful. He was surrounded by smart people whose lives were a series of solved puzzles, except for the big one: What was the point of it all?

The one guy who seemed different was Joe Nguyen. He seemed unfazed by the endless series of abstract challenges and unaffected by the boredom around him. If everyone else appeared in 16 colors to Raefer, Joe was at least 32 shades. No, that wasn't it—he was actually kind of a drab person. But his drabness was in sharper focus than the others, like he had more pixels.

Now he found himself alone in the caf with Joe, who sat quietly a couple of tables away, head down studying his bowl of synth pro chili while unenthusiastically spooning bits of it into his mouth every so often. Despite Joe's outward diffidence, something radiated outward toward Raefer. Was Joe trying to connect with him?

"How's the chili?" he asked Joe.

"Manufactured," said Joe, grinning. "To pretty low standards."

"What's the point of standards if they're not low?" Raefer said. "No one needs standards to make good shit. Just make it good, right?"

"Shhh, people will think you're not an engineer if you ain't authentic with standards and protocols," Joe said. Raefer could feel that Joe enjoyed their ritual display of youthful cynicism.

"Maybe we should take all standards out of CivPro," Raefer said. "Let people just go hog wild. See how fucked up the world turns out."

"Right, not like the real world…"

"Listen to us, we sound like our parents."

They traded bios. Joe's family were third-gen Americans who'd built grandpa's floor-sanding hustle into a decent sized real estate development company. He'd had a pretty ordinary middle-class upbringing. His family had hoped he would be more interested in business, but his sisters had those genes. Joe was the kid who hacked the family vid account when he was six.

"Not just a vid zombie, though, eh?" Raefer asked. "You got some serious math skills."

"Guilty. It just comes to me, really. Math is so clean. People are so messy. If you just let go of all that stuff, math is, I don't know, almost obvious. Right?"

Raefer knew what he meant. Math didn't have motives. It didn't say things it didn't believe or know weren't true. Or worse, knew weren't true but still believed.

"I guess I see both sides," he said, wanting to see how Joe would react to what he said next. "Most people don't care about gravity or statistics or the stuff math explains. I think they get frustrated because it feels as far from being about people as anything can be. When they ask what it means they really mean, *What it does it mean to me, or to anyone?*"

"No, I get that," he said, though Raefer could feel he didn't, and that he was disappointed in Raefer for saying it. For a guy who seemed to be more of an empath than most, he didn't seem very empathic. Raefer filed that away, changing the subject as he sensed Joe was annoyed.

Raefer smiled. "So what do you like to do when you're not hacking vids?",

His idea of a good time was building and programming his own judo robot.

"Seriously, I know it sounds super wanky," he said. "But think about it: My robot has to anticipate its opponent's intent and moves, come up with a response in three-dimensional space, and execute it in milliseconds."

"Interesting," Raefer said. "How does one robot anticipate another robot?"

Had Joe found a way to give machines empathy?

"Vids. Every robot judo match is on the Net somewhere. You can use image analysis software to understand how a particular bot is programmed. Like any other software, the maker leaves his mark."

"Oh, for a minute I thought you were implying that your robot had some kind of empathic skills. That would put it a step ahead of the other bot."

"Feelings?" Joe said dismissively. "That's the whole point. Robots don't have feelings. They just do. Stimulus, response. Very clean."

And yet, I can feel your mind, Raefer thought, *and it wants to connect with mine. What do you do with that information,* he wondered. He hadn't come across anyone like this before.

"I'll take your word for it," he said.

"Don't," Joe said. "Come to Brighton Gardens next month. My bot's fighting. You'll be surprised how cool it is."

Why not? Raefer thought. I'm feeling other empaths more and more, and I want to learn more about what makes all of us tick.

"Sure, I'll be there."

A NEW SCHOOL OF THOUGHT

Water Eye
June 4, 2049

Adno needed to purge herself of doubt and despair after the recent events. First, hearing that Far Flier had stepped down from the Guardian Council chair had been a blow. He had violated some of their most important rules and that was shocking. More shocking was how eager some of the other Council members had been to see him gone. Then her mentor, Diver, was summarily reassigned by Tanoch, head of the Ambassadors. And now, Tanoch was giving her a trial as Ambassador to the humans and sending her across the solar system back to Water Eye even though she had years of training left to go. All very confusing. Yes, all of this called for renewal.

"Don't the waters make us feel strong today?" she broadcast to her school. "Come race with me along the fast, cool currents rising from below."

TheManyLargeLoudBlueSchool turned toward her, waiting for her lead. She focused them on feeling the mood of the water. Somewhere, a deep river passed over volcanic vents. Warming, it began to wind its way toward the surface, bringing with it trillions of tiny creatures that lived on material shed by the redfish that lived in the warmer waters above. Now those redfish would feast on the tiny creatures, growing and shedding old cells that would then feed more tiny creatures in the deep. Larger creatures would prey on the enlarged redfish schools, and Adno's school would feed on them.

She was at the front of the school, leading them. She could feel the pressure of the water being pushed by the rest behind her, pushing her forward. The currents led to the surface, where the suns now shone through the clouds. She broke the surface, her speed taking her in a graceful arc back down into the water. The school followed, again and again, until they tired, lolling about near the surface, rolling in the warmth of the suns. Adno could feel the deep contentment of the whole school, their place in this sea firm and known.

And what was her place now? The school had chosen her only a few years ago to represent them in the Guardians. While the school had no leaders, its members looked to certain people for advice and direction. She was now part of that group. She let them see her thoughts and memories of the recent events. She felt their agreement over her concerns. She thanked them for their thoughts of support.

"But I will need also your strength and help with my new task—acting Ambassador to the humans of Earth. The head of the Ambassadors, Tanoch, has given me this to do, but he does not believe I can. Help me prove him wrong."

"I will help!" Arman, her egg sac brother, said. "But it has been many years since I touched the minds of land dwellers. So many odd sensations, like being tickled on the belly by a school of little gold speckled min. Quite amusing."

"Egg brother, so happy it pleases you," Adno responded. "And these Earth humans are not like the land dwellers on Traveler's Perch. They have never flown without machines, and they are not yet fully entangled with each other. Can you feel them in my mind?"

She sang the humans' song to the school. "Yes, they are not fully developed, but is it not wonderful to feel their lifeness? To feel how another kind feels joy?"

The school hummed with pleasant sensations. Mixed in, rude jokes began to emerge about that old fart, Tanoch, who had doubted Adno. Did he not understand that she had their strength behind her, that these birds and beasts who lived in ones and twos on the land could sing melodies, but not the symphonies that swelled their waters?

"The land dwellers don't know how to combine so many melodies in a harmonious way," she reminded them. "They won't understand how we can join as TheManyLargeLoudBlueSchool and still each be free as our own minds. They have not traveled from birth in our great schools, wandering the vast currents together, taking turns looking for danger, steering, exploring. They are enhanced now, each of them their own school of sensors. So they will never swim this current with us."

"And what is it you want us to find, egg sister, in this current?" Arman asked.

"I am still learning," she said. "But right now I must learn more about why he has put me in charge of the humans and pushed Diver out. Something is wrong."

She explained that she would give them all access to the archives of the wormhole interface. They could process the last 10 years of data with the hundreds of minds in the school. They could all put that at the back of their minds while they went about their lives. Within a few days they would know what was to be known. With dark skies for the next few nights, they wouldn't be hunting anyway. That would give them plenty of time to mine the archives.

Later, she swam to the wormhole interface that had been modified for underwater use and installed on Water Eye long ago. Tanoch used it to connect one-to-one with her, but Adno had learned to do something her ancestors had not even thought of, and that no other Guardians had even imagined. Just as she was able to entangle with many others in the TheManyLargeLoudSchool, she could entangle as multiple threads through the interface. She created hundreds of connections, making short work of copying the archives with her enhancements. Even as she felt it enter her mind, she flowed streams of it to her schoolmates.

It didn't take long for her school to find the weeds where the truth lay, waiting to be eaten. In his youth, Tanoch had been an Ambassador to a people called Yunx, an assignment that had ended with the Yunx blowing themselves up. That was known to all the Guardians, who accepted that Tanoch had done the best he could, given the Yunx's tragic history. What had become hidden in the weeds of time were Tanoch's indiscretions.

Tanoch had fallen in love with a young Yunx, MunzKizzFron. The young man was not a particularly notable empath and his fate had no impact on the survival of the Yunx in any of the timelines that the Guardians could examine. Nonetheless, during the final apocalyptic decades of the Yunx, Tanoch had rescued MunzKizzFron no less than seven times, transferring him to new timelines each time, in hopes that Munz would survive longer in the new timeline. Tanoch had made several reports that were less than truthful to hide this ethical lapse. He had mostly succeeded in that endeavor.

But now it had become clear that Hankori, too, had uncovered his secret. Adno suspected that Hankori used his knowledge to force Tanoch to replace Diver with her. And there was more. Hankori was occasionally entangling with humans other than Raefe or Lina, ones far off the radar of the Ambassadors. Something was definitely going on and now she had a way to find out why from Tanoch himself.

She waited for a few days, letting her mind plot the course through these new waters. On the third night of the new moon, she found Tanoch through the wormhole interface.

"Tanoch, I swim the waters looking for the guidance you have left for me, but I cannot find it."

"Guidance? What are you on about?"

"The currents bring news of big changes in the Council. How is a lone swimmer such as myself to know which currents to join?"

"The Council is none of your business. I've told you before. Just keep an eye on Raefe and Lina."

"I have, Tanoch. But there are people interested in Raefe for reasons I cannot glean. And I wonder if Raefe is in danger again."

"Why? Even after we had transferred him to this new timeline?"

"Yes. People hostile to him are watching him, I fear. I feel their presence in the waveform."

"Oh, what crazy theory are you on to now, Adno? Who would want to harm him?"

"People who understand his potential."

"What humans understand that, besides his partner?"

"I said 'people,' not 'humans.' That enlarges the pool."

"What are you suggesting? That a Guardian is involved?"

"No, but could it be someone from one of our worlds, but not a Guardian?"

"Ridiculous!"

"All the same, can you ask Timelines for advice, as a backup measure?"

"Not a chance! We can't be shuttling him from timeline to timeline every few months."

"Oh, forgive me then. Rookie mistake. I thought perhaps Raefe might be in the same sort of jam as MuzzKizzFron."

Even through the wormhole, she could feel a surge of fear and embarrassment from Tanoch. She counted to three before he began to answer her.

"Muzz? Why do you mention him?"

"As your subordinate, I study your work. I noticed that you had him transferred seven times during your work with Yunx. I assumed he was a critical player in their world, much as Raefe is on Earth."

"Muzz is nothing you need concern yourself with."

Half the school was listening in, amplifying his emotions, filtering out noise. At that resolution, she could see a complex of emotions trying to hide from her. Ah, now it was clear—her suspicions had been correct.

"No, you are right. Your love life is really not my business. But I am still confused about Guardian policy. If it is possible for you to transfer your lover seven times, why is it not possible for me to transfer Raefe twice in the interests of helping Earth? And if the need arises, do I have to learn how to use the Timeline interface myself, or is there someone who helped you who will help me?"

His fear was strong now.

"What do you want?"

"I want to know why you removed my mentor, Diver, from her assignment to monitor Earth and put me, only a trainee, in charge. I had thought perhaps you would become my mentor, but you give me no help. All in all, I am tempted to believe you want me to fail, and therefore, you want Raefe and Lina and the rest to fail. Is that true? Or shall I make a special appeal to the Council to discuss this openly?"

"I don't think that will be as helpful as you think."

"You think I am an ignorant fish who doesn't understand what happens on land. But I have found my way across great oceans, and I will find my way through this, too. Just tell me what you know."

"Alright. But you don't bring it to the Council. Agreed? That would work out badly, trust me."

"I can accept that for now."

She felt his relief. He had been resisting her questions out of self-preservation, not allegiance to Hankori.

"Certain people on the Council want your project to fail. They pressured me to put you on it. My misadventures of the heart with Munzz gave them leverage to insist."

"But maybe they have other ways to help Earth fail, no? After all, even without me or the Guardians, Raefe and Lina might succeed."

"They don't tell me, but I fear you are right. I've picked up some whispers that might mean that they will harm them. Or at least him."

"Whispers? What exactly did these whispers say, and who was whispering?"

"I can't tell you who. But I'll tell you what, and then you must leave this subject. This conversation itself is dangerous. Perhaps these same people have found ways to listen to our waveform without us knowing."

Adno had asked her school to monitor the waveform for ghosts. They signaled that all was clear.

"I think we are safe for now. I have taken precautions. So, what is it you may have heard?"

"There are certain people on Earth who can entangle but are not truly empaths. You know that happens in many species, but it seems more prevalent among humans. I suspect that certain Guardians are recruiting these people to further their own agenda, not that I'm fully aware of what that is either. Raefe could be well be in danger. I'm not positive, but I think it may be in motion now."

"Thank you, Tanoch, now I can do my job. Your secret is safe with me. You should think about how you want to redeem yourself after 1,000 years of service. You have made mistakes, but are you willing to work to overcome them?"

She felt him snarl.

"Well, give it some thought. Can I trust that our conversation will remain between us?"

"Yes, yes, don't worry. I'm not eager to show that my students' students are now more clever than me."

He broke the waveform abruptly, leaving her swimming in tight circles, amped up and eager to strike back before it was too late.

FORMAL
INTRODUCTIONS

Water Eye
June 5, 2049

Once, Adno had ridden along on Diver's waveform when the avian and Lina connected. Neither Adno or Lina had ever felt a mind like each other's before. As part of her training, it had been a big step for her to feel the mind of a species few Guardians had ever touched. Adno had not entangled with all of the other Guardian species. Few of them had. But in the loose culture of the vast Guardian planetary network, every young person got a basic idea of what entangling with any of the other species would be like.

Now it was time for Adno to draw on those experiences and her general abilities to establish her own first contact with the human. She left the school, circling her favorite reef, quieting her mind. She had put the interface in the center of the reef, a place where she felt at peace and could best still her nerves.

She found Lina's mind. She made herself feel like a warm, gentle current. Surprisingly, Lina recognized her mind instantly.

"It is good to feel your thoughts again," Adno said.

"I didn't really get to feel yours when we met. You are different than Diver. Do you look like her?"

There were no mirrors or cameras on Water Eye, but everyone knew what they looked like through the eyes of their school members. Adno let her see those views: her three-meter-long body, a deep, shimmering blue, tinged with silver along the bottom, and bright red markings near her eyes. Her long, wing-like fins, their edges lined in a goldish green, folded tight to her side, her forked tail with its short streamers bunched close together, like toes on a foot.

"You live underwater!"

"Yes, my whole planet is water except for a few small islands. But

I have been to Diver's world, too. We share the same suns. I lived in a water tank there, but I know what a land world like yours, and land people like you, are like."

"Just when I get used to one part of this incredible journey, something happens that makes me think I will never run out of surprises."

"Diver says the same thing, and she is 400 years old," Adno said. "I'm not even half that."

"You must have other surprises to tell me," Lina said.

"Yes, I wanted you to know that I am now taking over Diver's role as Guardian Ambassador to Earth. I am interested to know what is happening with you now. And I will also be contacting Raefer."

She hoped Lina would not ask too many questions about Diver. Adno had decided she would tell her, but not before she had a plan to help the humans. Otherwise, she risked Lina withdrawing completely, hiding her mind in fear. It was a good decision. Lina was full of enthusiasm for her new community. People were beginning to entangle with each other. She had learned how to create a long-distance waveform with Raefer. He had met people who knew other people in another part of the continent she was on who might want to be part of this. It was all so much to take in, but Lina was happier than she could ever remember in the past.

"These other Africans, who also know people in Raefer's part of your world? They might be important. I will encourage Raefer to try and make contact from his end, and you should do the same."

Lina sensed that this wasn't just an idle thought. This one was more attuned to danger than she had expected. She immediately asked what was wrong.

"We monitor many thousands of minds on your world who show a little bit of empathic abilities. I am concerned that some of them may be manipulated by powerful people who will hear about what you are doing. You understand that Citizens of Nowhere may be seen as a threat by the powers that rule your world?"

"I guess I see that. Mostly we just worry about the local bandits. And there aren't really 'powers that rule our world.' Everything is very broken up, even the powerful fight each other."

"Forgive me, I have much to learn. Let me say it another way: I think there are some powerful individuals who are aware of what you and Raefer might be able to do in the future, and who are considering perhaps stopping you now before you even figure out what that might be."

"And you think the New Voodo Army can stop them?"

"No, I think the New Voodo Army can be part of your waveform. And the bigger and stronger your waveform is, the safer you will be."

She could tell that Lina didn't really understand what that meant. Adno was frustrated—she had much to learn about communicating with these humans and no time to learn it. Right now, she was just scaring Lina.

"I apologize if I'm frightening you," Adno said. "This is all a little new to me, so we will learn together how to share our thoughts and make new ones. For now, I just want to suggest that hiding completely, as some of your school wants to do, is not possible. Sorry, I mean some of your fellow Citizens. Anyway, hiding from the local bandits is good. But so is taking a chance on finding allies as both of you try to fight the bandits around you and bigger bandits who might come from farther away."

"I see your point," Lina said. And without hesitation, she found Raefer and now their waveform contained all three of them.

Adno had heard much from Diver about Raefer, but his mind was still a surprise. Lina's was strong and focused, like a sunbeam cutting through the shallows on a bright day. Raefer's mind had the same colors, but it was less of a beam and more of warm, bright sphere extending outward. Adno was excited to feel this—this sphere was the sphere of entanglement, the spread of his mental energies out toward others.

She could see now that the two of them would be very effective together. His strength would be engaging others, hers going deeper with them. In her world, everyone had both these qualities. It was fascinating to see that in a less developed species, individuals might have impressive but incomplete abilities to entangle.

So this is why I am here, she thought. *Not just to encourage their current abilities, but to help them connect in richer ways.* She would swim in their school, leading them to the best currents, nudging them there, strengthening their current from behind when they took the lead on their own.

"Lina was telling me about the New Voodo Army," she said to Raefe. "Have you found out anything new about your old acquaintance, Alton Winchester?"

"A little," Raefer said. "After my friend at work told me about the NVA, I did look up on Alton on the net. He's in the area. But you know, I don't have a strong memory of him—we only had just met before the tidal wave came."

"Can you remember a conversation you had?"

"Yeah, I think so," Raefer said. "We talked about coffee…"

"Right!" Lina said. "Because I used to hang out with him at that little outdoor stand. With the people who lived above us. Wow, I'm remembering a lot of old Lina's world now."

Adno and Raefer could feel her memory of Alton.

"Oh, yeah," Raefer said. "Things are getting a little clearer for me."

"Good," Adno said. "The more you can recall, the easier it will be for you to connect."

"Connect? What is it you think I should do?" Raefer asked.

"I feel your desire to have a master plan to guide your actions, but we can't always see the end of a voyage that we are already on. I suggest that things will get easier if you can start creating a network of people you are connected with, who might share some of your goals. Lina is already doing that, and Alton has connections with the NVA. If you connect with him, you will have the start of a large and potentially powerful network. Then, together, you can figure out what to do."

"I just hadn't been thinking in those terms," Raefe said. "I was thinking Lina is more the people person, and I could find ways to use technology to help her. Supergeek to the rescue!"

This was what Diver had told her about humans. They had trouble seeing that technology was not separate or above people, or the other way around. How could a person who worked on technology that connected billions and depended on hundreds of millions to even work, not see that a lone hero unconnected to everyone else could not accomplish much?

"Yes, maybe you will be Supergeek to the rescue. But how will you do that sitting at your machine? I can feel that your real superpower, as you humans like to call it, is not coding, but connecting. Even though I never felt your mind before now, I felt it instantly when Lina connected."

"You don't really know me," Raefer said. "Diver said a lot of the same things. I'm just not the guy who other people follow. It's not that I think coding is better, it's just the only way I know to help."

She let his words sink in while her enhancements desperately cross-reference the cultural archives of his species with his own cultural favorites. Talking about her school wouldn't do, she needed to reach him in his world. She felt a momentary surge of panic but then, there it was, just what she had been looking for.

"The guy other people follow in your world often means the people with power, and that often means the power to punish or harm. You have a different kind of power. You are a fan of the vid star, Robby Rob?"

"Yes!" Raefer said. "Wow, you really can tell my thoughts."

"Is Robby Rob a great actor? Musician? Thinker? Leader?"

"No, I guess not," Raefer said. "He's just a cool guy."

"You think he's a cool guy because Robby Rob has a knack. All of his guests feel he understands them, that he's on their side. It's not an act, he really is. And they flock to that."

"You're saying he's an empath?" Raefer said.

"A raw one. He doesn't know it. He just thinks he's good at getting people to talk."

"Where are you going with this?" Lina said. "Are you saying Raefer should be a vidcaster?"

"No, not the point," she said, sighing to herself. "As you've become more comfortable with your abilities, Raefer, you are becoming a person other people will feel that way about, too."

"Well, that would be different," Raefer said. "But so what?"

"Imagine if Robby Rob had Goodstuff Benjamin and Lina's friend Edna on his vid. They would each feel more open to talk about what they were trying to do. But if it were you in the room, you could actually help them to connect more deeply, to feel deep down that the other was vital to them."

"I think she's right," Lina said, her enthusiasm palpable. "Already, in our camp, we are having that experience. The other day, Edna and I were eating with some of the elders, and they were disagreeing about how we will get our food in the coming months. I wasn't really paying attention, but I could still feel that the two elders arguing the hardest both based their thinking on experiences from their past. Neither knew the other's experience, and neither considered that maybe that wasn't really relevant. I think Edna felt something of the same from them. At least, I felt that from her. And then, somehow, their argument turned into exchanging their stories. And they found a way to agree on a new idea."

There it was, Adno thought, that bright ray of light breaking through the water.

"This makes me so happy that you are already learning how to influence those around you to do better," she told them. "You are both off to a great start. What I hope you see, Raefer, is that you can be that person whose presence will create a kind of mental field that's like a wormhole between distant minds. And you can also be a guide through that wormhole."

He wasn't completely convinced, she could feel that. But open to it, at least.

"Well, I'm not sure about all of that. But I will find Alton and talk to him about the NVA. At least, it will be cool to meet another person besides Lina from my other life."

***

The next day, Raefer found Alton on the Net. He owned a bookstore in a West African neighborhood in Arlington, at the end of the Red Line subway. It was a modest store that seemed to serve the part of the community that was involved with the politics and culture of Africa. On one side several customers browsed the racks of small puters that showed vid trailers for each book. On the other side were old-fashioned paper books, covers worn and ragged, but no one was looking through them.

And there was Alton, sitting behind the register, sipping a cup of tea. The loose bushy 'do Raefe had known had been replaced by a more moderately thick, neatly trimmed head of hair. The prison-style jumpsuits they'd worn on the reconstruction project were, of course, gone, replaced by calf-length loose hemp pants and a t-shirt with the alternating green and white vertical stripes of the Nigerian football team. Raefer got a vibe from him of a core of solidity ringed by curiosity and a bit of mischief.

"Do you have any books by Goodstuff Benjamin?" he asked, keeping his voice neutral.

"Yes, several. Is there something in particular you're interested in?" Alton answered.

"I have a very good friend in Kenya," he said. "She is doing a lot of work there with people who've lost their homes and land, and she was telling me about him. Just curious. You know how it is when you have a friend who's totally into something, and you have no idea of what they're talking about."

Alton looked a bit skeptical. Raefer realized he had just offended him slightly, as if the man's idol was a curiosity or some vid celebrity. As if displaced people were this week's buzz on the net.

"Do you want to know about the man or the ideas?" Alton asked.

"Sorry, I didn't express myself very well. Mostly, the ideas. My friend and I talk a lot about what she does, and I'm thinking of moving there to be with her, maybe help with her work. But until I met her, I'll be honest, I didn't know much about life in Africa. Except I do work with a guy from Nigeria, and I've also heard his perspective."

"Which is?"

"Not very informed, I think. That's why I want to read more."

He felt Alton's attitude shift slightly toward the positive. Goodstuff Benjamin had written a kind of beginner's book about the New Voodo Army that was a good way to get introduced to his movement.

"But if you're interested in the displaced, that's not just Nigeria or even Africa," Alton said. "You should read *One Billion*."

He handed him a tablet of essays from Benjamin and a host of other authors, none of whom were familiar to him. The blurb explained that in a generation there could be a billion people disposed by rising tides and economic crisis, and that the world needed to start acting now if anything was to be done about it. It had been published five years ago. We've been asleep, he thought, dreaming of a world that is already fading away.

"I feel embarrassed that I've never even thought about this. I like to think I pay some attention to things outside my own little circle. It's not that I don't know about the climate and all, but one billion? You think they're right about this?"

"Could be even worse."

Something bubbled up in the back of Raefer's mind.

"You sell a lot of these?"

"Some."

"What I mean is, are there people in this area who are involved in this? I want to read the book but I feel like it's the kind of thing you want to talk to people about. Not just, hey, I read this book and fuck, we're in trouble."

Alton smiled. "Read the books, we'll talk."

"Yeah, okay, hit my Voice with them."

Riding his bike back to TechTown, he felt the weight of it. Lina was plugged into something enormous and powerful. Did she even know that? Were they part of another tidal wave, a human wave that could match the destruction of the Earth with the construction of something new? He thought about Adno and all her water analogies. She would understand what it was like to feel the water at your back, pushing you higher and faster and farther. He wanted to know that feeling.

PRIMED FOR BATTLE

Traveler's Perch
June 8, 2049

Hankori was furious. Bad enough he'd had to pressure Tanoch just to tell him what Adno had done. But worse, that fish had somehow planted the notion in Raefer's mind that he should somehow throw himself completely into Earth's continuing downward spiral. As if some half-crazed hardly grown nobody could somehow halt the tectonic forces that had built up in human society for ages. Idiots!

He calmed himself. He was a Guardian, in fact, head of the Guardian Council. He had resources. Knowledge.

Raefer had still not done anything, really. He was busy reading a book by Goodstuff Benjamin, one of Earth's many quirky, charismatic leaders. This Benjamin was not going to save humanity. His ideas would never reach beyond his small part of the planet. His followers would never find common cause with enough other groups to have a big enough effect, or to sustain it long enough. Hankori knew firsthand that the fractiousness of humans always got in the way.

Nonetheless, Raefer might succeed in contacting Benjamin. That might lead to connecting with Lina's friends and other groups in the area. It might take a decade or two to fall apart. And in that time, the Guardians would yet again find cause for hope about Earth and reason not to forget that planet. And Permanence would be slowed down yet again.

He would make sure this went no further.

He found Joe Nguyen's mind. Fortunately, he was asleep. He scanned his memories and found the conversation with Raefer about the robot battle. Hankori smiled and began weaving suggestions into various parts of Nguyen's mind that would produce the desired effect. Now, it would only be a few days before the matter was settled.

ROBOT WARS

Water Eye
June 10, 2049

Adno had been in touch with Diver through the wormhole interface. While her old mentor evaded discussing her dismissal, she was helpful enough in filling in some of the missing details of her time monitoring Earth. And Raefer himself had exceeded her expectations, having already made contact with Alton Winchester. All in all, Adno was feeling more optimistic.

"I'm proud of Raefer," she told Lina. "He has so much empathic strength, but he is slow to see how much he could do with it."

"Most of his life, his abilities have been an affliction to him," Lina said. Adno felt it as a scolding. Lina was protective of Raefer and wouldn't welcome criticism of him. She'd have to learn how to navigate that.

"Ah, I think I understand a bit of that," she said. "My thought in saying it wasn't to criticize, but to underline how we all can work together. Now that he's taken this step, you can support it by making contact with the New Voodo Army from your end. When I entangled with Raefer, he thought of the NVA as a bridge to you, to being part of what you are starting to build with Citizens of Nowhere. If you also connect with them, it will help him to feel effective and involved."

"OK, I see that," Lina replied. "You know, you seem more involved in our lives than Diver. I'm not used to that."

"Diver flies the skies on her own or with her partner. I am used to swimming in a school of many. But things are also changing, and that's part of why I am more involved. You are beginning to attract attention, and with that comes risk. I want to help you build connections. That will help you more than anything as you begin to attract opposition."

Lina will respond to this threat, Adno thought, even though she doesn't yet know what it is. Her old attraction to Raefe is beginning to take hold in her relationship to Raefer. She feels the affinity between their minds. But she also senses the connections that could arise from their shared bond. She's attracted to the idea of being part of something new, something that might just change the world in a wonderful and unexpected way.

The urge to change things was strong in humans. They had remodeled the very rock and water of their world into so many strange shapes. Over the millenia, that had led them to lose much of the ability to live without technology. Those who owned and drove the development of technology always urged a turn to technology every time a problem arose. Diver had stressed that, and Adno saw it now firsthand. She also saw that most humans still had little access to technology and so less attachment to it than their leaders.

Adno reminded herself not to judge. Her people had no need of buildings and machines. Their technologies were organically based, integrated with the reefs and mats and other large-scale lifeforms of Water Eye. Life was infinitely creative, but it took sophistication to fully grasp its innovations. The land-based species in the Guardians could never quite believe that they had been able to reach out beyond their seas with these technologies. But they had never lost their love of feeling themselves ride the currents and winds, of enjoying their place in the natural order.

The humans would have to make a reverse journey, balancing their love of clever things with re-igniting their love of connection to each other and the natural world. She would have to be patient in shepherding them if she were to accomplish her mission. For now, it was enough just to keep close tabs on Raefer, making sure nothing went seriously awry.

She followed his mind as he went to Brighton Gardens to watch Joe Nguyen's robot do combat. The place was an abandoned warehouse that had been turned into a small sports arena. It was typical of the many places where humans engaged in one of their many forms of ritual, nonlethal combat in the center of a large room. The walls pulsed with light panels, the raucous, rhythmic, repetitious noise the humans called music filling the air like dense fog. The place was packed with young humans in a riot of artificial decorations, their voices loud. She imagined that if she were on the other side of the wormhole, the room would be saturated in their scent. Distance was sometimes a benefit.

Raefer's mind searched the room, looking for his coworker, Joe Nguyen. It was odd that she knew him too. She hadn't actually entangled with Nguyen, but she had absorbed his history from the archives. His ability to entangle was real, but he seemed to lack any interest in using the ability to actually connect. It would be interesting to see the effect they had on each other.

Tonight, the humans would only fight by proxy. Mechanical devices that looked like hybrids of human, animal and machine were paired off against each other in a form of combat. The goal was for one robot to hold the other one to the floor for five seconds. Failing that, the robot was awarded a point for each time it forced the other robot out of the circle they fought in. There were other, more arcane rules, but she wasn't here to fathom the deeps of robojudo.

The human handlers had built the machines, programmed them, and partially controlled them during the match. Some of the robot's moves were autonomous, the result of the software the handler had coded. Some were directly instigated by the handler. The match tested the handler's skill as a builder, a programmer, and an operator.

It all seemed quite unsatisfying to her, all this focus on these strangely limited machines. But the humans were yelling and cheering. Electronic skin decorations—what they called nanotats—glowed and blinked as images of snakes and serpents, tigers and eagles roamed the skin of some of the crowd. All the natural hues of human skin were there, as well as some who covered themselves completely in blue or green paint. Hair was also turned in to ornaments projecting from their heads. Some even wore skin-tight suits that made them look like other large animals. Her enhancements identified them as various predatory animals.

Her enhancements also suggested that the eyes and body movements of many of the crowd were indicative of chemical alteration. Her databases now fed her more details. The loud music pounding the walls of the room was Reg-K, a hybrid of contemporary Asian pop music and 20th-century Caribbean sound. The crowd was moving spasmodically but enthusiastically to it. Their motions reminded Adno of what it felt like to swim through a narrow channel where the currents had created swirling rapids that wanted to toss you this way and that. There was a wild joy to snaking your way through that, and she thought that was what the humans might be feeling. Maybe they weren't so hard to understand after all.

The music suddenly got quiet by a half. It was time for the next match and Joe's robot was up. She tuned into his mind lightly, not wanting to disturb him. He was not as bland as he usually felt. He seemed pleased that Raefer had come. He motioned for Raefer come closer to the circle.

"Hey, man," he yelled. "Sit over there—you'll get a better view. Watch how fast my bot is!"

She was just about to lightly entangle with Raefer, interested to see their relationship from both sides, when she felt something strange. Another mind wafted across her consciousness. A distinctly nonhuman one, in fact. A mind more like Diver's or Far Fliers. Now she was on high alert. She let her school feel her thoughts.

"Arman, egg brother, do you feel this?"

"Yes, I feel your alarm and agree with it. Something odd is happening."

"I will monitor Raefer and Joe. Can you listen for the other mind and learn what you can?"

"Egg sister, we will ride this current where it leads."

The fight had begun. The other robot belonged to a female, very pale-skinned but with bright yellow-green hair. She had so many metal parts that Adno wondered if she herself was a robot/human hybrid. But the metal seemed more ornamental than functional. Humans had a very complicated relationship with their bodies and the artifacts they created, and she hadn't quite decoded all of that yet.

The crowd cheered as the robots charged and bounced off each other. This happened several times. Joe pushed some buttons on his controller and the robot rolled to one side of the circle, jumped several meters straight up, and came down behind the other one. One of its arms lashed out, knocking the opposing bot down. Joe's bot whirred and moved toward the downed bot.

She felt Joe's excitement. She noticed him looking at Raefer, who was quite close to the downed robot. She felt a fleeting thought in Joe's mind—*I've got him now*—accompanied by a surge of anger. He was ordering his robot to miss its opponent and hit Raefer!

Without thinking, she blasted Joe's mind with "STOP!" He hesitated, confused, not sure what had just happened.

"The other mind noticed what you did," Arman said. "How can that be?"

She had an idea, but they could discuss that later.

"No matter what, you cannot let him control Joe," she thought back to Aman.

She found Raefer.

"Adno here," she thought, letting him feel her urgency. "Get out of this room now, and leave the area as fast as you can. You are in danger. I will explain later."

Raefer got up to go, but Joe noticed. Joe suddenly seemed uninterested in the bot, not watching as his opponent's machine got up off the floor into a fighting stance. Dazed, Joe began fiddling with his controls. She tried to read his thoughts, but it was as if he was walking in a dream.

"I can't stop this mysterious mind," Arman said. "He's ordering Joe to launch a program in the bot. It seems like it's some code that this other voice has already arranged to be embedded in the...oh, no! It seems he's preloaded it to kill Raefer!"

Adno felt the other mind through Aman. Now she knew who it was and what she had to do.

"Join with me Aman!" Their antagonist would not recognize her that way.

"Hankori!" they blasted the other mind. "You are in violation of Guardian law. Leave the human now before we are forced to incapacitate your mind!"

It was a bluff, but it made him pause. In that moment, she let Joe feel that he was doing something terrible, that the robo controller was dangerous, that it might explode. He yelled, as if in pain, and threw the controller on the floor. He jumped up and down on it until it was a pile of junk. Sounds of grinding gears came from his robot, which teetered and fell over.

She felt the fury in Hankori's mind as he realized he had been thwarted. It was a level of rage she had never before experienced in anyone's mind. And then he was gone.

Now she heard Raefer's mental cries through the wormhole.

"What just happened?"

"Someone was using Joe to try and kill you."

"What! That's crazy. Who would do that?"

She wasn't ready to explain all of that until she knew more. "I'm not quite sure yet, but you won't be safe here. Go somewhere where no one would look for you. Entangle with no one. If you feel a mind other than me or Lina, don't connect. In the meanwhile, I will make a plan to keep you safe. By the morning, I will tell you what it is."

"Goddam it, you're not going to move my head to another timeline, are you?"

"No, you are in just the right timeline you need to be in. But we need to find a way to safety for you."

She felt something break inside him, releasing buried emotions to rise to the surface, while others sunk out of sight. He was outside now, out of sight in the shadows on the side of the building. His breathing was tight, his muscles taut. She felt a surge from his mind.

"This shit is real, isn't it?" he thought to her. "All this future-hangs-in-the-balance stuff that I wanted to think was down the road, maybe so far down the road it wouldn't matter. It's starting already. I need to get to Lina. I just need to figure out how to pay for it."

It was a good idea, she thought. Let this crisis move things forward.

"Good, and I think I know how to help with that. When you awake, I will have news for you."

She would find a way. But first, she replayed the incident in her mind. She had to be sure. Yes, it was Hankori for sure. She replayed his rage when he realized he'd been thwarted. Her first impression was right—his mind was filled with brutal images and malevolent intent. And there it was—she'd missed it the first time. His anger was focused on Diver, then Far Flier. Not familiar with her, he had assumed her more experienced mentors had stymied him. And he meant to get even.

CLEARING HER MIND

Diver had spent several weeks buried in work. Now she was ready for alakh, the thinking sleep. She hoped to awake knowing her mind about Far Flier and their future. She arranged her room for maximum quiet. She removed herself from all entanglements. Finally, she disconnected her enhancements from all communications. She was alone with her mind.

She sunk deeper into the trance of alakh, watching the movie of her life as if it were someone else. For more than the last 100 years, she had been the bright female whom everyone liked. She was the person who had energy and promise. Still, her accomplishments were minor. Despite what Far Flier thought of her potential, she was sure that she would never join the Guardian Council, much less lead it as he had. She was not a pathbreaker.

Recent events had shown how unpredictable life could be. She realized now that she couldn't know what the future would bring, with or without Far Flier, or the Guardian Council. Perhaps she needed to take stock on her own terms.

She had engaged with Raefe and in just a year had brought him very far down the road to becoming a change agent. She had helped him through his initial trials with separation from Lina. Adno said they were now a force to be reckoned with and she had started them down that path. No one had recruited a new civilization to the Guardians in centuries yet she had taken the first steps to doing just that. She caught herself basking in this anticipatory pride for things not yet done and scolded herself. This desired outcome would take luck and the contributions of many others.

Still, she had surprised herself with her strength, perseverance, and skill. These would be her pillars, no matter what she undertook. She realized that Far Flier had said these things to her many ways, many times. And now she knew that he was not just acting the teacher, but also the pupil. He needed her.

Not just him. If what he had said was right, the Guardians needed her. Although he was only in his late middle years and not yet old, he had lost some of his hope and strength. Hankori was cunning, and she knew he had allies planted in many places. Far Flier had held Hankori off, but it was only a matter of time before he retreated to a place from which he would no longer be able to stop Hankori in whatever it was he was doing. And she was sure that what he was doing was needed stopping.

Connection, people, life—these were fundamental things she would fight for, not a list of achievements she could recite with false pride. The swirling thoughts in her head had spiraled down to this. She knew she should emerge from alakh now and walk that path.

It was nearly midnight, but she reached out to Far Flier. As he made his way to her room, she let him feel her alakh. She opened the door for him.

"We will make a child, and we will make a new Guardians," she said. "I will do this with you."

He embraced her, letting her feel his joy and sadness.

"You must realize," he said, "that our life will become much harder."

He let her know what Adno had told him. They were losing their battle to keep the Guardians on the right track. And they were in danger.

"I don't even know how to think about that," she said. "It's been millennia since anyone in our world has been in danger from anything but the kind of random events that killed my parents."

"I feel the same. It's like we have been transferred to a new timeline, where the Guardians are not what we know, and dying of old age is no longer assured. But remember, we are not completely alone. Adno is proving far stronger than either of us thought," he said. "She has offered to shelter us on Water Eye."

"Even if we want to go, how will we get there? What story will we tell?"

"She holds something back from me, but she has found a way to influence Tanoch, believe it or not. She can persuade him to assign us to her world as mentors or some such excuse."

She had not anticipated this during alakh. Yet, nothing she had thought of then was tied to this place. Nothing in this place was worth their lives. Nor did she wish to stay here by herself. She had found the current she would fly on, she would follow it where it led.

She took him wordlessly to her bed. After they had made love, Far Flier guided her in completing the creation process. In the next few weeks, he would nurture the egg he had fertilized and received from her. His body, with its enhanced nano gene-repair tech, would remove any mistakes, correct any serious diseases, build an energy transfer layer around it and wrap it in a protective gel.

When it was done, he would return to her, and they would perform the ancient ritual of transferring the embryo to her. Then her body would take over, and grow it until it was ready to be born. The time spent in both their bodies would allow the baby to immediately join their wave function, and its connection with them would pave its entrance into the larger community.

She knew that there would be pain and discomfort involved for both of them. Long ago, her species had tried to abolish all that by birthing children outside the body. They had learned the hard way that evolution had embedded in them the physicality of creation and birth. Both for the parents and the child, there were so many unforeseen and undesirable consequences to losing that experience. So they had contented themselves with merely making it safe.

In the early morning hours, they smiled and sang the first songs of new parents-to-be together. To feel such a chorus for the first time was an experience worth a little discomfort. She felt the excitement of knowing that they would also be reborn, in a way, in a new home and a new life.

GOING NOWHERE

Somerville
June 11, 2049

Raefer had fled Brighton Gardens in something of a panic, over-whelmed by the thought that Joe had actually tried to kill him. Joe, to whom he thought he had felt some kind of connection. He was lucky Adno had been watching, or whatever it was she did. But why had she even been watching? Did she do that all the time now?

He had hopped on to a motorbike taxi and mumbled TechTown, not knowing what else to say. Where could he go where he wouldn't be known? He thought of his work buddies, Herbie and Rod. What could he say to them about showing up close to midnight, if they were even home? The Raefe part of his mind felt calmer, slower.

I've been through worse, he thought, in the other world. An image of angry water filling Union Square flashed from Raefe's old memories. He tried to follow it but it faded. He tapped the taxi driver on his shoulder.

"Change of plans. Union Square."

The night flew by, buildings and people, cars and bikes and every hybrid of the two. He wanted to feel the energy of the people but Adno had warned him not to entangle. He withdrew into himself. Even the noise of the city whistling by on the bike seemed to recede. Then they were stopped.

"Union Square, guy," the driver said. "Fifty-seven bucks."

He told his Voice to pay the driver's and dismounted. He'd been here many times, but never really took it all in. This was where Raefe had lived before his life had changed forever. Raefer wanted to feel what that was like, to know that he had done that before and survived. His Raefe memories were still with him, but they had blurred at the edges, connecting themselves to his own memories. Sometimes they had rewritten themselves to blend, sometimes disappeared, but most of them were still there.

He was facing a throng of people at a Brazilian taco stand, laughing and kicking around a soccer ball. They weren't TechTown people, he could tell—wrong clothes, wrong music, different energy. They were the kind of people who didn't have careers, who worked odd jobs here and there and hustled in between.

This was where he and Lina's friends hung out, where the coffee stand they frequented in the old life was. He walked toward the harbor. An image of Raefe's TinyStack bubbled up. Traffic was whizzing by where it would have been, right under the overpass. Where he and the woman he had never met slept together in some kind of glorified shipping container under a highway.

He walked by and up a side street that went up a hill. From the top of the hill, he could just see the edge of the Mystic River. More images from Raefe's life appeared. Seawater was surging up the Mystic, pushing the river higher and higher, as if some great god was pushing up from below. The river was higher than a house now, even as it spread sideways over its banks towards him.

He was paralyzed with fear, not certain that he was imagining this. What remained of Raefe was reliving this even as Raefer experienced it for the first time. Time hung as the waters approached him, as he felt himself lifted up on to the highway, and relived the terror that had engulfed Raefe.

And then it was done. He was still Raefer, but he had now felt to his core what had shaped Raefe. And now that was irrevocably a part of him, no more the strange murmuring of a guest in his mind. The Somerville he knew lay in front of him. He would have to find his way in it and the rest of the world. Starting tomorrow—for now, he would have to find a place to hide until Adno contacted him.

He could see houses with the little HouseHotel signs saying Vacant scattered around the landscape below. A room in someone's house or apartment would do tonight. He asked his Voice to find him one near.

He paid the money and got a code that would open the door. No one was around. The room was in a basement, the door in the back. He sent the code from his Voice and the door opened into a low-ceilinged room, a single bed along the back wall. He kept the light off, letting the moonlight coming in through the casement window show him the way.

He lay in the bed, feeling like a guitar string vibrating endlessly. Slowly, the vibrations faded and he fell into a deep, dreamless sleep.

Hours later, he felt warm fingers touching his mind. It was Lina.

"Are you OK?" her thoughts exploded in a burst of concern.

He peeked out of the basement window. A sliver of peach light, bleeding into blue and then indigo. There was no water in the street, no killer robots nearby.

"Strangely, yes," he thought. "Adno has been in touch?"

"Yes, and I have been busy all morning here. Or rather, some of the Citizens have. What do you think you should do?"

"I'm not sure yet. I'm still trying to understand what's going on. Why would someone try to kill me?"

Adno had explained some of it to Lina while he slept. There were people who feared what they could do. Powerful people who discounted their ideas publicly, but privately believed that they were a threat, or at least an unwanted nuisance.

"And for that they would kill me?"

"It's more complicated than that and I have a feeling Adno isn't telling me everything. Long story short, they had help from a Guardian."

"What! I can't stand it. We get help from people who are super intelligent and supposedly past all of this madness and now they're trying to kill us, too?"

"I know, I had the same reaction. But then I thought, well, they're not angels or gods. That's us who put that on them. I guess there are always people who are out for themselves at any cost."

"But how can we fight them? They're a billion miles from here, and anyway, what would we even do?"

"Nothing. Adno says she can protect us. It's a matter for her people and she's confident they can defeat this rogue Guardian. She says just focus on humanity."

"Well, that makes it simpler," he said, letting her feel his fear turn to anger and sarcasm. He didn't think he'd ever forget the sight of Joe Nguyen freaking out at Brighton Gardens, knowing that he had escaped death by robot by seconds, thanks only to Adno. What if she wasn't around next time?

"You're angry, I understand that," Lina said. "I'm even glad, it will make you more alert."

"Yes, I'll have to be. Empathy alone isn't going to be enough."

As a lone empath, he was vulnerable. Empathy would only carry the day if it was embraced by huge numbers of people—people who had each other's backs, who could move bigger rocks out of the way than one person, who could extend their eyes and ears everywhere they needed to be. Like the people Lina was with.

"I think Supergeek is going to hang up his cape and take a trip to Africa," he said.

"I'm so glad! The Citizens have reached out to Goodstuff Benjamin. The NVA has its own network. When the sun is up where you are, they will contact the man you know, Alton Winchester. He will get you here. Don't worry about the details—it's all sorted between the Citizens and the NVA."

They were quiet letting each other feel their thoughts of their worlds coming closer, ending one phase, beginning another, a beginning that was in some ways a reunion, in other ways a renewal, and still more, a completely new path for both of them. But it was one that would soon bring them face to face, and they let themselves anticipate the excitement of that.

He would become a Citizen of Nowhere and trust his fellow citizens to help find that way. No more pretending that he could work within the corpo world, a little off to the side, but part of the machinery. If he was in the machine, he could be crushed. Lina had seen the truth, that the old world was a death trap. From now on, he would travel on the margins, meeting the ones who no one cared about, seeing what they were doing to survive, what new ideas they had.

He would help them build a new world, out on the edges, a world where people no longer thought only about themselves, but existed in a web of purpose and connection, of freedom to explore and probe and experiment. As the center shrunk with each catastrophe, the edges would pinch in, until they were numerous enough and strong enough to fill the center. It would take years, but what choice did they have?

REUNION

Kenya
June 17, 2049

The last few days had been a blur, hiding, letting Alton make the arrangements for him to go to Africa. He had never taken such a long plane ride before, trapped in the air, the buzz of 200 other minds his only accompaniment. After landing in Nairobi, he took a taxi into the city center. From there, it was a six-hour bus ride straight down the A3 to Garissa. From vids and school, he expected to see a necklace of bustling small cities extending out from the capital, filled with low industrial parks made of dozens of agritech plants. For the first hour, he felt like he'd never left Nairobi as they drove through endless neighborhoods with people packed into a random patchwork of shanties, container houses and tent cities. He guessed more people lived here, just on the eastern edge of Nairobi, then all of Boston.

But the houses thinned and then there was nothing for a while. Flat in every direction, most of the trees had been cut down for firewood or farming long ago. An hour out of Nairobi, the air had turned hot and dry. He'd once been to Arizona, and this felt like that. Suddenly about 200 kilometers from Nairobi, Mwingi City rose up out of the dust like a mini Nairobi. And then it was gone and they were back to hard-baked dust with the occasional small village.

And that repeated itself, one small city after another. Then they pulled into Garissa, a town like so many towns at the end of a road. His puter said Dadaab was only another two hours away, but his puter didn't know that normal traffic east of Garissa had stopped a decade ago. Between Garissa and Dadaab, drought had driven out even the smallest village farmers. Bandit gangs had taken their place, some of whom were affiliated with remnants of the jihadi militias that had plagued the region decades ago. They made dirt bike runs to attack trucks or the market in Garissa, and then disappeared back into the scrub. All in all, a dangerous place, he thought, anxious about Lina's safety.

At the bus station, four men with motorcycles approached him. His stomach clutched for a second and then he sensed they were friendly. One grabbed his bag. Another introduced himself as Malik in halting English and explained Lina had sent them to bring him to Dadaab. Malik gestured to the back of his bike, and Raefer hopped on. He noticed two of the men had short machine pistols slung over their chests. He wasn't sure if he should be happy or concerned that they were quite relaxed about being armed.

Twice, they skirted a village by riding off road. He tried to ask why, but the noise of four dirt bikes with ancient, rusting mufflers made it impossible. He could feel something between wariness and fear in his companions' thoughts.

It's begun, he thought. The heat, the drought, the breakdown. It's already happened here.

And then there was a bit of forest and the land rose gently. The forest thickened. They reached a ridge and there it was below, the remains of Dadaab, where 400,000 people had once lived. He could feel hundreds of minds below. They felt ordinary, just people going about their business, and that made him oddly happy.

And there was Lina, only 100 meters away talking to some people. She must have sensed him because she turned, a huge smile on her face. He hopped off the bike, yelling his thanks to Malik as he trotted toward Lina. He grabbed her up in big bear hug. She was warm and lean and shorter than he had imagined. Gone was the riot of curls Raefe had known, replaced by neat rows.

"Easy," she thought to him. "Public affection's not so great here."

He relaxed his hug and she moved back just slightly. They stood grinning at each other.

"Come," she said, "Let's get you some water."

The dining tent was empty and they sat down. He took a long sip of water. Their minds were fully engaged with each other and it felt somehow odd. And then he realized something.

"There are four of us here," he thought to her. "The two of us who were lovers, and the two of us who have just met."

"Lina meet Raefer," she thought.

"Raefe meet Milima," he replied. "I think you're going to like her."

"Sitting in Union Square, talking fugee biz with Kayam, I never imagined we'd be sitting here," she said.

"How's the coffee?" he teased.

"What coffee?" she said. "The heat has killed off most of the lower elevation trees. The high-mountain beans are too expensive for locals—they get shipped off to Europe. Sometimes we get some from Ethiopia, but bandits have ripped off the last two shipments."

"Doesn't seem right, no coffee practically in the place where coffee started."

"No, my love," she said. "All is not right here."

He could feel her sadness, different than what she had felt in their old life when she thought of the Efricar Holocaust. Further from anger, but wider and deeper. He stared out from the tent. Past Dadaab, the trees were low and sparse as far as he could see, which was all the way to the horizon. There, the line between land and sky was smudged by dust. It reminded him of the beach just after sunset, when water, clouds and sky all converged in slatey blur.

"You thought it would all be jungle and mountains," Lina laughed.

"Yes, majestic," he grinned.

"You sense it, too, the beginning of the changes that destroyed our first life," she said. "In a generation or two, the fertile coast will be underwater. And this will be a vast desert, a young Sahara."

"And Nowhere will be nothing?" he wondered.

"Nowhere will be everywhere," she answered. "Millions, maybe billions, of people will be like these people. Wandering with no destination, no home."

"Will it be like the East African Holocaust of your other childhood?"

"I don't remember much of that. I can sense a good deal of it from you since we came to this timeline—your memories of my telling are strong. I can feel some of them, so I know what you are asking. Not to mention that in this very place, my mother's relatives were part of a slaughter of 11,000 people a generation ago. But no one knows what the future brings. These people have so far avoided death from Shabab, their own governments, and now even the Chinese. But when there are tens of millions of them, what will happen?"

He remembered something from The Slide, or at least his dim memories of his parents' tales. No one had a plan beforehand. Sometimes hope just meant having a plan that might work. But what was Nowhere's plan? More Dadaabs?

"I feel like we have the beginnings of a notion of a start," she said. "Now that you're here, we have time to experience this place together, and talk to decide the way forward. I have learned patience from these people."

He looked skeptical. He had seen many sides of Lina, but none patient.

"Don't worry, Raefer," she laughed. "It can be learned."

"In only a few months, you've made a completely new life here. I sense from the others here that they see you as a leader, that they respect you. I'm in awe."

"This empathy that I learned from you, it is wondrous," she smiled. "Thank you." She reached over and took his hand.

"I don't know if I have much more to offer," he said. "I'm just a kid who's good at coding. Usually, if there are more than three people in a room, I'm uncomfortable. I get quiet."

"And yet from billions of miles away, super intelligent aliens could sense your potential, could sense that the rest of us need people like you. Now."

Aliens who had nearly killed him. For an instant, he wanted to run. To flee back to his little apartment, to his silly little routines with his work buddies at lunch, to his old job, where nothing really mattered. No, that wasn't right. He never wanted to lose this feeling. He stilled his mind, staring out at the village around him, unsure of what to say or do or even to think.

"It's hard enough for me to believe that you need me," he said. "I'm a 'me' person, not an 'all of us' person."

"You're not selfish," she said. "I don't believe that."

"No, you're probably right," he said. "The 'me' thing—it's not selfishness. Honestly, I think it's more that I don't usually think of myself being in situations where what I do matters that much to other people. You know, it's like, I have friends, but it's always 'hey, if we see you at the club great, otherwise, catch up with you soon.' And here I am, in Africa, with hundreds of people who lived through more than I could ever imagine. Really, who cares what I think?"

"They don't care that you're from somewhere else, that you're white as bleached cotton, that you're not a Muslim, or not a goat herder, or any of the rest of that. That's what Nowhere is about. The only thing that matters in Nowhere is what we can do together, today and tomorrow."

"You said that Nowhere could use help figuring out how to grow," he said. "How can I help now?"

"These people are so close to entangling, as the Guardians call it, they are right on the edge. I feel like the two of us together can push them over that edge. And then, who knows? Something truly remarkable could happen."

Could it? He wondered to himself. Could they all change their way of life together? Could they help them change this anarchic hum of many minds into a comfortable web that kept them all connected?

"Well that would be remarkable, and great," he said. "For the first time, all these voices feel inviting, not overwhelming. Maybe something truly spectacular has already begun to happen."

They left the dining tent, and walked across the camp to the tent where he would be staying. Feeling the minds of the people all around, he understood now that no one needed him to be a leader, much less a chief. Lina wouldn't be that either. She would be the practical one, the one who helped them use their empathic abilities to craft a new way. He would be a catalyst, he would be the one who helped them all connect. No, that wasn't it either. He would be the one who helped them understand how connection changed everything, how truly wonderful and powerful it was. Lina knew better how to help them sort out how to use that power. That might take years. He would inspire and teach, she would guide and shape. He felt her fingers brush his palm as they walked, their path now clear.

Later that night, they walked back up the hill into the forest.

"I think it's time we introduce new Lina to Raefer," Lina said, pointing to a glade of soft ferns.

Not a stranger at all, thought Raefer a few minutes later as they left normal conversation behind. Old memories, new thoughts, the ancient delight of warm bodies, the soft battle between rising passions and the desire to make it last forever, their occasional cries all mixed in a sweet gumbo of forest bird calls.

Lying on the ferns, Raefer began to drift off, the warm breeze and Lina's warm skin merging and lulling him. He began to dream of Lina, naked and glowing, flowing over him, enveloping him. He felt the warmth that was his love for her flow from his mind, down his spine, and through his sex into her. At the same time, he felt her love flowing back toward him, a whirlpool of sensations and emotions where they were joined. Old Raefe guided him, showing the part of him that was strange to her all the places that gave her pleasure. She responded by letting him feel how he felt to her. He returned the favor, and, in the dream, they both broke the silence with a laugh.

The laughter woke him up. He opened his eyes and realized he hadn't been dreaming, or even really sleeping. Lina had mounted his drowsy body as they lay there, but this time their minds had joined, too. Now he could see her, the forest, and the sky but had no wish to be distracted from the allness of her. He felt like a newly blind man who had discovered that the world could be seen through touch and taste and smell. As he thought that, he felt her thinking the same thing, and their bodies moved together without hesitation or doubt.

Finally, sated, they lay back, still breathing together. It was night, but the sun would come up on their new world.

MEETING OF THE MINDS

The next two days flew by. Here they were, Lina and Raefer, to-gether for the first time since being in another world in Somer-ville. *We have a lot to learn about each other,* she thought, and that felt like something to really look forward to. Especially as she sensed that with each hour that passed, the two of them were both becoming more sensitized not only to each other, but to all the minds around them. And they were starting to feel more tendrils curling out from the rest of the Citizens toward them and each other, as well.

"Some of them, like Edna, are so close to being able to entangle," she said replied. "They finish each other's sentences so often it's more like someone started the other person's thought."

"I asked Adno if she could nudge them over the line," he said, "but she won't. She says they made an exception with you and then by con-necting us, but we must find our own way. Otherwise, it could turn out badly. I realized that it was one of the first times I felt an emotion like anxiety or anything negative from her. Not sure what, but I definitely got the message that she's not going to help us with that."

But I can, she thought, and she decided to surprise him.

"What was that?" he asked.

"That was Edna's daughter, Fatima."

"You can feel her mind that way?"

"Yes, I have been around her for many weeks and know her mind well. But we have grown closer, too. I wanted to see if I could do that, connect your mind to hers through mine. And it worked?"

"That wasn't just me feeling your idea of her? That was her?"

"Yes, she is a very intuitive person, like her mother, so it was easier with her."

"But she can't feel your thoughts?"

"Not yet," she smiled. "But I have an idea."

Later, she bumped into Edna, who reminded her that today would be her daughter's coming-of-age ceremony. The Citizens were slowly developing their own rituals and festivals that took bits and pieces of each other's cultures and melded them into occasions that all could enjoy. This would be Lina's first experience of this one.

"You will come to my daughter's ceremony this afternoon, after Friday prayers?" Edna asked.

"Yes. Is there anything I need to know?"

"No, just look for the tent with the red banners near the dining hall at the far end of the camp. Everything will explain itself. Here, we have so many different traditions we do not worry too much about doing things just so. It is enough to do them at all. I will be with the mothers, and we will sing. Fatima will drink a special tea we will make her, so that she can hear the truth of what we sing. And then we will dress her, and she will return to her family and friends a woman."

And able to entangle, thought Lina. She felt Raefer in her mind, excited by her plan.

"You realize how big this is," he thought to her. "To see if we can create a whole new kind of human relationship?"

"I'm trying just to think about it like a new kind of puter message," she said. "One that doesn't need a puter."

When the time came, Lina had trouble calming herself, unable to make small talk with the other women. Then the ceremonial tea was served, and Lina found herself slowly being more drawn into the group.

She had thought through carefully what was about to happen. She would concentrate on Fatima, reaching out, gently touching her mind. Raefer would be in the nearby dining hall, pretending to read a book while monitoring what he could of the other women. Now, maybe, they could take a first step in creating the kind of world the Guardians seemed to live in.

Edna and a few of her longtime friends began the ceremony. Edna spoke in Swahili, but some of the songs she and the other women sang were in other languages Lina didn't understand. Some also sounded like Arabic prayers. Each had its own rhythm, its own melody that allowed others to feel its meaning even without words. After a while, the room was filled with a feeling of common purpose and serenity. Finally,

Fatima was brought into the middle of the tent, all the other women around her in a circle. She wore her normal clothes, except for a new red headscarf.

Edna said more words in a language Lina didn't know, but she could feel had something to do with being a woman. Then Fatima began to sing those words and more in the same language. The song was long, and Fatima fell into its rhythms, her voice now speaking from somewhere inside her.

Lina found Fatima's mind easily, and the ideas of the song began to snap into focus. Lina heard thoughts of creation, of every woman's part in the creation of the world, and of the worlds to come. Lina could feel Fatima's joy. When Fatima was done, she sat quietly, a huge grin on her face. Another woman began a song, this one a bit racy, about a woman and a man. Certain lines brought laughter from some of the women. No need to translate, Lina thought.

Lina calmed herself and focused on Fatima's mind. "I am happy for you," she thought, repeating the thought as in a chant. After a minute or so, she felt Fatima register her presence in her thoughts. The girl was a bit alarmed.

"Why does it seem like Lina is in my mind," Fatima asked herself.

"Because we are in each other's minds," Lina answered.

"Oh, my mother never said anything about this. Is this part of being a woman? Sometimes it feels like the aunties are in each other's minds," Fatima thought.

"No, this is just you and me," Lina said. "We have made a strong connection since I came. I could feel your thoughts easily."

"Can you read other people's minds?" Fatima thought. "Can they read yours?"

"It's not really reading. More like feeling your emotions. You seemed open to it, so I thought I'd try. I think the tea helped."

"What if I don't want to share my thoughts with you?" Fatima asked, concerned.

"Can you feel this part of your mind?" Lina asked, touching a certain part of her thoughts lightly.

"Yes."

"Focus on that and make that the center of your thoughts." She felt Fatima's thoughts gradually fade way. She made eye contact with her and made an "OK?" face.

The group was now singing another song, one that seemed to be about going forth and facing a new day. Perhaps the ceremony was almost over. She might have only a little time left with Fatima. She touched Fatima's mind again and felt her touch back.

"We will talk more later, Fatima," Lina thought to her. "For now, I just wanted to say congratulations." She felt Fatima's "thanks."

Lina was drained. She stayed long enough to eat some of the little cakes on offer, and then wandered out of the tent. She felt Raefer reaching out to her.

"I think that went OK," Lina said.

"You were able to entangle with her?" Raefer said. "I got distracted by the other women's minds."

"Yes, and she with me. I showed her how to block her thoughts, too. And then she initiated contact again. But it was exhausting."

"For my part, I could feel other minds sort of paying attention, but no more. I think they felt a disturbance, like a breeze, but nothing too upsetting."

"Good."

She walked to the edge of the camp, wanting to be alone and regroup. She sat on the ground, a tree between her back and the camp. Some large birds were perched on a tree in the distance, their occasional squawks managing to sound both languid and menacing. She could see they were taking turns feeding on a dead animal below them. The warm breezes felt good and soon she felt herself slipping into a dreamless sleep. She awoke suddenly, as if her mind had sensed danger. It was almost dark now and the light was falling like a soft dark curtain. She realized someone was standing in front of her. Lina made herself very still and quiet.

"Who are you?" the stranger asked. It was Edna's voice.

"What do you mean? You know who I am."

"Milima Kawambai Yang, now Lina. But who are you really? Are you a witch?"

"Why would you say that?"

"In the tent, you touched my daughter's mind."

"She told you this?"

"No, she said nothing of this. I felt it."

"You can feel other people's minds?" Lina asked.

"Yes, a little. Not like a witch, but a little."

She wonders if I am trying to control her or Fatima, Lina thought. I can feel she is both afraid of that but excited that it might actually be possible to understand someone that deeply. Even if we fear it, we still have that hunger to understand another without doubt.

"I'm not a witch. I feel other people's feelings, sometimes even their thoughts. And sometimes they can feel mine. I think all of you can almost do it. Your troubles have brought you together. And your ideas have made you open to each other."

"Why did you touch Fatima's mind?"

"I feel her thoughts all of the time—she is like a radio broadcasting. I wanted her to feel mine. To talk and feel each other's emotions better."

"Can you feel mine?"

"Yes, sometimes."

"And doing what you do—it's not dangerous to her?"

"No, it's not that different than when you feel a deep connection with someone. Only now, it's in words and it's alive—you're trading your thoughts and feelings in a deeper way than talking."

"Why?"

"Because if we could all do this, we could heal our wounds and be stronger. We could learn trust. And who not to trust."

"Teach me to do this."

"I want to. But I don't know if I can. Will you trust me and wait until I'm sure?"

"I feel an urgency. She is my daughter. I want to protect her if she needs it. If you teach me now, I won't say anything until you want me to."

"I will need help—our connection is not yet strong. I might need Raefer to help."

"He can do this, too?"

"Yes, he showed me how. He is very strong this way. Will you come to our tent around 10? We can see what we can do."

"I will come with Fatima. I don't want her to feel alone in this."

"I want you to know I would never hurt Fatima. Raefer and I, we have been hurt, too. Everything we do, we want to find a new way to heal. We want to prevent all of this, and worse, from happening to the whole world. The whole world will be Dadaabs if we don't find a different way, and maybe this ability is part of that way."

"If you are telling the truth, I will help you. But for now, you should be careful who you say what to. It is not only friends who want to know our thoughts. The imams, the police—these are people who have asked many of us for our thoughts, and hurt us to get them. Do not assume that everyone will trust you because they can feel your good intentions. Some will take that as a trick and they will hurt you."

***

Adno had been watching events unfold through the wormhole interface. This might be her first assignment as an Ambassador but all of Guardian history told her that she was witnessing the first of what would be an unstoppable spread of empathy and entanglement through the population. It might not save the humans. Empathy would not stop a nuclear weapon from wiping out Dadaab and preventing the spread of deep entanglement. Less dramatic events could drastically slow progress, even to the point that Earth's problems could still prove decisive. But unchecked, the humans were on their way toward a new level of interconnection.

She needed to understand how the Guardian Council would react. It would be hard for her to hide from them, but she had taught Arman and others in the school what they needed to know to find out. And they had told her what she needed to know.

Tanoch continued to talk out of both sides of his mouth, helping her when she pressed him, helping Hankori when he did the same. He had lost his way, responding only to fear now.

He was right to be afraid of Hankori, now that she understood that he was involved in something truly large and bad. She would find out what it was, but for now she was troubled that he still harbored such rage toward Diver and Far Flier. She would become his target someday, she knew that was unavoidable, but in his arrogance he paid no attention to her at the moment. And she would turn that against him to thwart him again.

Tanoch was not happy when she made her new request, but she would not let him slip from her teeth. In the end, he was forced to agree. He would send Diver to Water Eye to help her. She neglected to tell him that Far Flier would slip aboard the ship and accompany Diver.

Once the ship was underway, she took a chance and found a way to observe Hankori in the waveform unnoticed. He had just heard the news of Diver's departure, and was beginning to suspect that Far Flier was hidden aboard. She had not expected him to be happy, but the depth of his hatred was staggering. He was thinking about whether there was any way he could destroy the ship in space. It had been so long since someone in the Guardian worlds had killed another person in anger that there was no clear record of the last murder. Even on Traveler's Perch, no ordinary citizen had in more than 9,000 years. That the most powerful of the Guardians, the de facto head of the Council, was raging in his own mind over how to do kill Diver and Far Flier shocked her to the core.

And he felt that shock, just for a second. She felt his mind snap like the jaws of a hawk on a smaller bird. But she was gone, and he was no wiser.

Water Eye was a big place. Now that she was alerted, she would hide them well, and Hankori would never be able to hurt them there. But she would need all of her skills, and her school's, too, to prevent him from destroying the Guardians.

In the blink of any eye, she had gone from a trainee in a tank to shadowing the most dangerous prey in the largest ocean, hoping to attack before being eaten. Her skin felt electric as she raced through the waters, ready for anything.

BREAKING WITH TRADITION

Daadab
July 10, 2049

Raefer had wandered from the shower tents toward a small wooded rise just outside the camp. The pink light of dawn was slowly giving way to the grey yellow of early morning Kenya, the stand of trees no longer foreboding silhouettes. He sat on a boulder and watched the camp come to life, feeling the hum of hundreds of minds waking. Since Lina had entangled with Fatima, they had also taught Edna, and now it was clear that minds were beginning to reach out and find each other, even if they weren't quite aware of it. And some of them were. Adno had been right: Connection was strength.

"You know there is one last thing you must do," he felt Lina say in his mind "to become a part of this, not just my friend, or a friendly observer."

He let his emotions speak for themselves. The past three weeks had remade him completely. Was he Raefer? The old Raefe? Or someone totally new? Whoever he was, he had never felt this sense of calm and purpose before, and he was pretty sure the other Raefe hadn't either. For the first time, he felt that the Guardians were not insane to entrust him with this mission. A few weeks ago, he hadn't even believed that his empathic powers would ever really count for much.

"I had the same doubts," Lina said. "I was on a path to consider only the paths of being African, like my mother, or Chinese, like my father. I had never considered that the world offered more choices than those I was born into, and definitely not that it would give me entirely new choices."

"You thought about it a lot more than me," Raefe thought to her. "I've never thought about much more than 'Should I get another job' or 'Maybe I could get a better apartment.' A new way of living—that wasn't even something I was interested in books or vids about."

"And now we must make that happen," Lina said. "We will never want to turn our backs on that."

He walked back down toward the camp and her. "At least we hope, right? I know my parents had all sorts of idealistic ideas when they were young. They used to say 'Shit happens.' I guess it will to us, too."

Lina handed him a cup of tea and they sat eating ugali, the Kenyan corn porridge that she had been raised on.

"We won't let it slip away, will we?" Lina thought, half asserting, half asking in hope.

"No, I don't think so. Is today the day Alton and Goodstuff are coming? It's a good day for me to make my choice. You are right, it's time for me to commit. I will become a Citizen today. What do I do?"

He had reached the tent. He could see she was all smiles. "No papers to sign. When you feel the time is right, just announce that you want to join. They will ask what to call you. That's it."

Before he could think more about it, the Nigerians arrived. Raefer was caught short by Goodstuff. He had expected a tall, imposing figure. Benjamin was slight, a bit disheveled, and seemed somewhat absent-minded. Raefer embraced Alton.

"You are doing well?" Alton asked.

"Very well. And I have you to thank for it."

"I have a feeling you will pay us back in your own way."

"I am going to try."

A Citizen who had once been Nigerian showed the NVA contingent around the camp for a while, and then they all settled down in the council tent. If Nowhere had a capital, it was this modest tent, with its skinny aluminum lawn chairs and odd bits of furniture to put food and drink on. Edna came, along with Ahmed and some of Nowhere's other unofficial leaders.

"Welcome to Nowhere," Ahmed said, leaning back in his chair and opening his arms wide, as if to embrace them all. Raefer smiled at his ancient threadbare Amazon Chase Investments t-shirt. He must have gotten it 10 years ago after the company was liquidated and its corporate swag became a tax-deductible donation to Africa's future. Such was the corpo idea of contributing to world development.

"We have long thought there might be much we could accomplish together," Ahmed. "So, we are pleased that you have made this journey so that we can begin to get to know each other."

"We have, of course, heard about you, too," Benjamin said. "Some Citizens here have occasionally sent word back to their Nigerian families about their life with Nowhere, and we are intrigued. And honored to be allowed into your camp. Of course, your secrets are safe with us."

"We appreciate that," Edna replied. "Nowhere has been careful to stay in the shadows. We hold no territory as our own—we would leave this camp in a day rather than fight for it. You, on the other hand, are very public in your activities."

"Yes, but we understand your position, too," Benjamin said. "We have had to fight because neither the generals nor Boko Haram have given us any other choice. Submit or die. There is nowhere for us to hide in Nigeria, at least not for the many thousands of people who follow us."

"How many people do follow you?" Ahmed asked.

"We have a few thousand hardcore members," Benjamin said. "And about 100,000 followers. And maybe a million who look to us for answers and will participate on occasion."

The Citizens considered that, letting the weight of such a lot of people sink in. They had been careful to keep their numbers in the hundreds or low thousands.

"We, on the other hand, have turned away from being large," Ahmed said. "Our thought was that at some point, others would create other groups like this in other parts of Africa. By staying small, we avoid attention from the authorities and the jihadists."

"Yes, and you make it less attractive to people who might want to subvert what you do and become warlords," Benjamin said, nodding approvingly.

"And how do you avoid that?" Lina asked.

"First, let me say that there is no guarantee," Alton said. "If people want to do bad things, they can be stopped, but not always before they do damage. Still, we take many precautions. Power is very divided in the NVA."

"What he means," Benjamin said, "is that Goodstuff can ask, but he cannot tell. Neither I nor anyone else with significant authority can at the same time control our money, our arms, or our policy. It would take nearly a dozen people to agree on all of that to come close to having an authoritarian regime in the NVA."

"And then they would have to deal with the rest of us," Alton said. "In each NVA village, people can survive economically with little or no help from the others. They have their own arms to defend themselves. And money is really not all that important to us—we have ways to feed ourselves and take care of most of life's other necessities as well. "

"Being a dictator of the NVA is just not worth it," Benjamin chuckled. "Not that I personally have ever had that aspiration. But we try to think about the future, too."

"Still, you don't know what is in someone's heart," Edna said. "We all have trusted people who have betrayed us."

"Yes, that is a sad part of being human," Benjamin said. "Only God knows our hearts, and who is he, exactly?"

Edna gave Lina a short glance. Raefer could feel that she was expressing both that this is where Nowhere could be of use and that it was not yet the time to discuss that.

"Ah, but if we cannot know God, maybe still we can know each other?" Ahmed said, smiling. "I am an optimist about that."

"Perhaps," Benjamin said. "You will judge us by our actions, though."

"Ultimately, yes," Edna said. "So tell us more of what you are doing and how we might benefit from your ways."

"Alton, you are the engineer," Benjamin said. "Explain what we are trying to do."

"Gladly," Alton answered. "It's about combining healing the environment with providing food and shelter. In Nigeria, we face a century of petrochemical pollution that has not only made farming nearly impossible but also transformed cities into cancer farms. Western corporations will never do more than put on a show of cleaning it up. And now we have Chinese and Brazilian corpos and who knows who next coming in—it never seems to end. So, we do things like plant thousands, eventually millions, of mangrove trees to filter the chemical pollutants from the waters around Lagos and other heavily affected areas."

"Cool, but not that original," Raefer said. He wanted to see just how prideful the NVA was, and how open they were to other directions.

"But here's where we are being innovative: We harvest the parts of the mangroves that actually absorb the pollutants. The plants grow back, and it actually helps them live longer to be pruned like that. We have simple processes—crushing, burning, that sort of thing—to separate the pollutants from the plant. We purify them through a variety of simple flotation filters, and we're left with a menu of stuff. Heavy metals, sulfur, phosphorous, organics—we can produce these things for less than chemical companies with their mines and refineries. Some we don't sell—we just use them to make construction materials. Others we barter to get stuff we need."

"Cool and original. Even better," Raefer said. "So, you interact with global capitalism, but are really outside the system of debt and currency."

"I'm not sure if that has anything to do with us," Ahmed said. "Nowhere has no lakes of sludge. We have mostly new desert, dried out by the rising temperatures."

"Yes, and like us, you won't get any help from the countries that caused these new deserts, to adjust to them or to undo them," Benjamin said. "But our religion is not The Gospel of Sludge."

Everyone laughed.

"Our gospel," he continued, "is to fix our problems with the materials we have at hand, with methods we can understand and adapt. Our goal is not profit, it is change. It is surprising how much more you can do when you make that choice."

"For example," Alton added, "East of here, there are large areas that have not only become very dry, but very windy during certain seasons. We think these areas could be electrified via wind and solar that would power mineral dehydration to yield water to feed greenhouse-based agriculture. We have power technology that is simple, cheap, and easy to maintain. It's not the greatest in efficiency, but this is the tropics, not Denmark. We have more sunlight than we know what to do with. If we can develop that, all the dirt farmers would have plenty to eat and then some to barter for manufactured goods or animals from other regions."

"But if you come with your army, there will be trouble," Ahmed said. "The bandits only tolerate us because we don't oppose them."

"Unlike Boko Haram, the bandits' claims to having their own territory are fake," Benjamin said. "We know from our own sources that the only land they can occupy is exactly these deserts that are growing in the east. Neither Somalia nor Kenya will let them out of those areas. They will die there, hungry and thirsty."

"Hmm, you may be right there," Ahmed said. "But what does that mean for us?"

"That if we come, and you join us, that someday we will have to invite them to also participate," Benjamin said. "They will have to make a choice."

"This man does not lack for courage," Ahmed chuckled. "Edna, what do you think?"

"When you want to roll the dice, you do not put all your money down on one throw," she said, smiling. "We have contacts in Shabab. Like Ahmed, I had not considered what you are saying about how they are penned in. But I also know that they are growing old and desperate—they are not the heroes to the young, angry men they were years ago. There is a small village on the western edge of their territory—Mangai—Lina, you know it. Perhaps those villagers and some of us and some of you can begin a small project, and at the same time talk with the local Shabab about joining in."

"I like that idea," Benjamin said. "Time may not be on our side, but we cannot always run in a straight line."

Raefer realized that the entire time he had been in the tent, he had not felt anger or suspicion from anyone. Skepticism, yes, but they had all listened to each other and not been burning to find fault with the other. *We have already begun,* he thought. He saw the smile on Lina's face and didn't need to read her thoughts to know that she agreed.

Later, at dinner, he stood up.

"Today has been a very good day, watching the New Voodo Army and Citizens of Nowhere begin a new chapter. I owe my life to both groups. It was New Voodo Army who rescued me from danger and brought me here. And the Citizens who have made me their guest. I know from Lina that you have been kind and allowed me to stay longer than guests usually do, understanding that I come from a long way off, in many ways, and that I have difficult decisions to make, which my life has not really prepared me for. And so, I want to say that I have never felt so welcome and so hopeful as I did when I awoke this morning, and now this day has confirmed that. What I mean is, I want to become a Citizen of Nowhere, if you will have me."

He felt their approval and heard them banging the tables in agreement. Edna stood up.

"You are of course welcome. And what shall we call you, new Citizen?"

"Raefe."

It was Raefe's voice that he had heard that terrible evening that he had escaped from Joe's robot. Raefe had melted into him, but he had also changed him in ways that Raefer never could have.

At last, he heard Lina's thoughts: "We are together again."

PART III

CLOSE TO THE EDGE

Dadaab
September 19, 2081

Raefe and Lina looked out across the plain of Dadaab. In all the 32 years that they had been here, they had never seen 10,000 sets of eyes looking back at them from a sea of faces of every sort. The First Worldwide Congress of the Dispossessed was about to start, and you didn't have to be an empath to feel the high expectations.

"Did you ever expect to see this?" she asked Raefe, squeezing his hand.

"Some days, yes. But not that often," he acknowledged, smiling.

Yes, we can smile now, she thought, *at least for the moment.* The last 32 years had included many dark days, especially in the middle years. After his arrival in Africa, they had an almost normal married life for a while. Des and Nyssa had come and handling twins had joyfully occupied much of their time. But as the twins passed into school age and no longer required constant attention, Raefe had sometimes lapsed into long periods of self-doubt. He seemed concerned that the children would suffer from their considerable empathic powers, as he had.

That concern passed as the twins prospered, but Raefe wasn't always sure of his place in this growing movement. He had periods of depression, although fortunately they were short. Then he'd wake up one day, suddenly outward looking, and be off to meet a group who were "doing interesting things," as he liked to put it. And weeks later, he would return, highly energized after teaching them to entangle and become part of whatever it is this was. To him, though, it was often the reverse that was exciting: He had become a part of their world.

As he felt more and more empaths in the world, he had gained strength. In the last decade, that had become more the rule than the exception. He had done amazing things in bringing together groups that had never been united before. She had eventually come to accept that he had become the spiritual leader and public face of their movement, no matter how lost and rumpled he often seemed to her.

Lina had also had periodic crises. Empathy didn't always assuage egos, and she found she just wasn't that diplomatic with the many eccentric characters they had dealt with around the world. But she never felt as alone as Raefe often did. All along the way, she always felt surrounded by strong friends. And they had her back when her failings threatened to upend things. Over time, she had become the one who people counted on to turn all of their dreams into plans and their plans into reality. She wasn't sure how, but she had come to accept that, too.

And there were Edna and Alton and so many other smart and strong and good people from around the world who had become their friends and comrades. And so, year after year, the movement had attracted rag tag groups of people who no longer had a secure place, or any place, in the dying world of global capitalism. They had become strong enough to call them all to this place to talk about the new world they would build among the ruins, even as stones continue to tumble down around them.

Up front, on stage a band played "Wet Feet on Desert Sands," the song that had become the anthem of fugees everywhere. Lina looked at the band and felt a thrill of kinship. Like her, they were living proof that the old ethnicities and cultures were breaking down, blending together. She added her voice, and soon, 10,000 people were singing as one:

We leave our homes
In the sea
We walk the streets
With wet feet
Our feet water the deserts
That we meet
We are the future
That we greet
Hey, Ho, Forward We Go!

Over the din, the amplified voice of Lina's old friend Edna could be heard. She welcomed them as the representatives of the one billion people who had become dispossessed by rising seas, rotting nations, and an economic order whose leaders no longer even pretended that they were doing anything more than looting the house burning down around them.

The crowd hushed, letting the weight of a billion fugees sink in. Edna's litany was undeniable: the failure of rice farming from new monsoon patterns and extreme heat in Southeast Asia; the 400 million boat people from Bangladesh to Shanghai; the chemical holocaust of food supplies in West Africa. Even the formerly privileged had suffered—Miami was just a string of small, mostly deserted islands, Phoenix was uninhabitable for the summer months. Millions had flocked to cooler climes where they lived on the streets, often in thrall to corporations that used them as occasional dispensable labor.

"The old homes that we had in the old world are gone," Edna said. "Many of you never lived in that old world, before the ice melted, before the seas rose, before the rains stopped coming. So you feel the truth of what I am about to say: We will never have that home in that world again."

She talked about the new world they were already building. The Citizens, the New Voodo Army had just been the beginning. Already 70 million people across Africa had built their own economy, their own social institutions, and their own homes in the wastelands deserted by the profiteers, false prophets and thieves who moved on to easier plunder. The Rising Tide was doing the same among the boat people in Pacific Asia. The Urban Gypsies were organizing the urban fugees of Northern England. Almost weekly, groups were popping up in India, Brazil, Russia, and many other places where life had become problematic. Even in continental Europe, home of capitalism, the Republic of Holland, now an island itself, had made a radical departure from the past, offering citizenship to people all around the world in hopes of forming a new kind of nation not tied to territory.

As Edna finished, Lina could feel the energy of the crowd, eager to get on with it. She reached out to Edna.

"That was fantastic," she thought to her old friend. "I think they feel ready to do something new, something great."

"I feel the same from them," Edna said. "Now if we can just get them to figure out what that is and agree on it."

"Oh, that," Lina said, laughing. "But there are thousands of empaths here. This is the largest gathering of empaths in human history, as far as we know. That has to count for something."

"And if things go well, there will be even more by the time they leave."

***

Raefe wandered through the gathered, their emotions like conversations overheard while walking through a crowd. He remembered the first time he had felt someone else's feelings. It was supremely odd, yet there was also a sense of familiarity. You thought, oh my, no one else thinks like me. But eventually you found the greater truth: Our feelings are unique in the same way as our appearance. No two people look identical, but plenty of people resemble each other. Like one of those old-fashioned police sketch kits—you could make up almost anyone's face by assembling a handful of bits from a few dozen choices. Feelings were the same way, if a bit more expansive and complex.

He had read a 20th-century novel that had a scene where a child draws a picture. This took place before puters, and the girl had to use a piece of paper instead. And she didn't have a light pen with a color wheel. Apparently back then they gave little children crayons, pen-shaped pieces of colored wax. They would come in sets. This little girl had a set with only 12 different colors so she couldn't draw all the flowers in the garden properly. She wanted the box with 100 colors. With 100 colors she could draw most anything and it would look real.

He had found that most people had about 100 emotions, but even then, they came together, diverged and overlapped in an endlessly fascinating and fluid display. The difference between any two people was not just which colors they displayed or even how intense each was, but how one could amplify another, or tamp another down, or, well, even after all these years, he hadn't really figured it all out. Everything affected everything, that he knew. They were all woven together, more like a tapestry than a drawing. Or maybe more like an electronic circuit, each component affecting the others in nonlinear ways.

Nonetheless, he had become fluent in the nuance of human emotions, and to the extent that the heart and the head were aligned, it helped him greatly to understand what other people were thinking. He had traveled to meet groups, large and small, whose members were desperate for deep and fundamental change. He had listened to their grievances, their hopes for the future. He brought them news of Nowhere and all the other groups popping up in the shadows of the dying world all around the globe. In every place, he had met others with empathic potential, and, if they were willing, he had helped them to

learn entanglement. With Adno's help, he had located thousands of po-
tentials and been able to help most over the threshold to be able to use
and control their empathic powers. The day was drawing near when
their combined power could sustain a global waveform.

Still, few here knew what he looked or sounded like. Outside of
Dadaab and the Nigerian village that he and Lina had lived in for a
while, Raefe had carefully avoided the limelight. His skill as an empath
had enabled him to communicate more deeply with people. It had also
shown him how many people feared such closeness. Sometimes their
fear could lead to violence. But not here. Today, he was among friends.

He sat quietly on the edge of a group from North America, a rumpled middle-aged man in a big floppy hat and long gauzy sleeves, still
vainly trying to protect his too-pale skin from the fierce equatorial sun.
He had visited North America many times since coming here, but it
was nice to listen to people from the de facto capital of global corpos
compare their experiences and share their ideas on a way past that.

"We live on the new coast," a middle-aged woman said. "Our town
used to be the hilly section of a big city that was part of the old state of
Connecticut. Now there are only a few hundred buildings left standing above water. You can walk down the main street right into Long
Island Sound. You can go inland from our town, but not up or down
the coast. We're cut off by bays both east and west."

He noticed that her shoulders were tattooed with a riot of colorful
birds done in smart ink that changed colors in a complex, repeating
pattern. It was a design that had been popular years ago, and the smart
ink suggested that she had once lived a very comfortable life.

Raefe had first begun noticing the formerly comfortable displaced
and deposed in numbers about 10 years ago. Middle-class life in the
west had always had its casualties. A series of economic and political
crises had often ripped through the middle class with disastrous consequences. Until recently, though, the comfortable had always expected
a return to comfort, if not for them, for their children or friends. A
generation ago, the upper middle classes had even begun genetically
engineering themselves, aping the ultra-rich. They felt sure that would
keep them competitive and that the arenas of competition were more
permanent than the competitors.

And now, they were beginning to see what had at first seemed like
just bad luck for more and more people was really the rotting away of
the foundations of middle-class life. Now, most of them lived increas-

ingly anarchic lives in which old rules no longer applied. They had lost their pass into the arena, or the arena had collapsed. The woman from Connecticut was certainly feeling that.

"What I used to call Connecticut no longer exists," she said. "Most of it was ceded to DigiBrands in exchange for managing a long list of potential disasters. They cherry-picked what they could and now the rest of it, and us, are just an annoyance to them. We're more No One than Nowhere."

Raefe smiled. "How about Someone Somewhere?"

She laughed. "Some Some, I like that. Anyway, there's a large farmer's cooperative about 200 kilometers north, along the Connecticut River. With the new weather, that's actually a very fertile area now. We buy food from them, and smuggle it in to avoid DigiBrands' taxes. We think in a few years, the sunken town will become like a reef, so we're investing in fishing gear and shellfish farming supplies. At least we'd be able to feed ourselves."

"But food's not enough," shouted a wiry young man from Pittsburgh. He was an unremarkable young black man, hair cut in the current fashion of thin orange sides, a braided row circling the back of his head, and a paintbrush wedge of curls standing up on top. Raefe noticed a triangle tattoo on his neck, a barcode from one of Brightstar's prisons.

"We got the New Confederacy in what used to be called Appalachia. Some parts of the Midwest, too. They're hooked up with Billy Warren, who's basically taken over the old Koch empire. They actually tried to blow up one of our dams to force us back to coal electric! We had good contacts with some farmer's co-ops south of Cleveland, but now Warren's people want us to pay exit fees for the food to leave Ohio. And then there's some biker gangs roaming through western P.A.—sometimes they ride into neighborhoods on the edge of town and just take whatever they can. If the area's not mostly white, they might burn it down. All down the line, we're dealing with this kind of shit."

And they wanted to know what to do. Always. What was Raefe going to do? Or the Citizens? Or anyone?

"What's your plan to fix this?" a middle-aged man demanded of Raefe.

"You're the plan," Raefe smiled. "This is the plan." He waved his arm toward all of the other small groups. He could feel their resistance.

"You've come all this way because you're desperate," Raefe said.

"For hope and for answers. There is every reason to be hopeful. What we just sang a little while ago—*We are the future that we greet*—that's not just a nice thought. Here, and in other places around the world, we have been discovering that what society has torn asunder, we can repair. You all know that I've been preaching and teaching empathy for 30 years. It's not a parlor trick. Every day in Nowhere, we deal with each other with a much deeper understanding of each other's hearts and minds than we ever thought possible. And we accomplish so much more when we can see past the fears and misunderstandings that support racism, ethnic conflict and just plain bad blood among people."

As always, their first reaction was a collective groan. He waited, and sure enough it came:

"So what are we supposed to do, sit around and sing folk songs together?"

"If that helps you find answers, yes. But we are after something much, much bigger. We have to start thinking differently, stop pretending that our problems just need the right magic spell to fix, the right set of magic keys on our vid game controller. We have to change history. We have to change the way we live, and the way we live with each other. Thirty years is like 30 seconds for that. But we have to start."

Some people from outside North America had wandered into the group. A young African woman helped a frail old Somali man stand up. He spoke in halting English.

"You Americans, what do you fear the most? Terrorists? Do you believe I was a terrorist?"

Raefe could feel that that they were skeptical.

The old man continued. "In 2058, I was the commander of a group of bandits in Somalia. My father before me was commander, back during the last days of the Islamic State. I was raised to believe you are all devils. Not just Americans, not just white people, not even just people who aren't Muslims. Anyone who didn't follow our narrow way was less than human. We did terrible things to people who we didn't consider people. And you probably think I shouldn't even be here. How could a man like me change?"

"Yeah, how?" answered an angry voice from across the room.

"Because people from this camp came to my village and taught us to see inside them and inside ourselves. Not with magic, but with our own hearts and minds. And each day that we practiced that it became deeper and more second nature, it became harder to do what we had been doing. It became like killing ourselves. And then one day, we understood that we didn't need to."

"So nice to see you, Aaden, after all these years," Raefe said, pleased that the old man had made it. "Aaden's village is the center of a new way of life in his region. Free from constant war, they've created new ways of growing crops. They have built an entirely new society. You've never heard of it, because they are as far off of the grid as you can get. But we all can learn from it."

"But what these people want to know," Aaden's young companion said, "is whether we've renounced terrorism. Whether those men still oppress woman, gays, people of other faiths. I am Casho, Aaden's grandchild. I wear a scarf covering my head because it keeps the sun off me, but I can take it off any time I want. At home I have never covered my whole self in the ways my grandmother did. I live with another woman and everyone knows that. Neither I nor any woman in our region has been mutilated in my lifetime. I could say more, but let me just say that any of you would be more safe in our village than in your own. Maybe even better fed."

Raefe felt a murmur of approval, a sense of relief.

"OK, that's impressive," one of the doubters piped up. "But we're not villagers, we live in cities. The people who threaten us are not small groups of bandits. They're mega corpos with mega cash to buy off opposition and armies to crush the rest."

Alton was sitting on the edge of the group.

"I lived in the US for a long time, and then here, mostly in Nigeria, where we had many of the same corpos. The thing is, they couldn't stop the seas from rising, or the land from dying. Their money became increasingly worthless. And their armies were our relatives. Empathy has proven more effective than bullets in organizing against them."

Raefe felt nods of agreement on that. The military had often been the employer of last resort during hard times.

"And that's good," Karl said, "but you can mean all the best for me and still not understand my world. Or you could still have opinions I just don't agree with. You want to organize the whole world, except for a few. You can't possibly know the minds of everyone."

"You have a point," Alton said. "But what are the alternatives?"

"I thought you could read our minds," he said, looking at Raefe. "Can't you do that somehow for all of us, at least, here this week?"

"In fairness to Raefe, that doesn't really seem practical," Alton said. "He's just one person."

Raefe was smiling ear to ear.

"It's OK, Alton," he said, "I think Karl has just given us a fantastic idea. If we can know each other's thoughts, than why not literally put our minds together to arrive at a plan we are all behind. You see, something new and wonderful is already happening. I will speak with the organizing committee and figure out how to implement what you are suggesting, Karl."

This was the most exciting thing he had heard all week, Raefe thought. He could sense the group was excited too, but also skeptical, with a dose of the constant fears that they had brought with them from what had become of their daily lives. But now he saw a way to send them home with a sense of hope and possibility.

JUST A FEW ENHANCEMENTS

Traveler's Perch
September 21, 2081

Hankori reached the back of the cave and found the boulder that stood a meter in front of another passage. Unless you were standing right next to the back of the boulder, you couldn't see the opening. He remembered the day long ago when he had gathered his closest allies to plan Permanence here. Amazingly, they had been able to keep their secret. But they still had a long way to go on the project, and he wasn't going to relax just yet.

They were close to creating immortal beings. They needed a way to test the technology. He had to have access to test subjects on Earth. And he needed Putnomo to enable that. He initiated his own waveform in the secret subchannel that Putnomo had created to link the wormhole interface network and found the big quadruped walking through tall grasses on his world 453 lights years distant.

"How goes the work?" Hankori asked.

"Slowly, I must admit," Putnomo answered. "We can all be recreated as waveforms in plasma. We've mastered that technology. But allowing us to manipulate the material world in that state is proving tricky. We have big obstacles, still."

"Yes, yes, it's hard. I get that. But have you made any progress?"

Predictably, Putnomo went through a long litany of all the progress they hadn't made. Well, at least they weren't 20 years away, his usual estimate. Now they had closed in on 10 years away. A mere sprint to the finish line.

"I'm not surprised, given the difficulties so far. All the more reason my next request becomes important."

"What's that?"

"I'd like you to develop a package of enhancements for the humans.

Life expectancy, 1,000 years. Ability to entangle with other enhanced beings without our help. You can absorb some of the minor details."

He opened his mind to allow Putnomo to scan them. Putnomo could scarcely disguise his disgust. He protested that everything about the request was illegal, unethical, and highly dangerous. Hankori calmed him down. He only wanted to try this on a small group of humans. Just one to start would do. Putnomo sputtered and spat and put up objection after objection, but in the end, he agreed when he finally understood that he would be able to test some of his ideas on this group of enhanced humans.

Now that he had settled that, he reached into the wormhole interface network and found his main agent on Earth, Billy Warren, in the midst of a dream. The man was abhorrent, but with his money and power he was uniquely suited to this phase of the project. And he liked human beings even less than Hankori, so he would have no objections to Hankori's plan.

In his dream, Warren was sitting in one of those old-fashioned diesel train cars he unaccountably loved, looking out as the scenery passed by. Hankori sat down next to him.

"Pretty, isn't it?"

"Oh, hey, Hank, nice to see you again. Yeah, it's something, ain't it. See those deer up on that ridge? Those Hot Earthers want to put windmills up there. Scare the damn deer off. Not on my watch!"

Hankori suspected the deer only roamed the ridge in Warren's dreams, the woods they roamed in actuality having been ravaged by rising temperatures and forest fires. But it was Warren's fierceness of purpose and determination that made him attractive, whatever his other flaws. He could deal with Warren's delusions later.

"Yeah, I know what you mean, Billy. There are a lot of small minds in the world. But I have something that I think could be what you like to call a game changer, Billy. I wanted to run it by you."

He gave Billy a glimpse of being enhanced. How he would be virtually immortal, how he would be able to read other people's thoughts at will. And he hinted at more to come.

"Wow. Are you saying you can help me become like that, Hank?"

"Just so, Billy."

"And why would you do that?"

"Because I believe in the world you are fighting to preserve. We've lost our way, lost the fighting edge. You'll bring that back, but you need time. And I can help with that."

"And what do you want in exchange?"

Hankori smiled. Warren wasn't exactly the sentimental type.

"Humanity is nearing its end. The planet can't support billions more people. And the culture is lost in a mire of egalitarianism, on the one hand, and blind tribal strife on the other. I know you know that not every person is equal, that some can see further and accomplish more than others. And if humanity is to survive, it must recast itself based on those people. I want you to start that process, to bring together other people like yourself, and with the knowledge that these gifts will be yours, develop a plan to reform Earth based on the best of you."

"You're right that we are mired in those things. Even among the elite, there's no agreement about the way forward. But I have some ideas about a core group that could potentially accomplish this, especially if we have access to the things you promise."

Warren proceeded to tell Hank that Ken Robertson had sounded him out about a plan to create a formal meritocracy of the elite.

"The best, the brightest, the richest, and the rest be damned," Warren said.

"You bring them together, and I'll deliver," Hankori said, and broke the connection. Robertson's willingness to write off 99 percent of humans was just what he'd hoped for. If Warren and Robertson could deliver that, and Putnomo could do his part, Hankori could finish the Guardian tradition of passive involvement. Permanence would not eliminate the need to monitor lesser species for impending threats. But this way, they could reliably transform worlds to reduce their threat to future generations. Maybe they'd blow themselves up down the road, but at least the Guardians would always have a backdoor into those worlds to neutralize them as a threat.

And the best part, he thought, was that he had Warren on the hook. When it came time to find subjects to test out Guardian immortality technology, Warren would be far too dazzled by what he was being offered to worry about the cost.

FULLY MINDFUL

Dadaab
September 22, 2081

Lina smiled to see her children Nyssa and Des, now grown, sitting in one of the discussion groups, listening intently. She could feel their passion and their desire to speak, but the twins had learned long ago to listen first. That was the culture in Nowhere before she had arrived, and it had never wavered.

The discussions were going well, many ideas had come forth about how to organize more people. Even better, people were full of ideas about how to organize the world they would build in the coming years. They had reached the point where people were starting to repeat themselves. After three days, it was time to move to a consensus. Raefe had convinced the organizing committee that it was time for bold action, and now he would explain it to the crowd.

"We are on the verge of something big and new and full of life. And very human. The other day, one of you asked how we break free of the cycle of a few deciding for the many. Why, he wondered, can't we use this empathic power I'm always going on about to decide together how we want to move forward. And now, we are going to try that, for the first time, as far as we know, in recorded history."

The organizing committee had identified a group of about 100 strong empaths who collectively had been involved in all of the discussions. They were a diverse group, with members from every continent. They had been tasked with absorbing not only the ideas, but the hopes and fears of all the delegates. They would then entangle to use that deep knowledge to come up with a set of principles and tests that could guide them for the foreseeable future, as well as point to the most immediate steps that the Dispossed would need to take.

The crowd enthusiastically embraced the idea. Raefe let their energy wash over him but he also probed further, trying to find the roots of their mood. They were optimistic, buoyed by their days together, hopeful. The Congress would be a success. But the next hours would determine whether it would be an historic occasion, or just an important one.

MAXIMUM LIQUIDITY

Diver loved sitting on this rock after fishing. She had her own name for it—Hawk's Haven—but she knew Far Flier would think it sentimental and silly, so it remained her private name. Whatever Far Flier might think, it was a good name for this solitary rock, standing 20 meters high just off the beach. From the top, she could see the silver flash of bait fish far out into the water, the ripples where blue trout disturbed those schools, and the swells of Adno's people as they herded the blue trout into the shallows, where they could feast on them as needed.

She stripped off her flight suit, lounging on the rocks while Prime dried her. At first, the sky on Water Eye had seemed nothing like Traveler's Perch, even though it was the same solar system. But after more than 30 years, it had become just as familiar as the views of her first 450 years.

She had been surprised at how hard it had been to acclimate to this new place. Her mind had traveled so many places through the wormhole interface network, she hadn't understood how different it would be to stand on a different piece of rock, with a different sky. But she shuddered to think about what would have happened had Adno not warned them of Hankori's plot. Adno had cajoled Tanoch into sending them on a supervisory visit. On arrival, their ship conveniently malfunctioned, preventing them returning. Hankori had at first insisted on rescuing them, but they made a very public plea to remain on this world, they loved it too much to leave. He had been forced to drop the matter and settle for their permanent exile from Traveler's Perch.

She had given birth to Antithikos just after they had come here. From the time Anti was old enough to recognize the world around him, this was that world, and he took to it well enough. When he was hungry, when he wanted to sleep, when he wanted to play—these became the new rhythms of their life. A few years later, just before Far Flier had undergone her transformation to female, the two of them had bred Marilon. They had both spent much time in the water while carrying the egg, hoping to acclimate Mari to it. And it had worked.

After she was born, Mari took to the water like an alaktar, the marine birds of their home world. Diver, Anti and Flier were typical of their species, broad across the shoulders and long in the arms but slight in the legs and feet. Mari was longer in the leg and shorter in the arm—that gave her a powerful kick in the water. Even her enhancements adapted themselves to be as adept in and on water as on land and in the air. For Far Flier and Diver, it was a pleasant and surprising reminder of just how flexible life can be, a message they had perhaps needed in their sometimes lonely exile.

As she trudged up the hill, Diver could see the place they'd called home for these many years. When they had come, Adno's people had adapted an underwater reef structure for them, grown from engineered corals. Diver and Flier had rigged up a system of pulleys and ramps to bring it out of the water and up here on the ridge in the middle of their small island. They had become the first intelligent land dwellers on Water Eye. Unlike their homes on Traveler's Perch, it didn't morph to meet their needs. It had taken some getting used to, living in a structure that never changed. Since then, they had changed it in little ways, decorating it with shells and branches and pieces of the bright blue stone that stuck out from the rock here and there on their island.

Her reminiscences were interrupted as her family's minds begin to brush hers. Far Flier felt like an image she had glimpsed in one of the human's minds—was it Raefe or Lina?—from an Earth story about someone living all alone in a forest who kept a candle in the window in case strangers were looking for warmth in the cold nights of their winter. But there was something unsettled in her children's minds.

"My fierce mother mother," Anti greeted her. "You've been fishing."

"Fierce?" she protested. "So you only want to eat leaves now?"

"Why don't you let Adno's school bring us fish?" Mari asked. "It's nothing for them. I can even swim out to them and retrieve it so they don't need to come all the way here."

"I do let them bring us things," she said. "I let them bring us things from the deeps and from the bottom, things we cannot get for ourselves. I like fishing."

"We should teach our children to hunt, don't you think," Flier said, laughing at the whole familiar conversation. "What kind of person is it who must ask another species to feed them?"

"The kind who lives on the world of water, father mother," shot back Anti, who was always embarrassed at his parents' insistence on their old-world rituals, a world he and Mari had never walked on.

"And who has something on his mind that he's not telling me?" Diver asked. "Out with it."

"You see children, it is exactly as I've told you," Flier laughed. "Fishing sharpens your mother's sight. We have been talking with Adno, and she brings news about the Guardians."

"Oh," Diver replied. "Good or bad?"

"Quite bad," Flier said. "Hankori has resumed his secret project and she has been able to glimpse some of the outlines of it. He wants to modify the humans. Not all of them, but she hasn't figured out why, or how many, or even how. But he has Putnomo working on it, and that wouldn't happen unless it was challenging and significant."

"He's a fool," Diver said. "Every 10,000 years or so, some madman like him steers the Guardians in that direction and it never ends well. I can't stand it! Stuck here on this island, cut off from the Guardian waveform, watching your life's work, and what was to be mine, dissolved in an acid of egotism and foolishness. Even after these eons of learning and peace, to know that this can still happen."

"We'll have to trust that Adno can prevent this," Far Flier said, but Diver could see in her eyes that she was worried as well.

"Our moms are distraught," Anti thought, letting only Mari know. "It's painful to feel them."

"Exiles on a world they don't really understand, robbed of the purpose they prepared centuries for," Mari answered. "I want to tell them that it's not as hopeless as they think."

"Yes, it's time," Anti agreed. He opened his thoughts again to his parents. "Don't count out Adno. She is more powerful than you think."

"I know you admire her," Diver said. "But she's just one person."

"No, she's not," Mari said. "She's one person among a whole school. We used to fly as flock, but even then, it was a few dozen people and we were solitary much of the time. Not Adno's people. They live their entire lives in the school, all the time. She has the wisdom and strength of her whole school, and sometimes, her whole species."

Diver suddenly understood the many small things that had puzzled her for years. "You've learned to join their waveform, Mari, haven't you?" she said.

"I always been part of it. When you and father mother would swim with me inside you before I was born, I wasn't just learning to entangle with you."

"So we are the only two people on this entire planet who are not part of this constant organic waveform?" Flier asked, her head tilted back and beak open with incredulity. She laughed a deep, long laugh.

"What's so funny?" Anti asked.

"For centuries I was the head of the Guardians, this grand, self-important, galaxywide association of highly intelligent species, and after 30 years here, I had not noticed that, in the very place where I live, evolution has taken another jump. That the technology that makes the Guardians work is not even needed here. If that's not funny, I don't know what is."

They all laughed. Diver was happy to see Flier peek out from the laconic nest she had lived in since arriving here.

"Yes, sometimes we are just straight lines for that cosmic joker, the universe, eh?" Diver said. "But that's extraordinary news. What does it mean?"

"A few things," Mari said. "One, there's hope that this is not an isolated ability that just Adno's people have. There's me, and..."

"There's me," Anti said. "When I was little, and Mari just born, I also became part of their waveform through her."

"Anything else you want to tell us while we're revealing secrets you've kept for decades?" Diver asked, trying not to be annoyed.

"Yes, some other things," Anti said with a hint of embarrassment.

"Well, let's get it straight from the source," Mari said.

They felt Adno's presence.

"I apologize for keeping you in the dark, Diver, who is my mentor, and Flier, who is my hero," she said. "But I had my reasons. When I brought you here, it was because I had learned that Hankori had actually assembled a shadow organization within the Guardians, and that they had a plan that was secret from us. I was concerned that they might have developed capabilities like my people that would allow them to mine your knowledge. I thought it best to protect you from this."

"We would never have told them," Flier said, angry and disappointed that her loyalty would be questioned.

"No, of course not," Adno said, pausing to consider her next words.

"But you might not have known you were being probed. But now, with Anti and Mari so strong, and always near you, I can hunt in the deep without worrying about this. And, to be honest, we need your wisdom and strength now, so we need you to be part of this waveform."

Adno had pieced together the outlines of Hankori's plans. He continued to see humanity as an obstacle to his grander ambitions, which still remained obscure. She had come to realize that Joe Nguyen had just been the tip of the iceberg. And now she had discovered his Hank ruse.

"And Earth? Raefe and Lina? The other, weaker entanglers?" Diver asked. "What will happen to them?"

"We are making plans with Raefe and Lina," Adno said. "Already, they have been able to make a school of 10,000 humans, thousands of them entangled. And 100 of them are acting as a single mind, charting the way forward. We will not abandon them."

Diver felt the joy of that. "I am so happy to hear that. And happy for Raefe. I remember that he was nearly mad from the voices he heard before he understood his abilities. This is a giant step forward for the humans."

"And we're behind you. Whatever we can do. We won't let Hank, or whatever Hankori hides behind, destroy it," Flier said. "Hankori will no longer glide unharried on the currents, free to dive for his prey whenever he wants."

Diver smiled. Usually she was the one to call up such ancient images. Flier was calling on her inner strengths, and Diver knew she had many. Hankori would come to regret what he had done to Far Flier, of that Diver was sure.

"You see that she is still the hunter," Anti thought later to Mari.

"You were right," Mari replied. "I get annoyed at her ferocity, I take it as her disappointment that I never learned to fly, to be the bird she sees herself as. But I see now that it wasn't about me, it was about her exile and frustration."

"They gave up everything for each other," Anti said.

"And for us, too," Mari replied. "I sort of knew that before. But I see now that it was also bigger for her and father mother—their very ideals and life's work threatened."

Anti was silent, watching the play of the wind on the endless water, little whitecaps flashing like a school of jumping silver anok fish. "We have always felt part of something bigger, too. But it was a comfort—

all we had to do was swim, so to speak, with the school…"

"…And now we must be more," Mari finished the thought. "A more we don't understand yet. A more we must become."

THE COLLECTIVE
CONSCIOUS

Dadaab
September 25, 2081

"As far as anyone knows," Lina said, "This is the first time in human history that 100 people have joined their minds together for a common purpose. Yes, we've all been to a concert or football match or some other event where everyone felt at one with everyone else there. But we will be attempting something more ambitious: creating a platform for the next phase of society. You have all been selected because you are high empaths, already able to entangle with others. For some of you, that is an everyday thing. For others, a rare treat or even something you only suspected could happen. Regardless, we will learn together.

"So let us begin with what keeps us alive—breathing. Let us breathe together as we build our waveform."

She looked around at the people in the big tent, some sitting, some standing. She began the age-old Buddhist breathing meditation, in, out, in, out. She felt the air pass over the hairs in her nose, cool, warm, cool, warm. Her mind reached out to the man sitting across from her, a giant of a man with a huge black beard, very Slavic looking. She could feel his breaths, deeper than hers, but also more labored. She reached out to the corner of the tent, where Nyssa sat with a large drum, gently striking it with her palm. Her breathing and Nyssa's were similar and the drum began to follow them. She felt the big man adjust to the drum. She could feel him reach out to others in the room, and them to others. After a few minutes, they were all breathing a little differently than on their own, and all together. Nyssa had stopped actually playing the drum, but they all sustained a drumbeat in their minds and could hear all 100 drumbeats synchronized.

"You are the conductor," Nyssa thought to everyone, "and you are the instrument. We are the orchestra."

"We are now a living waveform," Lina thought. "When you think to the group, we will know not just your words, but much more of what you are feeling as you think these things. If you speak from sadness, we will know that. If you are confused or happy or angry, we will know that."

"We have come here in emergency mode," Raefe said, "to try and do something to stop the awful forces that threaten us like floodwaters behind a weak dam. We cannot stall history much longer. Anarchists, socialists, communists, greens, libertarians, gene splicers, space colonizers, ordinary liberals, people who just meant well—despite all of their efforts, this moment of crisis has arrived, and we must make it a moment of positive decisions. A new era is upon us. Let us now put the most powerful mind in human history to the task of defining it."

***

Raefe looked at the other 99 delegates who had labored for two days on a final document of the meeting. He remembered seeing a picture of his father's high-school graduating class, all the students lined up just like the delegates. No blue gowns, and very international looking, but they had the same look on their faces. He could feel it. They sensed that their lives would now enter a new phase, that they were somehow freezing a moment in time that would only live as a memory—the moment when the world changed. Unlike his dad's picture, these delegates hoped it would change for everyone, not just them.

They had decided to speak as one, and without introduction or fanfare, they spoke in one voice, their entanglement aiding precise synchronization of their words. No microphone was needed, as a powerful grand piano of humanity spoke with only its thoughts.

"For 500 years, much of the world carried out a great social experiment that combined three core ideas: our economies should be based on private property, our governance on individual rights, and our knowledge on scientific learning. These three notions have not always been honored equally, and they were often accompanied by hypocrisy of the worst sort, but they have shaped society for centuries. While they have promised progress toward social equality, the primacy of property has often thwarted that even to the extremes of human slavery.

"But this period in our history is coming to a close. Private property has become corporate property. Corporate property has become corporate power, and corporate power has usurped individual rights. At the same time, individual rights may be exercised in ways that are not informed by scientific learning, and so we do many things, even innocently, that are harmful to us and the world. Scientific learning has been extremely effective at helping us understand the physical universe, but less adept at helping us understand our own conflicts. How can we be rational and racist? Believe in equality and subjugate women? Science has been all too quiet on this front, and all too easy for corporate power to bend to its will.

"After 500 years, we have to say that these three pillars of our world no longer provide safe supports for human life. In fact, the clash between these three pillars is part and parcel of what we now face: that human beings will die off in huge numbers, or even become extinct, as so many other species have in the last 100 years.

"We must embrace the truth.

"The age of the nation is over. Transportation and communications have rendered the concept of living and dying in the same place obsolete. People, goods, and ideas must flow freely and safely across the globe. We must develop governance systems that enable this.

"The age of private property is over. Climatic disruption has rendered the ownership of property irrelevant. How can we fight for property rights when the sea can seize our property in seconds? How can we fight for a land that can be turned into a desert as the rivers that water it dry up? What value is ownership that cannot stop these things from happening? We must develop economic systems that recognize that property rights only make sense when they support human rights, not just individual rights. The need to protect owners of capital so that they might innovate for the good of all is no longer pressing. The world is awash in capital but poor in the will to use it to address the real needs of the vast majority of humans. The goal of commerce must shift from making profit for owners to making life better for everyone.

"The age of social rights must begin. Science has shown us that human beings have many differences among them, but none that make one human being entitled to claim a better life than others. We must develop economic and political systems that ensure every human's right to clean water, sufficient food and the same access to health care, education and other social benefits as any other person. Every person is socially equal to every other person on Earth, and no laws or customs should abridge those rights.

"A new age of human science is needed. Today, we know that rationality and logic are powerful tools to understand nature. They've shown us that our minds don't only think in that mode. We, along with other animals, have deep mechanisms of both empathy and antipathy, as well as other emotions that strongly influence our behavior, often without us realizing it. We must develop the wisdom to better understand ourselves so that we do not destroy ourselves.

"Nor can our newfound knowledge of how to manipulate our own genes be used to create greater inequality among us. We do anticipate that artificial intelligence and perhaps even artificial life will become more powerful and possible, but we insist that society as a whole has the right and responsibility to decide how to use these new capabilities. They too, cannot become another reason for inequality.

"For that reason, we reject the notion, increasingly powerful among our elites, that space travel is our only hope. Space travel is a hope that can only be fulfilled for a few thousand people in this century, maybe a few tens of thousands in the next. Someday, humanity will outgrow this home. But today, we must save it together.

"A new age of human collaboration is needed. In the last decades, our ancient sense that we are somehow linked together has been confirmed. Now, hundreds of thousands of people around the world have become empaths, able to sense much more deeply each other's thoughts and feelings. This capacity, latent in many, if not all, of us, has led to peace and collaboration among people who formerly engaged in great violence, even genocide, toward each other. We call on people everywhere to support deep exploration of our empathic abilities, from the underlying physics to the day to day practices that enhance their use. Even if we cannot all master this ability, we can agree that in the balance between collaboration and competition, collaboration must be given priority if we are to survive.

"We believe that all of these goals are reachable and that the next centuries will be marked by the struggle to reach them. There are likely many ways to achieve them. We urge all people working for change to measure their efforts by how they advance toward this new world, and we offer our support to all those who contribute to that advance. Nature has given us the ability to evolve, and now it is up to us to do that.

"Toward that end, we proclaim a new free association of people to be known as the Citizens of Everywhere, whose goal is nothing less than the global transformation of human society to a new level of collaboration, peace, justice, and well-being."

Raefe's first thought was that he wished Kiko and Kayam, their old friends from the TinyStack, were here, and he began to cry, to mourn for the first time the world he had left, the world that had never had a chance to hear this. Sadness began to turn to joy as he heard the first claps, and then the cheers, and then all 10,000 of them chanting "Everywhere! Everywhere!" as their minds came together with a new sense of hope.

A NEW JOB

Green was pretty sure Hankori was up to something, asking to meet at that out-of-the-way café he seemed to reserve for moments when he was feeling particularly dramatic. Most likely, he had worked himself into a lather over the latest news from Earth.

Adno had ensured that news of the so-called Congress of the Dispossed made it not only to the Council, but the entire Guardian organization and as much of the populace of the Guardian worlds as possible. People on all the worlds were buzzing about the possibility of a new civilization someday joining them. That had to push Hankori's buttons. Every time it seemed like the humans were about to drown themselves or blow themselves up once and for all, they found a way to pull back from the brink.

Hankori would blame it on Far Flier and Diver, as he always did. Green could not understand his obsession with Far Flier, nor his enmity toward Diver. They had made mistakes, but they had done the honorable thing and retired to Water Eye. *Leave well enough alone,* he thought. He stepped off the train. There was Hankori, sitting at his favorite table near the edge of the cliffs. Immediately, he knew that Hankori had sensed his displeasure at having to make the trip out here to Cresilon's old plaza.

"You feel my impatience and wonder why," Green said after ordering a bitter tea. "I'm guessing that you are upset with all of the attention Raefe is getting throughout the worlds. I wonder why Earthly matters seem to always set you off. I prefer to look forward."

"On that we agree," Hankori replied, his emotions indicating that he wasn't interested in further discussion along those lines. "I have some thoughts that I want to discuss at the next Council meeting, and I'd like your opinion. I think this moment on Earth is actually quite fortuitous."

Green sipped his tea slowly, his emotions now pulled back behind a curtain.

"What's your plan?"

"Just the beginnings of one," Hankori said. "I've come to believe that it's time that we transform the Earth project to be one of active stewardship, not just passive monitoring."

"You want to remove the ban on active interference? Why, after all of these years of opposing any effort there?"

He hid his alarm. Hankori was indeed up to something. If he was admitting to the beginnings of a plan, it meant he'd already decided on a plan and was now lining up support and assistance. Green would have to be careful about how he approached him or risk becoming a target of the plan.

"We owe them something, I feel," Hankori said. "We've mucked about in their affairs on and off, probably done more harm than good. But we can bring it to a successful conclusion."

"I thought you were just interested in any conclusion," Green said. "I always got the sense that you thought them impossibly difficult from your time as Ambassador to Earth."

"My time? No, not at all," Hankori said, as if surprised. "I was referring to the mess Diver made. Contrary to popular belief, I did not spend my time as Ambassador to Earth wandering around in ignorance. Yes, a few things backfired badly. But I put in place initiatives that are just now bearing fruit. For example, one of the wealthiest men on Earth now considers it commonplace to converse with a voice in his head named Hank. He's grown quite fond of Hank and values his advice highly. Why not? I've given him knowledge no one else on Earth has, and it's made him fabulously rich and quite powerful. Of course, he doesn't know that Hank is me, an alien from an advanced civilization 20 light years distant."

Green stared at him for a moment, absorbing the notion that Hankori had been secretly involved somehow in Earth since his Ambassadorship more than 100 years ago. Every time he wanted to trust the man, something like this caused him the deepest of doubts.

"You are troubled," Hankori said. "You think it was wrong of me to do this on my own. But I have always been clear that leaders must lead, from wherever they can. This is not about me. I turn this project over to you with no reservation."

Ah, Hankori wanted plausible deniability.

"And what is it you want me to do?"

Hankori sent his mind some numbers. Thinking the numbers was like saying a code, and soon, his enhancements had accessed Hankori's plan and decrypted the contents. Unbelievably, he wanted to give the humans longer lives, bigger brains, nano meds and more. Green was to analyze various timelines where some of those had occurred naturally or through the humans' own efforts and determine which were most effective. Putnomo would then create a delivery system that worked through the wormhole.

Green was stunned. Hankori wanted to give them thousands of years of social development and biological evolution, all written in a recipe, as if it were one of their food concoctions. The humans could manufacture it and administer it like a cure for a mild infection.

"Hankori, you know this will create chaos on Earth. A society has to slowly absorb these sorts of advances. How will they suddenly feed and house people who live hundreds of years while new people are being born all the time? How will their economy adapt? No world has ever gone from theirs to this overnight, especially with 12 billion people."

"Absolutely correct,' Hankori said, as if Green had answered a test question correctly. "But you mistake my intent. Earth is not going to have 12 billion people for long, despite all the optimism about Raefe's progress. I don't believe they have more than a decade or two before they destroy themselves. I'm more worried about saving the best million of them with this program."

We are really in uncharted territory now, Green thought. And what more secrets is this man hiding? Now was not the time to argue or sound the alarm. He needed to think long and hard about next steps.

"You've given me a lot to sort through. I'll let you know what I come up with."

HIGH-LEVEL MEETINGS

Lausanne, Switzerland
October 14, 2081

Billy Warren could never get used to the Swiss. They took an inordinate pride in being small and disconnected from everything around them. Their happiest moments seemed to be when you handed them money—plastic, electronic, or paper, it didn't matter. He understood the emotion, but they seemed to have little ambition to do anything with it except accumulate it. Where was their creative spirit? Where were the mines, the bridges, the buildings? He'd be bored to tears living here.

Still, it had a similar harsh beauty to the West Virginia country he had spent his life in. Looking over Lake Geneva at sunset, the view was gorgeous, if empty. No boats and certainly no swimmers marred its surface. The mountains of the southern shore were reflected in almost perfect fidelity on its cold, still surface. With the Gulf Stream submerging, the storms that had brought the northern British Isles to their knees had still had enough in them to whiten the tops of the high Alps, glistening in the distance. If you wanted to, you could mistake them for glaciers.

The fate of the glaciers was not his concern. They had come, they had gone, life would go on. And someone would have to be at the top of that pile of life. That was a contest he understood, relished. Tomorrow, he would lead 14 of the most powerful businessmen and -women in the world toward victory in that struggle.

He felt a sort of mental throat clearing that usually announced Hank's arrival in his thoughts.

"You are ready, I see."

"Indeed," Warren thought. "We have a strong hand in the negotiations. Any poker player will tell you, the best cards bring the best luck."

He had gotten used to these dialogs with the voice who called himself Hank. At first, he thought he might be going crazy. But over time,

Hank had definitely given him insights and information that he could never know on his own. He had decided that Hank was some kind of super-hacker who had found his way into his MindsEye, the top of the line puter implants that people of his station owned.

"Who do you fear the most at these talks?" Hank asked.

"Fear? I don't really fear any of them. We're all basically on the same side. But if you mean, who's most likely to oppose me, it's the Euros, hands down. They still think we can make some kind of grand deal, some kind of hybrid between old-fashioned governments and corporate states. They're always going on about how they pioneered that idea back in the 20th century."

"It didn't work then either. All it did was submerge the elite in a morass of mediocrity," Hank said. "Held humanity back."

"Try telling them that."

"No, no point, I agree," Hank replied. "But I think we have some aces up our sleeves."

And before Billy could ask what, Hank did one of those fire-hose brain fills he sometimes did. Billy's mind was flooded with a vision of a new order, of superhuman leaders who were nearly immortal.

"This should be an effective argument for you," Hank said. "This is what the people here today could become if they adopt your plan. In the coming weeks, I'll be sending you more detailed instructions on how to create this technology. You'll need to enlist Ken Robertson to build it."

Hank had given him a hand full of aces, and no one could top them. He walked back to his room and watched a vid. By 11, he was sleeping like a baby.

In the morning, they all gathered on the far terrace, the sun now just peeking over the distant mountains. They had rented the hotel in its entirety, no tourists, traveling salesmen, or prying journalists. They all had MindsEyes, no need for assistants cluttering up the meeting.

Billy looked around at the group. There was Alden Hayashi, who commanded a powerful set of Pacific Rim financial services firms that was the only realistic counterweight to the Chinese government in the region. From the Americas, Mario Munoz had amassed a fortune in financial services and privatized governmental services throughout the US, Canada, Mexico, and the smaller Central American countries. Robertson, of course, whose DigiBrands represented a century of mergers between ancient tech giants like Apple and Microsoft and a host of consumer products and communications companies. Ilana Romero ran Brazil's PetroBras empire—one of his main competitors in the resource industries—but also a string of South American telecommunications and biotech manufacturing companies.

The Euros had a committee of five men and women, a mix of old and new money, that were backed by Daimler Siemens, Philips DeMag, Fiat, United Financial Services, and several other large Euro conglomerates. Wang Ya Chen presided over China's giant mining, manufacturing, and electronics concerns. Adnan Arjan led more than 1,000 companies that dominated the Indian subcontinent, as well as parts of the Middle East and East Africa. Prince Ibn bin Ibn held the keys to the Saudi royal treasury, which had managed to survive the decline of oil and now had its fingers in many pies throughout the Middle East, Africa, and around the world. And Susan Mbuto owned many different businesses throughout sub-Saharan Africa.

"Ladies and gentlemen, let's get started," Billy said. "It's been a while since we've met, and I think we all feel that we are approaching a turning point. We've continued to make progress in replacing traditional governments, but recently we have seen a new kind of opposition, in fact several new kinds. Can someone from Europe fill us in on the Holland issue?"

Dieter Freundlich had been wearing a hole in his seat waiting for his chance. While it was already a couple of years since the part of the Netherlands that included Amsterdam had been islanded by rising seas, the impact was still being felt, he explained. The new island had declared itself the independent Republic of Holland and was granting citizenships to anyone in the world. In exchange for paying modest taxes to the republic, these citizens gained a social safety net, legal status, and a willing defender of their rights. They were now the fastest-growing country in what used to be known as the developed world. And they were draining potential revenue from all the large Euro corpos.

"But isn't Holland likely to attract citizens who are a revenue loss?" Robertson asked, puzzled. "Take out more in social benefits than they put in?"

"Yes, but that's not our problem. You are confusing us with what's left of the European Union," Ericka Weinsberg of Daimler Siemens said. "We have achieved something like your autonomous zones in North America with very few social obligations. We may collect less revenue than you do, but we still do collect some, and it adds up."

"As well, it creates a very difficult situation to navigate," Freundlich continued. "Everywhere we operate as a company now, we have a strong position, and we have a single adversary—the local government. Now there is a third party, Holland. As a former nation state, they understand our moves and motives, and they are able to play our game, divide and conquer, some of the time."

"Only if you let them, right?" Warren interjected. Could these Euros really be afraid of slogans and t-shirts? "What armies does Holland have to back up their claims?"

"Well, I think that's the point, Billy," Freundlich said. "The whole country is potentially an army, with troops everywhere."

Wang Ya Chen reported that the Chinese government was particularly concerned about the concept of Holland guaranteeing citizens' rights wherever they lived. His group encouraged the Chinese government to pursue a policy of opposition, with the side benefit of diverting the government's energies from their incessant campaign to dominate his companies.

"Is that a generally acceptable strategy, then, to encourage the local governments to clamp down on Hollanders within their borders?" Warren was growing weary of this topic. The Euro delegates had hoped for a more vigorous united response, but looked at each other and nodded agreement. "Ok, let's move on. Mbuto?"

"We sympathize with our European colleagues. Africa is also seeing some wild cards. The biggest of these has just concluded a meeting of 10,000 people in Dadaab. They claim to have 70 million members globally. I believe they will solve the Holland problem, in a way. Holland will join this new group, which calls itself Everywhere and also offers a universal citizenship. But they are much more ambitious."

Her MindsEye broadcast to theirs a report on the Dadaab meeting, including their new mission statement.

"These people ever set foot in my territory, I'll shoot 'em on sight," Warren growled.

"Their leader is actually from America," Mbuto said, "Raefe Epstein Miller. Although he married an Afro-Chinese woman 30 years ago and has traveled the world ever since. He's a bit of a mystery."

"We see his followers in our country," Romero said. "He's worked with Favelas United, coffee-worker groups, all sorts of marginalized people. Mario, you must see his followers in Mexico, no?"

"Yes," Munoz said. "For a while, they called him El Poco Jesus—

the Little Jesus—but he made them stop."

"The mullahs have kept him out of Iran," Adnan said. "What is it that his followers are attracted to?"

"He preaches empathy as a strategy to build a new type of society," Mbuto said. "His followers say he teaches you to look into people's hearts and know what they really feel."

This was all old news to Warren. If only he and Robertson had succeeded 30 years ago in killing the kid, they might not be having this conversation. Still, he was just one weird guy.

"Jesus wept," Warren said. "Are we getting weak-kneed over some guy who reads palms now?"

"We had that attitude, too," Hayashi said. "But I don't think we can afford to anymore. He's wreaked havoc in Asia."

About five years ago, Miller showed up in Japan. Before he arrived millions of people lived along the coastline, fishing, living in boats. They were organized along ethnic lines: Chinese, Japanese, Filipino, Malay, Korean, Taiwanese. They fought each other often enough to neutralize them as a threat either to corporate or state power. Miller had gone from port to port, preaching this empathy. Now, if you went to the coast, you'd see thousands of boats flying the Rising Tide flag, ethnic rivalries gone. And they were hostile to corporate powers.

"That seems to be what he's trying to do with Everywhere," Mbuto said. "His wife helped form it, too. She was part of Citizens of Nowhere, but it was a very small group when she joined 30 years ago. Now, well, you see they pulled together a meeting of 10,000 people. Not a demonstration, a meeting. The people were sent by other groups to attend. So it's really a much larger and widely dispersed group they represent."

"Well, this sounds like a problem for our security team, eh?" Warren said. Heads nodded. That was them giving assent to whatever was necessary to neutralize this odd threat. "Ken, can you have Brightstar liaise with everyone else's security people and come up with a plan?"

"Sure," Robertson said. Warren would talk to him later. They'd put a stop to this guy quick, this whole movement would collapse. That was the beauty of hero cults. Take the hero out, there was no cult.

"All right, I think we've covered the high-attention items we had on the agenda before the meeting. Some things have come up just recently, though, and I'm going to exercise host's prerogative to put some new things out there. Ken, I think it's time for your presentation."

"Thanks, Billy. As leaders of various corporate states, we've all been faced with multiple challenges. You've all confirmed, though, what is our most serious challenge—alternative citizenship that promises them both material benefits and a sense of belonging. I put to you that we have to compete on that playing field, and Billy and I have a proposal that does just that."

The room was silent for a minute as their implants processed his proposal. They would form a new global corporate state called Liberty. Unlike Holland, only the people they picked could be members. And their goal was to concentrate power, not to expand membership.

"I think this is brilliant, Ken," said Hayashi.

"Thanks," Robertson replied. "You will all note that Liberty is specifically designed to cripple our opponents' funding. Citizens of Liberty must pledge not to pay taxes to any other entity. We want to ensure that Holland does not recruit too many high wealth people by appealing to their do-gooder side."

"Your proposal indicates that Liberty's governance will be by executive committee of this body as founders," Freundlich said. "No messy, ultra-democratic parliament. So it differs from Holland in that way. But how does it differ as far as benefits to its citizens go?"

"It's a totally different beast," Robertson said. "It's clear from the start that Liberty will protect private property and not interfere with personal freedoms. But it will also not be a welfare state. Citizens will have to provide for themselves, but they won't have to provide for large numbers of unproductive people. It's a nation of doers."

"I'm not sure that makes it competitive with Holland," Freundlich replied. "And in some ways, it sounds like another Citizens of Nowhere, just with an annual membership fee. They have neither that nor taxes."

"Property, Gerhard." Billy said. "We protect their property. We will be the last great protection for those who have bothered to accumulate property. Don't you think the world's property owners will welcome the chance to right the ship and stop the never-ending assault on their rights? Surely, they'll see that's the only way to continue to grow as a society, to restore the profit motive to some place of pride?"

"Agreed," Adnan Arjan said. "But we are putting this approach into what is basically a hostile environment. We won't win everyone over. There will be multiple futures out there for the taking for some time."

"We don't have that kind of luxury," Wang Ya Chen said. "We're looking at massive relocations from our most developed, populous areas—hundreds of millions of people in China alone —and to many places that are strained for water or other resources. That will not happen easily or peacefully."

"Let's not get carried away," Warren said. "We're not here to solve the entire world's problems—just ours. Liberty is designed to stanch the wound while we prepare the second phase."

"Right," Robertson said. "If you look past the first five to 10 years of the plan, you'll see that we anticipate only partial success. We expect that we will recruit several hundred million of the world's wealthiest people to Liberty. That will give us both legitimacy and power to fend off local opposition for some time. As of now, there is no coordinated international opposition that can oppose us in a forceful manner."

"And when they do?" asked Illana Romero. "Because in South America, we fully expect the Capoiera Communal to challenge us."

"Well, we haven't completed the Phase 2 plan yet, but the outlines are simple," Robertson said. "We divert some of the revenue we collect from citizens to build self-sustaining, underground communities in secret. Once we've gotten about 50 percent of the way with that, we accelerate it by threatening to disrupt the key goods and services our businesses provide outside the corporate states if governments and other entities don't pay us higher fees."

"And when they stop paying?" Romero asked.

"Look, we can play Ouija here all day," Warren interjected. "Long story short—the wealthiest people in the world are going to build themselves private underground luxury cities and disappear while the rest of humanity tears itself apart fighting over a shrinking pie. After a century or so, we'll resurface and the whole world will be Liberty. We can reclaim the Earth, and forget these crazy ideas about going to other planets."

"And who will do all of this?" Freundlich asked. "Who will build these cities, keep them running? Where will all those laborers come from?"

"That's easy," Robertson said. "They'll come from my factories and yours. At long last, we'll have a world where robots do all the work. We'll cut deals with engineering talent to let them work off their membership fees so that we can continue to develop the software, but other than that, it'll be robots making robots to do what we need them to do."

"But what if humanity hangs on?" Freundlich asked. "What if after a few generations, sure many have died, but many remain and are not willing to give up?"

"This is a very interesting discussion, but I think I can contribute a clincher to it," Warren said, "Ken and I have been working with some amazing scientists who can make being a Liberty citizen a very long-lived proposition for those who merit it. And that will guarantee a stable core of like-minded people who can guide Liberty through the difficult times ahead."

"What are you saying?" Freundlich asked. "That you have some kind of fountain of youth drug?"

"Much more than that," Warren said. "I'm beaming you a description of a package of technologies that will enhance any human who installs them. We won't know how long we can live until we actually use them, but more than 300 years is a safe bet, and it could range higher than 1,000. And that's without the mental and physical decay we now expect in our later years."

The room was quiet as they absorbed the news. Questions swirled in their minds, but no one wanted to say no to the prospects Warren had introduced.

"Well, if there are no objections," Warren said. "Let's move on to talking about how to implement this plan."

URBAN RENEWAL

Newcastle, Northern England
October 28, 2081

In the month since Dadaab, Raefe had been trying to strike while the iron was hot and make some leaps forward. He was eager to follow the Everywhere declaration out in the world, to rally people around it. After 30 years, he felt that they were on the verge of something huge, and he wasn't going to just sit in Dadaab and bask in the glory of it.

Their movement had taken root among the traditionally dispossessed of the modern world, often the poor of the old colonized world. Where Everywhere would still be challenged was in the former empires of Europe and the United States. There, empathy battled privilege, or even just the illusion of it, for supremacy in people's hearts. In Dadaab, they had all leaned away from getting in the middle of that fight. But many people had come from those places to the summit. So Raefe had come to Newcastle as a further step toward becoming a fully global movement.

Gordon Brown, the leader of the Urban Gypsies, had been at Dadaab representing Northern England. The Gypsies had been around Newcastle for about 10 years, heavily influenced by the New Voodo Army's example of economic self-sufficiency. They tried to rally the urban poor to organize their own benevolent economy within the belly of the beast, as they referred to ordinary capitalism. And they had made progress but still faced an uphill battle. It was Brown's idea for Raefe to come, and he had eagerly accepted the invitation.

"Lads, you all know of Raefe Epstein Miller," Brown introduce him. "We talked at the Everywhere meet, and I asked him to come and help us sort out our next steps. So now that he's here, what do we think is holding us back?"

"Bloody Northern Guard, that's what's in the way," a young woman said in a thick Scottish accent. "Sorry, I'm Claire. We spent years here in the shadows, building up a whole way of life. We put pressure on the government, on the big corpos, we just had one demand: If you're not using it, give it to the people. We took old buildings, old telecoms, anything they weren't making a profit on, and we turned it into stuff people could use. No charge. We trained people to maintain it. And we were making a difference. Then the bleeding Northern Guard came along."

Brown explained that about 100 years ago, the London government decided the North was a cancer on the United Kingdom. After years of neglect, Brian McDornish, a local Manchester pol, got the idea in 2063 of Northern England for the Northerners. He blew up a few London bank branches and became a local hero.

"C'mon, Gordo, he did more than that," a dark-skinned man in his forties named Ganesh said. "I was with McDornish in the early days. Everyone in our block was. Northern pride! Yeah, he had the Hindus and the Geordies and whoever else singing songs, instead of trashing pubs every night."

"Well, it's true," Gordo said. "But it turned to shite fast enough. Two things happened: Southern England was taken over 100 percent by the corpos, and they drew a line from the Wash down to the Bristol Channel and said, 'Everyone north of there, you're on your own, you poor bastards.' Just like that, we were Brexited from the United Kingdom. And then McDornish, he saw himself bringing a new Saxon order to the North. He declared the Republic of Northern England with himself as chieftain. England for the English and all that. That was back in 2073."

"And now?" Raefe asked. "He wants the Gypsies to pay tribute?"

"Exactly," Claire said. "Last fall the Newcastle Shipping Company decommissioned a cargotainer ship. The Gypsies got the idea that is could be housing for 1,000 people. The shipping company said we could have it for 30 years, free, just for taking it off its hands. But McDornish insisted we pay rent for the docking space.

"We told McDornish to stuff it," Gordo said. "A week later, there was an explosion on the ship and it sunk. No one was on board, thankfully."

"Ganesh, you said you used to be with McDornish's crowd," Raefe said. "Why not still?"

"Me and my brother, Mikey, we were street kids in Little Mumbai in '64. McDornish recruited us to be soldiers for him. Filled our heads with all this nonsense about being real Brits, not like those Muslim bastards. Us and our mates—we weren't even against the Muslims. Played football with 'em, some of us had Muslim girlfriends. But he made it seem like real Northerners, they wouldn't stand for them, so get with it."

And then Court Street Community Center happened. It was a harmless place where mostly Muslim kids played vids after school. A group of McDornish's followers set fire to it on Tuesday afternoon when it was full.

"I was there, you know," Ganesh said, and Raefe could feel he was ashamed that he hadn't done anything to stop it. "I watched those white boys cheering while the place burned, those Muslim kids trapped inside. I felt in my heart they would do the same for some other brown boys like me and Mikey when it suited them. All that talk of how we could be real Northerners, like we weren't already. Born and bred, is me and Mikey."

Raefe could feel the anger and tension in the room. How many rooms had he sat in like this the last 30 years? The frustration of the dispossessed was the same everywhere.

"Gordo, how can we make a dent in this?" Raefe asked. "Where can we find a crack between McDornish and his followers, and widen it into a crevice, and then a canyon? What about these people who would have lived on that ship? Aren't they mad about that?"

"Yeah, some are," Gordo conceded. "Even some of his Geordie followers, old Saxon stock. There's a bunch Tyneside, they were washed out by a storm surge, and they're basically homeless, living in the rubble."

"Can we get down there for a chat? You all know I'm not talking about a fight. I'm talking about empathy, understanding what's really in their hearts and their heads, and maybe even them seeing that with us. Gordo told me you all have had some training in that, but not really a chance to put it to the test. This might be the time, eh, to see what's really in their heads?"

"Don't know as I want to," said Claire. "Bloody scary what's in some of their heads."

"I know, that's our first reaction," Raefe said. "And maybe it is scary, but unless you start to understand what makes them tick, your choices are to ignore them or kill them. Both have unpleasant consequences. The dead always have mothers and brothers and children who will grow up to hate you."

"Aye," Gordo said. "Can't argue with that. Half of us are here because of what they did to our families in the past. Let's take a pass on revenge. That dish is always on offer. Let's go down Tyneside tomorrow and talk to my wife's cousins. They would have gotten space on the boat, too, so that's something to talk with them about. They're not keen on me, but they'll not kill us for fear of Janet. "

That got a big laugh—wife Janet was not to be trifled with.

"So let's do something new," Raefe said. "We'll chat, but if I give you a nod, it means I'm going to do what you've been learning about. I'm going to try and create a connection between all of us in the room, all of our emotions. If they start to freak, I'll handle it. But are you game?"

The nodded mutely, not sure what they were getting themselves into but willing to try. They left early the next day, hoping to pass across the line into McDornish territory before most of his foot soldiers had slept off their pub night, but there were some about.

"You see the Guards over on the east side of that big building?" asked Gordon, the Gypsies' leader. "They're hardcore, call themselves Vikings. Some of the others are just wankers."

Raefe looked, but he had already felt the harsh glare of violent energy coming from the small groups Gordo was pointing to. How many times in the last 30 years had he witnessed a band of desperate armed people filled with that exact feeling? Some, like the Gypsies around him, gave off a more complex set of emotions: a hope that by fighting they could end fighting, a longing to wake up without the feeling of threat all around them.

But many, like these Vikings, had drunk, long and hard, the cocktail of violence and power that seemed to be the unofficial drink of every dissolving society. It was all too easy to put a gun in someone's hands, and all too easy for armed bands to believe that guns inoculated them from the end of the world as they knew it. By the time they found out they were no more effective than the idols of the ancients, it would be too late.

They walked in the shadows of abandoned buildings down a long avenue going toward the Tyne. Downhill toward the water had been the worst address in many places since the glaciers had started falling into the sea, and this was no exception. The buildings had been flooded multiple times, although now they were dry. Toward the end of the avenue, there was a small courtyard, with apartments all around it. The first floors were empty. Gordo took Raefe and Claire and Ganesh up the stairs. Raefe could feel eyes from all corners, wisps of contempt and fear but also inner conflict. Some people wanted to like them, he could feel, except they had been told not to.

The stair opened up to a little landing, and off the landing, a neat room about four meters square. Janet's sister Margaret, a pale woman in her late twenties, stood in the doorway.

"Gordon Brown," she said. "Janet said you'd be here. With friends. Come in." She waved them in with her hand. A bunch of relatives and neighbors sat on folding chairs, balancing tea cups, making small talk.

"Janet says you want to talk to us about burying the hatchet," Margaret's husband, Sean, said, moving past the pleasantries. "You're wanting us to put in a word with the Guard for you?"

Raefe could feel that Sean wasn't totally sincere, but he wasn't sure about what. It felt like they were being tested. What was the bottom line here, Sean wanted to know. Were they here to surrender?

"With the Guard, maybe, yeah," Gordo said. Raefe could feel he didn't mean it, but had decided to defer that issue. "But mostly, we're thinking, hey, it's a shite life right now and we're all in it. Hard enough to find kip and keep dry. What are we fighting about?"

"McDornish says you're not for the Northern Republic. Maybe you're for those bloodsuckers in the South." Raefe could feel Sean was calm, a bit proud, a bit stubborn.

"Sorry, could I just ask? I'm new here," Raefe said. "It's really me that wanted to meet with you all. I know Gordo from the Gypsies and all that. But when you say 'for the North,' what's that mean to you?"

"You know, build up the North," Silvia said. She had the look they had when they passed their mid-twenties, a deepness under the eyes, a permanent frown starting to set in the eyebrows. "We've had centuries of neglect up here. Then the South basically threw us out. So now we're on our own. All for one, and such."

"Well, I heard about the ship that the Urban Gypsies were fitting up for people to live in," Raefe said. "But now I hear it was blown up. What was that about?"

He had played dumb on who blew it up. He wanted to give them space to tell their own version. If nothing else, he was curious what they had been told.

"Don't you know?" Margaret asked. Raefe felt it more as "how dumb are you?"

"We hear different things," Gordo said. "What do you think happened?"

"Your lot blew it up," a man named Ron said. "Didn't want to pay your taxes. And you want to blame it on McDornish, make him look bad."

He said it without rancor, but behind the voice Raefe could feel that Ron was McDornish's man in this group. He had the Northern cross tattooed on the back of his neck, a blending of the Celtic cross and the Nazi Iron Cross. It was the Northern Guard's emblem, but before them, it had been a popular local symbol going back to the days of NeoSkinheads. How long had he had it? Raefe couldn't tell. He could feel the Gypsies bristle at his display of loyalty. Gordo's band was struggling to control themselves.

"Well, I can tell you we didn't," Gordo said. "On my children's lives."

Raefe could feel Ron weighing whether to call Gordo a liar, and Gordo cocked like a pistol in case he did.

"See, here's the thing I came here to try and understand," Raefe said. "A thousand people could have gotten out of the flood zone, gotten a decent bed to lie in, sleep without worrying. How could either side think that paying a tax, or not paying a tax, or getting credit or not getting credit, or any such bullshit, was more important than that?"

Ron had clammed up. He was angry, but words weren't his battlefield.

"I can see that you're not from around here," Silvia said. "Or you'd know that who's to blame is always what people here care most about."

"Because mostly, things go ass-up here and somebody is always to blame, right?" Raefe said. "Somebody except the people who created the mess in the first place."

"You sure you're not from here?" Silvia said, laughing.

"I'm from a hundred heres," Raefe said, smiling. "You'd be surprised how not-unusual this place is."

"Never been nowhere else," Silvia said. Raefe could feel she was reasserting her privilege as a local. Ron looked bored, said he was going out for a smoke.

"Hey, we've not met," Claire said. "I'm Claire. I'll save you the trouble: born in Scotland, lived here since '73. We all have our list of those to blame. We all know we've got some of it right and some of it wrong. And we don't usually want to be told which is which. Right?"

"Sure," Silvia said.

"But here's the thing," Claire said. "How are either the Guard or the Gypsies to blame for the Tyne taking our homes and flats? I mean, maybe those wankers in London, sort of, but how are we to blame for that?"

Raefe felt the silence as thoughtfulness. Claire had gotten them past the posturing, she had sensed a way in. He could feel that she knew it, and she was excited by it.

"She's got a point," Sean said. "It's bigger than either side."

"It is," Ganesh said, quiet until now. "But it's not so big that we can't do something about it. That's all we're after. Right now, we can't get nothing done because of the Guard. We just want a stand down. We don't make no money off of these projects, so we got nothing to pay the tax. And not to get too technical, but there's no law says we have to."

There was a bit of a giggle. Raefe realized they all thought that following the law was a humorous idea. When had the law ever helped them? Ganesh had understood that and played that part down enough without surrendering it.

"'Cept when someone's holding a gun on you, then it is a law," Gordo said. "So we know you all think the world of Brian and you're proud of the North standing up. We just want it to be a real stand up, something more than a football song. We want it to mean we live better. Brian will make his own way, never you mind, but down here in Newcastle, we need to make ours, too."

Raefe could feel that the ice thinning from the Tynesiders. They were impressed that the Gypsies had stood their ground without turning it into a punch up. And the Gypsies could sense that, even with their rudimentary training. He was impressed by how Claire had broken the problem down, how Ganesh had focused the conflict down to something manageable, and how Gordo had appealed to their best instincts. Now was the time to take it to the next level—he nodded to the Gypsies. It felt corny as hell, but he knew what followed could be life-changing for them.

It only took him a few seconds to find their minds and begin to entangle with all of the Northerners. For now, he would have to be a hub, connecting all of them through him. He let them feel the sincerity of Gordo's last statements about Brian and Newcastle. They'd seen that he didn't like McDornish at all, but that he would go down fighting

for Newcastle and everyone in the room if it came to that. Someone let
out a small gasp.

"What was that?" Silvia said, a startled look on her face.

"You're feeling Gordo's emotions," Raefe said. "You've heard of empaths, right?"

They all nodded.

"I'm one," he said. "I've been working with the Gypsies to help
them understand that we all have much more in common than what
divides us. I know, you've heard that before. But have you felt it? Deep
in your gut? That's when we get past the 'How do I know you're not
lying?' part."

Sylvia stared at Gordo. "You have kids, don't you? I can feel that
you carry that weight. And that you miss them. Don't you see them?"

Gordo stared at the floor, weighing his words. He looked up, his
cheeks hardened but his eyes shiny-moist.

"They're gone. Superflu epidemic in '78."

"It's why you're so angry at the Guard," Margaret said. "I never
realized that before."

She turned to Silvia. "Janet tried to get them treatment, but at that
time, you couldn't get a Health Services card for Northern England unless you swore allegiance to the Guard. And he's too proud to do that
if he doesn't mean it."

"And you don't all mean it," Claire said. "I see that now. You want
it to be true, all that Northern pride stuff, but you have your doubts."

"But we all do what we have to do to get over," Ganesh said. "And
then we try to be hard about it, because it hurts to admit we've been
made to do something we didn't really want to do."

The room was quiet, just the city's sounds in the distance. Raefe
had been around this block before and this time it was going well. Every step forward brought the possibility of a step backward, but not the
inevitability. And he could feel that this place would never be quite the
same after today. The Gypsies were ripe for this, they had been hungry
for it.

"Well, it's something to get used to," Sean said. "But I see now that
it's rubbish that you Gypsies are just losers and druggies trying to wreck
the Northern Guard. I can feel what pains you, and it's not a hell of
a lot different than our lot. That's a start. I feel like maybe we've been
looking at things the wrong way."

Several heads nodded.

"Just rubbish," Ron said. "Or witchcraft."

Oh, Ron, Raefe thought. *You really don't understand. Now they can feel your defensiveness, how you're worried that all the favors McDornish promised you might evaporate. They can feel your selfishness, not your dedication to the cause.* The ground had just shifted from allegiance to McDornish to allegiance to each other, and Ron had missed it. Raefe had seen this, too, many times before and always felt the same sadness for the people who couldn't let go and join the waveform.

"Funny, Ron," Silvia said. "Witchcraft, really? Feels natural to me, like when you have a close mate and you can see on their face or how they walk what's eating them. Only more so. Why are you so dead against it? Maybe they're on to something, maybe we were meant to know this about each other. I'm all for the Northern Guard, but who's to say they have all the answers? Maybe there are other ways, too. Doesn't have to be all one way, does it? How does that help us?'

"Jesus Ron, what have you done?" Margaret yelled suddenly.

Raefe felt it too. Ron was thinking about danger and how to save himself. He had set them up somehow. He had a mental image of a man looking through a gun sight. The glass cracked and there was a thud just behind Raefe's head. He started to yell a warning, but everyone in the room knew what gunfire sounded like. They all hit the floor.

He thought to Gordo, "What now?" but everyone in the room heard it.

"We'll get you out of here," Sean said. "We'll be fine. It's you they want, I'm thinking. Silvia, take them out the back!"

Silvia was pulling Raefe's wrist, Sean rolled across the floor toward her and the stairs. He sensed their plan and nodded, the three of them bolting down the stairs with Gordo following through twisted half ruined alleys. Sean must have grown up here, Raefe thought, he runs through here like a child at play. He could feel the anger Sean had at Ron.

"We were blind," Silvia said, sensing what he had. "We've got a lot to sort out now. I can take you to the edge of the district. I don't know if we'll ever meet again, but if we do, it will be as friends."

OUT FOR A DRIVE

October 28, 2081

Silvia had taken them out of Tyneside, and now Raefe, Ganesh, Claire and Gordo were back in Urban Gypsies territory. Now it was Raefe who was feeling the same fear that he had read in so many other war-zone victims. He had been around fighting on and off in his years in Dadaab, but he had never personally felt what it was to be like when someone was firing at you, trying to kill you. He remembered that Alton's friends had rescued him from an attempt by Joe Nguyen, but no shots were fired then. That was as close as he had come.

"You're mighty calm," Claire said.

"Far from it. I've sensed this feeling in hundreds, maybe thousands, of people over the years. Not the same when you're feeling it yourself."

"Seeing yourself through a sniperscope?" Gordo said, and Raefe knew he was asking from personal experience.

"Honestly, I feel like I'm wearing crosshairs on my forehead, like a new tattoo."

Claire put her finger up in a "wait" gesture. She pulled a small device out of her pocket. It took Raefe a second to realize it was a very old Voice, before they made them to fit in your ear. She held it up to her hear and listened and grunted and listened and grunted for a few cycles.

"Right," she said. "Plan C, just in case they're on to Plan B. We're to get you out of here, go south. You're not safe in the North anymore. And after the Guard find out you've been turning their supporters—that was brilliant, by the way—you'll be even less safe. We have a few friends in the Guard—keeping their options open—and they say someone's put Brian on to you. That wasn't a random shooting back there. The Viking Squad, Brian's best, have been sent out to find and kill you. Must have hit a nerve with your Everywhere theme song." And she started singing "Wet Feet in the Sand" as if she was on a Net singing contest. Ganesh cracked up.

"Don't let her kid you," Gordo said. "She's shite with a gun, too lazy to work. We just keep her around for laughs."

"Seriously, though," she said. "We can get you to the border, but getting over it will be tough. Can your lot help? Any friends in the South?"

The few they had were scattered and disorganized. Raefe remembered a boy from Dadaab who fancied Nyssa when they were teenagers. He had gone off to the University of Lagos and been seduced by United Financial Services in London.

"Maybe. Give me a few minutes to think this through."

He found Lina's waveform.

"Things have gotten ugly up here. The Urban Gypsies are doing good work but government here is little more than organized thugs. Someone took a shot at me."

"No! I can feel you were not wounded, but you are hurt."

"Yeah, I've felt this in so many other people. We can always talk about how people hate us, but when someone actually tries to kill you, it's deeply shocking. In my head, I know that happened before, with Joe. But it seemed like a robot was trying to kill me, or at least that's how I chose to think of it. So yeah, I'm a bit shook up. But, hey, they missed. I think I sensed someone aiming at me and leaned instinctually."

"The survival value of empathy. But this is new, eh? The Northern Guard would never target you on their own, I don't think. They're not exactly checking the Net for news of the world, is my guess. Which means someone, somewhere else, asked them to."

"You may well be right, although I didn't sense that from anyone there. Meanwhile, the Gypsies want to get me out of Northern England, go to the South. Do we have any contacts there that can help? I can show my fake passport at the border and maybe get in, but I won't last long down there just on that. You know what kind of identity tracking and surveillance the corpos have in the UK."

"You're thinking of Manfred?"

"Right! Couldn't remember his name. Does she keep touch with him?"

"On and off, now and then. He's married, midlevel in UFS, not happy she tells me."

"Well, here's a chance to act on that unhappiness. Talk to her and see what you guys can come up with. Try not to scare her, if you can avoid it. Anyway, we're probably headed out of town shortly."

He turned to Gordon and Claire.

"Let's say we do have a contact and they can help us. We're working on the details. What now?"

"Hang on," Claire said. "You called your people? You have one of them fancy subvoc Voices implants?"

"Claire," Gordo said. "He does it with his mind. Empathy. That's what I've been trying to tell you all these years."

"Thought it was just hype until now," Claire said. "I mean, I felt it all in that room Tyneside, but I thought that was the size of it. You can teach us that?"

"Some people can learn," Raefe said. "My wife and I have a very strong bond. Most people can't do that over distances like we can. Not yet. But with people you can see? Yes, if you have the inner abilities. And you both do. I could feel that you were able to sense those peoples' feelings up in Tyneside. But we can always teach you to be more aware of what other people feel. Everyone can learn that."

"Maybe we'll play tricksies on the go," Claire said. "Let's get moving out of Newcastle at least."

SOUNDING THE ALARM

Dadaab
October 28, 2081

Nyssa was angry with Raefe. He always treated her and her brother, Des, like little kids. They had tried to talk him into letting them go to Newcastle with him, but he shut them off. Yes, they were all empaths, so she knew he was being protective. And he knew she resented it. And none of that had changed his mind. But now he needed her and Des.

"Dad's in trouble," Nyssa said. "He's in Newcastle with the Urban Gypsies and someone's shot at him."

"Isn't someone always shooting at someone in Newcastle?" Des said.

"Yes, but it's not random. The Gypsies have intel that someone's put a hit on him. They need to get him out. Mom wants me to see if Manfred can help."

"Will he?"

"Maybe. Worth a shot."

"I'm going to let Adno know. She'd never forgive herself if something happened to Dad and she could have helped but didn't know."

"Yeah, alright. I've got to go to the comms tent to contact Manfred. See you later."

Citizens of Nowhere had become a huge presence in Africa, but they had maintained the discipline of migrating and hiding. At any one time, Dadaab was no more than a few thousand people, and many of its small buildings were tents, hidden in clumps of forest that the Citizens had restored with careful use of many of the techniques they had absorbed with the New Voodo Army. Nyssa found her way to one of those outposts, the tent where they communicated with the Net and the outside world.

Des might be her twin but they were nothing alike. She was the athlete, he was the intellectual. She was the people person, he would have been shy but for his strong empathic abilities. It was Des who had architected their whole external comms to disguise the location of their Voice calls and puter connections. Calls from Dadaab would be inconvenient for many of the people around the world they talked to. Everything they did went through complex spoofing routines and bounced around many times before finding its intended receiver.

It was a cat-and-mouse game, but Des was good. And besides, he used his empathic abilities to glean details about infosecurity any time he had the chance to connect with someone from the corpo world.

And now I get to use all that to make what might be the most important Voice call I've ever made, Nyssa thought.

"Manfred, how are you?"

"Good, good. What's up?"

"You know, nothing much changes here. Was just thinking of you."

Manfred laughed. "Really? I won't even try to guess."

"Well, you know that old light-skinned man who was always on your case when we were teenagers?" She hoped he would catch on to her veiled descriptions.

"Yes, how could I forget him?"

"He's having some health issues. We sent him to Northern England. The doctor thought the cold would be good for his lungs. But it hasn't worked."

"Oh, I'm sorry to hear that. How can I help?"

"The doctor in Northern England thinks there is a hospital in London that might be able to help. But you know how hard it is to get from Northern to Southern England. We wondered if you might be able to help."

She waited while he thought about it. His tone had been friendly so far. Maybe that was just a businessman being neutral.

"I might. Can you tell me more about where he is and where he wants to go?"

"Not really. We had a call from him this morning, and, honestly, he sounded in a bad way, and we didn't ask too many questions."

"I'll tell you what. I have some business in Wales. Sometimes I like to take a tourist boat along the north coast. It's a beautiful view. They stop in Liverpool for tea and then turn around. It's a bit of an international place there. If he can get himself there day after tomorrow—say 3 PM—I can chat to him about what would work best for him."

"That's great, Manfred. Really appreciated," she said. "I'll let him know."

"Sure, always happy to help someone from the old days."

"You take care, Manfred. Good speaking with you."

She sighed. She had never known any life but this, always looking over their shoulders for bandits or government soldiers, always squinting at the future to find a way through it. She couldn't imagine what it felt like for her parents, 30 years on in this project. But for her, times like this were exhausting. She wanted to sink back into the warmth of Nowhere, the hundreds of minds a soft hammock she could lay back into. But last month, in all the excitement of 10,000 people coming together and their big manifesto, it had finally dawned on her that it would be her and Des who would see this through. Their work would take decades, and more generations after that.

She found Raefe's signature and connected.

"I don't think I'm in danger anymore," he said, exactly what she expected.

"You only say that because you want to protect me," she said. "I am an empath, too, you may remember. You put aside your own fear to reassure me. But in doing so, you avoid the rational response to your fear, which is entirely justified."

She felt his laughter.

"Caught!" he said. "No hiding from you. But you're not chasing me, are you?"

"No," she thought, taking the sharp edge off her response. Still, she let him feel just a bit of her annoyance that he was making light of it to protect her. "No, it's not a game of hide and seek, Dad. I'm trying to be the grown up here."

"Ouch," he replied. "I guess I deserved that. I feel like there's more where that came from, too, but this is probably not the right moment to have a family talk. But you're right, I have to take this seriously."

"That's good to hear," she said, and let him know what Manfred had suggested.

He conferred a bit with his protectors and they agreed on the plan. Keeping in mind that it could be a setup, they agreed that they'd have watchers and an extraction plan if it all went bad. Then she let Des and Lina know.

Des had been in touch with Adno and was a little amped.

"She's very concerned," he said. "She's going to use the Ambassador's network of human entanglers to scour the Net for any comms that might tell us more. She recently did an analysis of Earth comms and feels that something is in the works, something big. She's not sure what, though."

They all felt a certain relief knowing that there were things they could do. As well, they were struck with the realization that their week of freedom songs and manifestos had provoked a dangerous response, one that would not end here.

SAME AS IT EVER WAS

Greenbrier, W. VA
October 29, 2081

K en Robertson hadn't been to what used to be West Virginia since his college days, when he and some friends had whitewater rafted down a river that had since dried up. Pretty country was the way he remembered it, although it made him think of old English stories about things hidden in the woods. Maybe that was why he had politely refused Warren's suggestion that he take the scenic route down from D.C. through the mountains. Did he really want to chance becoming yet another kidnap victim being held for ransom by the White Power biker gangs that roamed the area?

Instead, he had taken a solar electric stealth drone one of his companies operated, quietly approaching Warren's compound on the old Greenbrier estate. The machine was state-of-the-art: bioengineered substrate that extruded its own carbon fiber reinforcements, real-time conformational adjustments, solar superconductors powering super-efficient, high-torque motors. Back in northern Virginia, an AI and his security team worked together with his MindsEye to fly him and watch for threats. They thought he was working on a top-secret merger with one of Warren's companies and that Warren had insisted on him coming alone. Well, that part was true. Anyway, he'd have to bring his security guy Lawrence into the picture at some point, but no rush yet.

"Put me down about 50 meters from the building with the blue awnings," Robertson subvocced to the flight team. His implants registered their acknowledgment and he felt the drone start to circle down to a landing. He could see Warren standing by himself near the landing spot, waving. The AI took over, and the drone landed silently and without so much as a bump. He stepped out and stretched, taking a deep breath. Robertson sniffed, trying to place what he was reminded of.

"Diesel? Am I right?" he asked Warren. "Didn't know you could still buy it."

"You are correct," Warren answered. "Some of the boys are partial to diesel vehicles. Refuse to trade 'em in on electrics. And they're free to do that down here. I've got a pretty big stash of the stuff. Keeps 'em in the fold."

Robertson had never understood Warren's obsession with preserving old technology. Had Warren started early enough, he could easily have converted his vast stock of coal and oil assets to something more modern and friendly and not lost a cent. But Warren hadn't, and now he had affected a love of old energy as if it were Renaissance musical instruments or mechanical clocks.

"Your guys all out in the woods hunting or something?"

"Something. Sent most of them up toward Beckley. Labor troubles."

"I'd have thought anyone with a job up there would be happy as a clam."

"I'd have agreed with you. But we live in a selfish age. People want to be paid just for waking up in the morning. Want the state to pay them more just because the state can get it from me. That's why I got most of the old counties of West Virginia to sign a maintenance agreement with my company. We decide what's a productive use of public monies now, not the politicians."

Warren had insisted he come down without giving him much of a reason. He sure hoped it wasn't just to listen to his usual little sermons. Not that he disagreed.

"DigiBrands is doing the same thing in the Northeast. Every hurricane, every flood, more taxes. Has to stop. I can't feed every homeless person."

"That's why the Liberty Plan is so crucial," Warren said. "And I need your help with it. Let's go for a walk."

Warren led them across the lawn, past the huge old mansion that had served as a golf clubhouse for the rich back before golf had fallen victim to water taxes.

"Did you know that over 100 years ago, the rulers of this country built a secret bunker underground in case of nuclear war?" Warren asked.

"Sure, everyone's heard that story. Have you ever found it?" Robertson asked.

Warren gave him a big grin. "Oh yeah, we've found it. Would you like to see it?"

"Sure," Robertson shrugged. Was this what the old boy had brought him down here for, to see some old 20th century Cold War relic?

They walked farther into the woods until they came to a clump of trees. Warren took out an old-fashioned metal key and bent down, brushing away leaves and dirt to reveal a round hatch with a lock. He put the key in the lock and turned it. Robertson heard a small click and then watched in fascination as Warren lifted the hatch.

"Works even if there's an EMP weapon," Warren said proudly, "unlike those fancy electronic locks you sold the government for $5,000 each."

"If there's been a big electromagnetic pulse, locks are the last thing we need to worry about," Robertson said. "And those locks are impervious to being hacked by anyone who isn't supposed to have access. DNA recognition plus some other pretty special technologies."

"I like that idea. But my main point is that things have changed since Lausanne, don't you think?" Warren answered. "Those Everywhere people have scooped up parts of the world that have more than chants and Net memes going for them. There could well be not only EMP weapons, but nuclear warfare in the next decades. Hell, could be happening right now for all we know. Come this way."

Warren guided him to the edge of the shaft. The hatch was just wider than a person, but inside was a shaft that was about 2 meters across. About a meter below the surface, there was a platform and they stepped on to it. A dim phosphorescent sort of light made it clear that the platform was a kind of elevator. Warren flipped a switch on the wall and they descended slowly. About 20 meters down, the platform stopped at the entrance to a side tunnel. Warren stepped off into it, waving at Robertson to do the same. At the end of the tunnel they entered a large chamber.

Warren mumbled something into a control panel and the room was suddenly brighter. There was a large console with a modern smart screen. This was no Cold War relic.

"I've got a secret that I'm going to share with you," Warren said. "But this has to stay between us. I know people say that all the time, but I mean it. Just me and you—no aides, AIs, whatever. You good with that?"

"Sure," Robertson said. People always had secrets in digital technology, and they never stayed secret for long. Information wants to be free, wasn't that an old 20th-century saying?

"I have an engineer who's an absolute genius. I rescued him from the Chinese government, and now Hank's my biggest fan. I've had him working on some of the stuff we talked about in Lausanne, and I need you to tell me if you can make this stuff at scale."

Robertson sensed a flood of images and data arriving in his implant. He let them stream in, his MindsEye absorbing one groundbreaking technology after another. Neurocybernetics, controlled epigenetics, polymorphic metabolic controls—advances his engineers would call science fiction. And it wasn't just theory. There were recipes, blueprints, manufacturing diagrams.

"You're telling me the Chinese government has figured out how to triple our lifespan? Integrate our minds fully with digital technology? Enable us to survive without conventional food?" Robertson asked, stunned by what he had seen.

"Oh no," Warren said. "That's all stuff Hank's team has worked on since joining me. The Chinese have no clue. Can you do it or not?"

"Well, it seems very thoroughly characterized. So yes, I think my people can."

"Good, that's good news. This is the key, Ken, you realize that? The key to us becoming more evolved, more powerful."

"You're full of surprises, Billy. I thought you were blowing smoke in Lausanne about some of this. I figured you had something up your sleeve. But this is Humanity 2.0, that's for sure. We can't lose with this."

"Glad you see it that way. But I need something from you, in return."

"What's that?"

"I heard from my guys in Northern England that your team messed up. You missed the target. Were you going to tell me?"

"We'll get him. He's just a crackpot. White guy who went native and thinks he's a cross between Jesus and Buddha. All that empathy stuff. He'd have more followers if he were a quack on a Net channel."

Warren smiled. "Yeah, I hear you. But even a quack can get a lot of ducks to follow him. One of my suppliers is getting hurt by this guy and his people. He wants him gone and so do I."

"We've got feelers out all over Northern England. We'll get him."

"Tell your people to check Liverpool. We've gotten some whispers from that direction."

KEEP ON TRUCKING

Newcastle, Northern England
October 29, 2081

"We're going to Liverpool," Claire announced as she put her ancient Voice away. "There are Gypsies there, and they say the Northern Guard has been quiet. No roadblocks, checkpoints, none of that sort of thing."

They had been hiding out waiting for their plan to evolve in a part of Newcastle where McDornish's cover was thin. The Northern Guard rarely ventured into this territory. Minutes later, Gordo arrived driving a Northern Electric box truck.

Gordo could see Raefe's puzzled look at the truck.

"We've got a rental agreement, you might say," Gordo said. "Very low rate. Gives us a ready reason to be on the road. You'll be in that truck, with Claire. She actually does work for Northern and knows the drill, so she'll do all the talking if it comes to that."

Raefe walked over to the truck Gordo had indicated.

"Where do you want me?" he asked Claire.

"You stay in the back until we put some distance from Newcastle. Can't have McDornish's men spotting you around here. We'll switch off after that."

There were six Gypsies in the back, sandwiched between boxes of spare parts for wind turbines. They'd pass a cursory inspection if they had to, but no more than that. Someone outside pulled the truck door down, and the inside went dark. Claire started the motor, and they were off, bouncing down the rough streets. He heard a voice talking quietly on a mobile, and the interior lights went on.

Gordo was up front with Claire, for now. Mikey and Ganesh cradled old British Army submachine guns with large magazines.

"For McDornish's gang," Ganesh said, as if reading Raefe's thoughts.

"Do we have intel on them?" Raefe asked. "What's old Brian, the true Briton, doing?"

"I hacked their shit," the one called Ea said. She sat in front of an impressive looking puter, scanning a variety of apps for signals. "He's in Manchester, as usual. But he's got small teams all about this area, looking for you."

"Drones first, Brian's Viking squad next," Mikey said. "Rape, pillage, and leave. Not this truck."

"Used to getting their way with people, that lot," Ganesh said. "It's what they know. Fighting the climate just confuses them."

The truck lurched as Claire pulled down a side road into an old abandoned barn. She opened the back door.

"Protective measures, lads," she said.

Mikey and Ganesh climbed up on top of the truck. Ea threw a roll of some kind of film up to them. They spread the film on the roof.

"It's a sticky metallic film," Claire explained to Raefe. "Usually the cop drones have infrared cameras. Can't hide the engine up front, but the film will block thermal emissions from you lot. It'll make the vehicle look more like a car than a truck. Confuse them, at least for a while. You're with me now."

"Will we see them, the drones?" Raefe asked her.

"Maybe, if the sunlight hits one. Normally they're too high and quiet. They're just watchers, no missiles or anything. Northern England's too poor to have a drone air force like the South does."

He climbed into the cab with her, and they pulled back on the main road. He touched her mind lightly. He could sense that she was calm, used to dodgey circumstances.

"You really work for the electric company?" he asked.

"When there's work, yeah. Northern's a bit of a part-time affair, you know."

"The company or the country?" he asked.

"Bit of both," she laughed. "But the company, mostly. McDornish's obsession with power doesn't always extend to electric power. Can't be bothered with how the plebes live, most of the time, despite all the yammering. He makes a show of it now and then, and you never hear the end of it. But day to day, he's more worried about ripping off the corpos down South."

"My impression, too. But you're from Scotland?"

"Aye, born and raised. Me dad was a tidal power engineer in Sofricar. After the war between the pro- and anti-Chinese factions in Kenya spilled over into Sofricar, he went to Scotland to catch on at one of the island power stations. He met me mum there—she was a clerk up from Glasgow to do the accounting and such."

Another fugee from Africa, he thought. If this Gulf Stream trend worsens and Europe freezes up, will the flow reverse? Will we all retrace our ancestors' steps and find the savannah again?

"Wow, so if you had stayed, you might be a Citizen of Nowhere by now," he said. "Strange world we live in. But you grew up on one of those remote little power station islands?"

"Was born there, but they went back to Glasgow after a hurricane wrecked the plant. Was hard times for them, and me, in the rough part of Glasgow."

"And from Glasgow to Newcastle?" he asked. The rough part of Glasgow was a walk in the park in Newcastle.

"Bad judgment."

"How so?"

"Let's just say I let a bad situation get to me. I never felt at home in Glasgow. Even though, eyes closed, they couldn't tell me from a snow-white highlander, people still would ask me where I was from. Ask any black Scot, you'll hear the same. Some go all the way back hundreds of years there, too, but no mind. Even the posh ones. Never had our own tartan, I guess."

"No better in Northern England?"

"Worse. But I was fooled by all that talk when the Northern Brigades rebelled against the City in '73. They sounded like proper revolutionaries to me, out with the old, in with the new and all that. Soon as I was done with school, I headed there. They all had Goodstuff Benjamin posters on their walls and the clubs played that Afro-punk remix of "Bloody Sunday" that was huge back then. Sounded good. Was good, long enough for a cuppa maybe. Then there was some trouble with the gangs and one thing led to another. And then it was the North for Northerners, even if half of them are Hindus now. And I was back to 'Where was you born?' Maybe if I were a little lighter and had a different face, I could have passed for a Hindu, but they saw me, and I was nothing but an African here to take what jobs they still had."

Her tale of industrial decline seemed odd out here in the empty countryside. Snow still covered the ground, and there wasn't much to see besides scraggly stands of trees every so often. Way off, he could see a cluster of smallish houses. A large balloon floated above the cluster, tethered by a sizable electric cable. Solar collector balloons were popular in sparsely populated areas.

Claire jerked the wheel hard down a side road.

"What?" he asked.

"Those balloons. Never know if they have surveillance cameras on them. They put 'em up high so the lads can't damage them."

"Strange, isn't it?" he mused. "There was no one here at all thousands of years ago. The whole place was a hundred feet of solid ice, like maybe Scotland will be hundreds of years from now, the way things are going with the Gulf Stream. Everyone came here from somewhere else. And it's just a shouting match about who's here the longest, who are the true Brits and so on. America's the same. The only true Americans are mostly gone and everyone else thinks a few generations qualifies them to keep anyone new out. Even those who weren't indigenous— the biggest group from outside North America are the descendants of slaves. Tell that to the NeoConfederates and they'll tell you God saved America for white people. Never ones to be bothered by the facts, our homegrown racists."

"Indeed. You think it will ever change?"

"Has to," he said. "Change or die, those are the choices."

"But how? I see these blokes risk their lives for McDornish and his bunch. And all they get out of it is what they call Northern Pride. You heard it at Maggie's. How do you fight that?"

"Any way we can," he said. "Any way we can get people to see that we can only survive the world we've made by banding together and making it right again. Human pride. Anyway, I thought you did a great job of getting them to consider that they were fighting the wrong fight, and on the wrong side of it at that."

He felt her resistance, the same resistance he had felt a million times over the last 30 years. Deep down, we know this whole human race thing is a long shot, he thought. But he still felt the power of connection and he was dammed if he was going to give that up and cry in his beer.

"But what's your plan?" Claire said. "We're risking our lives to get you South. When we get you there, what will you do to make me feel I risked my life for a good reason?"

"You already answered that. You've been risking your life for years, just trying to walk down the street. There is no God or Jesus or Allah or Vishnu or whomever is going to lead us out of this wilderness. It's not me, either. I'm just the first guy to figure out he has empathic powers and see what can be done with them. If it wasn't for my wife, Lina, I probably wouldn't even have figured that out. No, there's just us. And there are a lot of us, most of us, even, everywhere. Many ideas about the future. We'll all figure it out, bit by bit. It will take generations, but there's no time to waste."

He could see that she wasn't persuaded.

"You want me to tell you that if we do such and such, in a few years, this will all be over and life will be great?"

"That would be nice," she said. "You think I'm stupid to want that?"

"To want that?" he said. "No, who wouldn't want that? To believe that there's a shortcut to that, that might be stupid. Your parents' country, South African Republic, they fought for four or five generations just to get the simple right for a black person to sit next to a white person in public, to be treated anywhere near the same. We still have that fight, and a whole world to change."

"And you think that's a fight we can win?" she said. "That we have enough troops, enough guns, enough guts?"

"No. The point of fighting is not that kind of winning, it's not destroying your opponent. It's changing what made you need to fight—hunger, oppression, or now, no homes, no water, no food. We don't have time to waste just to feed our thirst for vengeance. We have to find the connections that bind, not cleave."

"Yeah, that's righteous," she said, a half smile on her face. "Just wanted to hear you say it. But I still think you're asking us to fight human nature."

"Ah, but which human nature? The human nature of the first people who figured out how to make a fire, or a bow and arrow, and showed everyone else how to do it, gladly and for free? Or the human nature of the drug corpos, who get uni students to discover life-saving drugs for next to nothing, try them out on poor people and prisoners, and then patent them so only those who can pay through the nose can have them? What we call human nature isn't really natural. You can't find any other animal that is willing to kill half of its own kind."

"So back to nature, is it? A dog's life. I didn't have you figured for a back to nature type."

"Maybe I think we should go forward to nature, not back. I just feel it in peopl, that they could live without so much fear and hatred and violence. We have it in us, but we're trapped in a dance we can't figure out how to stop. I just want us to give it a go, to try, before we finally top ourselves as a species."

"Yeah, okay, I can respect that. Still, you might need a hard girl like me along the way, right?" she said, grinning at him. "Someone who can beat the drones and the Vikings."

"Yeah, probably," he laughed. "Then we'll have to figure out how to soften you up."

"We're almost to the ferry. You'll have the whole ride over."

HOW THE OTHER HALF LIVES

Liverpool, Republic of Northern England
October 30, 2081

Gordo had insisted that they scope out the area before letting Raefe wander about. They'd found a good vantage point up on Stanley Road and Gordo was surveying both docks with binos. Claire had gone ahead to the meet point.

"I'm not seeing anything troubling," Gordon said. "Claire's on my Voice saying OK on her end. You're good to go, mate."

Raefe walked down the hill toward the old schooner docks. A handful of brightly colored sail boats were there, tourists milling about. Manfred had told Nyssa he would be at the Beatles & Barbarians, a tourist trap of a pub that celebrated Liverpool's two most famous musical alums, though neither the ancient rockers nor the currently huge Viking shredders had ever frequented the joint. Claire was in the back, pretending to smoke a hookah in between sips of a huge brown brew. Manfred was at a table away from the window, sipping something clear.

"Manfred, good to see you," Raefe said, shaking his hand. "I appreciate you putting yourself out like this."

"Happy to help," Manfred said. "You and Lina were always good to me."

Raefe smiled. "I think maybe we were a little rough on you as a teenager."

"Ah, fathers and daughters," Manfred said. "I have an eight year old girl now. I'll probably be the same in a few years. No hard feelings. Anyway, this is all about much bigger things."

That's how they do it, Raefe thought. They think there are bigger things than children, because they only think of their child. They've lost the ability to think about all children, who will be all people.

"Not such big things, but yes, we have some serious matters to discuss. Myself and a companion need to be able to travel in South England for a few days, and then depart without being noticed. What do you advise?"

"Let me check the security situation."

Manfred had certainly come up in the world, Raefe thought, from the ragged boy in the NVA settlement. He was wearing a typical corporate one-piece suit, slate blue in some exotic technical fabric with short sleeves and legs that stopped fashionably just below the calves. Did it have an integral puter? Raefe couldn't see any ear-mounted eyepiece like everyone else used.

"Your suit a puter, too?" he asked.

"No," Manfred said, embarrassed. "UFS gives us implants. We subvoc to use it. Mandatory for employees above a certain rank."

"Implants, what will the rich think of next? Well, it was just a matter of time."

"And money," Manfred agreed. "Always that. Anyway, you're a popular fellow these days. UFS security was alerted by Brightstar to be on the lookout, high priority. Word is it came straight from Ken Robertson himself. But UFS is still Euroish, and they're not all that happy about Robertson. He's allied himself with Billy Warren, and UFS considers him a caveman with crackpot ideas. I don't think they'll be torturing people to find you. But they will use all the normal means."

Raefe was trying to decide if he was joking about the torture, but he didn't sense that. He'd been unpopular for years, but hurting people to find him? That was the stuff of local warlords, not global corpos. Then again, who did the local warlords work for?

"So in my opinion, London is still your best bet." Manfred went on. "With 30 million people, they can't watch everyone. Stay out of Central and The City. They're closed off to anyone under Level 10 or their certified employees. Too difficult to make that work for you. South London's your best bet, but it's tricky. Barking's all white, you could blend in there."

"No, that won't work for my friend."

"Maybe Bromley then. Every sort there. Not dangerous, mostly Level 6ish. Low-level managers, a few crafts types, and so on. Can you fake that?"

"Water engineer? Software team leader? Teacher? That sort of thing"

"Teacher and engineer, no that's Level 4 and 5 type stuff. A little down market. Is your companion female? She could be your wife, be an individual contributor. Especially if she's younger. Team leader, that's the right stuff."

"Okay, I think I can still talk that talk."

He would be playing at what he would have become if aliens hadn't changed his mind. He'd done it before. It was like wearing clothing that was the right size but didn't suit him.

"Alright, you're now Tom and Cecille Morgan and you've been transferred from Ilfracombe to the London offices of MiniWorlds, your old company from many years ago. You've been transferred a lot—check your new CV. That should cover you if anyone asks did you know the Smiths and so on. You should find a housing complex for new arrivals. New Opportunity Housing is the official designation. Certain wags refer to it as NO Housing. All perfectly normal, as it can take a year or more to find permanent housing in London. All South England citizens have numbered identity accounts. I've emailed yours to the account you set up for us to communicate, along with your stage 1 password. That will work for most everything except direct contact with the state. They do DNA scans. It'll take the week to set that up so that you can pass exit at Customs, so until then avoid being picked up by the coppers."

Money would be complicated. There was no cash in South England. He'd have to use his puter to pay for everything. But anything over 500 credits required DNA authentication. They'd have to stick to the New Opps hotels near the train stations.

"Shouldn't be hard," Manfred said. "You can find ones that cater to people not anxious to be found that will let you pay in advance each day to keep the total down. The area around the North Station in Bromley is best for that."

"Just curious, but why would a Level 6 solid citizen not want to be found?"

"Late on paying the bills, that sort of thing. Nothing serious but if you let your balances build up, they knock you down a level."

"And how confident are you that we'll go undetected?"

"Quite. Without going into too much detail, the group I work in at UFS does this stuff routinely. It can all be traced back to my boss, but not me. It won't be though. The security forces know not to poke into what UFS is doing."

"Well, very much appreciated, Manfred." Raefe realized Manfred was taking a chance and wanted him to understand he was grateful.

"Sure," he said, his expression now pained. "Nyssa probably told you my situation. When I came here, I thought they would all be these bright shiny corpos who were going to rebuild the world, and we'd all get rich doing it. They're monsters, though. They wake up every day trying to figure out how to make the most money off the end of civilization."

"You know your masters don't want to rebuild the world, right? They would be very happy ruling a world with only a billion people, if that's what it came to. As long as that billion included them."

"I'm coming to that realization," Manfred said, cringing at the word "masters." "But I don't see it changing. They have a lot of power and even more money."

"Topic for another day. Don't give up on Everywhere. They do want to rebuild the world, like you do. Just in a different way. So keep your eyes open, and thanks again."

"Right," Manfred said. "But before you go, there's something you should know. It's not just your lot that's banding together. The buzz is that the big corpos like UFS had a meeting recently. Hush, hush, future of the world, and all that. They have a plan. I don't know what it is, but you should. It's aimed at stopping your lot and who knows what else."

"That's interesting. We will do what we can. What do I do now?"

"Oh, here. I have two return tickets on the boat for you. You'll get off in Wales, and here are some train tickets to London, all as the Morgans."

"Will I see you on the boat?"

"No, that wouldn't do. I've got my own way of getting home. Not to worry. Hi to Nyssa—she was always smarter than me."

He stood up, gave a little half salute and was gone. He waited and walked down the street to the boat. Claire came a few minutes later.

"I heard from Gordo," she said. "He spotted half a dozen mercs trying to look normal at the Dublin ferry dock."

"My guy said Brightstar put UFS on to us. Still, we've got a way out," he said, waving the tickets. "Mrs. Cecille Morgan, so nice to of you to accompany your husband, Tom. Fancy a trip to Bromley?"

"Why, yes, Mr. Tom, I believe I do."

***

Two nights later, Raefe lay in bed staring at the ceiling in the temporary housing they had secured in Bromley. It had all gone as Manfred had predicted. Claire was on the couch in the living room, keeping watch in case anyone found them. Guns were out of the question, but she had a large kitchen knife within arm's reach. He sensed that she knew she couldn't protect him if a professional team came but was determined to make it hard on them. Only a few days ago, she had wanted to know why she should risk her life for him. Now she seemed willing to do it. He hoped it was for Everywhere, not just for him. But she probably didn't even know that herself. *There's no point in looking for pure motives, is there,* he thought. *Purity is not what we humans do.*

He reached out and found the warm mist of Lina's mind.

"You are safe?" she asked.

"Yes, as far as I can tell. No one knows we're here."

"Des is keeping an eye on Manfred. He doesn't appear to have sold you out in any way we can detect."

"Good to know. I think he is genuinely torn."

"Yes, although not torn enough to desert the corpos. So what is London like?"

He was startled to realize she had never been here. All these years, he had done so much of the traveling outside of Africa. She knew Johannesburg and Cairo like the back of her hand. But London, New York, Tokyo, even their old Boston digs, those had been his haunts.

"It's hard to describe. It's everything it always was—big, high-energy, young, amazing. And it's everything wrong with our world. You're assigned a level by your job, education, family, and income. That determines where you live and many more things."

"And they think this is a good way to live?"

"Some do, some hate it but keep it to themselves. I think Holland will have many applicants from Southern England."

He didn't really want to talk. He wanted to hold her, to breathe the same air.

"Me, too," she thought back. "And we will, soon. Gordo has been in touch with arrangements for you to get to Europe and then here."

He saw her memories of the arrangements.

"Soon, my love," he said, and drifted off.

PLAYING TELEPHONE

Traveler's Perch
November 17, 2081

Council meetings were one of Hankori's least favorite activities. Too much ceremony, too much deference to tradition. Even though he had consolidated control of the Council long ago, the Guardians and the people of their worlds still expected deliberation and consensus from the Council. Ultimately, he could steer them all in the right direction, but they could be a stubborn and tiresome bunch. And not everyone was always agreeable to everything that needed doing.

This session had at least yielded one step forward. He had talked Tanoch into swapping roles with Green. The old head of Ambassadors would now move to Timelines. No matter. Green had done already his job in using Timelines to pick the technologies that would be most useful to Warren's group. Soon Timelines would have little to do. With his acolyte Green in charge of Ambassadors, he could control that group more closely.

After the meeting, Hankori and Green walked through the quiet corridors around the Council chambers.

"Well, that went well," Hankori said. "I'm pleased that you will be heading the Ambassadors now. That group has needed leadership for some time."

"I appreciate your sponsorship," Green said.

"And I look forward to your support," Hankori said. "I trust you will resolve the situation with Adno, once and for all?"

"Yes," Green said. "While I think she's more competent than you give her credit for, I've come to see that the whole little group on Water Eye as a tear in the waveform. They simply add nothing positive to the overall effort. By the way, how did the summit go on Earth?"

"Quite well. Warren can be very persuasive, especially when he's promising them an entire world and immortality."

"I still don't quite understand why you are bothering with this. Why not just let nature take its course?"

"Sometimes you lack imagination. Did you think we would just be sending the humans plans for making drugs and gadgets?"

"In fact, yes. What are you saying?"

"We will have to remake them. Change their genes, the way they raise children, their whole society."

"Why?"

"You, yourself, pointed out when we last discussed this that these technologies will have a big impact on their society. Your concern was well founded. We need to help them through that. And no, I'm not suggesting yet another bout of wasting our resources on humans. This will directly benefit our immortality efforts. Do you think that once we have perfected Permanence, we would just implement it on ourselves? What if it doesn't work as we had hoped? What if there are unforeseen consequences?"

"I've wondered all along about that."

"There will be millions of humans, living in a controlled environment. Their breeding will be controlled by us, as will their food supply."

"You're not saying we would use them as test subjects?"

"I'm saying exactly that. They will be our living laboratory. You seem dismayed."

Green couldn't quite hide his shock from Hankori, but he was trying to soften it, to couch it as concern.

"We're going down a road here that is very dangerous."

"Green, my friend, we have been on that road all along. You are only now seeing that."

They walked in silence until they reached the door to the street. Hankori strode off briskly, feeling Green's troubled eyes on his back for some time.

***

Adno had been fighting off irrelevance for years, ever since Hankori had taken over the Council. Tanoch generally underestimated her, but at least he thought she was needed and should be allowed to continue. When the waveform carried the news that Green had taken over her department, she had expected the worst.

And Green wasted little time in delivering it and little effort in disguising his real plan.

"Who shall I brief on the current status of things on Earth?" she had asked him.

"You can just file a report, and I'll see that it's passed on," he had replied.

"To whom?" she asked, affecting an innocent curiosity.

"Not sure yet," he thought back to her. She was about to challenge him when she noticed the undertone of hesitation in his thoughts and unease in his emotions. She distracted him with platitudes about being ready to serve in any way while letting her thoughts follow his deeper. She didn't get very far before she could feel him shut off those thoughts to her, but enough to know that this hadn't been his idea and he wasn't entirely comfortable with the situation.

"What do you want me to do for now?"

"I'm giving that some thought," he said. "It's just my first day and I want to look over the whole department and think about what's best overall. Perhaps you can use this time to enjoy being with your own people."

"Own people indeed," she thought to herself. At least he hadn't called them fish, as Hankori sometimes did. But it was definitely Hankori who had put him up to something and she was going to find out what. Meanwhile, she reached out to the exiles on Water Eye.

"The moment we all feared is close," Adno said. "I've been reassigned from Earth."

"To what?" Diver asked.

"That's just it. Nothing. And no one is taking my place. Green has taken Tanoch's job, and he's running things for Hankori, no doubt."

"I've been monitoring some of the Guardians back on Traveler's Perch," Mari said. "Something seriously messed up is going on. Can you guys listen to this?"

She sent them her memories of Hankori's recent conversation with Green, and some of Hankori's memories of his conversations with Billy Warren.

"Can you believe this?" Antithikos said, his thoughts tinged with anger. "The Guardians are the greatest accomplishment of intelligent life in the entire galaxy. For thousands of years, our worlds have lived in peace with each other. On each world, our societies have lived without the plagues of crime and war. And this one person is perverting all of that, turning it into a criminal mockery."

"I share your anger," Far Flier said. "And now I wish that all of the Guardian leaders of the last millennia, including me, had done less to hide the fact that Hankoris have come and gone in our history. Not often, but not never. And now it will be our turn to fight back."

"We have to tell Raefe and Lina," Mari said.

"No!" Flier said. "With Hankori and Green in charge, they'll know everything that goes through the wormhole interface."

Anti and Mari looked uncomfortable.

"You should not worry about that, Flier who has flown between planets," Adno said. "I, who have also flown between planets, can swim far distances with my mind. With many minds. No Guardians will know."

"What are you saying, Adno?" Diver said. "Is this one of your watery metaphors, or do you know something you haven't told us"?

"When Mari explained to you how our people have always been entangled," she replied, "she did not tell you the entire story. Because I learned to entangle without the wormhole interface network, I don't really need it. Once I learned to sing the Guardian waveform, I was capable of finding it without Guardian technology."

"This changes everything," Flier said. "We have a secret weapon, Diver! We can fight back!"

"Yes, although it is not completely secret," Adno said. "It was because of this ability that I was able to find, with the help of The ManyLargeLoudBlueSchool, secrets that Tanoch was not eager to reveal. And that was how I was able to engineer your trip to Water Eye."

"I've always wondered about that," Far Flier said. "Well, at least we can still communicate with Earth. But is that enough? How can we help the humans fight this murderous plot that Hankori is launching?"

"We are not helpless father mother," Mari said. "Hankori thinks he has determined the next phase of the Guardians. But I think he's wrong—we are the next phase."

"What do you mean?" Diver asked.

"We never envisioned this day, but here on Water Eye, Adno has not just been doing amazing things with her school. Anti and I were raised here, with them. Not only that, but when you carried us, you were still frequently in contact with Lina, even while she carried the twins."

"What she's trying to get to," Anti said, "is that pretty much everyone on this planet except you can communicate with Raefe, Lina, Des, and Nyssa without the wormhole interface."

"Ah, the universe continues to tickle us," Diver said. "But this is great news. We must bring Raefe and Lina into the picture."

***

Lina bolted awake. Raefe's slow slide into sleep ended abruptly. Suddenly they were both part of the waveform Adno had created. She was there, along with Des and Nyssa, and Diver and Flier, and Anti and Mari. It was somehow stronger and more vivid than their normal connections.

"We have news for you that's urgent, and some other matters, too," Adno said.

"Go ahead," Raefe said.

"Yeah, ready here in Dadaab," Lina said.

"We want you to know that something rotten is happening with the Guardians," Adno said. "They are ending their guardianship of Earth. I've been reassigned."

"We've kept you out of a lot of Guardian politics over the years," Diver said, "because we had no thought it would deteriorate so badly and you had enough on your minds. But now you need to know. Flier was pushed out of the directorship some time ago and a man named Hankori took over."

"We can deal with his plans for the Guardians," Flier said. "But in the meanwhile we're pretty sure he's interfering with Earth in a big way."

Adno filled them in on Hank's influence on Billy Warren and how Warren had recruited Ken Robertson.

"Robertson? Now things are starting to make sense," Raefe said. "It was his security forces that were trying to kill me in England."

"And we've heard through other sources," Nyssa said, "that the corpos recently had a secret meeting of global leaders. They can rarely agree on what kind of water to drink, so it must have been important."

"We can stop worrying that our efforts are insignificant," Raefe said. "The Declaration of Everywhere seems to have stirred the hornet's nest. We have resources here. Now that we're alerted, we can try to find precisely what they're up to and when."

"We will help however we can," Adno said.

"It seems like our two struggles are converging on a single crisis,"

Raefe said. "But you know, I'm puzzled. This conversation feels different than usual. Somehow closer. Is something different?"

Adno explained that they weren't connected through the wormhole interface.

"You're saying that the eight of us, and maybe all of Adno's school, can maintain a waveform across these great distances, but outside of the Guardian network?" Lina asked.

"Yes," Anti said. "Just so. I'm not entirely sure why. My guess is that the Guardian network is actually a simplified, artificial version of a vast natural set of entangled connections that span the galaxy, if not the universe. I don't understand the physics of it. Do our thoughts ride through extra dimensions? Do they make the long sought cosmic strings vibrate, something else? But I know it's real. Once we show you how to initiate the connections, you'll see it's actually easier to use than the Guardian network."

"This changes everything." Raefe said. "From what you say, Adno, Hankori has always underestimated all of you on Water Eye. And he thinks humans are little better than insects. Whatever we decide to do, we'll have the advantage of surprise. And numbers. There are millions of empaths here now, but they mostly connect with people they can see in front of them. I'm guessing that no one but you guys know just how far humans have come in the last few years."

"Just what we thought, old friend," Flier said.

WIRED FOR THOUGHT

Barcelona, Republic of Catalan
January 12, 2082

Since Adno had alerted them, Des had been leading the effort to probe what the corpos were up to, but to little avail. Whatever it was, it was well hidden from the Net. In the end, Nyssa had suggested they try Manfred again, maybe push him a little harder. And here she was, ready to give it a go.

Barcelona's Cathedral Square was packed, as usual. Hopefully, she could persuade him, or at the worst, try to read his thoughts. She and Des were the only ones that really knew him. Empathy was strong, but empathy plus her knowledge and prior connection with Manfred was more power than Raefe or Lina or anyone else could bring to the task. Everything was riding on her ability to get Manfred to cooperate and to tell if he was genuine or setting them up.

She had carefully chosen a small café in front of a nondescript boutique hotel in the far corner of the square. From here, she could see all entrances to the square. Manfred might recognize her, but he wouldn't notice Des in a million years. Her brother was sitting on a blanket selling souvenirs just outside the church with a little sign around his neck indicating he was deaf. Raefe's hasty return from England had featured a zig-zag tour of Western Europe escorted by some pretty tough acquaintances who had been summoned to make themselves invisible around Cathedral Square. If Manfred was playing her, he'd regret it quickly.

She had spent the day before shopping for just the right clothes for a young Barcelona woman. It was unlikely anyone but Manfred would recognize her. In dark red harem pants, retro football trainers, a baggy vintage Real Catalan team shirt, oversize sunglasses, and a sheer white headscarf, she fit right in. She could see Manfred scanning the square for her. She had expected the full masterful young corpo uniform on him, but he was dressed down in sweats and trainers. She let him search for a while, reaching out to touch his mind. He seemed calm but a little tense. To be expected, she thought. If he was part of some plan to kidnap her, he was better at hiding his emotions than she imagined he should be. Finally, she made eye contact and waved him over.

"Look at you," he said, "a proper little Barca girl."

"And you," she answered, "slumming with the tourists. Been awhile, eh?"

"Yeah, I saw your dad recently, but what's it been, 10 years now?"

"Just about. You're looking well."

"And you! Africa still agrees with you."

"Most days, yes. Dad says Europe has had its ups and downs for you."

"More like ups and then downs," he nodded a bit ruefully. "Here in Catalunya, you can't really feel the tremors that are shaking the rest of Europe. It's a bit like the last glacier in the Swiss Alps. You can hear it groaning and cracking in the distance, but you don't know whether it will just melt away or come tumbling down on the villages below. Back in Philips DeMag, you can watch the ice tumble down the mountainside from your kitchen window, as it were."

"Sounds like Kenya! Where do you think things are going, Manfred?"

Manfred gazed out over the plaza, eyes strangely vacant. She was just about to clear her throat to jog him back when he abruptly turned to her.

"You think that because I have neural implants and have some minor responsibility in the technocracy, that I know things like where it's all headed? I don't. I hear things, I can guess things. That's all."

"Nyssa, I've been monitoring his mind," Des thought to her from his post. "He was just connected back to Philips' computer network. Looking something up. Couldn't tell what."

"We're not in danger?" she thought to him. "He wasn't signaling someone?"

"No I don't think so," Des said. "But I'm paying attention. What I need you to do is get him to access the network again. I think I can hack the system through him."

"Sorry," Nyssa said, turning her attention back to Manfred. "Don't take it the wrong way. I think of you as a friend. We're all caught up in this. Last century, they had a saying—'Rearranging deck chairs on the *Titanic*'—and I don't want to be that person. None of us do, to be the person yelling 'Water!' as the ship sinks. Anything you can tell me that will help us avoid that is very much appreciated."

"My boss's boss took part in some kind of big corpo meeting recently," he said. "I told your dad about it when we spoke."

"Right, in Lausanne. We know who was there, but not what came of it."

"You can expect that there were layers to it. The first layer is a big public show of a plan to show they're on top of things. After that, things get murkier. And more threatening."

"How so?"

"The corpos' business model has evolved as the crisis has deepened. Fifty years ago, their model was get as much money out of the system in the short term as they could. But then they realized that governments were weakening faster than them, and their model switched to fostering global privatization, with the top corpos consolidating regional power. Now they have a problem. Nowhere, the NVA, the Dutch Republic, all the smaller imitators. They're taking people out of the tax pool, the job market, and even the consumer economy. That's eating into the corpo revenue stream. And their costs are rising, with the waters and the droughts and the rest of it."

"So, a new business model? Is that what Lausanne was about?"

"Precisely. I don't know all of the details but I know where they are stored. I know you have people who can hack their way in."

She could sense that he wanted them to get the information. His emotions were a shifting complex of annoyance, anger, sadness, resignation, and a small sense of satisfaction. But the more she let them wash over her, the more she suspected that the anger and annoyance were at his corporate masters. The sadness and resignation were just his ground state for how he viewed the world. And the small satisfaction was that he was here, helping her. *Hack away,* he seemed to be feeling.

"I wouldn't know about hacking," she smiled. "But if you want to message me with links to where I might learn more, I'll see what sense I can make out of it."

"I'll do better than that. A week ago, just before you called, I got a visit from a top exec at Philips DeMag. He was at the summit. Turns out they've been keeping tabs on our occasional little interactions for years. No worries, always useful to have contacts, they say. Anyway, Philips DeMag wants you to know the plan. They don't trust me with it. But they want you to know. It must be horrible if they've opted out.

I'm going to transfer some info to a neutral server. Later I'll send you a key. Then a location. I have to spread it out to avoid the security bots."

Ah, so some of the anger was at their lack of trust, she thought. *And at whomever was so abhorrent even they didn't trust them.* Nyssa struggled to control her emotions. So bad that DeMag had opted out? She knew it would take time to find the data, decrypt it, and so on. It was going to be a very anxious next few days. But Manfred was doing his part. He had that far-away look in his eyes again that must mean he was using his implants.

"There, it's done. Expect the rest within 48 hours."

Des was telling her that he had gotten what they needed and that he agreed with her read of Manfred's emotions and loyalties. If they were being played, so was Manfred.

"Thanks," she said. "I know this can't be easy for you. And if you need asylum, you know where to find it."

"Thanks, Nyssa," he said, the sadness now seeping into his voice. "I feel like that old Greek myth about the kid who flew too close to the sun. We can never lead the life we should have, you know?"

"But we can leave the life we shouldn't have," she said. "Just say the word."

"You take care," he said, abruptly standing. He squeezed her shoulder and walked off without a glance backward. She thought of his face to remember it, realizing that she might never see it again.

SECOND THOUGHTS

Green had found Putnomo in the waveform.

"How go the preparations?" he asked the old quadruped.

He felt a surge of grumpy energy and then a string of numbers.

"There, that's better," Putnomo said. "Been wanting to try this trick out—using your genetic code to encrypt our entanglement so that only your mind can understand it. And I've transmitted the same to you, so that only I can understand you. Never know who might be listening."

Green wondered if he meant Hankori or that busybody, Adno.

"Why all the secrecy?" he asked.

"Because you want to ask me if we're really doing this and if it's really going to work."

"So I'm not the only one who's having doubts?"

"No. But to be fair, I have no doubt," Putnomo said. "What we are doing is wrong and can't possibly have good consequences. I just didn't have a choice."

"Our mutual friend has threatened you?"

"Yes, but it's my own damn fault. And you?"

"More flattery than fear. What are we going to do?"

"We could do nothing. It's doubtful that Hankori's human friends will succeed. I tried to tell him but he wouldn't listen. You might as well give a child the blueprints for a fusion reactor and expect them to build a working model."

"You're speaking from personal experience?"

Putnomo laughed. "You know well my species' talent for physics. The humans are somewhat less talented, however. And what is your role in this?"

"Well, when I was still in Timelines, he had me run a lot of quantum computing cycles to figure out the most efficient way to sabotage the entire Earth power grid, among other things."

"You mean the thousands of power grids that actually don't form a single power grid."

"Precisely. Pragmatics aside, I don't know if I can go through with this."

"I have made my peace with that" Putnomo said. "I am old and want to live my last decades in comfort. If I don't help him, he'll find someone else, even if it takes another century. He will not be denied."

"I'm sorry you feel that way. He's only one person. He needs people like us to help him."

"Well, I'm going to do what he asked but I didn't say I wouldn't help you stop him."

Putnomo might be a laughable figure sometimes, putting on airs, but his people were truly born to physics. Putnomo had already seen that Timelines were the way out.

"He wants you to transmit a vast amount of information," he had explained to Green. "That will take a vast amount of energy. Energy and time are related, just as matter and energy are related. If the energy source undergoes selective phase shifts, the transmissions will all go to the same place, but not to the same timelines."

Green didn't entirely grasp it, but the upshot was that it would look like the transmission was going well, but certain bits would go to random other timelines, where there would be no one to receive them or understand or act on them. Putnomo would adjust the central power source to make these phase shifts in response to certain bits of code to render the message unusable in the exact best way. Afterwards, no one would know what had happened, other than that the transmissions had been useless. Green could say he had done his part, and no amount of investigating would uncover what had happened.

"You'll do me the favor of never telling anyone that I've told you this," Putnomo said.

"And you'll return the favor?"

"Of course." And he broke their connection.

POWER FAILURE

Once Manfred had shown them the files, they had set to work analyzing them. They were vast and difficult. Des created a way for Adno's school to absorb them, and soon thousands of minds were at work, each linked to the other in a way that made it easy to connect the dots. Des stayed connected with the school most of the time, fascinated to learn their techniques. Now he was taking a break.

"You are with the school all day and night?" Nyssa asked him. "Are you aware of them?"

"Yes and no," he said. "It's a bit like having a day dream, or like when you drive a car and are thinking about something completely different while driving. It's hard to describe. More and more, I'm not that aware of it until I find something interesting."

She remembered a teacher they had in third grade who had the most boring voice. She droned on forever, but you still had to listen for the nuggets that would be on the test. It was a funny memory and she shared it with Des.

"Just like Mrs. Odipo?"

"Yes, that's a bit of how it is," Des said. "And this time, there is a really big test. But you know, I think I'm close to another breakthrough."

He explained that between his long stretches as part of Adno's school and his intensive work on the computer, he was beginning to learn how to entangle with computers. After all, minds and computers both used electromagnetic fields to store, transport, and manipulate information. They both depended ultimately on quantum effects to function. They might be very different, but they had that in common.

He hadn't figured it all out yet, but he was getting faster at traversing the data. He had nearly unraveled the whole plan that Manfred had given them. It was nothing less than the oligarchs trying to become a new species of supermen ruling a planet rid of most of the humans they would become superior to. If they hadn't known better, they would have thought it was a script for some new action vid. But the corpos were serious.

"We have to tell everyone," she said, quite alarmed. "This cannot happen."

***

"We now have the big picture," Nyssa said to her family and their friends on Water Eye. "The magnitude and insanity of this plan is way beyond Warren or the other corpos, so we think Hankori must be involved."

"How many people are they talking about?" Raefe asked.

"They had been talking 100 million, then 10 million," Nyssa continued. "Now they talk about one million. The best sense we can make out of it is that they are having trouble recruiting."

"And that takes us to the second aspect of this," Des said. "We think they are promising people that if they join, they will live for 1,000 years and have all sorts of powers."

"He's promising to give them the enhancements that we all have," Flier said. "Genetic remodeling, nanobio maintenance, organic computing elements, the works. This is truly madness. In our long history, no Guardian has ever broken that barrier or even suggested it on this scale."

"But there's more, outside of the docs Manfred gave us." Des said. "I told Nyssa that I've been learning how to access networks with my mind. For weeks, I've been slowly meandering through the inner nets of UFS, which took me to DigiBrands, which took me to Warren's own nets. And I've discovered something."

"Wait, you were able to do all of that through your empathic ability?" Lina asked.

"I can't explain it," Des said. "It's not about empathy, since we're talking computers here. But I think it is about entanglement. The truth is, organically, our abilities are based on quantum interactions, not human-level concerns."

"You may be the first person in the galaxy who can do this," Raefe said.

"Unfortunately, that's not true," Des said. "Mari and Anti have told us that Hankori is conducting secret research on transforming his species and others into a kind of living computer."

"Tell us what you have found," Raefe said.

"You should be receiving the full data," Des said, "but the short of it is that Warren's cabal is planning on sabotaging the Nets worldwide. Their goal is to accelerate chaos here on the surface."

"We seem to be doing that all on our own," Lina said. "Why would they want to speed it up?"

"In part," Des answered, "because he's a bit of a sociopath. But their group is not doing so well attracting recruits to the new world order. So they want to shock them into joining through fear. They've created a super computer virus that will bring down electric power grids worldwide. They're also selectively targeting banks outside their own, some governments, military Nets, and a bunch of other targets."

"What do they think will happen?" Lina asked.

"They've done sophisticated modeling of the impacts," Des said. "They hope that what's left of the world economy will disappear. The only corpo-level businesses that will still function will be theirs. No governments or military large enough to matter will be able to respond. People will be living in a world where they no longer can buy and sell food, clothing, or water from more than a few klicks away, and only by bartering. More than two billion people will lose their jobs within a month. And the entire world will be in the dark, not knowing exactly what happened or why."

"And here's the worst part," Nyssa said.

"Yes, I was getting to that," Des said. "They will leak out small dibs and dabs that suggest that it was Everywhere that did this. They're still deciding whether to go further and say it was empaths who did it."

"I've been waiting for that," Raefe said. "All these years, somehow we've been able to live without being a secret but without being in the spotlight."

"We're not ready for this," Lina said. "We're still a year or two from Everywhere having the numbers and organization to take on something like this. Although, I'm not even sure I know how we would do that."

"We think we know how," Nyssa said. "Thanks to Adno."

"Adno's people are all entirely entangled with each other all the time, without the interface networks the Guardians use," Des said. "Yes, they live as a school, so that makes sense. But that doesn't mean other empaths can't do that."

"We felt something like that at the Congress," Lina said. "And Edna's people have been exploring that for years."

"And now Anti and Mari have learned it from Adno's people, and we have learned from them," Des said. "And now we can teach it to thousands, millions on Earth."

"We don't have time to teach it," Raefe said. "We have to demonstrate it. We have to show how we can use this power to stop this plot. And we have to convince people that they can use this power, along with us, to change their lives, their world. Now is not the time to be meek."

Nyssa could feel her father's spirit growing. Those who didn't know him tended to misjudge him as a dreamer. And she could feel Lina beaming at his intensity.

"Well, Dad," she said, "all of us can make plans to stop this plot in its tracks. But it's going to have to be you who tells the world about it."

"She's right, Dad," Des said. "I have some ideas about how to use the Net to entangle with people, sort of like our own local wormhole interface. And Mom can put out the world to get our allies in position to intercept the corpos as they scurry to their holes. But..."

"...As many people on Earth as we can reach need to hear the truth," Lina finished his thought. "And that means leading millions, maybe billions of people, to entangle for the first time. And that means you, Raefe."

"Yes, I think you're right," Raefe said, and Nyssa was surprised how calm he seemed. She saw a fleeting image in her mind of a giant wall of water approaching a storm-sieged beach, and then the wave passed and she was looking through someone's eyes at the same beach, waters calm and sun bright off the water. And she knew that light was the joy filling Raefe and Lina.

THROW THE SWITCH

Traveler's Perch
March 7, 2082

After nearly half a year, Putnomo had finally finished with the technology package that would enable Hankori's plan for Earth to work. What they once referred to as Permanence had now been named Phoenix Cresilion. Hankori loved the name, which he had created by fusing an old Earth story about a bird who was reborn from fire and ashes with the story of Traveler's Perch's last emperor, Cresilion. Green could no longer hide from the fact that Phoenix Cresilon meant ashes and domination for Earth.

He had been dreading this day since his talk with Putnomo, going back and forth about whether or not to do as he was asked or as he knew in his heart was right. Hankori had manipulated him time and time again, pushing him to this moment when he had become a crucial player in this insane plan to destroy Earth. Green admired Hankori's brilliance and the Permanence plan still had its attractions. Some days, he even thought it was a good idea. The other days, he thought it would never happen but that they would learn many valuable lessons along the way.

But none of that prepared him to help slaughter 12 billion people, nor to doom a million survivors to the fate of microbes in a lab dish. He had anguished over the whole prospect but Hankori had never questioned the morality of it. Why bother? Hankori had come to believe he was a god, or maybe even God. His desires were automatically moral, his victims just unhappy accidents.

Green had also come to realize that he himself was seriously flawed. He had been ambitious and vain. Before Far Flier's fall, Green had looked up to him in a way that he now realized was just envy. Hankori had read him very well and led him slowly along the path until it seemed like there could be no turning back.

But Putnomo had given him exactly that way back. And now he

had to take another chance.

He found Adno's signature and connected to her through the wormhole interface network.

"How are you, Adno," he said. "It's been a while."

"You miss me, boss?" she said. "Can't get along without me?"

"Something like that," he said. "Listen, some things have come up back here on Traveler's Perch that I thought we could chat about. But they're personal, and maybe it would be best to have a more private conversation."

"Well, that would be easy if I were there or you were here," she said. "But I don't know what you have in mind."

"I have in mind that you know other ways," he said. "Let's just say that over the years, certain things have happened that could only be explained that way. It doesn't bother me, so I never mentioned it. To each his own, and all that. But this would be a good time to let me in on it."

She cut the connection. Was she spooked? Or making preparations? Only seconds later, he felt her signature, and like that, they were connected outside the network.

"OK, what's the big secret?" she asked.

"Hankori hasn't just decommissioned the Earth project," Green said. "He's got his own plans for Earth, and quite frankly, they're insane. I don't expect you to do anything about them. That's my problem. But I want you to know. Candidly, I want a witness should this ever come to light. Are you willing?"

"Depends."

"On what?"

"On whether you are going to tell me anything useful." And then she told him exactly what Hankori's plan was, in fair detail.

Green was stunned. "How do you know all of that?"

"You think I am a stupid fish that swims in circles all day on a silly watery planet with only a few smart birds like yourself to look after us. My people have entangled for their entire existence. They can entangle in the millions. They can combine their powers in many ways you are ignorant of. We use these powers to help life, and I used them to help Earth when that was my job."

"Earth will need my help, as well," Green said. "Hankori asked me to prepare instructions for the humans that will allow them to destroy their power grid in a matter of minutes, never to work again. I know how to prevent that."

"Then prevent it you should. And I will be your witness. Afterward, you will want one."

"Thank you."

"And what will you do to stop Hankori from destroying the Guardians?"

"Why do ask that? What is it you think he is going to do?"

"He wants all the Guardian people to become immortal, to become pure energy."

He had indeed underestimated her.

"You think that is a false goal?"

"I am immortal already. Born into my school, I have the memories of all who went before. And those after me, they will have my memories. I live a very rich life. But I also get to feel the cools of the water, the lights of the planets, the beauty of my mate partners. Why would I give that up to be lightning in a bottle?"

"Your school will die off someday."

"And so will the universe. Frankly, it will get bored first."

"You have your own view, but the rest of us don't live in schools."

"You already live in a school, just one that is not self-aware. Your school could evolve these forms of thought and being in time. You could help. We could teach. Your choice."

Green was confused. He had thought she would be a good, simple-minded witness. Now she was asserting that she was a higher life form.

"You've given me much to think about. For now, I just want you to know this. I hope you will not share our conversation with people who would take it the wrong way. The consequences could be dramatic for me. And I wish you and the humans luck. Just remember that I did what I could."

"My school will remember this forever."

LOCATION, LOCATION, LOCATION

Greenbrier, W. VA
March 8, 2082

Warren sat on the porch of the old Greenbrier mansion, a 200-year-old bottle of Cognac on the little table next to him. It would be a long time before he watched a mountain sunset like this again. He let the liquor feel the warmth of his hand on the snifter, shaking the glass ever so slightly. He raised the snifter and let the brandy touch his tongue. Nectar of the gods.

And tomorrow, they would become gods, after a fashion. He would board his private jet and fly out into the middle of the country to a place where earthquakes and floods hadn't happened for centuries. He would descend deep under the Earth to the amazing underground city they were building.

Around the globe, his colleagues would do the same. In the end, they had decided against one large colony. The Asians wanted to stay in Asia, the Americans in America, the South Americans had picked somewhere in Brazil, and the Africans in Africa. The Euros, well they had fallen apart. No stomach for it. He had agreed to take some of them on. Hell, America's best days were as a European refuge, so why not?

"You seem pleased with yourself." Hank again, always Hank.

"Yes, my friend, it's been a long time coming, and we're almost there. At some point, a celebration is in order."

"We are ready with our preparations. Your people will get all the info I promised. But you still have not delivered Raefe Epstein Miller."

"Miller? You still worried about him and his hippy-dippy friends?"

"You think he is a joke?"

"I think he is a fraud. No one can read people's minds. Or transmit thoughts to them."

"How do you think it is that we communicate?"

"I don't know. Some kind of advanced electronics?"

"You have a lot to learn, my friend. But many years to learn it. Good luck tomorrow."

"Thanks. I have thousands of people working on this. I always favor that over luck."

NOT SO FAST

Dadaab
March 8, 2082

Des was now effectively the tactical commander of Everywhere, armed with the knowledge Adno had provided. His links to thousands of people and computers around the world gave him an immense field of knowledge. He knew where all the leaders of the corpo plot were at all times. He could see into their comms networks, their financial movements.

He knew that all of Everywhere was counting on him. Part of him was ready to freak out, but then he felt Adno's school behind him. He understood now that it was impossible for him to be alone, and he was surprised how good that felt. Other than Nyssa, practically no one had ever come close to understanding him. Even Raefe and Lina had never really been able to see the world through his eyes, as much as he had felt their love and affection. Now, in the school, he had achieved a most satisfying view of the full complexity of the situation they were faced with.

"You are good leader of school," Adno said.

"I thought you were the leader," Des replied.

"Oh yes, of my school. You will see in time that a real school has no leader, or it has leaders everywhere. That is its strength. I meant leader of your school, the humans."

"God, I hope not." Adno didn't always get how humans worked.

"You are funny for a human," Adno said.

Adno had trouble understanding how billions of humans couldn't be a school. What could it even mean, she had asked him, to be an individual among billions of similar creatures? But she had good news for him.

"We have confirmed that our friend on the Council has done his part," she said. "Isolated parts of Earth's grid will shut down, but it will remain a coherent worldwide system, your Net. You will not be thrust into the cold deeps."

"Excellent. Dad has absorbed your lessons. I feel very good that he will be able to link up with millions of empaths around the world. And that they will be able to sustain a waveform for long enough for our message to the whole world to get out."

"What about the corpos?"

"They're all headed to their mouseholes. I'm tracking their every move and Lina's mobilized people in Everywhere's network near all of their destinations to intercept them."

"You are right to do that. They are the past. You are the future. Keep your mind on that."

GREETINGS

Earth
March 9, 2082

Raefe woke before dawn. Somewhere, it was daylight and people were active. He reached out and searched for their signatures. He felt them swimming by in the thousands, small silvery lights in the dark. And then he saw a brighter glow, another empath, one of their trained band. He reached out to him and now they resonated. They moved together and found a third, a fourth, and their wave began to grow. Soon it swelled beyond even what they had done at Dadaab.

Within an hour, they had built a wave that circled the globe. Countless minds touching each other, feeling their common bond, understanding the task they faced. They were ready.

Des had hacked into the world's vid and voice Nets. Whatever Raefe chose to communicate as speech within the waveform, would also be broadcast on the world's Nets.

"People of the world," Raefe said. "This is an emergency broadcast. I speak to you today as a citizen of Everywhere. Millions of people around the world are reaching out to you. You are hearing my voice because their minds are connected to each other and to the Net. And through them, you are experiencing my emotions and the feelings of all of us who are connected.

"I will explain in a minute how that is happening, but first, I have some shocking things to tell you. It's no secret that the world's largest corporations have increasingly taken over the running of the world. They use every crisis to force governments to give them more power. They use that power to benefit their owners, even when that harms the rest of us.

"What they have kept secret is that some of the world's most powerful corpos have banded together and have a plan to take over the world. I know, that sounds like some low-rent vid plot. But we have posted the documents that prove this on servers around the world and you can read them for yourself. What they say is that this secret cabal wants to build underground cities for themselves and perhaps a few million followers, take their money and resources and disappear underground, and then wait until the rest of us have destroyed ourselves fighting over the shrinking supply of food and water to come above ground and reclaim the Earth for themselves."

He gave them some time to look up the docs and then continued explaining how this would take many generations. The documents discussed the long-life treatments the super-rich would give themselves, but he had decided not to dwell on that for now. There were more immediate threats to deal with.

"But they will not succeed. Just before our broadcast, citizens of Everywhere were able to penetrate this Net attack and disassemble it. This cabal, led by Billy Warren, Ken Robertson and a dozen other corpos around the world, has been thwarted. Fellow humans, for the first time this century, we have averted a major disaster that could have led to our extinction.

"Both nature and the corpos will continue to threaten us. But we have learned more than just how to disarm massive computer attacks. We have learned how to connect with each other at the deepest levels.

"Some of you are concerned, I can feel that. But I assure you that you will not lose your sense of self, your individual will, or any other such thing. You will be you, standing in a chorus of billions, hopefully humming joyfully as you see fully for the first time that your fellow humans really do want the same kind of things that you do, regardless of how different they might appear, that though we may occasionally threaten each other, we have gotten this far because, deep in our cells, we do know how to live together. At this moment, no one is in charge, no one is giving orders, no one is making you listen to this. You can leave the wave at will. But you can sing your own notes too, if you want to alter the tune. This is not about conforming, it is about informing. So as you feel those first thoughts, reach back out to them and welcome them."

He saw Lina across the room, her face beaming. She had let herself be swept off of that drowning beach so many years ago, not really knowing what was happening, just for this moment. He could feel the world vibrating between the many other Earths that existed on other timelines. And now he understood that the energy of that vibration was being organized and modulated by the waveform of his fellow humans, up to their chins in the mud of the swamp of greed and fear they had unintentionally built for themselves. Now, with full intention, they felt themselves ever so slowly rising up out of that swamp, into the brightness of day. A brightness that was now Everywhere.

ACKNOWLEDGMENTS

This book began as a conversation with my old friend Effie Weisstein about the state we humans find ourselves in. He asked me what I thought about writing a book about a guy who lives in the near future when the world is truly falling apart from climate change and social divisions. Much of what you have just read stemmed from that initial conversation.

So this began as a book of ideas, but it needed characters, conflicts and a reason to hope. It turns out two were better than one when it came to ponder those things. Soon we fell into a rhythm of me writing, him reading, and the two of us talking every month or so.

For me, this was a new experience for fiction writing. In my professional life as a journalist, I was used to a highly collaborative environment. But like most fiction writers, I usually thought of a work like this as a solitary, almost secret task. In the early stages, I would normally have not mentioned it all to anyone.

Eventually, I would have workshopped some chapters, carefully sifting through the feedback for useful ideas. Eventually, I would have enlisted a few trusted readers to give feedback. But the experience of brainstorming with someone who came at the project more concerned about the ideas than the execution proved to be very interesting and ultimately inspiring.

Writers sometimes refer to people as "their muse," but Effie was more than that, a partner in the enterprise. He was free with ideas and critiques, respectful of my creative impulses, and a constant prod. Together, we did something more than what I might have done on my own. I encourage other writers to consider these kinds of partnerships.

I had much other help. To Sara Rivera and the gang at Grub Street, your encouragement and criticism of the early stages of the manuscript got me past my initial doubts and headed in the right direction. Many thanks to Melanie Wittes and Charlie Collinson for slogging through the first draft and helping me to see the book through others' eyes, and to my editor, Michele Seaton, whose unsparing criticism and praise were absolutely invaluable in making this a book that people might want to actually finish. And of course, Layla Schlack, whose final edit helped clear away the clutter that I had left along the way.

Throughout it all, my lovely wife and talented writer Julie Wittes Schlack was a source of constant support and steady counsel, as is her wont.

I began this project with Effie in 2015, and events were soon to outstrip even our dim view of the state of the world. As I neared the finish line with the book, I felt propelled by the struggles of the ordinary people caught in the meat grinder of the American immigration system. Their travails are nothing less than a preview of what will befall many of us if we do not face the changes we have wrought in the climate with more unity and compassion. The hostility, violence and dehumanization they have been subject to lent an urgency to making whatever small contribution this book might make to finding humane answers to the vexing questions the human race faces in the 21st century and beyond.

OTHER ANAPHORA LITERARY PRESS TITLES

*The History of British and
American Author-Publishers*
By: Anna Faktorovich

Notes for Further Research
By: Molly Kirschner

*The Encyclopedic Philosophy of
Michel Serres*
By: Keith Moser

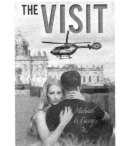

The Visit
By: Michael G. Casey

How to Be Happy
By: C. J. Jos

A Dying Breed
By: Scott Duff

Love in the Cretaceous
By: Howard W. Robertson

The Second of Seven
By: Jeremie Guy